PROMISED & PURSUED

L.C. PETRA

PROMISED & PURSUED

BOOK ONE

THE RECLAIMED BALLADS

L.C. PETRA

EVOKE PRESS

Editing by Kate Black @bitchnbooks

Cover Design and Title page art by Rachel McEwan

Interior Art by @art.bymikki

Print Paperback ISBN 979-8-9993626-0-5

 Formatted with Vellum

CONTENTS

A NOTE FROM THE AUTHOR

Thank you for picking up Rasha's story! This book is a work of fiction, written with the intention of keeping the tales of the gods and goddesses from multiple cultures alive. The story you are about to read is deeply inspired by Norse mythology, Vikings, Scandinavian and Arctic Circle tribal history, pre-christianity. Within the pages, you'll find graphic adult content, including explicit sexual scenes, violence, non-fatal injury to a companion animal, minor animal death in rituals, oppression against women, off page sexual assault (not to the main characters), and death.

To the young woman I once was - to the good student, the people pleaser, and the always available - May she Rest In Peace.

1

RASHA

Celebrating Yule with the four clans is going to be a disaster. Tonight is the winter solstice, and to match the endless dark, my face is wet with black lines of paint, representing the years I have held the lead huntress position in my clan. Resisting the urge to fidget with the heavy antler and holly crown sitting over my red hair, I wait for my brother at the front gate of the Aske Stronghold. All four clans chose me to be the Maiden of Yule and light the massive log that will burn throughout the next twelve nights of Yule feasts.

Harald, the Jarl of Aske, invited all the Vikings to his stronghold to celebrate the customary cycle of death and rebirth. It is an honor to be chosen as the Maiden of Yule, and I fully intend on leading our people through the darkness of winter one way or another.

"I need you to stick to my plan for the next twelve days, Rasha," Jorvik, my brother, says with a smug smile. Fluffing the long, fur cloak around my creamy white dress, we walk to the ceremonial circle built in the middle of the village. Jorvik has been traveling back and forth between the clans for months. When my clan arrived here last night, we were shocked when Jorvik told us that Harald agreed to bend the knee to a King from across the sea. And that the huntresses were purposely kept in the dark by my brother.

"I will not be forced to marry someone I don't know." I walk faster to catch up to my friends, but Jorvik quickly loops his hand through my arm to yank me close, not letting me get far. His blue eyes, the same as mine, sear through me in a harsh stare.

"Harald is the most powerful man here, and you will marry him on the last night of Yule. A union blessed by the gods," he mutters. My freedom is now intertwined with the livelihood of all the Vikings.

"How many times do I have to tell you, no," I reply, plastering a smile on my face for those who walk with us.

Jorvik regularly tries to sell me off, using my virginity and skills to entice different leaders into marrying me to boost his own political position. I've always found a way out of his ridiculous arrangements. Squirming against his skinny frame, I feel him dig his fingers into my arm.

"I am serious, Rasha. This is our chance. If you don't see that, then you really do belong out there." He gestures to the tips of the mountains peeking over the village wall and the forest beyond the fjord.

"I am a huntress, and I belong out there. Who will keep the balance of nature for the gods if not huntresses?" I retort, and he lets me go. Having exhausted every excuse in the dozens of our arguments on the journey here, I crunch through the frozen path determined to find my friends.

After tonight, I need to focus on my plan to find the tomb of the goddess Skadi. She relinquished her immortality to be a huntress and died on the fjord hundreds of years ago, according to the Ballads. Her tomb lies somewhere on this land, now owned by Harald. But feast songs retell a story about a great shrine built to honor her contribution to the clans, though there is no proof it ever existed. The real reason I agreed to come to Harald's Yule is the possibility that the tomb is real and the goddess's bow is buried inside.

If the bow holds any remnant of the goddesses power, I can earn my freedom and help our people return to honoring the gods. Leading my clan and whoever wants to follow, we will find the lost reindeer herd beyond the mountains, away from Harald and his new King.

"What did Jorvik say to make you all flustered?" Joanna asks as I squish myself between the two women.

"The same as always. He wants me to agree to marry Harald," I reply.

"That's not a bad idea, Rasha," Katrine chimes in, and my stomach churns. Katrine is a beautiful blonde with soft blue eyes. She enjoys spending her nights in the throws of any strong man who'll sweep her off her feet. Her father is a well established trader on our council, making Katrine and her mother free women. I envy her ability to fall in love, hunt, or choose to marry when she feels ready. Whereas Joanna, the severe looking brunette on the other side of me, is parentless like I am, and hunting allows her freedom.

"I have no interest in marrying anyone," I reply, and they both tense beside me. "You two cannot be serious? Do you agree with Jorvik that I should marry Harald?" I ask, feeling betrayed by the two women I consider my sisters.

"We want you to be safe," Joanna starts, but her voice drifts away with a gentle smile. Katrine doesn't give Joanna a minute to collect her thoughts before continuing the battering conversation.

"Harald is now backed by a King. We don't know what power the King holds. He could march right through the mountains and take all our land. He could make us comply in all ways. Rasha, you must think about everyone." Katrine's voice is determined like she practiced this speech in the women's longhouse. I was given my own room in the Aske Stronghold, so I didn't have the pleasure of this conversation earlier.

"I have a plan," I whisper, wanting to keep my voice down around the building crowd.

"Your plan is to pray to a goddess whom everyone has forgotten," Katrine argues.

"Not tonight, Katrine." Joanna comes around my other side to send the best withering stare she can muster at Katrine. "Rasha is the Maiden of Yule, and we should pray to the gods and the goddesses. A Jarl and a King cannot replace them."

I lean my head against Joanna's boney shoulder in thanks. Katrine halts her arguing and pretends to fix the holly and evergreen crown on her head. The huntresses and women, eligible for marriage, wear earth-like crowns, absent of the antlers on mine, so the free men of the clans know who they can pursue. Tonight is a more subdued evening with a feast, while the night of the Wild Hunt is when unions between couples ignite.

The village streets are packed with people and their families. Children hold lanterns and palm sized carvings of their favorite gods. Little girls are wrapped in fur blankets in their father's arms. While tentative women walk through, pouring ale and mead into horns.

"Here is our beautiful Maiden!" the Jarl bellows my introduction as the three of us walk into the ceremonial circle.

"At least he's attractive," Katrine whispers in my ear, and I stifle a smile at her persistence. The Jarl is attractive; she isn't wrong. Broad and strong, his dark hair is tied back, and he has a full beard.

"Thank you for being so generous with your land and welcoming all of us," I loudly reply while a hundred eyes watch me break from my friends to walk up to him. Harald dips his chin in harmless acceptance of my position and opens his arms wide. I glance back, the strangest sense of needing my brother to know I am trying overcomes me. Instead I find him shaking the hands of other men around us.

"Rasha, you are not what I expected," Harald says.

"What did you expect?" I ask with a smile on my face. Harald tries to slip his hand around my waist, so I turn to him instead. He looks me over, his roaming eyes pausing at my full breasts and curved hips in a way that makes me want to crawl out of my skin. Closing the fur cloak over my dress prompts him to clear his throat.

"I was told you are a heathen. A hunter who prefers the mountains and camping together with throngs of unwed men and women," he says, making me shiver, more from his comments than the bitter cold.

"I am Viking, the same as you," I reply. Walking around the circle in the dying sunlight, I have no interest in arguing with

Harald over what kind of woman I am. The cloudy sky turns a deep shade of violet, welcoming the darkness that will be the canvas for our ritual. Every winter, we wait for the northern lights to shine across the sky. In my lifetime, they have never been seen, and no one knows why. I wonder on quiet nights if we have angered the Immortal Realm or if they have forgotten us?

"To the Maiden of Yule!" A collection of our clan members shout and cheer when they see me round the circle. Seeing so many friends who made the six day journey to be with me and our huntresses warms my heart, giving me courage. The sickening feeling that this might be our last true Yule we celebrate without an overbearing Jarl and a power hungry King stomping over our gods propels me to take up a torch.

"The first night of Yule is celebrated on our darkest night, and I am happy to honor it with the four clans," I yell, trying to make my voice as loud as possible as people's cheers hush into silence. "I give my life to our gods and goddesses during the time of little deaths so that we may enter a new life cycle." I finish the prayer while around the ceremonial circle, Vikings clink their horns together and stomp the bottoms of their torches into the ground.

The huge Yule log is set up on a massive stack of smaller branches and filled with kindling. Finding the best area, I stash my torch deep inside and quickly slide my knife out of the inside pocket of my cloak. While everyone repeats their prayers and shares hugs with their family members, I slice my palm open and squeeze my blood on the Yule log. The fire hasn't made its way around yet, so I draw the only runes I know on the peeling bark.

Please, Freya, help me fight back. Help me find Skadi's bow and reclaim our freedom.

Flames begin to lick the tips of my fingers, and I pull back as the orange and yellow blaze engulfs the wood. Standing in the heat of the growing fire, I let the wind bring swaths of warmth to my cloak and dress, ushering out the cold left by Harald and Jorvik. I have no idea if our mother goddess heard my prayer or if the bow is real, but I have to try. I cannot let Jorvik marry me to Harald and let the Vikings be overtaken by a King.

5

After a moment, I turn around and wipe the blistering wetness from my eyes. In the first moments of night, the crowd is buzzing with the promise of a feast. People start dancing, linking their arms together in front of the Yule log, and give their own thanks for another year of survival.

"Very good, Rasha. While everyone heads to the stronghold for the feast, I need you to get to know Harald," Jorvik says, putting his hands on my shoulders to prevent me from walking away. Katrine and Joanna are lead away by men I recognize from our clan, and suddenly, I am afraid I missed my moment to escape. My eyes water when I try to refocus on Jorvik's thin frame, dark and lithe in contrast with the bright white and yellow flames.

"We have eleven more days for that," I reply. Attempting to walk through the crowd, I know Jorvik is right behind me. Opposite of where everyone is going, there is a wall protecting the village with a patrolled gate further away from us. I would love to slip out and enjoy the peacefulness of the forest, but Jorvik will never permit it. So I stop walking and hover in the empty circle.

"He agreed to marry you because you are a virgin, but it would be in your best interest to seize his heart." Jorvik's voice cuts through the sudden stillness of the disappearing crowd.

"I can't believe you. You've gone behind my back for months, and now you want me to play nice? You have no right to sell my virtue for your own interests."

"For all of our interests," Jorvik spits back. He closes in on me and pulls the ties on the top of my fur cloak. The silky fur opens, and he flicks my chin up to pay attention to him. Behind my brother, I see Harald waiting by the burning log, and my heart plummets.

"Get your hands off me," I grind out, low so Harald doesn't get a sense of our conversation. Jorvik ignores me and pulls my red hair off my exposed neckline.

"Go, enjoy your night, Jorvik," Harald commands. My cut palm stings, and I curse at my stupidity. I asked the goddess for help and let myself be distracted by unrealistic dreams when I should have been planning to leave the ceremonial circle as soon as I lit the log.

Gathering my heavy dress in my hands, I squeeze the fabric tightly, hoping it will stop the blood and seal the wound before Harald sees. Jorvik gives me a stern stare and walks away, following the last of the families leaving to go to the feast, till I can no longer see him.

I am left with Harald watching me. My tight dress does little to hide my strong, curved body. Walking around the sparse trees to avoid him, I have no idea why he agreed to marry a woman with nothing, but he seems far too intrigued.

"Do you want me to chase you, little Rasha?" he asks as I duck behind a tree and come around the other side to where he stands.

"Now that we are finally alone, I want to know what kind of life I will have here if I agree?" I have never been interested in finding a husband, or even laying down with a man, though that has never stopped them from finding and wanting me.

"You will pledge yourself to me and the King in good time," he drawls. I wind my steps around the next thick tree, but his speed is overpowering. Suddenly he slams my back into the tree trunk as his hands squeeze my shoulders. "Word in your clan is that you like to disobey your kin and your council."

"I am the lead huntress and the Maiden of Yule. I didn't receive those titles by wronging my clan." There is no submitting even if I wanted to. I hold his stare, and like I predicted, he can't peel his eyes away from my breasts as they rise and fall against the tight fabric in tune with my erratic heartbeat.

"I expect you to be a virgin." His voice quiets, and he dips his forehead closer to mine. For the first time, I can see his parted lips, feel his hot breath on my cheeks, and I am not sure of anything anymore.

"I am, and I wouldn't lie. But why is that important?" I ask lightly, not to sound too defensive.

"Because our marriage needs to be valid in the eyes of the King."

The mention of the King again flusters me. Adding another man I must submit to only further resolves my need to find a way out of this in the next eleven days.

"Why?" I look for an opening around his big arms, but there isn't one. Pushing myself around him, I hope he will concede and step back.

"First lesson, Rasha." The dangerous edge in his voice unnerves me. Harald takes my wrists and holds me fast against the frozen bark. The reality of trying to do what Jorvik wants me to do comes crashing down. "I am not to be questioned. You will bow before the King, and you will get on your knees for me."

"Harald," I whisper, refusing to give in or fight back. Hearing his name, he lets go of my wrists to feel up my body. Under my cloak, I feel him run his cold hands over my breasts, wasting no time taking what he presumes to be his. Shuddering against him, I try to move again, but make things unimaginably worse.

"I will marry you whether you're ready or not. Everyone will hear you scream my name, and we will be the first clan of the new religion," Harald grunts through his words, and my mind floats from his hands trying to gain purchase on my legs to the idea of the new religion he speaks of.

"What new religion?" I ask, and he stops.

"What difference does it make? You are a virgin, which is what the King said I needed to find. He will reward us for banishing the old gods." Harald roughly grabs my chin, bringing my face closer to his. The desire to be kissed is long gone, if it ever was present, and I struggle against him.

"You can fight all you want, but your days are numbered." He pins me to the tree and watches me struggle to get away from his grasp. Not kissing me or trying to make me submit, but holding me there to show he is more powerful. To make me never forget this moment.

"Let me go," I force the words out.

"I can be kind, but you have to earn my kindness," He drops me onto my knees. The snow numbs my hands, constricting the slit in my palm until I don't feel anything. Reaching through the slush, my fingers hit a rock and pick it up. Regaining my footing, I see Harald already turning around, making it the perfect time to swing.

"Did you hear that?" he asks, as if he wasn't just threatening my womanhood. My hunting skills click into place, and I hide my hand, holding the rock in the swaths of the cloak. The clash of metal on metal rings out through the forest. Looking at Harald for a split second, I am glad he is the Jarl, and this is his problem, but he doesn't move.

"Shouldn't we see what's happening?" I ask, dropping the rock and tying my cloak to prevent the icy wind from further numbing my skin.

"Vikings get drunk and fight. I'm sure it is nothing," he casually answers. I watch him look down the row of the solid pine wall to where the gate is, waiting for a glimmer of starlight reflecting off a blade or the warning bell in the guard tower.

I don't move a muscle, expecting to hear shouts or footsteps. My ears strain to listen while Harald marches off to his stronghold. As I turn to fain dutiful behavior, I hear the awful, guttural sound of an animal in pain.

"Harald," I whisper, but he's already gone. The animal cries again, and my heart fractures. Nothing makes that noise unless they are close to dying. I'll be dutiful tomorrow.

Harald will be furious because I am not following him to the feast. Leaving the Yule Log burning, I bolt down the perimeter, looking for an opening in the wall where I hear the crying animal. I don't know this village like I know mine. Holding up the cloak and the dress so I don't trip over every icy rock and snow drift, I wait to hear another sound.

This time the sounds of fighting urge me on. Thinking better of running toward danger unarmed, I find my knife in the pocket of my cloak and take a wider path around where I last heard the scuffle of bodies. The evergreen trees closer to the gate make it impossible to see the night sky, and suddenly, I am enveloped in the shadows of the wall.

Turning back the way I came, I squint to look for the tall flames of the Yule log, hoping it will guide me back. Realizing this is a fool's errand and I have no business trying to break up a fight in the middle of the woods, I look for the path back, and in an instant, I am pummeled by fur and claws.

2

RASHA

Fear fills me to the brim as I hit the deep snow and sharp rocks. Using every ounce of my strength, I push the crazed animal off my body. I roll to my side, but the heavy creature comes for me again. Massive paws and curved claws rip through my dress as I kick against the solid, furry mass. Trying to get to my feet, I feel no pain but hot and sticky blood coats my hands.

"Stop," I say through my teeth. I don't want to anger Harald or Jorvik with my foolishness. Screaming out here in the dark will certainly get me in trouble or worse. Men from the gate are rushing into the forest, and I need to move in between longhouses to stay unseen.

"I'm not going to hurt you," I add, willing my panicked breathing to still. An animal's instinct to survive runs off fear. My ability to stay calm is what makes me a good hunter, and maybe if I can get this particular animal to relax, we can either part ways, or I can help it.

Adjusting my eyes to the shape of the prowling animal across from me, I slowly walk backwards in between two longhouses. Wisps outlining its ears and bright amber eyes follow me from side to side as I drop my knife in the snow. It's a lynx, but not like any I've ever seen. Three times the size of the lynxes I've seen out in the mountains or snagging chickens out of the village coop, this lynx cannot be from this world. Raised, thick fur glows in the moonlight, revealing a deep, long gash in its side.

"Is that what all the commotion was? Were you eating an awful bastard? Or did they attack you?" Speaking in an even tone, I don't get any closer or move away as I wait for it to decide what it wants to do. "Freya is flanked by two lynx. Are you supposed to be a sign?" I ask another absurd question, and the great animal stops in its tracks. Winded from running and fighting, its legs shake until it lays down a few feet away from me.

Now what, Rasha?

My useless morality urges me on in this strange endeavor. Carefully, I move through the snow toward the lynx, trying to see if any of the men from the attack are still at the gate or if anyone has come to look for me. But all is quiet.

I've killed many animals with bows, my axe, or various pointed blades. Always doing what is necessary to make the kill quick and painless. We make sacrifices and offerings to the gods before our hunts and bless our feasts when we return with full sleds. Putting the lynx out of its misery should come naturally. I take a breath, settling my uneasy chest, and another feeling stirs in the dormant depths of my heart.

"You're very pretty. If Freya heard my prayer and sent a sign, you must be a girl?" I ask, sweetly. Kneeling down beside her, I gather my torn dress and finish ripping off a section where her claws separated the seams. Her huge amber eyes track the smallest movements. "I am going to help you, but we can't stay out here," I explain, as if she can understand.

Taking the strips of the heavy cotton dress, I don't look at her while I press my makeshift bandages into her wound. A ground shaking growl escapes her strong jaws, but she doesn't move.

"We can't leave a trail of blood, or they will find you," I keep talking as I work to close the wound. Taking a loose pine branch, I sweep our footprints away, covering our tracks. Burying the bloodied snow deep against the crust of the earth as my fingertips grow numb..

"Rasha!" Joanna's voice wafts through the trees. The lynx perks up, moving her massive paws to right herself. She instantly turns her head and tries to lick the bandages.

"Don't do that," I scold, quickly using my hands to make sure the bandages are still tight. The move, unfamiliar to the wild animal, causes her to stumble away, showing me her sharp fangs.

"Rasha!" Joanna calls for me again. We both turn towards her voice, and I sense the lynx raise her back fur. I need a plan, and I need it now.

"Walk with me?" Asking the lynx to follow my lead is about as useful as talking to the flames. She lays back down in the snow listening to the wind carry Joanna's calls. I have no choice but to walk back through the frozen path where I find Joanna with a frightened look on her face.

"What happened?"

"Katrine is already on a man's lap, and I didn't know where you were. Harald came in demanding a drink. I…" Joanna looks at me in horror. Her brown eyes widen at the mess of my dress.

"No, he didn't hurt me. This is from something else. Joanna, I need your help." Gauging by her expression, she must think he forced himself on me and left me for dead out here in the snow, but neither of us will admit the threat to our bodies out loud.

"What are you doing at the gate?" she hisses, glancing over to the men pushing the massive door shut. They still haven't seen us, which is a good thing. It means they haven't seen the wounded lynx either.

"I heard fighting, so I went to see. I found a sign from the gods instead."

Joanna follows me back toward where I left the lynx. I can count on her quiet footsteps and her ability to blend into her surroundings without worry. We have worked together in all seasons, hunting in the mountains, and are able to read one another without speaking.

"Rasha, I pity the position everyone put you in with Harald," she whispers, and my gait slows to listen. Pity is not what I want to elicit out of my friend. As happy as I am to have her accompany me to Yule, I also don't want her to be bartered off in the same way. Joanna is a huntress, like I am, and we are tied to the mountains. It is where we thrive.

"Don't pity me," I answer. "You can't tell anyone what we are about to do. Promise?"

Joanna agrees, and I hold my arm back to keep her from walking right into the giant cat. I see her amber eyes before I see her body and let out a sigh of relief. A strange hope settles over my like a fresh tattoo sinking into my skin. By helping this animal, maybe my plea to the gods will be answered.

"Look out!" Joanna screams, and I wince. The lynx musters her strength to bare her teeth with a deep growl.

"No, no, Joanna. It's alright. We are bringing her back to my room. She's wounded." I talk Joanna down, stroking her shivering arms to turn her focus on me, her friend, and not the lynx who could gut us out of pure fear.

"I get not wanting to marry Harald, but is harboring a wild animal going to help you?" she asks, rubbing her numb hands together.

I unravel my hair from the antler and holly crown and toss it high, over the wall. The last thing we need is someone recognizing me as we smuggle the cat into my room.

"Freya's animal is a lynx, and I made an offering of blood on the Yule log," I reply, moving closer to the lynx. In awe of her regality, I crouch low and hold my hand out, hoping she'll sniff me. We train horses and dogs in a similar way, so maybe it will work for a lynx who wants to rip my leg from my hip.

"Please, let me help you. Joanna is a bit scared, but she's a good person," I say, scooting closer to her.

"I am not scared," I hear Joanna sputter.

Hot, feline breath comes in heavy pants, and I have an idea. Untying my cloak, I spread it out on the snow and pat the middle.

"What happened to her?" Joanna's timid voice comes from over my shoulder.

"Maybe the men attacked her, or she attacked them?"

"So you went to investigate? That is the opposite of what you should be doing," she chastises, ignoring what I said about making an offering.

"I thought it might be men from our clan suffering." I try to find a suitable excuse.

"You did not. You are looking for an out. I know you," she shoots back. I stand up with the edge of my cloak in my hands and let my face fall in an honest expression to my friend.

"Please, help me? If I have to choose between freedom and saving everyone, I will save everyone by marrying Harald. You should know me better than to question my commitment," I say, laying out the cloak so we can carry the lynx through the stronghold, but it will look like we are only bringing in extra blankets. Joanna rolls her shoulders and sighs.

"If she bites me, I'm going to kill her," she says, and the lynx hisses at the other end of the spread out cloak.

"We are all going to be calm," I reply, patting the cloak again, hoping the lynx understands the message. Joanna backs away, and I hold my hand out, trying with every ounce of will to lure the cat closer.

The edge of the village is deathly quiet while the three of us face off. Chilly winds and errant snowflakes take the hint and pause in the onslaught of winter around us. My breath stills in my lungs, and I stare at the tired, wounded cat. A million thoughts swirl in my mind. The most obvious is that Joanna is right, and I am purposefully causing a problem. I know this will piss Jorvik and Harald off. Maybe enough that they allow me to live in the mountains like the heathen I am?

Another, smaller thought sparks behind the many guilty and chaotic ones. Freya heard my prayer; she heard my call and sent me her lynx. A sign from the gods that the fight for our clan and our lands isn't over just because Harald says so. Maybe this once fearsome cat is going to…I watch her slowly sniff the cloak before laying down in a huff of fur. Well, maybe I am going mad.

"On three?" Joanna asks, and I nod, moving to the front of the cloak. We fold the edges in and count down to lift her solid body.

"What is going to happen to us if we get caught?" Her question comes out tight from her sudden exertion.

"Nothing because we aren't going to get caught. This is an extra blanket," I say, looking back to see the twinkle in her eye as we walk by the Yule log. The flames have fully engulfed the wide piece of tree trunk, making the air thick with smoke and char.

We pick up the pace and trek the way I remember through the village streets. Men and women are everywhere, but no one looks at us. With four clans coming together, there are many strange faces.

"Are there stairs to your room?" Joanna asks.

"One set and there's a side door, so we don't have to go in the front."

"Finally, you've said something that makes sense. I thought you were planning on unrolling our furry friend here, right in front of Harald, as a wedding present." Joanna chuckles under her breath and shifts the cloak to her other shoulder. A growl emits from inside the rolled fabric.

"What we do in this world comes back to us, so if the goddess wants me to heal this cat, I will," I say. My knees slip out of the long tears in my dress, and freezing winter air raises goosebumps along my thighs. My fur boots go up to my calves and make walking around in the snow bearable, but they aren't as tightly sealed as my hunting boots. My toes are starting to lose feeling from the cold.

"Rasha, the Maiden of Yule has come for a drink!" I hear my name when we are closer to the outer wall of the large stone structure of Harald's stronghold. My red hair and white dress must have given me away, even without the antler crown. A group of rowdy Vikings smash their cups together, letting foamy ale spill over. One knocks his cup back, draining the liquid and throwing it into a snow drift.

"Rasha, they say you are the best huntress. Come, show us how good you are with a bow," a tall, skinny man demands. I notice his tunic and vest are splattered in blood as he swings his axe around. Joanna keeps walking, urging me forward. My hands sweat as my grip slips, and I switch shoulders.

"In the daylight, if you ask the Jarl first," I answer and keep walking.

"What are you carrying? Let us take up whatever you need," the man's comrade offers, causing us to walk to the other side of the narrow pathway in between the forge and stronghold. Both men seem less inebriated than their friends who have already moved on from the conversation.

"Extra blankets, the Jarl's fortress is drafty," I say, skating around a sloshy puddle of ice. The side door of the stronghold is a few feet ahead. Both men look at us with lax curiosity, and I can't decide if they were part of the scuffle in the woods or if the blood staining their tunics is from another time and place.

"Oh, you must forgive me. My name is Bjorn," the thin man says, coming much too close to me. I can't back up or else I'll squish the lynx, and we will be caught. He continues to stand in my way, taking his time to look at the torn section of my dress.

"I don't think you've given cause for forgiveness yet," I say. Maybe it will make him think twice before attempting to hurt us if he thinks the Jarl has already claimed me?

"I forget that you really are a maiden and haven't known what it's like to share a man's warmth. But I can let the Jarl know your bed is cold."

"He'll be happy to set fire to your sheets," his friend sneers. I force my feet forward, and Joanna follows. We don't look back or stop until I reach for the curved handle of the door. Yanking it open, I gently put my side of the cloak down and peer in between the layers of fur.

The lynx's massive, round eyes stare back at me as if to say, *where am I?*

"I hate the men here," Joanna exhales, rubbing her sore hands down the front of her long coat.

"Did you see the blood all over them?"

"I did. But that doesn't mean anything when it seems they are ready for a fight."

I mull over Joanna's words and pick up the edge of the cloak again. It is easier to make it up the stone steps and into my room now that we are alone. The fortress, as I've been calling this strong-hold, is actually not as drafty as I pretended it was. The sealed stone walls hold in the heat nicely from the many hearths. Regardless, the fires I left going in my bedroom have died down, so the room feels like we submerged ourselves in a frozen lake.

We put the lynx down on the side of the bed farthest from the door. In case I have any visitors over night, I'll be able to hide her.

"She must know she's safe. Look," Joanna whispers. I unfold the cloak to see the lynx's eyes are closed.

"See, she's just like a barn cat." I smile at Joanna, replacing the fear from our walk up here. The lynx's breathing is peaceful, and the bandages have held tight. Going to the hearth, I add logs and allow for air to circulate through the embers, making the fire reignite.

"I should go back to the longhouse with the other women. Your secret is safe with me, Rasha." Joanna slips out of my room. Kneeling alone at the hearth, I sigh, wishing I asked her to stay. We've slept side by side many times on hunting trips, and it would have been a comfort to not be alone.

Peeling out of my wet dress and boots, I crawl into bed and cocoon myself in blankets. Between the heavy purring of the lynx and my weary bones, sleep takes me instantly.

3

SHAW

The last thing I told Aslaug still rings in my ears as I regain consciousness and realize where I am. Forcing my eyes open, I take in my surroundings. The feast for the first night of the solstice is in full swing. Warming spices and the pungent smell of roasting meat make my mouth water, but my jaw throbs on the exhale. Blood clogging my nose makes it too hard to breathe without leaving my lips parted.

"Who did this Shaw?" Harald's voice echoes, and my hazy vision makes him slide in and out of focus.

"Someone who didn't know I am unarmed," I reply. The two men holding me up let go, and my knees give out. Vikings around us briefly halt their drinking and dancing to survey the damage to my body while Harald and I exchange words.

Some stop to listen when I say my sled was attacked on the way to the village. I carefully provide limited details. The last thing I need is to make an enemy of the Jarl. It is most likely he ordered the attack on my wagon to begin with and is trying to manipulate my allegiance.

Through my swollen eyelids, I see several people murmuring to themselves, trying to hide their growing tension. Harald thinks he is above the needs of his fellow Vikings, ever since he aligned with the King. A King whom I hope to never meet.

When Harald ordered me to travel here, I fought with the decision to tell him no. Treating me like a subject is beneath both of us when I have made weapons and goods for all the clans without discrimination for years. I haven't spent all twelve nights of Yule with anyone since the time I spent with my own family.

The memories mingle with the pain searing through my probably cracked knee, bringing a sting to my eyes. My shoulders slump with each labored breath while Harald barks orders to the men who are supposed to be hauling me around.

"Get him to the medicine woman! Why are you just watching him? And where is Rasha?"

Long and lean, Bjorn's tunic is covered in blood, and there is no mistaking the snide smile across the face of the man I can't wait to pummel into the ground.

"Oh, Bjorn, have you seen her?" Harald asks of his second and closest friend. A Viking by the name of Erik helps me drag my feet across the floor, but I lean my head back to listen as we walk, hoping Bjorn will mention Aslaug or what I assume he stole from me.

"Rasha went to bed. We saw her with her heathen friend. Sadly, the brunette isn't as well endowed as your soon to be wife." Bjorn's voice answering the Jarl is the last thing I hear before the back door swings closed.

Whoever Rasha is, she has to be the meekest woman in their clan if she's going to be happy with Harald for the rest of her life. The dim light of the hallway does nothing to keep my spirits up. The last time I came to the stronghold the stone walls were not fully erected, and they asked me to teach their blacksmiths how to make the iron clamps that help support the towering walls.

"Who is the Yule Maiden this year?" I ask Erik, only to keep myself conscious.

"Rasha. Same one Harald's after. She's the one you'll be making the rings for. You are the goldsmith, aren't ya?" Erik asks, and I grumble a *yes* as best I can through the increasingly swollen parts of my jaw. The smell of a medicine room tingles my nose, and

I brace my arm in the doorway while he ducks between dark curtains.

"Siggy, you back there? Shaw is in bad shape."

"Too much to drink on the first night? That surprises me since the smith is…" Siggy's words stop, and I know she's seen me.

"I just need a tonic to sleep. I'll be fine in the morning," I say, but the stout, old woman helps me to a cot near her table of tools.

"Thank you, Erik," she mumbles, her glassy gray eyes wandering over my blood and bruises. "Lay down, your leg might be broken. When did this happen? I told Harald that bringing all the clans together was going to be disastrous." Her harsh words and steady hands exude the perseverance she's needed to stick with being a healer in a clan full of ungrateful men.

"I didn't even make it to the lighting. There was an altercation at the gate. I figured the log was already lit."

Siggy nods, pushing short strands of gray hair back into the coronet around her head. She helps me get out of my ruined tunic and hands me an herb soaked rag. I sop up the blood and clean my bruises. The eyes of one who has had a vicious life always has more to tell behind stern looks.

"I have no love for Harald, so what's on your mind, Siggy?" I ask, and she hands me a clean shirt.

"There is something happening behind the guise of this solstice. The woman who was chosen to be the Maiden is going to have her work cut out for her, and I fear she doesn't know what is coming. Her brother came many times to negotiate with Harald."

Rubbing my tender jaw, I ask, "Where is she from?"

"She is the lead huntress in the Beaivi Clan. That should jog your memory. Supposedly she's a virgin, and she didn't cower in fear like everyone else when Harald tried to use her moment for his own gain. I'll give it her. She has the spirit of a Valkyrie."

"She's either smart or foolish. With the King backing Harald, she might be better off as the Jarl's wife than a maiden whose days of hunting are numbered."

"Why are you really here, Shaw? If I remember correctly, you stay away from women of the Beaivi Clan," Siggy asks, mulling over our shared ideas of impeding oppression.

"Harald requested I make his wedding rings, and I have other business on the fjord."

"I hope your other business doesn't leave you this damaged. Your body isn't what it used to be," she says with a smile. A smile I remember from the first time I met her when her hair was a rich brown, and her eyes were clear and bright.

"Just a tonic for sleep, and I'll be fine in the morning, Siggy," I repeat as she searches for a slim wooden splint in her basket of bone setting equipment.

"You'll do as I say," she instructs. Taking various herbs and dried leaves off shelves, she adds a bit of one and a handful of another to a pestle before crushing everything. Handing me a small cup with the muddled tincture on the bottom, she finds a thick towel to remove the boiling kettle from the fire. Filling my cup with bubbling water, I let the heat soothe my aching knuckles and inhale the steam through my broken nose.

"I have to go back out in the morning. There's something I need to find," I explain, knowing panic is rising in my voice. I need to find Aslaug, my lynx who saved my life an hour ago, before one of these forsaken Vikings finishes killing her.

"Rest and I'll set your leg," she says as I bring the hot cup of medicine to my lips. The tang of the tincture burns as it slides down my throat.

Siggy places her arthritic hand over my chest to still my thundering heartbeat. She applies coats of salve to my shoulder, over the whorls of a blue tattoo, and mumbles soft prayers to the gods to watch over her room. The cot is warm, and the mattress bends with my body as I lay down. Siggy splints my leg, which sends blinding pain up through my chest, and I curse this whole fucking situation.

"Thank you," is all I can manage before my eyes drift closed.

A memory of the inky blue night sky from a few weeks ago blurs behind my swollen eyes. Bright stars aligned the way they do only once in a great while. There had been no signs for years, so I paused outside my cabin while I was chopping wood. It was the first indication that my journey out of banishment was beginning. Why now after all this time?

For days, I gave Aslaug all the reasons why coming here was a terrible idea, and all she did was stare at me with her big amber eyes. The lynx has kept me company through my darkest times. Shuddering under the blanket Siggy threw over me, my aching muscles urge me to get up and find her. I can't let her bleed out in the snow while I am safe and warm. But there is no way I'd risk bringing her in front of Harald's clansmen, knowing the King will order his Jarl to kill her. Anything resembling the Immortal Realm is a threat to his new found power.

She'll be okay, I tell myself and let the herbs in the cup drag me into a dreamless slumber.

CUPBOARDS OPENING and softly closing wake me from the deepest sleep of my life. *What did Siggy put in that tincture?* The shape of a much younger woman takes form at the corner of my bleary vision. Bright red hair falls over her shoulders and down her graceful back. She's in a woven tunic and pants, not usually seen on a lady. What am I thinking? I make a point of avoiding women.

Watching her through a barely open eye, I decide it's best to pretend I am still asleep since she keeps looking over her shoulder at the door. Her glances dart over me to the rows of tiny bottles lined up on the shelf. She must not know what she's looking for because she turns the bottles to see the colors of the herbs, instead of reading the letters Siggy wrote on the parchment.

Her blue eyes halt as we both hear footsteps coming from the hall outside the medicine room. I haven't seen eyes that crystal blue in decades. She returns to her task with determination, but her hands shake in fear. The better part of myself wants to ask what she's looking for. She seems healthy, so she must be here for a friend. But I can't get involved in anything until I find Aslaug and what was taken from me.

As she turns, I close my eyes, trying to breathe as a sleeping man would.

"I know you're awake." Her voice a whisper. I smile like an idiot and fold my arms over my chest, keeping up the ruse.

"I don't want to know what you're up to, so I'm keeping my eyes closed."

"Is that so?" I feel her body move towards me. "What happened to your face?"

I open my eyes slightly to see her worried brow hovering over mine. A hand that has seen work reaches out to touch the side of my face, but she thinks better of it and recoils.

"By the way you're sneaking around, I should be asking you the questions."

The color in her cheeks rises to match her crimson hair. "I'm not sneaking around. I need to help someone who can't come here." She presses her soft lips together in thought. Another shuffle of foot-steps outside the door sends her on high alert.

"What do you need, and I'll point you in the right direction." Sitting up, I feel stiff and sore as I stretch my legs over the edge of the cot. I swing my knee joint, making sure I am whole once again, and tuck the wooden splint under the blanket so she doesn't see.

"How do I know you'll give me the right combination?"

"Should I find Siggy, the medicine woman?" I counter, and she sharply inhales, letting me know that is not an option. "What happened to your friend?" I ask with a less accusatory tone.

"She has a fever from an infected wound," she admits, crossing her arms over her chest.

When I stand up, she takes two steps back, knocking her elbow into the work table. She is different from the little, old lady who patched me up last night. The two of us in the low ceilinged room take up much more space. She has nowhere to look but up at me, and I am overcome by a captivating, yet not ideal, vision for this particular interaction.

Clearing my throat, I avoid her full lips and intense glare as I gather the herbs she needs. I find a tiny spoon and scoop out different amounts for bringing down a fever into a small pouch.

23

"Every few hours, apply these herbs in a paste. Can you do that, or would you like me to go with you? I can carry your friend here. Siggy is a kind woman," I offer suggestions. The red headed beauty stuffs everything I laid out in the inside pockets of her tunic and folds the fabric back down over her hips.

"Thank you for your help." Without waiting for further conversation or a moment of awkwardness, she leaves. I never asked her what her name was. Finding another jar full of dandelion root, I muddle myself fresh tea and think about the ways I can gracefully alleviate the strain in my pants.

4

RASHA

The lynx woke up along with the rising sun and whined. While I slept, her massive, furry body acquired a fever from her infected wounds. I know from experience that if I don't tend to the fever she'll die, and my prayers will be for nothing. What I didn't expect was for a man to be sleeping in the medicine room. A strong, slightly alarming man who looked like he took a beating last night as well.

Leaving the medicine room, I keep my head low and stick to the side of the hallway with the windows to pretend to look at the scenery, instead of wishing others good morning. The staircase to my room is empty, making my heart lighten, until I round the corner and see Jorvik pacing outside my bedroom door.

I'd tip toe back down the stairs, but he's already seen me.

"Good morning, little sister. I've been out here for ten minutes knocking," he scolds.

"I figured you'd be tired after last night."

Jorvik searches my face for clues to my whereabouts, and I try to remain neutral. He still smells like ale and smoke from the fires. It doesn't look like he's changed his clothes from last night either, and

I'm not sure that is a good thing. Jorvik likes to bed women, so I am astonished he's outside of my room this early.

"Where have you been?" he asks.

"I went to bed early after you left me in the woods with Harald. And this morning, I went to get herbs from the medicine woman."

"Why do you need them?"

"You don't want me to bleed on my wedding night do you?" I snap back with something I know he thinks is vile to make him back down, and it works. He levels me with a look of disgust and turns away.

"What did Harald say when you two were alone?" He switches to the conniving portion of this morning's meeting.

"Nothing unusual. Now if you don't mind, I have to braid my hair." I push past my brother, looking for the key under my tunic. The only good thing Harald gave me is this room that has a locking door. Though I'm sure Harald didn't give me the only key, at least it allows me to keep Jorvik out. I click the heavy iron key into the lock and feel the gears shift.

"Rasha, you need to participate in the feasts. Dance with Harald at the very least. Make everyone believe you're making an effort at unity."

"Why? You really think the clans are full of idiots? They know what is happening to their way of life." I start to close the wooden door in his face, but he throws his foot and arm in the doorway.

"They need to see you happy so they can be settled with letting Harald lead us all."

"Let me participate in the archery competition or today's games, and you'll have a deal. I'll dance with Harald. But he has to participate in the Wild Hunt fairly, or all bets are off. It is for the gods to decide our partners."

Jorvik narrows in on me, looking for another way around my request. I need him to leave before the lynx wakes up.

"I'll pour his drinks and sit on his lap. I'll lead the women in a dance at the Divination Ritual too." I pile on the negotiations, waiting for Jorvik to pounce on my appeasement.

"Alright. The archery competition is to honor the goddess Skadi.

Supposedly, her tomb is somewhere by the fjord," Jorvik explains, and the goddess's name unearths diluted stories I remember our mother telling us. "But Rasha, I will hold you to your word. On your best behavior during all the evening festivities."

"Deal. Please go wash. You smell like you've had too much fun." I push him gently, and he trots back down the stairs. Maybe I shouldn't shut down the idea of being the Jarl's wife if it comes with the benefit of keeping Jorvik at arms length.

In the safety of my locked bedroom, I take the pouches of herbs out of my pockets. Carefully walking around the low bed so the lynx isn't startled, I crane my neck to see if she's still alive. Those big eyes of hers are closed, but her belly rises and falls with each breath. It doesn't take me long to mix the herbs and add melted snow from the windowsill, creating a paste with the mixture.

Replenishing the water in the bowl I was supposed to have breakfast porridge in, I push it to her, and she wakes, eagerly lapping up the cold water with her prickly tongue.

"You didn't happen to attack a man with no beard and hazel eyes did you?" I ask, and she peers up at me with no response. Stretching her huge hind legs causes two bandages to fall off, revealing a streak of red deep in her fur.

I don't usually spend time with predatory animals because they always try to kill me before I kill them. Bears and wolves are two we steer clear from while hunting deer and moose, but lynx are elusive. Watching her pad around the room reminds me of a barn cat searching for something to jump on to. Sure enough, she tenderly raises her front paws and looks out the window.

"Get down before someone sees your pretty ears," I say. Coming to her side, I take a breath and stroke her massive head until she sits back down. Her fur is soft and dense to the point I can't feel her skin beneath, which keeps her snow proof. She doesn't move while I scratch her head, dragging my fingers down to her shoulders until I hear a quiet rumble.

To be safe, I burn the bandages in my fireplace and apply fresh medicine to the long cut that barely missed her internal organs. Feeling over her body, I can tell her ribs are certainly swollen, and her front paws show signs that she defended herself against a knife or a small axe.

The men outside the stronghold would have surely boasted about facing off with such a formidable creature, but they've said nothing. Jorvik isn't the type to listen to hunting gossip, so I'll have to keep my ears open today. The man in the medicine room had wounds as fresh as the lynx's, but I saw no bite marks which confused me. Also his kindness is out of place for the group of men living here.

I am here to find the bow. Not help strangers.

Shaking my head, I try to clear my memories of last night so I can focus on today. When our parents were killed, Jorvik brought me to the Beaivi Clan, thinking it would be the best place for us. I made myself useful in any way they asked, not to make Jorvik proud, but to keep from being beaten. If I was the first one to bake bread for the day or clean the most rabbits, then I'd be valued.

So much for value now. I shrug and add another log to the fire. Leaving all of my food and water for the cat, I change into hunting leathers and a long, fur-lined tunic, braiding the sides of my hair while leaving the rest loose down my back. There will be plenty of nights to look like the wife of a Jarl, but today I want to look like a huntress.

Making my way through the stronghold, I try to memorize the square layout in case I need to make an escape. It is different from what I am used to. All the clans live in wooden longhouses in various parts of the mountain range and deep valleys where the fjords meet the sea.

Big stone structures are new and expensive, so one this large is solely for the Jarl and he friends. Reaching the bottom of the stairs, I am greeted by an open space big enough for horses and wagons or sleds. Around the sides are the bedrooms and meeting rooms, although I've only been shown my room and the long Feast Hall at the back.

From an outsider's observation, it seems silly to make the Feast Hall along the back because there aren't many places for people to run if anything were to happen, say an attack or a simple kitchen fire. But Harald is following his new King's example.

It's not very efficient if you ask me, which they won't, because I am a woman.

Katrine and Joanna are huddled in a corner, chatting. Joanna spots me first and hides a grin. I pray she hasn't told Katrine what we did with the lynx; she'll want to involve her fur trading father.

"How did you fare last night?" I ask, taking charge of the conversation. Joanna looks at her boots, tucking a loose piece of brown hair behind her ears. On cue, we look around the square to see if Harald or Jorvik are following me. We are all well versed in steering clear of my brother.

"I danced the night away, which would have been more enjoyable with my friends by my side," Katrine says. When Joanna and I don't reply immediately, Katrine lets out a huff of frustration. "You're the Yule Maiden, and you spent all night evading your Jarl," she scolds, and I bring my arms to their backs, leading them out of the open double gates.

"I spent plenty of time with him," I admit, my body tensing at the memory of our moment alone.

"Not in front of the rest of the clans. We feasted! We danced!" Katrine shares and Joanna chuckles at our friend's lamenting.

"We can feast tonight. And between the Divination night and the Wild Hunt, I have no fear that all the eligible men will be primed and ready to catch us," I reply with a shaking breath.

"I overheard Harald's council say they will have the Wild Hunt closer to the end of Yule because a Seidr told them it would have a better outcome." Katrine raises her eyebrows up and down for emphasis, breaking our seriousness. I giggle at how much Harald is still relying on the gods and our ways while declaring to anyone who will listen that he is the King's new best friend.

Counting the nights in my head, I try to figure out a moment that I can duck out and look for Skadi's tomb. Joanna and Katrine continue chatting about the possible men that caught Katrine's eye last night and a match for Joanna.

On one hand, I do want to be with my friends. I want to share a drink and dance until I am sweaty and happy. On the other hand, I need to find the tomb and the bow, and there's a lynx with a fever in my bedroom. I wish I could tell Katrine, but she never takes me as seriously as Joanna does.

Joanna leans forward to grab my attention as we walk. I know what she's asking. The three of us share everything. At home, we all sleep in the same longhouse, but what I did last night and the secret I am keeping needs to stay between us. Shaking my head, I silently beg her not to tell Katrine about the lynx. I need her to understand there are things I don't plan on sharing with everyone.

"Today is our chance to shine," Joanna thankfully blurts as we come to the edge of the open field. Most likely a field they aren't growing food on this year, so it has been turned into an arena for the games. The sun rises late in the morning and will set early, giving us a short window of light and meager warmth.

"Do you think Harald will let women participate in the games? He has been rather brutish about women from other clans doing anything on his land." I wearily look around at the hungover group. Women are not dressed for the games. They are covered, head to toe, in long cloaks and fur trimmed dresses. Their arms are laden with pitchers of ale and trays of hot food.

In our clan, men and women are allowed to take up any position in the games during Yule or in any of our holidays. We value the strength of all of our people. Here, the Jarl is turning a vivacious group of Aske women into nothing better than a collection of servants.

"Harald, the Maiden is here." I hear someone alert him to my arrival, and I separate myself from my friends. Harald is covered in thick furs, the tails of the animal skins dangling from his shoulders.

"What a beauty she is. Isn't she?" he asks the surrounding men, and they look me over like a pack of wolves waiting to tear a doe limb from limb.

"What games are we playing today?" I ask the group. Usually, Vikings throw knives and wrestle, but even crafting the finest axe or carving gods in wood can be a judged event.

"Jorvik and your clan sung your praises with the bow, so the archery field is yours," Harald says. I know I need to play nice, so I walk straight through the men, making a show of standing directly before him, and I bow my head.

"Thank you," I say in the shared breath between us. He runs his teeth over his lips, making me sweat it out. His fat fingers run along my ribcage as he guides me up to his eye level. He kisses me gently on the cheek, his coarse lips and beard scratching my cold skin.

"Tonight, Rasha, I expect you to be by my side," he says.

"I expect you to treat the women the same as the men, and I'll gladly sit by your side." I catch his stare and force some form of happiness or lightheartedness over my cheeks to my wide eyes. "Please." I hate saying it, but the thought creeps into my head that maybe Harald knows more about the tomb. Will he be willing to share his information if he thinks I am willing to be his wife? I know it's wrong to falsely lead someone on, but my choices are limited. After a beat, Harald adjusts his heavy belt and nods his head.

"You can participate," he says, and I turn away, letting out a sigh of relief.

"Joanna too?" I ask before I can stop myself.

"Yeah, let her have a go. We can make bets as to who she'll have to tend to if she is outshot."

"Only if you have your own women participating to make the bet fair," Jorvik interrupts. His voice is like a hammer hitting an anvil. Joanna and I swivel to find him standing behind us. She looks at him with new eyes, and my heart sinks. Jorvik is only playing by the rules of men, not showing weakness or submissiveness. He doesn't care what happens to Joanna.

"Am I playing by your rules?" I lighten my voice and give my brother a bow in the absurdity of our situation.

"Don't embarrass the men. Throw a shot or two in humility," he whispers at my back as I walk to the weapons station.

"Relax, won't you?" My temper flares. He raises his hands in defense and walks away.

The weapons station is abundant, another nice feature of living with a clan receiving funding from a King. I am always practicing with my bow or an ax, but Jorvik uses all the coin we receive and provides me with what he sees fit. If I became the Jarl's wife, maybe I'd be able to make my own purchases and find someone to train me to make my own weapons? Piling on the positives keeps me going when I'd rather run off into the woods. I don't want to think about not finding the tomb or come to the conclusion that Skadi is a myth.

When we reach the table, the men preparing the weapons hesitate to give us what we require.

"I know you are the Maiden, but did Harald give you permission?" a man asks us.

"He did," I reply, and his face lights up. The men behind him breathe a sigh of relief while an uneasy feeling sits in the pit of my stomach. What has Harald done to everyone here to make them so fearful of disobeying him?

"For you and your friend. My name is Leif. If you need anything else this week, you are welcome to ask."

"Thank you. Do you make the arrows yourself?" I ask Leif. He smiles, his beard cut short and his brown hair braided tight to his skull.

"No, we have blacksmiths. I am a wood worker by trade. Actually, there is someone you might like to meet later. He smiths in precious metals."

The horn blows to start the competition, and I scoop up the bows and quivers to walk with Joanna into the field.

"These are nice," Joanna acknowledges, taking an identical bow to mine from my arms. Much longer than our bows at home, these are made for men with a heavy draw on the string. Our work is cut out for us.

"Archer's ready!" the judge shouts, and we take our positions. Joanna is next to me, and a man from Harald's clan is on my left. Another two men flank us, all looking to show off their skills and maybe gain the gods favor.

Taking up a sturdy stance, I narrow my vision down range, across the gleaming white snow, to the small target on a hay bale. Bending down for an arrow, I feel the weight of the long shaft in my palm and line it up with the grip. All my worries sink into the snow and ice as I situate my left hand on the front grip and pull back the heavy cord to string the arrow. My cheek rests against the bristles on the end of the arrow, and I let my heartbeat slow.

Nothing in this moment matters except the target at the end of the range.

"Loose," the judge says, and I let go. All my fear and guilt flies away as the arrow rips past my cheek and across the field. The judge walks from target to target and places a flag at each that hit the center. The man to my left doesn't get a flag and slaps his hand against the bench before stomping off, leaving Joanna, the two remaining men, and myself to shoot in the next round.

Again, we ready ourselves, and I release a second arrow, knowing by the almost silent sound of the wood splitting air that I hit my mark. Joanna lets her nerves get to her and misses the target completely. So does the man closest to me. Not showing anyone any favor, I keep my eye on the targets at the end of the field while the judge calls to set the last two closer.

With Joanna and the two men gone, I glance over, only to be stunned. The handsome man from the medicine room this morning stands with a foot on the bench and the bow gently balanced over his knee.

"I thought you were injured," I say, turning back to the field.

"And I thought your friend had a fever," he responds, watching Joanna run to be by Katrine's side. My gut rolls over, and my palms start to sweat. Who is this man? One minute, he's bruised, laid up in a medicine room cot, and another, he's drawing back a bow with no effort at all.

"Different friend," I reply. I can't help myself. I turn to catch his stare. Hazel eyes, no different than this morning, reflect back at me with the same attractive smirk. His form is perfect. He is not bothered by the crowd that's gathered or the soft snow swirling around us.

"Archer's ready!" the judge shouts, and another surveyor sprints away from the range.

I set my last arrow and ignore the way he pulls back his string with little effort, lining up the feathers and his fingers against his healing cheek.

Focus, Rasha.

My calloused fingertips take up the crafted arrow. All my muscles scream in protest from carrying the lynx up to my room. Planting my feet in the snow, I make use of the fresh powder to dig my heels in, and we wait for the horn.

The wind tickles my nose, sending tiny flurries around the back of my neck, and I fight the urge to shrug my shoulders.

"Loose!"

We let our arrows fly before the judge finishes the word. The two arrows shoot down the line like they are one. He hits his target with such velocity it falls over, and the crowd goes wild. My arrow hits dead center along with the two previous arrows, and my heart resumes its nervous pitter patter.

"Impressive," he says, holding out a hand for me to take.

Gripping the bow tighter, I don't know what to say or do. Technically, we have a draw, and we could go again.

"We tied," I say, giving him my hand. He brings my cold knuckles to his mouth, planting a hot kiss over my skin.

"My name is Shaw. You can have this round. I am sure you'll have another opportunity to beat me."

"Rasha," I answer, and my mouth parts as winter air infiltrates my lungs. His stare deepens like he's frozen in thought. Before I can ask why, he takes both quivers and both bows to the weapons station, leaving me standing awkwardly in front of the cheering crowd.

5

RASHA

All the women who were watching the competition, along with Katrine and Joanna, thunder onto the field to congratulate me. Trying to see where Shaw went over their pretty braids and fur covered hoods is impossible, so I succumb to the easement of celebration.

"My heart is still pounding!" Katrine shouts, giving me a good pat on the back.

"You're playing with fire, going head to head with a man while Harald is watching," a woman I don't recognize says in warning. She wears the colors of the Jarl, so I assume she lives here.

"The man I tied with doesn't seem interested in what Harald thinks." I keep looking behind us to see if Shaw is still around, and nearly half the women giggle.

"The smith is the strong, silent type," a woman with brown, loose hair chuckles. "He's everything Harald is not, but Harald invited him here as the goldsmith for your wedding rings. My name is Enora, and this wet blanket is Ingrid."

"I am advising her to be cautious. As we all should," Ingrid whispers, her small frame shivering under a big cloak.

"We've lived here our whole life and never seen anything so amazing," Enora exclaims.

"So are you going to tell me what you know about Shaw?" I ask, pressing my lips together to stifle my need for information.

"Only if you teach me how to shoot like that," Enora replies. I raise my eyebrows at her boldness. Finally, someone around here who isn't scared of challenging men. Following the group of women off the field, I give Jorvik a sweet wave. I earned this moment, and I've missed having company to talk too.

"I can teach you. Though I am alarmed that Harald and his men haven't trained you?" I ask, and a few women behind me fall silent.

"Harald recommends we tend to the fields and our chores. But…"

"Enora. Hush," Ingrid says, wedging herself between us. Glancing to my other side, I see Katrine and Joanna are hanging on the women's admission that they truly are held back from learning crucial Viking skills.

"We cannot talk out here where anyone could overhear," Ingrid explains. The women's longhouse is in the middle of the village, giving us a beautiful view of the roaring Yule fire on our way. Embers smolder underneath, melting all the snow in the ceremonial circle, and the tall flames send plumes of white smoke into the cloudy sky.

"It feels like a storm is coming," I say to break the awkward silence that followed Enora's mention of the King.

"I wouldn't mind," Joanna adds. "Twelve days of feasting is exhausting. A few days of being snowed in and napping would suit me just fine." She lets a tiny grin perk up her thin lips, and I wonder if she's thinking of the lynx sleeping off her fever back in the stronghold.

We follow the women into the longhouse, and the instant smell of familiarity overwhelms me. Having double the amount of unwed women here means cots line the edge of the main room, and bedding is everywhere. I grin at how little Harald knows of his own clanswomen after accusing me of lying in a pile of my friends. I'm sure there were women here who cuddled together last night for warmth.

"Welcome, Maiden of Yule." Enora turns to face me, giving us all an outlandish, sweeping bow. "Our messy but comfortable home is also yours."

I step over bags of extra clothes and pillows strewn across the floor toward the circular fire pit in the middle of the open room. Women casually chatting with one another walk into hallways leading to their rooms, and others find an assortment of cups for hot drinks.

"So tell me, why does Harald keep you all from hunting or using weapons?" I ask, finding a plush seat next to the fire.

"The King gave him orders too," Enora starts explaining, but her friend interrupts.

"You are going to get us banished from the Wild Hunt or worse. Sorry, but I can't get into any trouble. My family needs me to marry," Ingrid says, unfastening her coat.

"I don't want to get you in trouble." I try to assure them, but it doesn't feel like Ingrid believes me. Katrine and Joanna come to sit, handing out cups of hot tea, and Enora grabs a flask, adding a bit of liquor to each cup.

"I have heard stories that the goddess Skadi is buried here. Does anyone know where?" I ask, keeping my tone casual.

"Skadi is disgraced, and Harald is going to be livid that you won that archery match. The people will be praying for a feast in your name now, and that will make Harald jealous of the attention you are getting." Ingrid is quick to explain.

"Why is she disgraced?" I bring the discussion back to Skadi.

"Think, Rasha. Harald may have the King's support and favor, but only if he can get the Vikings in line. According to songs we no longer sing, Skadi was a goddess who renounced her betrothed and the realm of the gods to live on her own."

"That sounds like a goddess we should be praying to, not disgracing," I retort. Enora's face lights up as she drinks, and the majority of the women nod in agreement. But Ingrid has a permanent scowl on her face.

Joanna perks up to add, "Harald and the King will force us eventually if we do not learn to live in the King's new ways. None of us wants to be wed against our wishes. But Jorvik arranged for you to marry, and therefore, you can protect us as best as you can."

"I know. I will always try to protect you. That is why I want to find the bow. It is a symbol of balance, and the other clan leaders will have to respect it."

"You don't understand." Ingrid keeps her light eyes urgently fixed upon me. "They don't care about the balance of the Immortal Realm and our world. The King doesn't believe in the gods and goddesses."

"Help me find the tomb so we have proof that we are not alone in this mountain range, that the gods are with us?" I am going out on a limb, which is dangerous, but there are too many women here who look at me like what I've agreed too will set the standard for the rest of them.

"That is impossible. The songs about the shrine and Skadi's bow haven't been sung in our lifetime. We can't read the scrolls if Harald hasn't burned them all already," Ingrid says.

Sipping the hot tea, I contemplate what to say. The after burn of the liquor in each mouthful radiates down my chest and into my stomach. Joanna and Katrine engage in other conversations around me while I try to find a common ground between Enora, who wants me to defy the Jarl, and Ingrid, who would prefer I teach all the women how to skin a deer rather than hunt one.

Slowly, the tension in the room unwinds as the women stock the fire pit with logs, and the room reaches a toasty temperature. I should find a reason to leave and check on the lynx, but Enora has something of the tip of her tongue, which makes me hesitate. Someone asks Ingrid to show her how to do a particular stitch for a dress, and she moves to help. Enora pounces on the moment and slides next to me in the pillows, putting her feet on the edge of the fire pit.

"Ingrid is scared. Please don't think less of her," she says as she fluffs her brown hair, each section falling over her shoulders in waves.

38

"What happened when Harald declared women could no longer hunt?" I don't want to ask, but need to so I can understand what I am up against.

"Any woman who didn't comply was killed in public. Over the summer, her mother was one of them."

"Oh, Enora. I don't know what to say."

"She is determined to marry a man who is on Harald's council to protect herself. Maybe Bjorn? But I hate that for her. She fears many people will be killed if they don't bend the knee once Yule is over. And there's more."

"That sounds like enough." My grip on the cup tightens as she continues.

"I've poured drinks for Harald's council, and well, I've stayed later in their rooms then maybe I should have." Enora rubs her own arms, trying to shake feelings that I know all too well. "Your brother, Jorvik, and Harald want nothing more than to see the King and attempt to sit at his court. Whatever that is."

Sighing at my predetermined fate, I say, "I know Jorvik's ambition will be the death of him and me."

"There are plenty of women who will follow you away from here," Enora encourages.

"If I don't have the gods on my side, it is going to be impossible to have the support of the men, and without strength, we are as good as slaves if I don't marry Harald at the end of Yule," I say, staring at the crisscross threads of the blanket over my knees.

"What did you want to know about Shaw?" Enora moves back to my original question.

"Did he pledge to Harald?" I ask, looking at the angle of the sun out of the longhouse window. I need to wrap this up and return to the lynx.

"No, and it pisses Harald off. Shaw lives alone somewhere in the Sacred Forest. He comes occasionally with weapons that outmatch all of ours, and he knows things that no one else does. Like when Harald was building the stronghold, Shaw came to teach the other blacksmiths how to make things like hinges. But he tends to disappear for years at a time."

"Well he bleeds like every other Viking," I reply, and Enora gives me a once over as she waits for any other details I have about the mysterious smith. "I saw him in the medicine room this morning, that's all. He looked like he got into it with someone, and then, on the field, he seemed fine."

"He is going to be very sought after by the women at the Wild Hunt because he never stays for the entirety of Yule. Luckily for all of us, we have days to prepare."

"Speaking of preparing, I should go." I use the opening in the conversation to stand and search the room for Joanna and Katrine.

"You can come here anytime!" Enora shouts after me, and I look back, giving her my warmest smile.

I follow the sounds of Katrine's exuberant voice down one of the hallways. She's sitting in the middle of a few women, retelling a story of one of our hunting trips where I took down a moose. Flicking her eyes over to me as I lean on the doorframe, she suddenly throws her body down in the blankets, pretending to be the moose. All the women clap at her performance until they realize I am standing there.

"I just wanted to let you know I was going back," I say, and Katrine scoots off the bed, taking the blanket with her to wrap around her shoulders.

"Do you want us to come with you?"

"No," I reply. Katrine shifts, blocking the rest of the women from listening to what we say. "You don't have to make me out to be larger than life."

"Yes, I do. If you are going to find that bow and convince these women to follow you, I need to make them believe in your abilities," she counters, pressing her full lips together till the pink turns white.

"I thought you didn't agree?"

Her voice drops to a whisper. "I don't want you to get killed. Either way, you need more than Joanna and I on your side."

Giving her hand a squeeze, I thank her for her support and leave the women's longhouse. Everyone is busy this afternoon, playing games in the field or finding comfort indoors with music and drink, so my walk back to the stronghold is uneventful.

Past the tall stone walls, I see the tips of the mountain range, and below lies the frozen fjord. The biggest obstacle in finding the tomb will be the weather and the lack of a map. If what the women are saying about how Harald feels regarding the gods and goddess is true, then he will have gotten rid of any of the texts talking about Skadi and chiseled out any of her runes around the village. I will have to find someone who's been here longer or outlived Harald's council. Wracking my brain for an idea, I stuff my hands in my pockets to keep them from getting cold, and my fingers hit an extra pouch from the medicine room.

The memory of Shaw's bruised face laying on the cot distracts me, and the way he shot today is also curious. Why would someone who seems like they have so much to offer any clan choose to live alone? The women said he is a smith, and smiths work in the forge right by the stronghold, so it won't be hard to see him again.

Taking the steps two at a time, I happily use the key to open my door and give thanks to Freya that I didn't run into any trouble on my way back. The fire still smolders in the hearth, and the cat is curled up close to the flames. Taking off my heavy coat and snow crusted pants, I gather the loose linen top over my head.

"Rasha." I hear his voice from somewhere in the room.

6

SHAW

The unmistakable whiff of Aslaug was on her clothes. I should have been shocked when I looked over down the archery range and saw the woman from this morning with a magnificent draw on a bow sized for a man. But shock is useless when much of life is determined by fate.

Her aim needed the smallest amount of assurance after seeing me jostled her nerves. A piece of my soul stirred back to life watching her. She looked taken aback that I would concede my win. Kissing her hand gave me the opportunity to seize an errant piece of hazel fur on her cuff, confirming my thoughts. She saved Aslaug and had a good enough heart to bring her medicine this morning.

One drink with Harald after the archery competition and the bastard told me where her room was. He also made no mention of the lynx or knowing anything about why Bjorn attacked me. I am sure it was Bjorn. His face might have been covered in the forest, but his sneer in the Feast Hall gave him away.

Since I am the one who taught the blacksmiths how to make the locks, breaking into her room proved easy. What I didn't expect was for her to take her clothes off without realizing I am sitting in the corner of her room by the fire.

"Rasha," I softly call her name, forcing myself to stop watching the most beautiful woman peel her clothes off her luscious breasts in the sanctity of her own space.

"What the fuck!" she shrieks and grabs a seizable knife off her night table. Choosing to not care about her partial nudity, she comes at me. My mouth runs dry with the same mixture of self preservation and utter desire from this morning.

"Why didn't you tell me you had Aslaug?" I stand, bringing my hands to a defensive position. Her anger changes to confusion in a heartbeat as she looks down at the sleeping lynx.

"Who?"

I jut an elbow to the curled up feline, and Rasha's piercing blue eyes stare back at me while she tries to put it together.

"Aslaug is the lynx. She's my cat."

"Well, then you should be thanking me." She twirls the knife over her knuckles and backs away to get a dry dress, turning her back to me. I am left standing like a hooked fish with my mouth open. Her spine is milky white with several raised scars, one following the curve of her ribs to where her breast falls. I shut my eyes completely.

"Shaw, you broke into *my* room," she firmly reminds me.

"You lied," I bite out and let one of my eyelids flutter open to see her toss her leggings off from underneath a dress that fully covers her. My knee aches as I sit, stretching out in the chair opposite her bed.

"How was I supposed to know the cat is yours and has a name? For that matter, why did you leave her to die?" She hurls the insult, and I am wounded. She is right. I didn't go back out last night to look for Aslaug. My gaze falls to the floor where the hazel and white, speckled, furry beast sleeps off her fever.

"Can I explain?" I don't spend time with women. There is nothing good that will come from getting involved with someone I cannot spend my whole life with. But with the way this huntress is looking at me, I wouldn't mind spending one night pretending my life is not predetermined by the gods.

43

"Go on," she says and proceeds to hang her wet clothes near the fire.

"I was attacked on my way to the gate. I told Aslaug to stay home, but she is a cat, obviously not a normal one as you can see. She must have followed me, despite my instructions. She saved my life when the attackers got the upperhand, and I told her to run. Harald's men will not be kind to her if she is discovered." I explain my story, letting the familiar level of disappointment and guilt seep from my bones into my heart where I welcome what I deserve. I left Aslaug to die. Maybe that is why the great cat chose a new partner? Have I learned nothing in the long years I have lived alone?

Rasha takes a settling breath, and I look at her perched on the bed, wondering how much I can trust a woman who's been brought here to marry the Jarl.

"I am sorry. I heard the fighting."

"You did?"

"It was after I lit the Yule log. I went as close to the gate as I could, and Aslaug, as you call her, threw her wounded self at me. Joanna and I brought her up here and no one else saw."

"Joanna knows too? The woman who shot with you today?" My nervous energy builds, and I stand.

"Joanna is my second and would never tell. Like I said, when I saw you this morning, Aslaug had a fever from the wounds she should stay and heal. But what I don't understand," she pauses and quietly comes around to the other side of the bed where I am. Needing to stand where the icy breeze comes through the uneven slats in the new windows, I wait for her to finish her question.

"I don't understand why you're healed." She reaches for the fading bruise on my jaw, and I wish I had grown a beard for this moment.

"Siggy is a good medicine woman," I answer, but I can see the dissatisfaction in her high cheekbones. My gaze falls to her lips, barely parted and glossy pink, as she touches the edge of my jaw.

"I didn't see you when you were first brought in, so maybe you are telling me the truth." Rasha's voice strains against another thought I don't have to be a god to understand.

"You cannot tell anyone else. Joanna is already one person too many. I am not beneath ending a life if I am betrayed," I threaten. Her face falls, and she leaves the shared space, taking her sweet scent with her.

"I would never tell Harald about such a lovely creature. But you owe me now."

"Maybe we can help each other?"

"I already saved her."

"Yes, but like you said, she'll need to stay here until she's healed, and with Harald trying to get in between these sheets, how long will I be able to trust you?" I ask, realizing I am passing judgement too soon.

"I don't care for Harald. Give me a little credit?" she answers, shivering from the fresh snow hitting her windowpane. Prompting me to add two more logs to the fire, I step over Aslaug as the lazy cat stretches out to show me her bandaged side.

"I owe you, so you name it. But in the meantime, Bjorn took something from me. I need it back, and I need to know if Harald has it or has seen it," I explain. Rubbing my hands through the cat's thick fur, I am surprised at how frail her body is. Years ago, I thought of her as immortal as Freya herself.

"That is a tall ask," Rasha mutters, pacing around her room in bare feet as her plain, dark-green dress drags against the floor-boards. "Bjorn is unpredictable from my short time knowing him. Why would he steal something from you when Harald could have asked?"

"Maybe Harald asked once, and I lied."

"That doesn't sound hypothetical. Also, if you want us to work together, you can't assume I am going to run and tell Harald." Standing at the foot of her bed, she wraps her arms around herself.

"I have omitted many parts of my life to Harald because he will not act in the Vikings' best interest if he knows the things I know."

"Which are? How am I supposed to find what Bjorn took if I don't know what it is used for?"

"Don't get ahead of yourself, and don't end up alone with Bjorn under any circumstances. If you hear him talking about a map to the mountain pass, come and get me. Alright?" I cannot stress enough that she doesn't need to put herself in danger. Rasha leans back on her bed, a multitude of scenarios running through my mind, ranging from delicate to downright wicked. I need to resist the urge to satisfy her in a way that none of the men here ever will.

"Tell me what it is you need the most?" Hopefully it is a task I can see through easily, and then we can find a safe exit for Aslaug.

"I need Skadi's bow," she whispers across the quiet space. My muscles tense against my clothes, too hot for a blacksmith who's used to smoldering temperatures. The bow? How could she know about the one thing I have been searching for over an eternity for?

"You don't know that exists." I slowly gauge how much she knows and search for what the gods have already laid out for her.

"It must. Why else would Harald be so keen on keeping women from hunting and refuse to give women in his clan any freedom. There must be merit to the ballad, or it would mean nothing to celebrate her. The King will force us to give up our land. I can take whoever wants to come with me to the mountains to live with the reindeer if I have the bow."

"You're ambitious," is all I can muster. Gathering her long, red hair, she lays it against her chest and combs out the ends. "Give me something that is not impossible to achieve. The bow is not real, Rasha. It's a fool's promise." *The lie is for her own good.* Aslaug's soul catching stare makes it harder for me to continue.

"There has to be a way to know for sure. A lynx this size came from the gods. There are stories and ballads of them sending animal guides to our Mortal Realm. Once, the reindeer provided meat and hides for warmth and milk to our children. There must be a way for us to live with them again," she persists, despite being flustered.

"After the Divination feast, we can search the fjord for her burial place if it pleases you. It will be nothing but a collection of stones long forgotten. But I should go now before someone discovers I am in the Maiden's room."

"I hate that title," she says, pushing off the bed and going to the door.

"By the way you handled yourself today, I'd say you earned it." I try to give her hope, even though her path to Harald seems set.

"I saved my virginity for the gods, not for a man to squander." Her admission settles in my perpetual guilt. If she only knew gods squander what they hold most dear too.

"They haven't forsaken you. That I can promise. Be careful with her," I say in parting. She checks to make sure the hallway is clear, and I give Aslaug a good head scratch before leaving.

The door shuts, and I wait till she turns the lock before pulling the hood over my head and leaving the stronghold. Her scent left my coat smelling like sweet evergreen and fresh arousal. Her fucking, full lips and determined, blue eyes will be impossible to forget.

Back in the forge, I light the kiln to keep the room warm and the irons hot. Giving the resident blacksmiths a break for the days of Yule wasn't only a nice thing to do, but I prefer to be alone. Reaching for the honeyed wine I hid under the cot, I let the thick, warm liquid settle me from the inside. My cock is hard, sitting useless in my trousers. Am I truly contemplating that she could be who I think? Taking a deep swig from the bottle, I lay down and pray for sleep.

Rest overtakes me along with snow and sleet. Waking up in the middle of the night to a blast of icy wind and snow piling around the doors, I race to pull the walls closed around the forge so the kiln doesn't lose its flame. My hands are frozen as I bring in all the wood I should have brought in earlier and stack it by the table to keep dry.

The storm howls, rattling the walls as sneaky snowflakes pour through the loose cracks in the wood. Can't a man have any peace in this life? Adding another layer of clothes to my tunic and trousers, I put my coat on and walk out into winter's fury.

The sun will not be up for another few hours, and in the frigid layers of falling snow, I won't have to worry about anyone following me. Thinking about Rasha, hopefully sound asleep with Aslaug high above me, I trudge away from the stronghold toward the fjord.

Watching Rasha with the bow, not just her beautiful form with the arrow, but how she defended herself and her people, I know why

47

I am here. I wish the stars gave me another task in redemption. After seeing what her clan, her own flesh and blood has done to her, it doesn't seem fair to put her through another trial. The gods are never wrong, and to bring a virgin huntress here, during this solstice, is not a coincidence.

7

RASHA

The next day is uneventful. I steal a leg of lamb and slip back up to my room as night draws near. Aslaug is immediately thrilled at the fresh, oily meat and happily chomps down on a good meal for the first time in who knows how long. It is good to see her in better spirits.

Everywhere in my room, I feel Shaw. His ability to break in without me knowing revolves in my mind, making it impossible to sleep. Maybe I want him to come back? A different type of thrill throbs in my belly when I remember how he looked at me against the moonlight. Then my heart sinks as I remember how quick he was to tell me the bow wasn't real. Everyone keeps saying it doesn't exist, but the way Shaw's face changed when I mentioned it, fuels my plan.

Tomorrow, I will have to sit outside with Harald at the Yule log, accepting offerings from Vikings in our clans, but tonight, I am left alone in my room. As much as I welcome the quiet, nights like this, when Jorvik doesn't return to our home, or I am the last one hunting on the mountain, makes my grief resurface like flowers I planted long ago, rising through the dirt on their own accord. Each beautiful petal reminds me how much our parents loved us, and how much I wish they were here to guide me.

The last lessons I remember about the gods were from our mother and father. They broke away from the clan when they married and established themselves beyond the mountain pass. After their deaths, Jorvik brought us to the Beaivi Clan and immediately I wanted to leave. I was too young to travel alone, and by the time I found a place out of the kitchen and into the hunting party, I couldn't remember the way through the mountains. In a decade, the landscape of the mountains and forest has changed, and the tiny cabin we lived in when it was the four of us is probably buried under piles of rocks and snow.

Aslaug follows me to the door of my bedroom. I'm not sure if she is trying to come with me or make me stay, but her paws still have raw spots, and Shaw would never forgive me if I let anything happen to her. Promising to return with more food, I take a chance at scratching her head the way he did and lock her inside for the night.

Letting my instincts carry me, I am already out of my room and down the stairs without dwelling on the consequences. Sneaking past the small groups of men drinking around the fire pits is easy, and in a few more steps, I leave the stronghold.

My red hair is braided in one long plait and covered by the hood of my fur cloak. The fjord is beyond Harald's wall, and at this time of night, no one will be traipsing through the snow. Searching for the tomb or the bow should be easy while they enjoy a fresh round of music and drinking on one of the less exuberant nights of Yule.

I thought of asking Joanna to come with me, but the risk of running into the women from the longhouse is too great. The less people who know where I am the less I will have to worry about endangering anyone on my behalf.

Now that I know my way around better, I find where the wall is weakest and slip through without alerting the gate guards. Wedging my shoulder and hip between the narrow, broken slats is hard, given my wide hips. It's going to leave a bruise, but I push through anyway and kneel in the snow to catch my breath.

Freedom is beyond this wall. Freedom is deep in the forest where I can disappear into the towering pine trees and evergreens. The icy snow biting into my knees and palms reminds me of my mother, harsh on the outside but always teaching me a lesson. She loved us and tried to give us a life away from a clan that only sought to chain me to a marriage bed. But Jorvik is staining her teachings. He is determined to live a life opposite our mother and father, as if he can spite their corpses with his strict adherence to clan rules.

Standing, I leave the dark snowy forest to my left and head for the fjord. It is tempting to run and never look back, but there are too many women who follow me as their guide through the season.

The water is frozen solid and will be for another few months, until the spring thaw, but that doesn't make walking over it easy. Gingerly, I step onto the ice. As I adjust my balance so I don't slip, I am suddenly knocked on my ass. Muscled fur crashes into me, and we slide across the ice. Reaching for her thick coat, I hiss her name into the never ending darkness.

"Aslaug, you can't be out here." Hearing me, she digs those piercing claws into the ice, and we stop sliding. Underneath, the thick layers buckle and sway with our combined weight. Pushing thoughts of being submerged in the numbing waters away, I find my footing and step away from the great lynx.

Turning her head without moving her body, she glares at me. I worry for anyone who actually crosses her path when she's in good health. The healing gash in her fur is still prominent from my view as I try to glide around her on the ice.

"What is that look for? I told you to stay inside," I chide, but she ignores me. Squinting to see the slowly drifting plumes of smoke over the stronghold, I look for a sign that someone could have seen her. Shaw will be furious when, or if, he finds out we are both out on the fjord. Thankfully, the trees along the bank are still, and I don't even see an owl or a fox.

Squeezing my eyes shut for a second, I bury the foolish hope that sparked when I met Shaw. That tiny flicker of anticipation he might burst through the woods is snuffed out by the cold. He is only going to bring me heartbreak, but his cat, on the other hand, might be helpful.

"How did you get out? Did anyone see you?" I ask logical questions, but she slinks away, walking gracefully toward the mountains and maybe the tomb. Having no choice other than following her, I try my best to slide and walk without slipping. In some places, the ice cracks underneath my boots, and my heart lurches, causing me to shuffle one way or the other.

The moon is three quarters of the way full, and the clouds out here are not as dense, giving me decent visibility in the dark. Feeling my hip for my knife, I double check its position, calming my nerves. The closer we get the more the wind picks up from the mountains, sweeping wet ice and snowflakes around my face until my teeth clatter.

"Are you sure we are going the right way, Aslaug?" I ask, bending down to brace myself against a harsh gust. Tucked into the tunic under my coat is a fire starter, but finding a place to block out the wind is going to be difficult, and making a fire might be impossible.

The lynx stops a few feet away from where the mountain looks like it sinks into the fjord. Sharp rocks stick out from the ice, and I have no way of knowing how stable my steps are the closer I am to where land should be underneath.

"Aslaug wait!" I yell as she leaps from the ice, using her massive back legs to land up on a dry ledge. She peers over the top as if to say *you next.*

I can't jump that high. My fingers are cold inside the pockets of my coat, and when I let out a hot breath, it instantly freezes against the cold air. Walking underneath the ledge, I keep my gaze on her, waiting to see what she does, but she's not looking at me.

Something beneath the ice has her attention. Using the protruding rocks, I slide myself around to look down at the same angle. The rocks are covered in layers of ice that melt where I touch, making my fingers numb. The walls of the mountain are sheer and flat for as far as I can see in the dark.

"I can't stay out here all night. I'll freeze to death," I whisper, trying not to totally break down, but I don't understand what she is trying to show me. The snow covering the mountains might be hiding an entrance but I might need to come back in the daylight to further explore.

Aslaug shifts above me, letting out a long whine, and pushes massive icicles off the ledge. Ducking under it, I narrowly miss a sharp piece of broken ice as it crashes onto the frozen fjord.

"Are you trying to kill me?" I question the cat but receive no response. Carefully gripping the side of the mountain, I slide back out and lose my balance. Struggling on my hands and knees, I see the shape of a longboat underneath the ice. Aslaug looks down at me, and I smile while her huge, glowing amber eyes watch me as if to say, *Don't you trust me?*

Chuckling, I wipe the ice off my cheeks and try to breathe properly. Below us is a funeral boat carved from stone, and I might not be the best at reading, but I know what a bow rune looks like when I see one.

"Why did you jump up there if the tomb is under the ice?" I ask, my voice bubbling out over cold, shallow breaths. Aslaug lays down, her huge paws hanging over the edge like she has been waiting to come here, and now that she's here, she is going to sleep.

I'll never be able to break through the ice to reach the stone boat, and my body is already succumbing to the plummeting temperature. I can come back tomorrow with Joanna and Katrine, or maybe with Shaw if he is in a good mood?

Gazing up at Aslaug, I have the strange sense she is waiting for me to do something. I pat my thighs like I am calling a dog from a herd of sheep, but Aslaug is too existential for such things. She opens her strong jaws, showing off those big fangs, and yawns.

"Well it is Yule, and during Yule, we make offerings. The only thing I have tonight is my blood," I say to myself, wondering if the great cat is even listening anymore. Taking the knife from inside my tunic, I carve the same runes I painted on the Yule log into the ice. My legs start to lose all feeling, but if I die out here, at least I won't have to marry Harald.

The cynical way my thoughts have protected me causes a smile to perk up my cold lips. Pushing my sleeves up, I slice my forearm open because I don't think my numb palms have any blood flow. I squeeze my arm and watch my hot blood drip down my elbow. The deep crimson fills the etched ice carving, and a fresh wave of dizziness overtakes me.

8

RASHA

Stay awake. Stay awake. Stay awake.

I need to move, but I am so cold. Rubbing my chest to try to warm up, I hear Aslaug moving on top of the ledge. Maybe she will be loving and come down here to cuddle with me so I don't pass out? Laying down on the ice near my carvings, I watch my blood trickle through them and realize how much I miscalculated my ability to withstand the cold. My hips and shoulders ache in defeat. Maybe I'll sleep and wake up to the sun warming me? The skin on my cheek is stuck to the frosty ground, making it painful to move, but I see someone coming.

"Aslaug!" Shaw's voice echoes in a harsh call across the fjord, and I swear snow rattles from the mountain. Ignoring me, she leaps off the ledge and bounds to her master.

Ripping my face off the ice, I can't tell if I tore my skin or not due to being mostly numb. I move my sleeve over the cut on my arm and steady my weight, trying to move my limbs. My pants are wet with ice and snow making my movements stiff.

Shaw watches as I slide around. He is going to have cross words with me about coming here alone, which is not how I pictured this night going. I'd rather keep the upper hand and make it to him with my chin held high. But without Aslaug to lean on, it is harder to balance. He sees me floundering, falling hard, and strides across the ice with his heavy, black coat engulfing his frame.

"What are you doing out here?" he says before he reaches me. I get to my feet, and he grabs my hips with his strong hands.

"I had to see for myself if there was a tomb. Are you out here trying to find the bow before I do?" My voice wavers in the cold, but I stay determined. He looks past me to Aslaug's ledge and shakes his head.

"You took her out of the room when you promised you wouldn't." He switches topics to scold me.

"I'd rather talk about the longboat at the bottom of the fjord that you should have told me about, since she is a grown animal and broke out of my room all by herself."

He turns to her, and I wouldn't be surprised if they were somehow silently communicating. Aslaug rubs her body against my shaking legs and beams up at him. His hand is firm around my waist, and I feel his muscles relax as he uses his other hand to pet her.

"No one has ever found the bow, Rasha. One tomb under the ice doesn't mean what you think," Shaw murmurs, bringing my body closer to his. I swallow the dryness in my throat. Opening his coat, he pauses and drops his hand from my side. "Warm yourself for a moment, and I'll take you back before we all freeze to death."

Did he come out here looking for me or for the bow to have an advantage over Harald? My thoughts are lost to the wind as I stand next to him, waiting for something to happen.

"Rasha, you can come closer if you want," he says, and I glide into his solid chest. Burying my face in the heat of his tunic, I feel his arms wrap around and cover me with his coat. His chin rests on my head while I let his body heat warm my lungs so I can take a proper breath.

"I wouldn't let anything happen to her," I finally whisper, taking in his scent of burning embers and pine.

"She is a gift from the gods. I have failed them in the past, so I am protective," he admits. His hands rub circles over my back, and I smoosh my face into the ties and seams of his tunic.

"Why didn't you say she might know the way? Is she trying to show me the tomb or what she thinks I need to see?"

"She is bringing you to those she greatly misses," he says. Our faces are so close that he could rest his cheek against mine. Our hot breath mingles, taking shape on the icy air and rising up around us.

"So there is a chance the bow is under the ice?" I ask again, trying to understand why he doesn't trust me.

"I'll explain, but first we need to get inside," he replies, letting go of my body against his. I back away and throw my arms out to find balance. Shaw seems to have no trouble walking on the ice, and despite grabbing my hands a few times to prevent me from falling, we manage to make it back to land uneventfully.

On our way to the wall, we find evergreen branches to wipe away our tracks and stay low to avoid being seen. When we are at the loose part that I came through earlier, Shaw kneels on one knee to whisper something to Aslaug. Brushing her head against my hand in her own form of goodbye, she takes off into the darkest part of the forest.

"Where is she going?" I ask in alarm.

"Where she will be safe. I'll check on her tomorrow before the feast. Besides, she needs to hunt, and it's safer for her away from the clans."

"You aren't worried she isn't healed fully?" I ask, wedging my body through the tight wooden slats.

"I am, but if she breached your room to find you, it means she is ready to be in the wilderness," he explains. It is harder for his bulky shoulders to fit through, but he does, and we throw our hoods over our heads to keep anyone still awake from recognizing us. The village is barren and quiet. Everyone is sleeping, tucked into their cozy beds in the longhouses for the night. Soon enough, we are standing in front of the stronghold.

"Do you have a tub?" Shaw asks, and I shake my head. Lingering together is dangerous, but I have no desire to go to bed cold and alone. He takes my hand, and we leave the double doors to meander around the side where the forge is.

"The forge has a tub?" I watch his hazel eyes catch my raised eyebrows.

"The forge is well stocked," he replies and opens the door for me to go inside. Adding a stack of logs to the bottom of the kiln, he pumps the air from the top to reignite the fire below.

"You should take off those wet clothes," he says as he walks around collecting things. Touching my wet pants, I find the ties with my numb fingers and struggle to loosen the knot. Getting naked in front of a man with the power to do anything he wants with me is a terrible idea, but he hasn't shown a hint of aggression or need.

I abandon the frozen ties and look around instead. Weapons in all stages of being struck and welded are everywhere. Swords and axes in various conditions line the tables and drying racks. Tools, crowd buckets, and black stained clothes are hung over chairs.

Shaw carries heavy pales of snow into a back room, and I follow him. He's already taken off his layers of fur and black suede, keeping only a white tunic on. Sleeves rolled up, he adds snow to a small wooden tub with a smoldering fire underneath.

"Thank you." My voice is small against the snow splashing into the tub. Over his shoulder, he catches me staring and puts the bucket down. Dipping his hand in, he shakes his fingers with excess water and walks over to where I stand.

"I didn't think you'd run off in the dead of night to go look for a bow. Are you always this impatient?" he asks, and my cheeks redden.

"I am not impatient. I need to find a way to stop this marriage and Harald."

My body is at odds with the cold and the heat from the fire below the tub. I shrug out of my coat and try again to take my frozen tunic or pants off. My fingers shake so badly I want to scream, but he'll think I really don't have any patience.

"Rasha, let me help you." His voice is soft like he is speaking to Aslaug. Letting my limbs go slack at my sides, I look off to the side of the room, trying to will all the arousal out of my blood. He takes a knife from the little table near his cot and finds the ties. I feel his eyes on mine, and I stare back. Without looking at my body, he cuts the ties and loosens my waistband.

I find the edge of my pants and shimmy out of them, breaking the palpable hunger between us. No one said I had to stay away from the touch of men, I only have to be a virgin, which is becoming less and less of a focal point. I don't need to be a virgin to wield a bow that might not even exist.

"Do you need help with the rest of it?" he asks, and my willpower dwindles.

"Go on," I whisper. This time I close my eyes as his rough hands trace the edge of my skin under the long, wet tunic. Raising my arms above my head, I allow him to pull the whole wet top over my body.

Being naked, wholly free, in front of him is a moment I might treasure till they light my corpse on fire. How can a sane man be this honorable? Taking my elbow in his calloused hand, he opens my arm to see the cut I made with my own knife, causing me to flinch.

"What did you do?" His question is quiet. Sudden nerves spread over my chest like I've made a mistake. Looking down at the cut above the crook of my arm my soggy skin still trickles tiny drops of blood.

"I made an offering," I reply. Whatever he wants to say comes out in a grunt, and he squeezes his hand around my skin to stop the bleeding. I am no longer aware of the difference between pain and pleasure.

My pink nipples harden in the drafty bedroom. We are too close. With his hands on the small wound, my desire for him to put his hands elsewhere is almost too much to bear. He lets out a ragged breath, forcing me to come to my senses. Stepping around him, I move into the steaming tub, thankful to be able to hide under the water.

"You could have died out there. I told you before I would take you. Can't you trust me?" The concern in his voice makes no sense. I don't know anything about him other than he cares for a creature gifted to him by the gods. I don't even know why the gods favor him.

"What do you care if I die? And why should I trust you? For all I know, you could tell Harald everything you've seen me do tonight and be rewarded. You are a free man. At any time, you can take your cat and leave."

"I am not free," he bites out and comes to the edge of the tub so we can properly glare at each other.

"That makes two of us," I challenge, bringing my forearms to the same edge, and we are once again touching. His tense thumb brushes over my ice-burned cheek like he's fighting to regain his composure but wants to feel me against his skin all the same.

"You have a clan that admires you and women who look up to you. Stop being so reckless."

"So rescuing your cat and trying to find a relic from the gods is reckless?"

He grinds his jaw together. "You're the Maiden of Yule. Act like it."

"Don't Maiden me. I saved myself to be worthy of being a huntress. To serve the goddesses. And all my prayers, all my sacrifices, have gone unheard. That's why I went out on the fjord tonight."

"Your prayers have not fallen on deaf ears. If you want a reason why I am fond of you, or why for the next eight days we should trust each other, I don't have one. But fate is foolish." He stretches to stand and adjusts his trousers to hide his hard cock bulging against the seam.

"Shaw, you don't have to go." I don't know what I plan on doing if he stays, but sending him away feels painful.

He holds his position in the doorway, finally gazing down at me. "I'll be right outside," he replies, taking his time to drink me in before leaving.

The water is exactly what I needed to thaw my frozen muscles. Rubbing my thighs and arms, my thick blood starts to flow again, and turns my skin a rosy pink under the steam. I don't feel the least bit ashamed that he saw me naked. Smiling to myself at how hard he must be as he waits, I decide I don't need to wash my hair. Getting it wet will only make me colder, so I lean my shoulders on the wooden edge and picture the fjord.

He knew where the tomb was because he found me. Which means, like I thought earlier, there is something of value under the ice. Settling in my new found satisfaction, I close my eyes and picture his hand cupping my breast instead of my arm, imagining the feeling of his calloused hands over my sensitive nipples instead of the warm water in the bath.

As much as there is a unique tie keeping us together, I cannot understand if it is fate guiding me to him or cruel temptation showing me I am on this journey alone. Jorvik is obsessed with forcing me to marry Harald, and Harald expects me to have my virtue intact. Fuck all the men who think I will be so easily pushed around.

9

SHAW

I must have lost all common sense bringing her back here and taking off her clothes. Falling for a woman, *sleeping with a woman*, is an idea I have long banished. I take a deep breath and grip the forge, letting the fire remind me of my task and purpose.

The Maiden should not excite me the way she does. The feel of her skin on my hand will drive me to many sleepless nights, as if I haven't been experiencing them already. I chose this torture by offering her a bath, I know because I can't stop the feeling that I need her.

Rasha comes out of the makeshift bedroom, looking divine in my shirt and pants. I knew those were the only clothes back there when I brought her here. *Fuck.* I should have taken Aslaug two nights ago to avoid letting her lead her to the tomb, but some pulls are unavoidable.

"You can wash. I won't run off," she says, the slightest grin lifting her lips.

"I will before I sleep. I want to show you something to make up for being..." she adjusts the shirt over her curves, and I lose my train of thought.

"Over protective," she finishes.

"Yes. Shall we try to trust each other?" I ask, knowing I am looking at the shadow of her full breasts. Rasha clears her throat, and I break from the trance. Taking a small smelting cup, I add it to the kiln and ask, "Have you ever melted silver or gold?"

"No," she answers.

"It won't take long. They are soft metals that come from the Ivalo River that runs inside the mountain. The ore of the gods."

"And they contain magic?"

"It depends on what you believe." Seeing the color come back to her cheeks makes me feel better about bringing her here, so I pull out something I've never shown anyone. "I've made each link of this chain."

When I lay the delicate chain, slighting bigger than a necklace, over her hands, it dawns on me she is the first person beside myself who has felt the links with her own fingertips. She twists the chain in the light of the fire, gazing at the reflections of silver and gold in each tiny oval piece.

"It's beautiful, but it's not finished," she points out, holding the ends in bewilderment.

"Hold it while I get a few things," I say, needing to remove myself from the idea that she could forge the last links with me, and maybe then this nightmare will finally be over? Is it worth taking the chance? She does have a fearlessness I haven't seen in eons. In the bedroom, I shuffle my things from under the cot and bring out the honeyed wine and little bag of precious metals.

"I know this is more than a trinket you've made, but I am going to guess you're not willing to share its purpose?" she asks, dropping the chain link by link into my palm. Explaining that I've crafted each link with my lifebond to act as a reminder of my penance is not something I planned to divulge. Slipping the weightless chain in my trouser pocket, I give her a handful of silver and gold nuggets to examine.

"That seems overly kind of you to not pry," I reply, and her smile knocks the air from my lungs.

"You offered your tub, and I might want another bath, so put it on the list of things we owe each other for. And I don't want to push when I have another agenda," she says, coming to the side of the kiln where I line up tools and gloves.

"What's your other agenda? I am not looking for Harald to accuse me of touching you." I can't help but chuckle at my lie when I already touched her, and I'll dream of touching her again tonight.

"Can you teach me how to smith? How did you learn? How is the map more valuable than the ore? Or were you better at hiding the gold and silver?" Back to the rapid fire questions means she's warmed up from the fjord and feeling comfortable next to me. The urge to keep her curiosity alive lights a fire within my soul.

"Well, I have a skill for mining, and I learned to smith to make a living. Drop the ore in the smaller cup that's in the fire, won't you?" I ask, and she does as instructed. "And Bjorn thinks what he took is more valuable, yes." Staying close to the heat of the forge, I can't help my need to be close to her again. So I come up behind her with the long rod to secure the lid on top of the smelting cup. We watch the black iron grow hotter than a normal fire, turning a deep shade of orange as the heat fuels the ore to melt along with my restraint.

"Have a drink?" I ask. She agrees, and we settle near the forge on a bench with the bottle of honeyed wine. She takes the first sip and scrunches her nose as she swallows.

"It's strong," she sputters, wiping the glossy liquid from her lower lip.

"I make it, so don't run around telling your friends," I add, bringing up a blanket over our legs.

"They find you very interesting. That's for sure. Those girls will be after you at the Hunt, so you shouldn't fear your bed staying cold."

"Tell me, what do they say?" I take a mouthful of wine and pass the bottle back to her.

"You live alone for one, which I find very admirable." Her blue eyes watch my lips, and I know she's trying hard to sound casual.

"Why?"

She drinks again, settling against the blanket. "Because I was raised in the mountains by my parents without a clan, and there are days I wish I could live alone in the forest again."

"It's not for the faint of heart. I have been alone for a long time," I answer, realizing there is much I don't know about her. But having her open up with that nostalgia coloring her memories makes me want to know everything.

"You have Aslaug." Her leg slides against mine. I tell myself she's cold, and the bench is narrow.

"I do. Let's check the cup." I move, and she jumps up with me. The excitement we seem to be sharing is nice for a change. When I came to help build the Aske Stronghold, most women were relegated to cooking, not learning to smith.

"Put the gloves on." I point to an extra pair for her to slide her hands into. "I know simple jewelry isn't exciting to a fierce hunter, but would you like to make something with me?" I heave the heavy pole off the kiln, and she follows my lead, taking the long tongs to remove the lid.

"Is it good practice to make arrowheads?" she asks, and I refrain from smiling at her persistence. I bet the next question will be if she can make arrows for Skadi's bow.

"It is good practice for anything you'd want to make in the future. Please, if you will place the mold on the floor in the middle of the room." I keep giving instructions that she follows without fail, and I pour the molten metals in the clay mold carefully, not wasting a drop.

"So now we wait for it to get hard?" she asks with a sleepy laugh, taking off the gloves and reaching for the wine.

"Making jokes like that means you are tired and tipsy, but yes it hardens." She giggles again. "Should I take you back to your room?" I ask, but she opens the blanket, and I sit close, letting our bodies relish in the heat.

"How about you tell me about Aslaug and the gods, since I'm tipsy and won't take anything you say seriously?" Her gaze wanders down my chest in a way that lays me bare.

Giving into my desire, I put my arm around her shoulders, and she leans her head into my chest. I take the wine out of her hands and set the half drunk bottle on the floor, wrapping her up in the blanket.

"Comfortable?" I ask, and she has the sweetest audacity to snuggle in.

"Should I be afraid of you instead?"

"No, Rasha. You never have to fear me," I whisper against her red hair. Feeling each link in my pocket with my other hand, I remember all the years I have avoided setting things right. My atonement is hammered and sculpted in one long lifetime of loss. Her breathing becomes methodic, and I shift my shoulder to see her eyes have closed. Listening to her calm heartbeat, a thought creeps in like a pit revealed after water is wiped from a quenched blade. Has she ever felt safe enough to sleep so soundly?

I continue talking to lull her to actual sleep. "Since you'll probably wander out in the snow to look for Aslaug, I'll tell you that I have been separated from my family for many, many years because I made a choice that killed someone."

Cuddled in my ribcage, sleeping off her adventure, her body becomes heavy against mine, and I know she won't remember any of this. I tell her the story of how in one moment I lost my family and my seat. Cast into the Mortal Realm, alone to suffer a worse fate than a quick death. Aslaug was my mother's last gift to protect and remind me that I can earn my redemption, one link at a time.

Rasha is exquisite in a way I don't deserve. As I gather her up behind the knees, she grabs my tunic while mumbling something I don't try to understand. The night is more than half over, so bringing her to her room is easy. The courtyard is empty, and I open the locked door without a sound. Tucking her into her bed, I see the mess Aslaug made with the window, clawing through the wood to release the latch that I showed Harald's men how to make a year ago.

At least the crazy cat didn't shatter the glass. While Rasha sleeps, I bolt the latch back to the shredded window frame, knowing it won't stay permanently, and add logs to her fire so she doesn't wake up freezing.

The cold air sucks the romantic fog out from under me, and I jog down the staircase to return to the forge. The crucible sits unopened in the middle of the room where we left it. She was so busy chatting and questioning, she didn't ask what type of mold I used, and although I would have been honest, it might be nice to surprise her. I feel ridiculous for thinking this way when Harald has laid claim to her, and I am only a blacksmith looking to get home.

Wishing Aslaug was here to listen, I find the right pry bar to open the lid. Smithing iron or precious metals takes patience, which I have a lot of since I have lived in the mountains for many centuries. I grumble at how torn I am between wanting to tell Rasha the truth and knowing she'll think I am crazy or trying to get between her legs.

Slowly loosening the lid to not crack the mold or jostle the metal, I vow to give her a few days to come back to the forge if she chooses. Once the lid is off, I use my bare hands to loosen the clay. The gloves are purely for show, and over time, I've gotten used to putting on all the proper protective gear to not raise eyebrows.

Brushing away the hardened clay with my fingers, I see the shape of a bracelet come into view. Still soft, it is the perfect temperature to engrave, and once the metal solidifies fully with the winter's frigid air, it will be set until it is reheated.

Closing the kiln quickly, I bring everything into the bedroom and set up the bench to begin. I have no set pattern in mind, using the tiny instruments I created myself to etch the delicate motif into the silver and gold. Before long, the strokes of the sharp tools create the shape of many antlers interwoven in scroll work that reminds me of home. Different curves and lines are revealed as I picture Rasha's body and how strong she is. How strong I will need her to be in the coming months. *This bracelet is for her.* Turning it over, I examine the hollow pocket inside the band that is exactly the same size as the unfinished chain I carry.

10

RASHA

Waking up alone is almost painful. I don't remember going to my room or saying goodbye. The last thing I do remember is listening to Shaw talk about his family. He might have mentioned his mother giving him Aslaug, which is all a fuzzy blur in my addled mind.

My arms and legs hurt from the near hypothermia last night, and my thighs are slick with arousal. I dreamed of Shaw joining me in the tub, making my heart further entangled than I intended.

Aslaug is gone, out in the forest, hopefully hunting and putting plenty of space between Harald's awful men and herself. I wait alone for the sun to fully awaken and the day of sitting with Harald at the Yule log to begin.

Sitting up, I pull Shaw's shirt off my body and lay back down. We smell like one another. Ice and fire, honeyed wine and holly berries. The combination is enough to make me want to pleasure myself.

Pushing the blankets off, I shiver in the cold air and pray to the goddess that I will somehow be released from the infatuation over-whelming me. I pray that my blood seeping through the ice is enough to awaken Skadi in any form and show me the way to her bow. Maybe Shaw really does have a map that is worth something? We could buy or bargain our way out of bending a knee to Harald and the King.

Shaw's hazel's eyes roaming over my naked body in his room take precedence in my tortured mind. We were slightly tipsy when I touched his chest, laid a hand on his thigh, and leaned into his powerful pull. He might have dipped his beautiful jaw into my neck or carried me to bed, but my memory is a blur.

I wanted to ask him to stay, that much I know. My hands travel over my body the way I wanted his hands to, caressing my stomach until my heart flutters against my ribs, and my legs fall open on the soft mattress.

I am alone.

The thought comforts me, and I trace the outside of my wet cunt. If I need him in this way, how will I agree to marry Harald? My chest tightens in panic, and I decide to let go of fearing what is to come. At least for this moment.

My fingers dip into my aching flesh, and I can't hold back the softest moan, encircling my clit till my breath comes in shallow pants. My taut muscles contract and throb to the point of pain as I slip two fingers inside, sliding in and out, giving myself what I desperately need. I find my own raw, untouched walls and delve into the blissful madness of wanting Shaw to be the one who stretches me. Splaying my knees open, I press my palm against my clit and continue working my fingers inside myself.

Cresting to an orgasm, I hear the wind rattle the window Aslaug broke, easily breaking through the loose lock. A cold, snowy gust kisses my sweaty nipples. The sudden chill takes me over the edge, and my legs shake while I come, squeezing my fingers with each clench and release.

Spent and laying on the bed, I decide that if I can't find the bow, I will sacrifice myself before I marry Harald. I will die before I let a man take away my womanhood.

Latching on to that thought, I rise to close the window and resist the urge to leave the village through the loose slats in the wall again.

I need to find a way before the end of Yule or I am going to die resisting this marriage.

I comb my hair, braiding it in sections and wind the plaits around my head to keep it off my face. The buzzing between my legs doesn't stop when I pull my leggings up, barely touching myself. Adjusting my breasts in the heavy red and green dress over my warm layers makes it hard to breathe, and I half curse ever meeting such a man. We will probably run into each other during the day or at tonight's Divination feast and I wonder if he woke up as needy as I did? Divination is always exciting. Who doesn't want to learn about their doomed future?

"Rasha!" Jorvik's voice bounces off the walls, and I stuff my knife in my dress near my rib cage before opening the door.

"Good morning," I briskly greet him as he strides inside.

"What happened to your window?" he asks immediately. He hasn't been here completely since the first night when we walked to the lighting of the Yule log together.

"It's fine. A raven got in looking for food," I answer, wondering if he will believe the deep claw marks are from a raven's beak. Jorvik rarely hunts or deals with animals, so hopefully he will have forgotten that ravens are opportunistic birds who wait to be presented with food.

"It's so hot in here. How much firewood do you go through?" Jorvik walks around the room, and I quickly slide Shaw's shirt under the blankets as I make the bed.

"I am alone, so I get cold." I shrink, using the same excuse I gave Bjorn that first night. He picks up the little, wooden carved statues that I placed on the mantle, given to me at various dinners by the little ones. Putting my fur cloak on, I tie the front up and wait for him at the door.

"Shall we go, or are you looking for something in particular?" I ask, standing in the doorway. I don't think Shaw or Aslaug left anything, but I never know what type of mood Jorvik is in.

"You've slept in this room every night alone?" he asks, walking past me into the hallway. Catching up to him, we descend the stone staircase, and I nod, but that doesn't satisfy him.

"I need you to show Harald you give a shit."

"I told you my thoughts on Harald."

"And you promised you'd be kinder, more malleable, but at dinner you've barely spoken to him. I heard from one of the girls that you were asking about the blacksmith."

"The man who I tied with in the archery competition?"

"Don't play dumb." Jorvik's anger spills over, and I straighten my shoulders as we arrive in the courtyard. "Today you will spend the whole day with Harald. And tonight too. He wants you, and all he needs is a little push."

"I am not a breeding mare. What else can I do to secure our clan's safety?" The courtyard is busier this morning as people collect their offerings and fill wagons with the extra supplies needed to set up the stronghold for the next week.

"Marry Harald. Accept his proposal. Give me a nephew. A son with our blood that I can use to unite us."

I swallow bile and bite my tongue. Obviously, Jorvik has thought through everything, planning down to the next generations of my blood and using them to manipulate me.

"Harald will take our son and send him to the King or outright kill you when you are no longer necessary. Have you thought of your own safety?"

"No, because I am working on having something he needs."

"Besides me?"

"Besides you." Jorvik keeps me in the corner so I have no choice but to hear him out. "I heard a rumor that your new friend has a map to the reindeer, and it was stolen off his person. Is that true?"

"Why would I know that? I don't need a map. I am sure I can find the reindeer herd if you ever allow me to stay out on the mountain like our parents taught us," I argue, keeping my tone low. No one is supposed to know about the reindeer herd. The last time they were found the clans hunted them to near extinction. Our parents were killed because they would never have given up the knowledge they had about the reindeer's migration patterns and because I was a reckless child.

"You need to find out from Shaw if he knows where they are."

"Aren't you worried if I talk to Shaw that Harald will take notice?"

"Maybe it is not such a bad thing that Harald knows he can be bested by another man? And that I, your brother and his advisor, will not be played. Now go sit for the daily offerings like the Maiden is supposed to. No matter who catches your eye, Harald will be your husband." He turns me around by my shoulders and sends me on my way.

Stuffing my hands in the pockets of my cloak, I walk out the front gates to see Shaw leaning on the wall outside the forge. His chin perks up when he sees me, but I keep walking. Being pushed and pulled by the men in this awful village will end as soon as I figure out how to break through the ice covering the tomb.

"Rasha is here!" I hear my name called and look around at the crowd gathering in the bright morning sunlight. A young girl runs through the snow, followed by a group of red-faced children all carrying boughs of evergreen and wreaths of holly.

Kneeling to their level, I open my arms as they bombard me with little hands and sticky smiles, giving me things they made themselves. Proudly beaming at me, one says, "You are the prettiest Maiden we have ever had." His blonde hair is half shaved, and his green eyes shyly look at his feet.

"Chin up," I say, raising his round face to see me. The women behind us pass him a crown made of spun holly and white washed bones set in soft maple branches. "Did you make this for me?" I ask when their nerves take over.

"We did," the boy says, and I tilt my shoulders forward for him to place it on my head.

"Go on, go help your parents. Leave the Maiden to her duties," Harald calls, stomping across the ceremonial circle. The children jump, and I grab the crown before it falls, straightening myself while the children run back to wherever they came from.

"You didn't need to scold them," I say, brushing the snow off the bottom of my dress. Harald offers me his elbow, which I take, and we walk to the newly constructed platform next to the Yule log. More wood and kindling has been added under and around the log to keep it burning. I look for where I drew the runes in blood, but the flames and cinder have already made it disappear.

"Children need to mind what their parents say and do as they are told," Harald says, helping me ascend the two step platform. Keeping my cloak tucked around my legs to hide my body, I take a seat and watch him sit next to me.

"Ruling with a heavy hand can come back to bite you."

"And what does a heathen from a hunting party know about ruling?"

I fix the crown the children gave me as if it is a real one and look over at him. He is well groomed today. His beard is combed and every finger sports a shiny silver ring.

"I know that a leader needs to be able to trust the people around them. And in return, those people support their leader. That's how a hunting party works. We work with each other."

Harald waves his hand, and one of his servants appears with two cups of hot wine on a wooden tray.

"No, thank you," I say, wanting to keep my head clear, but Harald passes me the cup and waves the man away. He takes a mouthful of wine and raises his cup, waiting for me to consecrate our moment. Gently clicking the glasses together, I take a small sip and force myself to swallow.

The red wine is vastly different from the sweetness I tasted last night. Harald is nothing like Shaw, not that I know either man well, but Harald's method is to gain favor through oppression. Shaw doesn't seem to seek favor or acceptance, and that is refreshing.

"What is on your mind?" Harald asks as the Vikings begin to lay offerings around us.

"Being a good vessel for the prayers of the people so that the gods might hear and respond," I reply.

Harald leans over to rest his elbow on the chair, moving close to me so I can smell his overly herbed soap and wax. His clothes are beautifully crafted, the fur edges sewed with delicate patterns on the trim of his tunic.

"The people are easily swayed. After this season, it will be our job to teach them to love the King," he whispers.

"Will the King come here?" I ask, barely raising my face to his.

"In good time. I want to make sure you are ready to receive a man of such status. Someone who walks in the likeness of a god."

We are interrupted by four men who carry a dead goat hanging off a thick wooden post. The large, curved horns scraping through the snow remind me of Odin.

"For you Maiden. For tonight's feast, we killed our best goat in honor of Yule," the front man says, keeping the post balanced over his steady shoulder. Harald claps, rising half way out of his chair to survey the creature. "The horns are the best of our herd and will make a fine mask for you, Jarl."

Harald roughly pats the second man on the shoulder. "A mask for the Wild Hunt in the name of Odin himself. Thank you, my friends." The men walk away, turning to head for the stronghold. Large goats take hours to skin and cook, so the kitchen will have their work cut out for them.

Pouring himself more wine, Harald strides across the platform and resumes his seat by me. The crowd grows larger around us as people leave baskets of fresh bread and apples at my feet, bolts of dyed cloth for dresses or tunics too. After a few rounds of wagons roll by, there is a lull in the offerings, and I nervously shift in my seat, wondering how best to ask Harald about the map.

"You look like you want another drink," Harald says, glancing over at me.

"I am alright, thank you. We have a long night of dancing don't we?" I put on my most cheerful smile.

"Will you finally dance with me?"

"If you treat the rest of the people with grace today." I offer a compromise, and he accepts.

"I would like to come to a place where you gladly perform the marriage rites, Rasha."

"How does it benefit me to marry you?" The bold question catches him off guard, and he props his elbow on the chair to lean closer.

"I am not a bad man. I want children and a prosperous clan. I want a lovely wife to warm my bed. Is that not what every Viking man desires? Is that not what you want? A man to protect you?"

"I don't need protection." I straighten myself against the back of the chair.

"Your reindeer herd will," he whispers.

"No one has seen the reindeer herd in years."

"Not in all your hunts?" he asks, quieter now as his eyes reach mine.

Determined to get a handle on the conversation, I respond, "We don't hunt that far into the mountain pass." I have never hunted through the pass because the Beaivi Clan is there to protect the mountain's earthly riches, not deplete them.

"Maybe we could come to an agreement. If you marry me and I give you the necessary support, you could hunt and find the herd for me?"

Sucking in cold air to keep my lungs working, I don't know what to say. He thinks I am naive, and will bargain time out in the mountains against the safety of the reindeer herd. Harald reaches over to find my hands curled in my lap. I clench my fingers in vain as he forces my hands apart, lifting my fingers to his mouth. Tension rolls through the rest of my body.

"Please, Rasha, I know there is more happening in that beautiful head of yours. The King will reward us for providing him the means to conquer these lands, and we will rule without having four councils and four clans. We will be one," he proposes, kissing my knuckles.

"Even if you gave me twenty of the best hunters, I don't know where the reindeer are," I admit as he rubs my fingers in a small effort to warm them against the bright and chilly day.

"What has your brother told you about the blacksmith?" He asks.

Keeping my gaze on the undulating fire in front of us, I murmur, "That he will make our wedding rings if I choose to accept your proposal."

"Jorvik surprises me. You know I thought he told you all of our plans. He is one person I know I can trust. Your face says it all, little Rasha."

"What do you mean?"

"It is hard to tell if you are lying, I must admit," Harald says, and I finally wiggle my fingers free. Tucking my leg underneath me, I lean to sit in the farthest corner of the big chair.

"What should I know about Shaw?" I ask, point blank this time.

"There is a map to the herd's favorite valleys, and I think he holds it."

"Well there is an easy answer to that question. He came here at your request, so why not ask him if he has a map to the reindeer herd?"

"Because he was beaten the first night for his resistance to my request, and he previously promised me no such thing exists."

"Harald, that means someone here is lying. No one has seen reindeer in decades, and it is the hunter's job to protect the balance of nature. If you threaten that, there will be vengeance." My honesty comes out in a rush, and Harald's eyes gaze at me while I stumble through putting the information together. "And if you want to accuse me of lying, then I can do the same. You might be cooking up this reindeer nonsense to leverage me into marrying you, when in fact, the reindeer are fucking safe and sound far away from here."

Standing up, I gather my dress around me and settle the long folds of fabric over the edge of the platform. I glance back at Harald with a distrustful glare, not sure what to think. Shaw is looking for the map that he thinks Bjorn stole from him. But can I trust Shaw over my own brother? He wouldn't have any reason to lie, but Harald and Jorvik have all the motivation in the world to try to manipulate me.

11

RASHA

Accepting offerings lasts well into the afternoon. Harald fidgets in his chair, asking me easier questions about life, which is nice for a change. Then he falls asleep after we eat small helpings of bread and hard cheese.

I don't mind the quiet or holding hands with those bringing even the smallest of offerings. Straw figurines are laid around the burning log, accompanied by short prayers and pretty songs. As the sun loses leverage against the thick, snow-laden clouds, the cold of the afternoon seeps through my cloak, finding weak spots in the seams of my dress, making my bones cold.

Longing for the day to be over and to find Shaw in the heat of the forge so I can ask about the map, I notice Joanna tip toe up the side of the platform so she doesn't wake Harald.

"He is napping so he can be lively at the divination feast." I roll my eyes, and Joanna dips her forehead into mine.

"Sorry we've stayed away. We've been preparing the costumes for the Wild Hunt. Wait till you see yours."

"It will be good to get that part of Yule over with."

Joanna glances at Harald, making sure he's really asleep and buries her face against mine.

"How is your furry bedmate?" she asks, the wisps of her brown hair tickling my neck.

"She left last night. There was an opportunity for her to escape, and it was best to let nature take its course."

"I am sorry she didn't lead you to the bow. But the women had another idea," Joanna replies and turns to the crowd that has doubled in size as we were speaking. "Rasha, the women have brought you, and you alone, an offering."

"I don't know what to say." My tender voice rattles over the words. Many women have come now, slipping through the ranks of men to fill in the empty places around the Yule log.

Stepping down, I am eye level to so many women who wear proud smiles across their faces. Many of whom have been quiet during the nightly feasts and held back at the afternoon games. Katrine blends in with Joanna to my right, and Enora steps forward.

"We made this for you," she says. My jaw opens at what is in Enora's arms. It's a long bow, cut from a yew tree and sized for a female. Carvings begin at the iron nocks and continue over the hand rest all the way down.

Taking it in my arms, I look closer to see the faces of Freya, Frigg, and Skadi depicted in the narrow wood. Enora wipes her hands on her dress, and I pull her into a tight hug.

"Thank you. You don't know what this means to me." My whispers are muffled in her fur hood.

"We want you to know we are with you," she replies, leaning back to give me a smile.

"Thank you," I repeat to everyone who is watching. The energy in the ceremonial circle is thick with unease.

"In the name of Skadi, I accept this gracious gift. May all the women prosper in their bellies, in their homes, and in their hunts," I say quietly, raising the bow above my head. The fire crackles over the massive log, spitting sparks and embers over the snow covered ground. Several people begin to whisper, and others cheer. The names of the goddesses fall from the women's lips in a chant.

"Skadi, Freya, Frigg. Hear our prayers. Accept our Maiden who'll lead us into the new year." It starts from the huntresses, with

Enora leading the chant, and it grows into a loud song, traveling into the next group of quieter women until even the husbands begin to repeat the words. Fearing the wrath of a goddess is something no man wishes upon himself when he has a child bearing wife to care for.

Clutching the bow, my heart stutters in the overwhelming love pouring out from the women who chose to honor the goddesses. Through the many unfamiliar faces, I see Shaw with his black hood over his head, golden hazel eyes staring across the expanse and into my soul.

"Rasha, what is happening?" Harald's hard voice snakes around my neck, and his hand is suddenly against my spine. Straightening, I start to walk away, but his heavy hand finds my shoulder, squeezing roughly, so I stay planted next to him.

Leaning back into his ear, I keep the bow tight to my chest. "They made me a bow to honor the goddesses during Yule."

"The goddesses and not the gods?" he asks, pinching my shoulder while I quake at the knees to leave.

"There were many offerings to the gods while you were asleep."

"You should have woken me," he snarls and lets go. Shaking out my shoulders, I don't see Shaw across from me, and my hunting instincts prick up my spine. Women and men take notice of our exchange and find other places to be, taking their wagons and blankets with them. The ceremonial circle becomes a congested collection of people.

Harald takes me by the elbow, and I have to move with him. Walking fast back toward the stronghold, I notice Harald's men collecting all the offerings and following behind us.

"I can walk," I snarl and yank my arm away.

"What did you say to them to rile them up like this?" he asks, kicking mud and snow around as he stomps in through the tall double doors.

"I am a huntress, Harald!" I scream in blind rage.

"You will be my wife," he yells back. The men bringing the offerings keep rolling by with the wagons, trying to avoid our argument.

79

"I am a Viking woman, and our laws state I need to accept you. You cannot force me." I say the truth I've been holding on to since Jorvik first told me of his plan.

Harald's temper simmers between the never ending cups of wine and my stubbornness. He paces around me like a rabid fox, not big enough to make the kill, but desperate enough he doesn't care.

"Rasha, come with me." His arms go lax at his sides, and I back up until I am standing on the second and third step. At this height, I can see the women who fled the ceremonial circle now gather at the open gate doors. His face relaxes as he realizes we are being watched.

"Where?" I ask, cradling the bow against my chest.

Harald lets out a frustrated sigh and runs his ringed fingers through his hair. Coming closer so I can hear, he speaks softly, trying to appease me. "I haven't made you an offering."

The crowd outside the stronghold pretends to sort the bread from the meat, but women who are taught to protect themselves are always listening. Joanna and Katrine are arm in arm with Jorvik and walk past us, but I wave them over.

"Would you put this in my room?" I ask the group, flashing a desperate glance to the women. Katrine loosens her arm and takes the bow, giving me a quick nod.

"I don't have a key." She spins two steps above me and holds out her hand. Fishing the iron key out from my bodice, I pass it to her and descend the last two steps to give in to Harald.

Jorvik beams as I pass him, completely satisfied with how I handled the situation, and I want to scream. But for the sake of saving the bow and keeping Harald from taking his anger out on the women, I'll entertain the Jarl.

"Where are we going?" I dare ask on our way out of the stronghold. Harald pats my arm, leading me around the corner, and my stomach contracts. I know where we are going. Plumes of smoke billow out of the roof of the forge, and the heat hits me, mingled with the anticipation of the conversation that is about to happen.

"The first reason I asked Shaw to spend Yule with us is because he holds a special set of skills."

The words I heard Shaw say to me days ago echo behind Harald's voice. We don't knock or announce our presence as Harald pushes open the door with a loud greeting. Remembering all the places Shaw and I were close enough to kiss, I step away from Harald and run my hand over Shaw's big black coat slung behind a chair.

"Harald," Shaw says, coming out from the back bedroom. His gaze travels around the room, landing on mine. "You brought the Maiden. What can I do for you, my lady?" My mouth smiles in acknowledgment until I press my teeth into my lower lip to stop myself.

"I want you to show her the rings or better yet..." Harald motions for me to come closer, and I do. Avoiding Shaw is like trying to stop falling asleep after a long day of hunting. The lure of our attraction is bound to be discovered, I force myself to remember I am here with Harald. But he is oblivious to what's between the blacksmith and I.

"What would you like him to make you? I commissioned rings for our wedding, but can he make you a bracelet? Or a lovely neck-lace for that pretty chest of yours."

Shaw's grip tightens on the handle of his hammer, and my throat closes as I try to breathe evenly. It's one thing for me to want Shaw to do unspeakable things to my chest. It is another for Harald to openly talk about adorning me in jewelry in front of him.

"The rings will be plenty. I wouldn't want to overstep. Are they made already?" I look between both men, and Harald grins with a satisfactory grunt. *Freya save me.*

"Have you seen raw ore?" Shaw asks, knowing we have already experienced these moments between us. I shake my head, and he pulls out the familiar pile of silver and gold nuggets, except the other night there were a few more pieces. Harald walks over to inspect the pieces too. His burly body overshadows mine, blocking the heat of the kiln, which is making me dizzy.

"Sorry we haven't found your attackers. You have enough to

make the rings? I've heard of shamans who add bits of the body, bone, or blood to enhance the marriage ritual. I need to make sure we are bound. Rasha here is going to satisfy the King with an heir for us. For the clans, Shaw, think of it." Harald finds my hips with his wide hands and situates my body against his.

"There are things I can add to the ore so the impurities are extracted during the melt. Flesh that is added must be freely given, and it is up to the gods whether it is enough for a true consecration," Shaw explains, walking around the kiln. He flips the head of an axe over so it evenly heats and rakes through the coals, making tiny sparks of fire rain onto the stone floor.

Ignoring Shaw, Harald turns me around so that we are close but not touching. His hands find my face in an almost loving way. My heart should feel light and full of happiness, but instead, my insides feel like molten iron is being poured down my veins, solidifying in my gut.

"We are not alone, Harald."

"He will witness our union along with the clans at the end of Yule. We have no need to hide."

"Thank you for bringing me here. The rings are more than I could ask for," I say as he caresses the skin of my jaw under his thumbs. I am not sure if I should play along or walk away. The last time I defied him it ended poorly.

"Give him your blood?" he asks, and I recoil. His hands travel to the back of my neck where my hair is braided. Taking a braid in his hand, he searches for the tie at the bottom, his fingers brushing the top of my breast. "How about a lock of your hair?"

"She doesn't have to decide right now," Shaw interrupts. "I won't melt the ore to make the rings until after the Wild Hunt since I have a few masks to finish."

"I would like your word, Rasha, that after the Wild Hunt you will agree to marry me," Harald says, the smokey air hangs between the three of us like a curtain of lies. My hands crawl around Harald's forearms, wishing for a way out of this moment. I pull gently, and he lowers his hands.

"Tonight is the Divination feast. We shall ask the gods our

future." Turning from Harald, I find Shaw focused on rolling the irons in the kiln. His shirt is rolled up, showing off his thick muscles and taunt shoulders. I am about to get myself killed. "You'll be at tonight's feast?" I ask, and he looks my way.

"I'm not one for feasting, my lady."

"Oh come now. You live alone. You work alone. You need to set your sights on a pretty woman for the Hunt. Why not start tonight? Rasha and I insist," Harald says from behind me, and I watch that tiny muscle in Shaw's jaw contract.

"That is kind of you. I'll find a place in the Hall once I clean up."

Not wanting the conversation to go further, I head for the door, holding out my hand for Harald, and he takes it. He assumes we've come to some sort of agreement, whereas I am happy to leave in one piece.

12

SHAW

The hammer pounds against the flat metal of a sword, sending sparks exploding in all directions. My shoulder muscles scream, but shaping swords and quenching freshly wrought iron is the only way I keep myself from pummeling Harald's face into the dirt.

Swinging the hammer again and again, my mind spins out of control as I think about when I would have gladly taken up the mantle to fight a man over the smallest grievance. Another flip of the hot metal against the simmering coal and I raise my hammer once more, letting the memory of peeling off her clothes run rampant.

The tip of the sword breaks away, scattering across the stone floor as I swear into the eruption of flames. My tools are covered in hot, white fire, fighting against the wind billowing down the open shaft.

"For fuck's sake," I curse, pushing the end of the broken sword into the hot coals and setting the hammer to rest. Ripping my sweaty tunic off my body, I run my grime coated hands through my hair and stifle a scream.

I need to open the tomb so I can finally make peace with what happened. That is why I am here. I know that's what the stars pointed to, but what I didn't expect is a woman in my way or a chance at finding a partner when I thought my love had been lost.

Kneeling at the forge, I lay my forehead against the scalding clay and stone kiln, drinking in the power from the wafting flames. My chest slowly releases the tension I haven't found an outlet for since I watched him manhandle her.

Finding the bow to bring to the reindeer herd would be easier if I didn't feel this allegiance to Rasha. She won't break free from Jorvik and Harald without a sizable fight. Wandering alone around the mountains all these years, I was certain my path to redemption would have nothing to do with earning love from a woman. Maybe I have gone too long without and now am so starved I am confusing my place within the realms?

Sighing, I drink the last of the honeyed wine, tasting her lips on the rim, and dunk my head in the freezing bathwater. I shave my face and the sides of my scalp to show off the whorls of blue tattoos. It's rare that I miss my form, but tonight, I wish in humility, of course, that I could stroll into the Hall as I see myself, not in the body I have been reduced to.

Choosing the finest tunic I brought with me, I lace up the sides, wondering foolishly what she'll think of the two embroidered lynx crawling up the soft fabric. My own suede pouch of Divination tools weighs heavy in my palm. By the time I close up the forge, there are many people outside because not everyone will be let into Harald's inner circle.

Vikings made small fires around the roads, leading from the Yule log to the Aske Stronghold, where they plan to drink and ask the gods to foretell their futures. Blending into the group going into the courtyard, I gaze up the stairwell, looking for her, when I know she is already seated in the Hall, but I can't help myself. I am a fool who wishes to know what she tastes like, regardless of how her love will damn me.

I see her pathetic brother before he sees me. Jorvik does a double take, making sure it is me, after bidding goodbye to a group of men and women who enter the Hall. Instead of blending in with the next group of Vikings, I remain still.

"You have no idea what it takes to make me falter, Jorvik." I deal the first unforgiving blow. Jorvik gives me his best intimidating stare and crosses the courtyard with his long legs and lanky frame.

"We need not be enemies." He meets me, and like a true politician, offers us a path forward into the Hall.

"Were you absent earlier today? You saw how he treated her. The women are Vikings. They have the right to hunt, to hold a weapon, and to choose a partner," I spit back.

"You live alone, Shaw. You don't know what is at stake here."

"I know that she is worthy of more than this. All the women are," I respond through my clenched jaw. My hand is wrapped around the hilt of my axe, but I cannot kill Rasha's brother.

"Look, stay away from her," Jorvik whispers, pushing his hand into my chest. I push him back without thinking, and he comes at me again. Taking the handle of my axe, I bash into his boney, little chest. Anger rushes through my arms and legs, making me want to split his head open.

Soft hands are around my elbows, and I stop, turning in the anticipation of seeing crimson hair, but I see a short brunette. Recognizing her from all the times I've seen Rasha in the village, I lower the axe.

"We are not fighting tonight, boys," Joanna scolds. Jorvik takes a number of steps back, keeping his eyes on me, which are the same as Rasha's. "I'll keep him company tonight. Jorvik, please calm down," the brunette adds, staying in between us. I slip the axe back into my belt and watch Jorvik turn on his heels and stomp into the Hall.

"I had it under control," I say as her face breaks into a cheeky smile.

"It's Joanna if you don't know," she replies.

"Shaw, but I'm assuming I've been the topic of a few conversations." I hold out my elbow, and she loops her hand around my arm. A small crown of holly with little red berries is woven nicely in her thin, brown hair. I have the urge to ask her about Rasha, but that seems too forward.

"Jorvik overestimates his abilities," Joanna murmurs while we head into the Hall.

"He has good reason to be worried. The women were very brave today, offering the hunting bow."

"They see her as their way out. I won't lie, I am afraid." She dares a glance up at me as we walk around cedar laced fires, the sweet smell making the overly large room cozy.

"I never thanked you for your help with the lynx. I appreciate your discretion," I reply, hoping she'll remember how brave she was that night.

"I wasn't surprised she found a strange creature in need. Rasha always ropes me into something crazy. She will find Skadi's tomb if it exists, I have no doubt, but will it be enough to protect us? That is my fear. The gods don't walk our land. We have to protect ourselves," she rambles on, and I lead us closer to the head table, finding an empty place at the end of one of the long tables. "Don't you think?" she asks, breaking away to sit across from me on a bench.

"Tonight we will ask the gods. That is what the Divination feast is for, isn't it? To ask for clarity on our lives and find a direction forward."

"I can see why she likes you." Joanna leaves the bemused smile on her thin lips, like she knows something I don't. Rasha sits at the head table with Harald on her left and her brother on her right. Our eyes meet for a heartbeat, and I return my focus to Joanna.

"She shouldn't like me." I lean my elbows forward on the table. The setting sun gives the Hall a golden, fiery hue. Dried apples and fruits hang against boughs of evergreen around every post and pillar. Mistletoe and holly decorate the tables, and basins of fire fight to reach the tall ceiling.

Joanna stays close, chatting about hunting and asking me a thousand questions about making the best arrows for taking down a variety of prey. I can't say I've missed this type of onslaught conversation, but she is rather endearing.

87

As darkness takes over and night befalls us, plates of food are cleared, and half the fires are snuffed out to create a smoky atmosphere. Pipes are passed around with a concoction of herbs made to enhance the rune readings, but I pass.

Harald stands, and the room quiets, and my gaze once again finds hers. She takes his hand to stand, but her blue eyes stay fixed on mine, like earlier today when I know she saw me in the ceremonial circle. I could have come forward. I should have supported her, but my path home stopped me. I won't let what I've done get in the way of helping her.

Clearing his throat, Harald opens the ritual. "Tonight we open the channel to see the divine. May you all find the answers you seek." Rasha pulls her hand away, opening her arms to the ceiling of the Hall where the stars and the never ending sky look down on us.

Rasha takes a basket holding little silver bells and passes them out with the help of a few younger girls. The ringing calls the Seidr from Vanheim to open the celestial gateways, letting the magic of Yule flow freely, or so the myths say.

It isn't lost on me that Rasha left the head table in the opposite direction of Joanna and me, so she'll end her walk with us. The sour tang of hot goat's milk mixes with the lingering smell of earthy holly and warm nutmeg. Taking out my own set of bone carved runes, I brush off the table, and Joanna scoops a sheep heart out of a bucket being passed around.

"Have you been keeping each other company?" Rasha murmurs against my ear while she drops the last bell on our table.

"Joanna has been enlightening." I dare to look up at those beautiful blue eyes as I slide down the bench so she can sit.

"I'm going to find a less awkward couple to read my runes with," Joanna says and takes her cup of goat's milk with her.

"If you like, I can ask her to stay?" Rasha's eyes dart between Joanna and I.

"Sit. Joanna is lovely, but I came tonight for you." She scoots in next to me. "Whose idea was it to come to the forge this afternoon?"

I ask, unable to move on. Rasha's knees knock into mine, and I take an easier breath knowing she's next to me.

"We fought in the yard after he dragged me away from the Yule log. Everyone was watching. He backed down and wanted to show me what he considered to be his offering," she explains. We both drink the goat's milk, cleaning our pallet for what is to come, and I move my legs to sit astride the bench. "I didn't know where we were headed until it was too late. I put us in a shitty position." The strain of her voice spurs my hand to find her thigh under the table.

"It's alright. We gave nothing away." Assuring the actions between her and Harald bear no weight, I rub her leg in slow circles, giving me a moment to look at her unapologetically.

Her beautiful face is painted with delicate lines and dots. All her luscious, red hair is braided around her head and down her back. Snuffing out the thoughts of undoing those braids and watching her unravel underneath me, I take the squishy sheep's heart and lift it to her mouth.

She doesn't hesitate to let her lips fall open to take a bite. Deep red blood drips out, coating her chin. I steady the flow with my finger so it doesn't drip down her cream dress.

"Do you really want to know what the gods have in store for you?" I ask in trepidation.

She holds out her hand, and I drop the bloody sheep's heart in her palm. She fights the urge to wipe her chin by pressing her red lips together.

"I do. I need to know if I am on a fool's errand." She brings the heart to my own lips for me to take a bite. The muscle is tough and porous, making blood coat my mouth with only one bite. Swallowing it, I move the cups and heart pieces away to lay out my runes.

"The runes talk in riddles," I say, though I know she is smart enough to know this. She lets a laugh out under her breath and flicks her mesmerizing gaze my way.

"Drop the runes in the bowl, Shaw. I didn't take you for a man who fears the future."

I refrain from telling her it's not the future I fear, rather it's what

I've done in the past coming to a head that frightens me. And our two paths are about to collide in a way where only one of us can see the end, which gives me pause.

"I'll do it then." She takes the little pile of bones and inspects them. "These are beautiful; where did you get them? All the ones we prepared are carved in wood."

"These are my own."

"And the bones?" Her fingers trace the lines that I carved years ago after filing them smooth.

"A secret I haven't decided to tell."

She releases a breath and turns to the table, putting the bone runes in the cup that is coated with leftover goat's milk. Covering the top with her hand and shaking the cup, her eyes close, lost in whatever prayer she has been taught. A compelling need to touch her radiates through my own bones and muscles until I reach for her back, and she gracefully leans into me.

Letting her hand go, I watch as she scatters the runes over the table, and they roll through drops of sheep's blood. The thick, white milk mixes with the blackish red blood in a pattern I see immediately. Rasha stands to look down at the future I warned her she didn't want to see.

"Shaw," her voice is eerily quiet. Standing next to her, my body shields her from the conversations around us, people detailing what they see in their own runes and laughing about who will die next in the winter's chill.

"I see it."

"It's the same shape of the bow rune that Aslaug showed me. But this…" Her voice breaks as she runs her finger over the splatters of red, covering the rune for death and deer.

"It's my future. We ate the same heart," I say, trying to make the outcome better.

"So if I choose you, we are going to die because of the reindeer herd? Shaw that doesn't make any sense, unless…" Her head whips around the room, looking for what I am afraid to ask. "Where's Harald?"

"He's looking for you," I whisper against her skin. "You should do this with him." I hate saying it, but I need to know if her outcome will change.

"What?" Her face is ghastly white.

"Or with Joanna. You don't want your future intertwined with mine."

"But Aslaug showed me the tomb. I didn't meet you by accident," Rasha says with newly developed panic. "The pull to you is so strong I can't stand it." Her confession comes like an arrow through the heart.

I want to kiss her and tell her I can fix this, but I don't think I can without giving up my only chance at going back. Harald is making his way around the room. He'll be here soon to read his own future with the Maiden of Yule that he has been promised.

"Rasha, the bow is only going to bring you pain." Her eyes flare in sudden understanding. She pulls away, which guts me, but she needs to let it go.

"So it is down there, and you lied. We told each other we'd be honest."

I sit, pulling her back onto the bench with me. "We cannot have this fight here."

She's like an animal in heat, caught between wanting to give in to me and fighting the overwhelming feeling to run into the forest where she'll never be found. Her strong shoulders are stiff with anger against mine, even though her hips fit nicely in my hand.

"Roll them for me." Rasha carefully picks the runes out of the mess and drops them into the cup she drank from.

"That's not a good idea," I reply, looking over her head to where Harald is one long table away from us.

"Roll mine or the ritual isn't complete." She is stubborn if nothing else.

"Where are all those pointy knives you carry, so I know where to block from?" I ask, and she grips my thigh for a change. Her nails pressing through my pants let my blood loose, and my cock grows hard. We sit closer, her back almost against my chest, and my arms could easily be around her body.

Covering the cup with my hand, I lean my leg against hers in a meager form of support and methodically shake the cup. The bones touch my skin, bringing long forgotten power to my physical form, and I can feel thousands of years of life moving inside the cup.

Taking in a heavy breath, I release my hand and hear the hollow bones rattle against the wooden table. We stay quiet, reading the runes that have made an unusual pattern in the already used trenches of blood and milk.

"I think that is for the Immortal Realm. And these are flipped over, which is bad," she says immediately, flipping the last so we can see. "This one is for…"

"That is a deer," Harald says, his shadow overtaking us. Rasha gets up as quickly as he appears, and the space around me runs cold. "Shaw, what is your future?" he asks, and I stand to meet him, height for height.

"He's going to die," Rasha cuts in, and I half choke. Picking up the runes, I nod in agreement, unsure of what he did or didn't see. Rasha finds a bowl of fresh water, and I drop all the runes in to clean them before stuffing them in my pouch.

"I am sorry to hear that old friend. We all must leave this world eventually," Harald says. With him renouncing our ways, it is nice to hear some concern. He wraps his burly arm around her, pulling her to him like he owns her.

"Shall we do yours?" Rasha asks him.

"I don't want to know my future. I'd rather have a dance," Harald announces, and I sit like the wind has been knocked from my lungs. The Seidr still flows through me, buzzing through the room with the ringing of bells from other families learning their futures. Puffs of smoke from men who care not for enlightenment curl around the tables and wood columns. What I need is fresh, cold air and to walk away from her, but the last rune is seared in my mind. One she didn't see.

13

RASHA

"I would love to dance," I say to Harald. I don't want to dance at all. I want to argue with Shaw until he tells me the truth about the tomb or until I kiss him to satisfy my curiosity.

"Your demeanor has changed, Rasha. Did seeing my commitment at the forge bring you happiness?" He slides his hands around my waist. I let him lead us into the middle of the Hall near the biggest of three burning fires to keep us warm.

"I don't like how you govern, but I did appreciate your offering." I step away from him so we form the beginning of two lines. Joanna and Katrine come to fill in the places next to me, and a group of men, including Bjorn, take up the spaces on Harald's side.

"You'll learn, like the rest of my clan. They are prospering because I know what is best. I have brought more coin to our mountains than any other Jarl. You should be impressed," Harald boasts and waves his hand for the music to start.

In the corner of my vision, I see Shaw take up a place at the end of the line. A glance to my right shows Joanna matches me with a bloodied chin and a weary stare, but Katrine, who somehow managed to keep her face clean, looks ethereal.

"Your future?" Joanna asks as we turn around each other, my palm to the back of her hand, then we switch to turn the other way.

"Confusing. Yours?" I mutter.

Joanna halts a beat before picking up her dress at the knees to kick her foot out opposite mine.

"Reindeer, Rasha. I saw reindeer."

"I did too." I watch as she switches places with Katrine and am forced to spin around Harald to get to the next set of women in our line. Keeping in time with the music makes it hard to continue a conversation, but that doesn't stop Harald.

"I don't need my future foretold to me by the gods," he shouts, loud enough for all to hear, kicking his feet the same as us and turning around two younger women. "I know in my heart that Rasha is my future. And the King will bless our clan with riches beyond what we can imagine."

"Harald is our future," Bjorn says, spinning Katrine around his body. She plants a quick kiss on his cheek and resumes her place with another woman, touching their hands together, and so on. Katrine dancing with Bjorn is certainly not in her best interest. He looks at her like she's his next meal.

Shaw is two men away from me, and the next two young women are thrilled to have a turn with him. As mad as I am that he lied to me, jealousy boils over in my blood as I watch one rosy cheeked woman drape herself around him in a twirl.

"Something terrible is going to happen before Yule is over. My runes foretold," Katrine whispers in my ear when we meet.

"I don't doubt that. Thank you for putting the gift from the women away," I say, bringing our bodices together and back out.

"I'll always support you. But please be careful." She gives me a little push toward Shaw. His hands press against my dress, finding my ribs effortlessly, and time halts around us.

"I'm sorry," Shaw says without pause.

"For touching those women?" The accusation falls from my mouth, and he chuckles in my ear.

"We are all dancing. Harald touched you hours ago in my forge, and I didn't cut off his hands." Shaw spins me around his body. For the first time tonight, I can see the embroidered lynx clearly stitched on his tunic. "I'm sorry I lied about the tomb."

"You have to stop protecting me." I find an ounce of anger through my desire.

"I'm not protecting you. If anything I will get you into trouble."

"If trouble means living with you deep in the forest, I'll take it." Another gush of honesty makes him hold me close.

"Rasha." His deep voice makes me forget why I am here in the first place.

"I am teasing. I need the bow, Shaw." We push against each other in unison with the rest of the line.

"You don't know what you're asking. A mortal cannot claim her bow," he whispers. I have no choice but to turn around him and walk up the line, back to my place in the front.

My chest heaves with information from the rune and Shaw, along with everything else I've discovered. Jorvik didn't tell me that Harald plans to seize the reindeer herd because he knew I would have stayed to protect them. The women in all the clans look to me to guide them. And Harald expects me to marry him in a week.

"Rasha?" Harald asks, and I blink over at him.

"I need some fresh air." I grab Joanna's hand and drag her up the side of the Hall, searching for an exit. Ingrid and Enora take our places in the dance so the music doesn't stop.

"Slow down. They are going to think we are in trouble," she hisses behind me.

"We are," I shoot back and push through a side door into the kitchens. Empty baking trays, coated in flour, sit in stacks on low tables. I walk to the window, throwing both sides open, letting snow and icy wind pour into the room.

"What happened?" Joanna asks, coming to my side, but it's hard to look at her. Each breath comes tight and strained. I need to fill my lungs with air, but my chest constricts instead of letting me breathe. Maybe I haven't recovered from the night out on the ice?

"Joanna, can I have a minute?" Shaw asks from the doorway, and she backs away. I grip the edge of the window, letting my fingers grow cold to feel something other than fear.

"It's okay Joanna," I tell my friend, and she takes out my bedroom key that I gave Katrine, passing it to me on her way back to the feast.

Resting against the window, I count to five until my lungs fill with cold air, and I release my first full breath. Shaw walks around the kitchen and gathers two cups from a shelf. Watching him yank the cork out of a leather flask, I focus on his hands as the amber liquid splashes into the cups. I count to five again, breathing in his scent, and welcome the familiar feeling as I listen to my heartbeat resume a normal rhythm.

"Can I apologize properly?" Shaw asks, holding out a cup. Calm settles around us, and I take the cup, cradling it, but not tasting the ale. Shaw drinks it down in one gulp. We all have our own ways of finding equilibrium.

"Why are you so desperate to keep the bow away from me?" I ask.

"Because the woman who finds and wields Skadi's bow will be hunted, not just by Harald, but the King, the other clans, and who knows what else. Skadi herself was hunted," he explains, sitting astride the bench. I can't help but sit too.

"If you didn't believe I was good enough to live up to the goddess, you could have said so. You didn't have to lead me to believe it didn't exist." Leaving the cup on the table, I curl my hands in my lap, and Shaw fits his fingers around mine.

"You are more than good enough, Rasha." He lifts my chin to look at him. "The bone runes were given to me by the Seidr herself. They don't lie. The runes have foretold that you will wield the bow, and I will die."

"I can't let you die for me. You owe me for helping Aslaug, but not with your life. How do we fix this?"

"You don't marry Harald," he says without restraint, intertwining his hand in mine. I laugh as my core rumbles in acceptance, and all I want is more.

"Joanna and Katrine saw reindeer in their runes. Maybe there are more women who share the same future as you and I? We gather everyone and leave before Yule ends while Harald is ill prepared to chase us down."

"I am not someone people follow or trust, and I still need to find my map."

"Harald asked me about the reindeer. He offered to give me a group to search for them."

Shaw moves away at my confession. Walking around the room in thought, he rubs his smooth jaw. I get the sense he's holding back again, unwilling to give me his trust.

"I didn't say anything about what you've told me. But I haven't seen any evidence that Harald knows about Bjorn taking your map." I spread my dress out around my legs. Jorvik's harsh words from this morning ring a bell in my memory. "Jorvik knows."

"Knows what?"

"He knows about the map. He mentioned something about having another meaningful thing to secure his position besides me. There is nothing else Harald needs besides the reindeer herd and a wife."

"He's not going to get either." Shaw crosses the room, sweeping the cold air with him. "We will look for the map tomorrow. Bjorn must have it, and I have yet to repay him for hurting Aslaug. Then we will leave."

"What about the bow?" I search his face for a hint that he wants more than my help. He reaches in his pocket and takes out a bracelet, the metal shimmering in the little light from the kitchens.

"This will show you the way if the goddess hears our prayers." His fingers find my wrist, roaming up my arm and softening my tense muscles. I open my palm as he traces the sensitive places on the inside of my forearm until he reaches my fingers.

Our eyes meet, and for a split second, I feel we transcend time. He makes me feel seen in a way that brings forth an ethereal part of me. Underneath my hard huntress exterior there are feminine pieces, soft and delicate, that beg to be let out.

"Shaw, I would give myself to you if you asked." The golden irises embedded in his hazel eyes flare. "The Maiden at the end of Yule is supposed to."

He slips a bracelet over my hand and up my wrist, dipping his forehead to mine. Our breath mingles, and I swear there are sparks in the air like those coming off the kiln.

"I know how the rituals are supposed to go. That is why I am giving you the bracelet. It's what we made the night I found you on the fjord."

I touch the beautiful piece of silver and gold, remembering the mix of ore and the honeyed wine. I move to see his whole body, the one I've welcomed in my dreams. "Thank you for making it for me." Running my tongue over my lips, I don't want to know the rest of my future or the hardship I am sure is waiting for me.

Shaw backs up, keeping my hands in his and says, "The ritual works both ways. A man needs to give himself up as well, so can you do me a favor?"

My chest caves in at the absence of his body next to mine. "Anything?" I force my legs to stay tightly closed.

He walks to the door, opening his arm to usher me out to the Hall. Walking past him back to the feast, I hear him whisper, "Don't get caught at the Hunt."

14

RASHA

"We all saw it. I've talked to the women who read their runes in any form of divination last night, and a reindeer was present in each of their readings," Joanna shares. We are having breakfast together in their longhouse. Many woke up early, like I did, itching to get out of our beds and busy our worried minds with a task.

"We cannot get ahead of ourselves. It is going to snow, and we must take part in the Wild Hunt. The gods must be watching for all the women to have similar readings," I answer. Gathering empty bowls and cups to put in a wash basin gives me a moment to weigh what it means that our runes were all similar.

"Ingrid and Katrine never came back last night," Enora says, coming out of the longhouse to where we set up tables to finish sewing our dresses for the Wild Hunt.

"Does Ingrid stay out all night? Katrine maybe." I look to Enora and find nothing but worry across her rosy cheekbones.

"Katrine stayed dancing with Bjorn because we wanted to give you a chance to slip away," Joanna admits, the edge of frustration on her tongue.

"I appreciate everything you've both done for me." I take her cup and fill it with hot tea, passing her the warm mug carved from a solid piece of wood. Bjorn does not treat women kindly. I let Katrine put herself in harm's way by going to bed instead of staying till the last fire died.

"Ingrid has already taken a beating from her father, so it is not like her to spend all night in a man's bed. She knows her father will throw her out of the clan," Enora says.

"Don't accuse anyone of anything until we have proof that something happened. For all we know, both women will traipse back here with marriage proposals by noon." Joanna tries her best to lighten the mood, but Enora doesn't budge. I don't blame her.

"Are you thinking about Shaw?" Joanna changes the subject with a little, mischievous grin.

"No, I was thinking of looking for our friends."

"Maybe when you go back to the stronghold you can ask around? Did you and the blacksmith exchange more than glances last night?" Enora's tune quickly changes.

"We haven't kissed," I confess, and all the women look at me, their mouths slightly parted as if I am withholding the truth. I should be looking for Ingrid and Katrine instead of gossiping about my feelings. Enora and Joanna lay out the dresses on the tables, securing needles and pins where the next rows of stitches need to be placed.

"But you want to." A younger girl who wasn't at the feast giggles, and a smile breeches my cheeks. Yes, yes I do want to kiss him.

"He has many talents, that's all." I try to make it sound less romantic, which makes them laugh more.

"No one will blame you, but Harald will kill him, so make a wise choice," Enora says from across the table where she adds white fox fur to the trim of her dress. We will all be hidden behind animal masks, which are being decorated at the next table.

"Rasha, I wanted to ask you something?" Joanna whispers, laying out her dress next to mine. Katrine did the embroidery on both our dresses because I have no sewing capabilities. The front bodices are open, and for the Hunt, we will tie them loosely, so if we are caught, the hunter has access.

"That sounds ominous, but go on." I find a collection of dull needles and start sharpening them on a whet stone. Keeping tools sharp is more my forte.

"Would you be angry with me if I slept with Jorvik?" she asks, and I pause to look at my best friend with the thin needle between my fingers.

"No, but is that what you really want?" I ask. Avoiding my gaze, Joanna looks down at the long loop of green and red thread she's rolling out to have enough for the bottom section of her dress. "He's my brother, and I would love nothing more than for us to be family in blood. But I know how he can be."

"I don't have anyone else who can protect me besides Jorvik," she admits.

"Oh, Joanna." I stop sharpening needles and wrap my arms around her neck. "You have me. I'd place a wager on Shaw stepping up if I asked."

"I'm sure you would fight till the death to keep me and all the women safe, but you need to live and be happy too. That's why I wanted your blessing for me to be with Jorvik during the Hunt. Maybe we can move on from this Yule with less bloodshed," she murmurs against my cheek, and I nod.

"Of course, you'll always have my support."

"Thank you." She squeezes my forearm. Her hand takes mine, and the bracelet falls down my wrist.

"Who gave this to you?" Her brown eyes narrow on the glinting silver and gold.

"He did," I point to Shaw walking up the field to greet us. Joanna drops my hand in honest surprise and buries her head in the rest of her embroidery.

"Good morning, care for a walk?" Shaw asks, and I hear soft giggles from the women coming in and out of the longhouse.

"Let's go before they enact their own ritual on us." I throw my most motherly scowl back at the group and leave with Shaw.

"I haven't been around such a large group of Viking women in a long time. Are they always rooting for a Maiden to be swept off her feet?"

"Is that what you think you're doing?" I question his boldness, and the first smile of the day breaks across his face, which I hate that I am about to change. "Apparently, all the women's runes depicted reindeer at one point last night."

"Are they sure?" Shaw's tone clips.

"Yes," I say on his heels as we hurry through the back end of the village.

Shaw glances over at me. "Sometimes we see what we want to see."

"That's not how the Seidr works." I am quick to defend the women, even though I am not sure what the runes mean.

"Think, Rasha. Maybe they saw the reindeer because they are counting on you to find the bow and save them from a life of servitude to Harald."

"Skadi taught Vikings how to hunt. We only see her depicted with reindeer and her bow. Doesn't that mean she didn't have a family or a partner? I always thought it meant we could survive like the ancients did, living side by side with the reindeer herd and the seasons." I am talking more to myself than Shaw, raising my face to his and waiting for him to dash all my thoughts like my brother would.

"Maybe Skadi isn't the only god at play here." He keeps our conversation open to possibilities. I am ready to ask another question, but by the way his brow furrows, I am not sure what he's thinking.

"So where do you think Bjorn hides out during the day?" I change the topic.

"First, you need to cover that gorgeous hair of yours." The compliment gets a rise in me as Shaw ducks in between the wooden houses and huts and takes a short, deep brown cloak from a line hanging in between the windows.

"We will return it later," he says when I raise my eyebrows at his thievery. "Bjorn has a room in the stronghold. I found out late last night when I joined the men for a drink."

"How are they feeling about Harald?"

Shaw shrugs, coming around the side where huge snow drifts have collected against the houses.

"They fear the King, and they question whether Harald can really keep him placated."

The idea of the King is so foreign to me that I have put the threat of another man coming to take from our land at the bottom of my long list of worries. As Shaw and I draw closer to the stronghold, I pull the hood over my hair and pray that we aren't caught.

"You are assuming he's not in his room?" My voice is a gargled hush. We wait for two men to wheel a wagon, carrying tapestries that will hang on the partitions for the Hunt, into the courtyard, and walk easily next to them.

"He's in the tavern with the men," Shaw explains, and I stay flush to his side so we look like one big group.

"How do you know?"

"Because we passed them when you were trying to work out the reindeer and the runes."

"Oh." feeling foolish, I try to remember the path we took to get here.

"Do you know what Harald does during the day?" Shaw asks as we walk through the dark hallways that outline the stronghold.

"He naps when he isn't mucking up every ritual and stomping around like an insolent child."

Shaw laughs at my description and takes my hand as we walk deeper into the dark hallway. At the end is a staircase and hallway that mirror where my room is on the other side. I assume Harald is the last room which takes up the shorter back wall over the Feast Hall.

"What if he keeps the map on his person?" I ask, tugging on Shaw's hand for no reason other than knowing this is a bad idea.

"One problem at a time." Shaw moves down the second level hallway, and sure enough, there are two doors to two bedrooms. Taking out a roll of leather from the inside of his vest, he lays it on the floor, then finds skinny tools and sizes them against the lock.

"Is this how you broke into my room?"

"I made the locks, so yes. Does that alarm or excite you?"

It excites me, but this is not the time to feel warmth between my legs. Meanwhile, Shaw kneels at the lock, putting his head at the level of my thighs. After a few short taps and the sound of the gear grinding, the lock pops, and we give the door an easy push to open it.

This room might not be Bjorn's, but it is certainly a man's room. Clothes are everywhere, as well as weapons and half drunk cups of ale. A woman's under things are scrunched up on the bed, and the sheets are twisted in a used way.

"Rasha?" I hear my name croak from a weak voice, and I freeze. My eyes refuse to register what I see while blood drains from my face.

On the other side of the room, Katrine and Ingrid are chained to the corner post. The post is flush with the wall and connected to the roof, so they would never be able to get out on their own.

"Katrine, who did this to you?" I muster every available ounce of courage to walk across the room without disturbing anything. Shaw turns to the wall to give us a moment of privacy.

"Bjorn and his friends. She's not awake. I don't even know if she's still breathing. Get her out first." Katrine's words are strong, but tears slide down her cheeks over the deep cut on her lip.

"You're going to be okay," I assure her. Kneeling, I pull her torn dress up over the deep bruises where no one should have bruises. There are so many wounded parts of her body that I stop counting. Smoothing her matted hair from her forehead, I ask, "What happened?"

"I started dancing with Bjorn. It's not the first interaction we've had, so he set his sights on Ingrid. But she's so young, Rasha. I couldn't let him take her alone, so I offered myself."

Shaw comes to Ingrid's side, pressing his fingers gently into her neck to see if she's still alive. I take the borrowed cloak off and put it over her body as she blinks awake.

"Rasha?" Her voice comes out like gravel.

"We are getting you out," Shaw says, and Ingrid tries to twist her tortured body to see him. Finding different tools, he starts to unlock the wide cuffs around her wrists.

"What if they come back?" Ingrid whimpers, and I want to cry, but that won't help her. The thought that several men did this to them while I slept safely on the other side of the stronghold makes me cough into my elbow, trying not to vomit.

The distraught woman brings her knees to her chest to cover herself as best she can while Shaw keeps a steady hand, making quick work of removing her chains. Ingrid bolts to the door, and I don't blame her, but I can't let her run traumatized through the village, not yet.

"Wait." I rush to her, trying to help her put her boots on. Shaw starts on Katrine's cuffed hands behind us. "Was Bjorn here? Is this his room?" Ingrid nods, her lips trembling as tears tumble out of her eyes. "Did they speak about a map to the reindeer herd?"

She's not the first woman to be found in this state, nor will she be the last. Holding out my hand, I offer her the dress she wore last night, trying to show any form of comfort. Sniffling, she looks from me to Shaw and back again.

Wrapping her top tightly around her chest, Ingrid says, "I don't know if this is Bjorn's room, but he was in here for most of the night. They talked about you more than anything, in between taking turns with us. How you will be next." She looks around the room as she speaks, like she is remembering her nightmare. "They talked about having land from the fjord to the mountains, and that no one would stand in their way."

"I'll bring you back to the women's longhouse," Katrine says, standing. My body shivers against the unforgiving cold in the room. When the men left, they didn't add a log to keep the fire burning, not caring if the women froze. This could be me at any time if I am not careful. If I stay here with Harald, I wouldn't put it past him to throw me to the wolves when it suits him.

"Everything will be okay. The men will be found and punished." Katrine keeps her voice even, but she sends a pointed stare to Shaw. Even though her own legs are shaking, Katrine puts her arm around Ingrid and they start down the hallway.

"It's okay to go with them and make sure they return safely. I'll bring Siggy to the longhouse. There's no sign of the map being here," Shaw says.

"Don't kill anyone before they stand trial," I add. Running down the stairs after them, my gut bottoms out when I see the long shadows of a man coming up the stairs. Reaching for the axe on my belt, I try to get their attention, but they are too happy to be free of that horrible room to notice. The light flickers against the stone wall, revealing the man's shadow, and Katrine screams.

"Run, Kat," I yell as loud as I can, hoping Shaw hears me.

Bjorn comes into sight. Planning to give them an opportunity to escape, I launch myself at him. Long and lean, full of slick malice, he sneers at me and lets them run down the rest of the stairs.

"Little Rasha, I was wondering when they would send you to rescue those pathetic bedmates." He puts his hands up, blocking my next move. I walk back up the stairs, and he comes for me. Knowing it is my one chance, I swing the axe. Bjorn with his stupid, lean body dodges, and I hit the stone wall. He punches me clean in the mouth, and I crash down a few steps.

My mouth is coated with my own blood. He steps over me, grabbing my hair on his way back up the stairs. Scrambling to my feet, I scream against his strength. The axe clatters down the stairs, well out of reach, and Bjorn yanks me toward the bedrooms.

I claw at his forearms, his hands around my hair, and kick with everything I have.

"Stop making such a fuss. I wouldn't dare claim your virtue and risk Harald's wrath, but that pretty mouth of yours is fair game."

"So is yours." Shaw hits Bjorn so hard I hear his bones crack, and he drops my hair. My eyes sting with blurry tears as I clamber to my feet to see Shaw land another bone shattering punch to Bjorn's gut. While Bjorn is doubled over in pain, Shaw takes a fist full of his tunic and drags him down the hall into the horrible bedroom.

Scrambling after them, I feel my face where my skin will eventually be swollen and curse at how we won't get away with this. Bjorn will tell Harald that we broke into his room the minute we let him loose. For hurting my friends and countless other women, I'd like to kill him myself.

Shaw brings him to the corner where the chains lay ready to be used again. Bjorn is quick and throws his weight at Shaw, clobbering Shaw's face. I close the door and turn just in time to block Bjorn from attacking me.

Driving my elbows into his arms, I feel him kick me hard in the stomach as I try to flee from his continuous battering. A glimpse of his face shows his bloodied and broken smile as he pulls me close to him. Moving away, I feel the cold edge of a knife against my skin and freeze.

"I can say Shaw killed you, and that would make all our problems go away wouldn't it?" he bites out, blood sprinkling my neck. I shuffle my feet and feel the pointed edge stick deeper into my flesh.

"Let her go and tell me where the map is," Shaw demands.

"I'll tell you where the map is if I can keep her tonight, or I will have to tell Harald his favorite blacksmith touched his betrothed." Bjorn drags the knife down my neck, and I squirm against my skin being opened. Shaw looks at me, then the wall behind me. Taking the hint, I reach back, feeling the wall until I touch the end of something, hopefully heavy and sharp.

"You took the map and left me for dead. Why?" Shaw asks, buying me time. Bjorn maniacally laughs at the question.

"I am not going to wait for a King to own me. I know what the reindeer herd is worth to Harald. Meat, milk, hides. I am going to use the map to get those mindless creatures myself. I'll gain a swath of land and a constant stream of women to fuck."

Shaw inches closer, waiting for me to grip the handle while Bjorn talks, thinking he has the upper hand.

"You are going to die, Blacksmith. Your future is foretold, I heard, which makes sense, because someone needs to be sacrificed. And you, lovely little thing, will entertain the whole clan once you are the Jarl's wife."

I don't wait for him to finish. Using everything in my shoulder, I swing the massive, double sided axe across my body. The movement throws Bjorn off, and he falters with his knife. But the axe is too heavy, and my swing takes both of us out at the hip.

Shaw moves like lightning, taking Bjorn's wrist and driving the knife into Bjorn's leg, near his crotch. Blood pours from the wound as he screams, but Shaw kneels on Bjorn's other leg.

"You have seconds to tell me where the fucking map is, or I'll see you in Valhalla when I get there." Shaw's voice is chaotically dangerous.

"What are you going to do with his mess, little Rasha?" Bjorn still has the nerve to speak to me.

"You gave it to Harald already didn't you?" I ask. He smiles again through the pain of his broken face and thigh wound, shaking his head. I look at Shaw who is ready to kill him, but Bjorn has a point. How are we going to vouch for what we've done?

"You gave it to Jorvik?" I ask, trying every road to get the information we need. He laughs this time, blood spurting out and around the knife embedded in his leg.

"You're fucking brother had it this whole time?" Shaw says to the both of us.

"No, as of this morning I made a deal," Bjorn says to Shaw, and then slides his reddened, conniving eyes towards me. "He'd sell you to the King if he could be the Jarl. Now fucking kill me," Bjorn finishes.

Shaw takes the knife out of his leg, ripping a piece of the bed sheet, and ties it around Bjorn's thigh. Quickly making a loose knot, he breaks the wood off the handle of the massive axe on the floor and twists the bedsheet around it. Clamping the wound shut, Shaw cranks the wood until Bjorn screams, writhing on the floor in pain. The bleeding stops, and for better or worse, Bjorn will live to fuck up another day.

"You need to go to your room and lock yourself in," Shaw says, and I protest, not waiting to leave him here. Shaw hits Bjorn over the head with the end of his previously unsheathed seax knife, and Bjorn slumps over, unconscious.

"I'll admit to finding Katrine and Ingrid. I can say Bjorn tried to attack me, which is true," I plead, not wanting him to suffer the consequences of the choices we both made.

"Rasha, Harald will know something isn't right. You can tell Harald you knew the women never returned after the feast. That will help, but I need to bring this coward out in the open and put it to a vote. No clan leader or Viking man will stand for having their own women locked up and assaulted."

"At least let me ask Jorvik about the map," I reply, and he rubs his hands. I didn't notice before, but he wears two iron bars over his knuckles. Taking the double rings off, he slips them into the pocket of his vest.

"Can I trust Jorvik to tell you the truth and not hurt you?"

"He's a lot of things, but he wouldn't hurt me."

"Stay in your room after." Shaw comes to my side, his gaze stopping over my bruised lip and swollen chin.

"Alright," I comply, taking his hand and pressing the palm into my lips. The rush of the fight still urges my body onward, but later I will crash. He pulls me close, letting his arms cocoon me like he did out on the ice. Breathing in the scent of embers, I wish I could count on him coming to my room tonight, but in light of what happened, I doubt he will.

"Promise me you'll stay in even if it snows or if the women come to your door. Keep them with you instead of getting into trouble. I'll see you at the Wild Hunt," he murmurs into my hair. I have no recourse, so I agree. Letting him go, I open the door and leave the room of horrors.

15

SHAW

The urge to kill Bjorn is strong as I haul his unconscious body over my shoulder and down the stairs. The courtyard is full of Vikings. Joanna is in the forefront of the group with Katrine. Her strength is admirable, though it kills me to know I did nothing while the horrors of last night unfolded. Ingrid huddles under Enora's arm as other women come to her aid, and the rest of the clans pile in to seek vengeance.

"Who is it, Shaw?" Leif, the woodworker from the archery competition, asks.

"Bjorn. He held two women from the feast against their will in his room with his friends. Go see the chains and the blood for yourself. He fought against me. Demand for a vote," I grunt through my explanation as I walk through the courtyard toward the medicine room.

"Where are you taking him?" The shouts of Vikings from all four clans cascade over me. Giving Leif an urgent look, I see him walk behind me to tell the crowd.

"He's taking him to see Siggy to get stitched up. Calm yourselves." I hear shouting back and forth. A riot during Yule or any gathering of cold and frightened Vikings is not far-fetched, but there is no way I'll leave Rasha here alone for that type of battle. I don't know what she has experienced in her life to know about men like Bjorn. The horrific thought that someone could have done to her what he did to the women sends me into a blind rage.

"Siggy!" I yell, but the little woman is already at her doorway.

"Come, come. What mess have you brought me?" she asks, standing back to allow me to toss Bjorn's limp body on her work table.

"I stabbed him."

She looks over his body, quickly gathering her bottles and jars of herbs while I tie his wrists to the table legs.

"What did he do to warrant you beating him within an inch of his life?"

"He kept two women chained in his room. Multiple men were there all night, Siggy. This is unacceptable behavior from a clan." I pour hot water into a clean wooden bowl, and she closes the medicine room door.

"You broke his jaw, and his side is swollen like you ruptured an organ," she mutters, waving me toward the hearth. "Bjorn is a troublemaker. I've already given treatment to a few women who came down here after being with him."

"Will you speak that truth to Harald?" I ask, knowing I am asking a lot for an elderly woman who relies on this stronghold to keep her safe.

"And your new friend, Rasha? Is she hurt?" Siggy slides a glance my way while she keeps working on Bjorn's leg.

"She isn't unscathed." I clean my bloody hands, scrubbing away all remnants of the piece of shit lying helplessly on the table.

"I saw things in my runes last night." She keeps her voice low, leaving Bjorn's open leg for a moment to come across the table.

"We all did."

"Isn't it time for you to remember who you are? Rasha is the most capable virgin in the last thousand years. Don't falter now that you've let your cock take over."

I bite back a laugh at the old woman who knows me through and through.

"Just keep him from dying so he can stand trial. I promise there will be rolling hills of flowers for you on the other side of the Vanheim when you meet your end, my old friend." I kiss her cheek and leave her to patch up Bjorn.

The courtyard is congested with people waiting for me to face Harald. Someone must have woken him because he clearly looks disheveled. Wearing none of the finery we're accustomed to seeing him in, Harald parts the crowd for me to walk directly to him.

"Shaw!" he yells, thinking if he is the loudest, then he will be believed.

I do the unthinkable and slightly bow to the Jarl to appease whatever cost I am to bear for today.

"Where the fuck is Bjorn, and why is everyone here questioning my men?" Harald seethes, invading my space, so I back up.

"Ingrid from your village and Katrine of the Beaivi Clan never returned to the longhouse last night. The women asked for help, and I found them chained up in Bjorn's room. Is that the type of Yule you're practicing here, Jarl Harald?"

The women have already spread the story around, leaving Rasha out of it. I have no need for games and have no intention of acting like these men.

Harald gets in my face again. "Where is Rasha?"

"Why would I know that?" I stare at Harald who is not processing what is happening.

Leif breaks into our stare down to say, "There are others, Jarl. Other women who have come forward. He needs to stand trial, or the gods will abandon us!"

"Where are they? Where are these women?" Harald asks, waving his arms around like a chicken.

"We are here," Enora speaks this time, standing in front of Ingrid, who shows plenty of visible signs of a struggle. Five others come out from the crowd, and my blood vibrates against my bones at the severity of what I've allowed to happen while staying here. The guilt that I could have stopped this makes me sick.

"Can you point out the men?" Harald asks, his true weakness showing.

"We will have justice for the defilement of our women!" another Viking yells, drawing his sword.

Harald leans to me as if we are in an alliance and asks, "What am I to do?"

Crossing my arms over my thumping heart, I give him the only correct answer. "Morals are not hard to live by when you strip your ego and desire from what is right and wrong."

"Trial! Trial!" the crowd chants, banging the walls and ground around us in a methodical chorus.

The higher ranking men from the other two clans close in on Harald, and I have half a mind to throw him to the wolves. Jorvik won't speak against him, even though Katrine's his responsibility. How he will look her father in the eye when he returns to the Beaivi Clan? I have no idea.

"You will compensate us for their virtue, and we will see those men punished before the Hunt. Our women will not participate unless we all agree on the eligible men."

An angry mob faces Harald, ready to put him on trial with his own men, but where would that leave us with the King? The King poses the greatest threat to our way of life, so it might be best to leave Harald in place for now.

"Agree, Harald," I instruct, giving him the nudge he needs. "What would the King think of this when he asked you to act with chaste humility, did he not? What about Rasha?" I ask, and Harald glances at me with panic lacing his narrow eyes.

"We will set this right by sundown," he announces and pushes through the crowd to the staircase leading to Rasha's room. My knuckles clench, missing the feeling of the iron bars that come in handy when I need to crush bone.

Walking out of the courtyard, I hear Enora thanking me, but I keep going. I have spent too much time laying low and going with the flow. Siggy is right. Fuck, Aslaug was right when she brought Rasha to the tomb. It is time to start the ritual I have put out of my mind for far too long.

After I collect my coat and stock the kiln for later, I follow the same path along the wall that Rasha and I took before and wedge my sore shoulders through the broken slat. With all the clans here, I would think someone would have fixed this, but I thank fate that no one has noticed. Harald's gate guard would be the first to accuse me of leaving and being guilty of beating Bjorn for my own purpose if I stroll out the main gate.

The overcast, lavender sky means snow is on the way. I pray it snows until the Wild Hunt, the women receive a respite from the feasts, and I have time to eavesdrop on the grumblings around the village.

Aslaug bounds through the deep snow toward me, and I kneel in a true genuflection for her.

"How are you?" I softly ask, stroking her clean fur. Feeling her stomach, I can tell she healed well, and fur is already growing over the scars. She arches her back and rubs my legs with her strong body.

"I am sorry, Aslaug. I wasn't ready. Bring me to the tomb?" She purrs. Deep rumbling emits from her square head and broad, furry chest. I don't care that the sun won't set for another few hours. There is no one that will dare venture out on the ice, and the village will be preoccupied with the trial.

My boots crunch in the snow as the massive cat nimbly trots through the untouched, white powder. The reflection of the mountain range on the icy fjord is the piece of the puzzle Aslaug wasn't able to explain to Rasha.

The Immortal Realm sits equal to the realm of men, but in between lies the Vanheim. In that limbo, Skadi's tomb exists because she existed in both realms. The soul of a mortal cannot pass through the Vanheim, even though I am learning that maybe the soul of a mortal can find the doorway.

I have waited so long to be able to return home. I need Skadi's bow to cross through since it is the relic that cast me out. Without honoring my penance, the scales are tipped against me, and I have never been willing to bring a partner into my problems. Maybe it has been my own foolishness that caused me to withdraw myself from the clan for all these years.

Rasha is different; she is more than I could have ever asked for. I can only pray she will not hate me for the ritual I am about to begin. Finding where she spilled her own precious blood is easy. The ice suspended her offering, waiting for me to return. Aslaug slides on her padded paws over to me with a mouthful of kindling, and I light a small fire to heat the edges of my seax knife.

"It is nice to have you next to me," I murmur to the cat while we wait for the fire to grow hot enough. Scratching her head, I peer down into the bottom of the fjord with Aslaug where the top of the stone tomb has lain untouched for a thousand years.

Heating the edges of the knife, I cut the ice around where Rasha's blood is encased and take out the empty amulet. I hand-made the smaller, more intricate piece to hold what I thought would be my blood one day. Sliding the filigree cover off, I lay it down and put the blood-filled ice over top.

Aslaug and I sit while I stoke the fire until the sun is barely visible over the tall trees, and the heavy clouds start to release fat snowflakes. Sitting with the great lynx reminds me of our struggles in the first weeks of being cast out. There were many cold nights in a body I didn't know was so fragile and many hungry days when I lost my way in the Sacred Forest, but Aslaug never left me.

"I am sorry for the pain I have caused you. For the loneliness I brought to you when it was only me to blame," I whisper against her thick, insulated fur. She leans her body against my legs, and I feel the journey coming to an end. But what will become of me when Rasha gains the bow?

A spark skates across the ice, and I sit up, watching the ice dissolve into water. Rasha's thick blood fills the well in the amulet. Between the bracelet I gave her with my hidden chain inside and the amulet now containing the blood of the virgin chosen by her people, she should have what she needs to claim Skadi's bow.

I still have the bone runes in my pocket. Taking the one out that Rasha didn't see last night, I turn it over in my hand.

Rebirth.

Aslaug's amber eyes stare up at me, and I grind my jaw, knowing exactly what she's thinking.

"I can't tell her. That defeats the ritual." Taking the rest of the bone runes out of the pouch, I smash them to powder with the end of the seax knife against the ice. Like I am adding root vegetables to stew, I scoop up the shaky dust and add the bits to her blood, swirling it till it mixes inside the small amulet.

"That should coagulate things so this works. If it doesn't, we will both die, and I don't know what that would mean for you," I say to the cat. She sticks close as I smother the fire.

Gazing at the trees, I ponder leaving Rasha the amulet and heading back to my cabin, knowing that either way, I will eventually hear what took place. But I asked her to wait for me at the Wild Hunt, and I still need my map.

The thought of her aroused and running towards me, when we both know my restraint hangs by a frayed thread, causes my cock to twitch. In a mask, I will be able to let out a fraction of who I am, but some urges are too primal to be quelled. She will need to stay a virgin longer than she thinks. Once she learns my true purpose, will I run the risk of damning the relationship I hope we have?

16

RASHA

A winter storm halts Yule for three days. Wind howls outside the stronghold, picking up snow and ice, till I can't see the wall or the trees beyond. Joanna and Katrine are in my room, fussing over our hair and masks for tonight's Wild Hunt. I told Katrine to rest and skip it, but she's determined to forget what happened to her in that room.

After the fight with Bjorn, I ran to Jorvik's room and told him everything. In truth, I readied myself for an outburst for my betrayal of spending time with Shaw, but it never came. Surprisingly, Jorvik was forthright in showing me the map, which is nothing like I thought. It's an antler with tiny drops of silver that form a constellation that appears in the night sky when the Northern Lights appear.

I stayed behind a locked door while they punished Bjorn and whoever his accomplices were. I didn't ask what happened to Shaw. I didn't utter his name after Jorvik showed me the map, and I certainly didn't allude to knowing anything about what went on when I was seated with Harald the next day for a somber midday meal.

The snow gave everyone a welcomed break, but my mind constantly thought of Shaw. He didn't come to my room, and I didn't leave the confines of the stupid square fortress, keeping my promise. This morning we woke to clear skies, but I fear everyone's emotions are still fraught.

"I know you are nervous, but this is supposed to be the best night of Yule. If nothing else, do it for me. I need new memories," Katrine pleas, laying on my bed and attaching tiny pieces of metal to her head piece. Her bruises have faded, and her lip is nearly healed.

"When you put it that way. Promise me when you go home, you'll tell your father everything?" I ask Katrine while we tie the front of my cream dress.

"I promise. Stop being the serious huntress for a second." Katrine hides her worry with a girlish grin, pushing up my cleavage in the bodice.

"She's right!" Joanna finds her excitement, bringing our crowns. "In the shadows, maybe Shaw will steal a kiss from his woman."

"I am not his woman." I push them away, hiding a laugh, and fix my red hair over the pointed antler crown around my head. I know this will be a pivotal moment no matter what happens. The eligible women who want to participate will have the opportunity to form a union with eligible men, and if Harald catches me, my chances of getting out of my own marriage will be almost non-existent.

We head down to take our places as the sun sets. The stronghold is a maze for the night, sectioned off with rolling partitions so no two ways stay the same, which creates plenty of dark corners for debauchery.

It took a few days for them to construct the partitions for the maze while the snow fell, creating a tundra outside. Looking up at the violet night sky, I don't think it is a coincidence that due to a storm, our Wild Hunt now falls on the full moon. The moon will connect us to the fates, just like the runes connected us to the Seidr at the Divination feast.

The Wild Hunt symbolizes Odin's everlasting hunt across the vast wilderness of the Vanheim. To honor him, before the chase begins, the men perform their own ritual. Cleansing their bodies, drinking, and using sacred oils, connects them to the gods and channels Odin's strength.

In my bones, I know there was a time where women were equal hunters to men, and men took part in being our prey. Scrolls in our clan depict an equal number of women and men chasing after their counterparts, and some years, they would switch so that the clans could marry into different families, making the bloodlines strong.

Men who are already married assemble to keep fire basins stocked and anything too terrible from happening. Mothers and wives come from the sides with trays of hot sheep's blood to consecrate our bodies in the name of Odin and Freya.

Harald drinks first and walks across to me, gazing up my body to the deer mask over my eyes and antlers sitting atop my head.

I shiver in a gust of snowy air and force myself to stand still. He dips two fingers in the blood and presses his fingers into my lips, dragging them down my neck until he reaches the clasp over my fur top.

"In the name of Odin, we hunt the quick and the primed." He takes a sip and gives me the silver cup.

"In the name of Freya, we yield to the strong and the voracious," I announce, making sure to turn to each side, including the women behind me. Taking a sip of the hot blood, I instantly want to vomit, but I swallow the thick gulp. Harald closes the space while the silver cups are passed around.

"You can run, but when I find you, I expect you to submit," he commands, and I recoil. Adjusting the soft fur around my shoulders, I cover the ties that reveal my skin.

"You have to catch me, Harald. Do not make a mockery of the gods when the past few days have been difficult." Looking past him, I watch men lift their masks slightly, but I don't see Shaw. The fires cast long shadows on the group, making it impossible to know who is who. Jorvik is somewhere in the fray, but his fox mask and reddish fur vest are easier to spot since I've seen him in it before.

In light of Bjorn, I would expect most men to be respectful or fear the wrath of Freya, but pipes and ale make for Vikings with a loose definition of respect. Those who lurk in the shadows worry me. They might not go as far as Bjorn and his friends, but the way we found Katrine and Ingrid still haunts me.

The drums beat in unison, drowning out the heart pounding fear rattling my ribs. I am the huntress and am rarely the hunted. Most men will try to catch me first because kissing the Maiden or having a moment to touch me will bring them good fortune in their future marriages.

From deep inside the maze, a horn blows, and the Hunt begins. Not waiting a moment, I bank left and throw myself down the first hallway, keeping my eyes peeled for men. Women follow me, giggling in anticipation of being caught, and take heed to run through the first alternate pathway in the partitions.

I quickly look back to see Enora and Joanna coming my way. The women brush into me as we pause in a corner of the stonewall, and I pull the partition in front to hide us.

"What is the plan?" Enora asks.

"Don't let Harald catch Rasha," Joanna confirms.

"But girls," —I grab their shoulders so they turn to face me— "don't get yourselves in trouble on my behalf. There are still men who will be kind to a wife. The gods are watching." I pull the partition open a fraction, slip in between, and run. It is best if I stay away from all the women and use the moonlight to track the direction I go.

All I want is for Shaw to find me so I can tell him that Jorvik has the map. Scratch that – I can't lie to the gods. I want him to find me so he can claim me in front of all the clans and put an end to Harald's demands.

Rounding the corner, I watch two more women run into from Leif, who has been nothing but kind. The smile on his face reminds me some still look forward to celebrating our rituals. *Not everything must end in bloodshed.* But still, my heartbeat threatens to burst through my ribcage.

"Little Rasha." I hear Harald's voice, but I don't see him. Spinning around, I feel my legs for my knife, but the clans agreed to no weapons, so I am defenseless.

"If it takes all night, I will find you," he says, and I whirl around, thinking he must be near me, but I don't see anyone. The wall rolls, opening another pathway, and Katrine darts in front of me. Grabbing my hand before I can register what is happening, she pulls me down the new corridor in the dark.

"Joanna is keeping Jorvik busy," she heaves, pushing her teased blond hair from her cheeks to fix her crown. "Think about giving in to Harald so he'll take you back to his room, and you could stab him?"

"Katrine!" I hiss, and she forces a weak smile. We assess the three ways we can go from here, and I try to figure out where we are in the stronghold by the angle of the moon.

"Running away all night is exhausting." She lets out a rattled breath.

"Have you seen Shaw yet?"

She shakes her head. "I haven't, but he seems like the loyal type." She pulls the partition slightly, giving us a view of an empty corridor.

"You're brave for being here. I should have told you earlier," I whisper, panicked that I might not be able to speak with her so freely any time soon. We keep moving, making sure the corridors are empty before running through, and I start to feel guilty for keeping her with me.

When we get to a cross, I give her hand a squeeze. "I'll go towards the sound of hunters."

"You sure?" she asks, but I'm already letting my feet silently lead me away, down zig zagging hallways. Plenty of people have started to lose themselves in one another. Slowing my frantic run to a careful walk, I can't help thinking Shaw must have left. He could have been accused of hurting Bjorn unjustly, and he left because what importance am I to him?

I hate this feeling. I didn't need to get wrapped up in his nonsense with Aslaug or the map to the reindeer herd. My purpose is to find the bow and make it through Yule without getting married. My face radiates embarrassment at how foolish I am for thinking he would want to catch me. To have a chance to kiss me.

"You are the Maiden," a voice I've never heard skates over me, and I raise my chin, only to collide with a man. *Fuck.*

"You can't be sure," I say, trying to give myself time to run. With the mask on, I have no idea who this is, but he isn't Harald, and he isn't Shaw. His clean hands and richly woven tunic place him in a council role, maybe the son of a clan leader? Either way, I am running out of places to hide.

Taking my chance, I bolt, but he has friends. Another masked man grabs my arm so hard it feels like my shoulder is about to dislocate as his leg snakes around mine.

"Don't hurt her," the first one says, sounding younger the more he speaks.

"We have her. We'll bring her to Harald to trade after I watch," his friend says, twisting my arm behind my back till tears sting my eyes.

"The gods are watching," I grind out through my clenched jaw. He throws me to the younger one, whispering how he wants to watch his friend use me. I let the young one run his hands all over my curves. Underneath his tunic, I see the glimmer of a hilt peaking out. We agreed to no weapons, and yet, he broke the rules.

Reaching around his body, I see him grow ridiculously excited, and he grinds his hips into mine, thinking I am starting to enjoy him.

"What's your name?" I ask in my best breathless tone.

"Ivan," he says, all too quickly.

"Kiss her. We deserve to taste her," the older man says, and I relax, letting Ivan's soft lips kiss my neck. Enthralled in his luck, he doesn't feel me slip his knife, which isn't tied tightly at all, from his belt. The curse of naivety is placing how you look before the practicality of keeping your weapons secure. I push one hand against Ivan's chest, and he smiles like he's about to be blessed by Freya herself.

"She has a knife? She broke the fucking rules!" the other man scolds, but Ivan admits his mistake.

"It's mine. It's my family's ritual knife. I didn't think it counted," he says to the man who wants to watch. Ivan's old friend has been teaching the young man to be an utter abhorrence. I recognize him as the partner Ingrid danced with before she left with Bjorn. He was in on it.

"You deserve to be killed along with the men who have been hurting the women."

Chuckling, he responds, "Harald kept you locked away so you don't know that none of those men were killed. Punished, yes, but they will live to fuck another day." My only response is to drive that fancy knife into his chest.

He's unarmed, and I am full of fury. Bones snap and muscles squelch as I take all my fucking frustrations out on piercing through his lungs and his fucking miserable heart.

Ivan runs. He doesn't try to stop me or help. I hear him vomit on his way around the partition corner. Wiping my hands, I keep the knife locked in my palm and roll the partition to cover the body.

More thudded footsteps come towards me, the wall shifting again, and I feel the heat of another man. Raising the knife, I see the blood stained metal catch the moonlight, illuminating both of us.

"Calm yourself," Shaw's quiet voice stops me cold, and I start to collapse. His hands wrap around my body, and I melt into him.

"I thought you left," I murmur, lowering the knife.

"I wasn't going to leave you," he replies, and I look at his mask, trying to see his eyes. Gently, he walks into me until we are pressed against the wall. "Is the person you used that on dead, or do I need to finish him off?

"Dead." My voice shakes, and I drop the handle of the knife, listening to it hit the ground. In the safety of his strong embrace, I unravel my tension. "It feels good to stand up for myself."

"I'm sure he deserved it." He lifts his mask a fraction and smirks before placing it back against his face. Hearing his voice makes me want to cry and rip my clothes off at the same time.

"Jorvik has the map. I saw it with my own eyes." I wait for his reaction, but he's gazing at my dress like he's seeing a spirit. "Shaw?" I ask, gripping his shoulder, but he runs his tongue over his lip, and my stomach throbs.

"The antler mask makes you otherworldly. I don't give a fuck about anything but you right now if I'm being honest." His passionate words ignite me. Stepping into his arms, I raise my eyes to meet his stare as he runs his hands through my hair up to my crown. I caress his forearms, reaching the band of the crown, and remove it, bringing it between us. Many sets of broken antlers make up the circlet.

Pressing my forehead into his, I can almost feel his smile when he realizes the antler with the tiny silver drops that mark the map is hidden among the other plain antlers.

"You amaze me at every turn," Shaw whispers, taking his antler map out of the Maiden's crown and pocketing it. My hands never leave his shoulders, daring to run my palms across his broad chest to his waist line. "Rasha, this crown belongs on your head." His voice interrupts my exploration. Bending slightly, I feel him fit the circlet back with the gentlest motion, moving my hair out of the way. I stand tall in his reverent gaze as his fingers skim my collarbones, and he pushes the fur wrap from my shoulders.

"You caught me. Take your prize." I can't help but move into him, my body overwhelmed and ramped up from our other encounters. He obliges with eager tenderness, slipping in between the ties of my dress. When his hands touch my skin, I choke back a moan, and he turns me around, pressing my back into his chest.

Arching my neck up to his shoulder, I know our lips are a heartbeat away from a kiss. Our masks knock together, and I glance at the intricate scrollwork in the shimmering metal that he must have done himself.

"Touch me," I whine as my impatience builds. Shaw's hands find my nipples, hard against my dress, and he rolls one through the fabric. My legs fall open around his thigh. I can't find the words to beg, but my body knows the way. His hands play with my aching breasts, finding sensitive places I didn't know existed.

"You smell like you're ready to be fucked, but I can't." He sounds strangled.

"I want this with you," I say, meaning it. I don't care if he ruins me, and Harald kills me. I want to feel something for one night.

"Gods, Rasha. I need you to kiss me."

"You don't have to ask." I turn around and loop my arms around his neck. In seconds, he hoists me up, and I wrap my legs around his waist. As my back bangs into the solid stronghold wall, a faraway thought reminds me the opposite wall could move, and we would be caught.

"Yes I do, and if you want to stop, I'll stop," he growls against my chest. Pulling my dress up, he takes fistfuls of my ass in his hands as I balance over his shoulders.

I don't ever want him to stop. I slip my hands over the strong edge of his jaw and crash my lips into his. Meeting me with equal ferocity, his mouth seeks to know me in any way possible. With every little whimper and moan, he changes his position. His hands slide up my back, molding us together. I need him beyond this night and these clothes and this mask. We kiss each other like nothing exists, except for his tongue swooping over my lips and my teeth nicking his skin.

His impossibly hard length rests against my core. Grinding myself into him, I know we are lost in the moment. Rough fingers caress my thighs, and my breath hitches in anticipation of him touching me where no man has.

Moonlight catches from a new angle, and the reflection of silver across the gold mask stops me. The crunching of gravel and snow as the partition rolls away raises the hair on my arms in alarm. Slowing each painfully hot breath, I know there is no going back now as my breasts rise and fall against his naked chest.

"The Maiden is mine." Harald's voice reeks of death behind us.

17

RASHA

Every muscle in Shaw's body contracts, ready to fight. Setting me down, he keeps himself in between Harald and me.

"She is fair game in the Hunt," Shaw replies, like he glazed venom over a sword.

"She evades me, and now I know why," Harald spits back.

"Rasha come." Jorvik is here, of course. He walks from the corner of a partition with his pants unbuttoned. Joanna follows from behind him, pulling her undone dress back over her exposed breasts. My brother doesn't even care to help her.

I don't move from Shaw's back, but I don't know if I can risk him getting hurt on my behalf.

"And who do you want, little Rasha? Who is behind the mask?" Harald asks, and I suddenly see a path without bloodshed. Stepping around Shaw, I place a steady hand on his back and pray to Freya he understands what I am about to do.

"I don't know who this man is. We are in masks." I muster every ounce of confidence and walk up to Harald. Shaw doesn't move; he might no longer be breathing, but I don't look back.

"She killed Axsel," Ivan shouts, picking up his family's ritual knife from where I dropped it.

"Is that true?" Jorvik questions. Ivan and two other men push their masks off to drag Axsel out from the partitions I rolled around the body.

"Rasha!" Harald yells this time, prompting Shaw to come to my side and take his own mask off.

"Shaw?" Harald spits, wiping his disgusting mouth with his sleeve. "So your plan before you die is to take the Maiden from me after everything I've done for you?"

"They kissed, Harald, which is nothing more than what you have done. Rasha is untouched as I promised she would be." Jorvik, ever reframing the problem, moves in front of Harald.

Shaw leans into me and whispers, "Whatever happens, you are worthy of what you seek."

I steal a glance at his unmasked face. The swirls of blue on his scalp are new but seem familiar. I can't place them as Harald begins his petulant barrage. Jorvik strides over to us as Joanna tries her best to grasp his shirt or hand to keep him away from me.

"What the fuck have you done?" he hisses in an awful whisper.

"She did what she had to do. Where were you to protect her?" Shaw takes over. He's twice the size of Jorvik, but Jorvik as stupid as he is, doesn't back down.

"Leave," Jorvik threatens Shaw, causing Joanna and I to exchange nervous glances. I mouth to her to go, but she shakes her head and folds her arms over her chest. Everyone is beyond stubborn when they don't need to be.

"I killed him because I recognized him from the night Ingrid was taken, and I was not confident he would be respectful to me," I say, leaving Jorvik and Shaw's staring contest to go to Harald. Harald is the Jarl, and he'll have to make a decision as to my punishment. Maybe, if I am lucky, he will choose to not force me into marriage now that I am a murderer.

His eyes narrow on my chin where the blood from his fingers once coated it, now consumed by Shaw's lips. I have an inkling Harald cares more about who I kissed then who I killed.

"Get the bow," he says. His dangerous glare roots me to the

spot. "Get the bow the women gave her and tell everyone to assemble at the Yule log."

Jorvik nods and runs to my room where the bow from the offering lays on the end of my bed.

"Leave, Shaw. You're already on a knife's edge with Bjorn, and I don't want to kill you," Harald says, finally looking past me to Shaw. I hear the blacksmith's boots, and I don't have to turn around to know Shaw is in Harald's face, ready to rip him apart for what's gone on during the sacred week.

"She is the fucking Maiden of Yule. You might kneel to a useless King and think of yourself as a mighty Jarl, but there is nowhere in Valhalla you can run from the gods when you're dead." Shaw's merciless statement excites me, but now is not the time to think about what other merciless things his hands can do. Walking away from Harald, he stops and takes my face in his hands like I am the last woman on earth.

"I'll be right back," he says. His kiss sears through my heart a split second before he lets me go and walks away. "See you at the fire," he says to Harald on his way out of the double gates.

Harald comes to me and slaps me across the face so hard my mask falls off as I try to stabilize myself. He yanks me up by the collar of my dress, and I hold the ties together while pulling away from his grasp.

"You didn't have to kill him. You have made a fucking mess of everything instead of waiting for me to get to you like I ordered," he sneers into my ear and drags me to the gate.

"What if he got carried away and took my virtue? Would you have still wanted to marry me?" I retort.

"Be honest, you don't want to marry me, and you never did. But your feelings on the matter are fucking irrelevant." He continues dragging me out of the gate and down the road. Trying to keep my feet underneath me, I see all the clans staring at me while they try to sober up for what is about to happen.

"Kill me then!" I scream and swing against his body, landing a good punch to his chin. He drops me in the icy mud. The snow seeping through my dress instantly makes the thin fabric stick to my legs.

"Here." Jorvik's voice makes me turn my head. He holds out the bow for Harald to take over my body on the ground.

"Tie her up. We will teach her a lesson, and I will marry her before this night is over," Harald says, and I force my legs to find footing. Taking two steps away from them gets me nowhere because Jorvik's arms are around my waist.

"You're such a coward," I seethe, debating whether head butting him is a good idea or if Harald will cut my hands off if I try it.

"You killed a man. You kissed the blacksmith, who is useless. I drew the map and it's locked away in my room. I told Harald you were with Shaw when he broke into Bjorn's room. You did this to yourself, little sister."

My body gives up at his admission and I sink to my knees. He betrayed me. Pulling me up by my armpits, Jorvik loosely pulls my arms around my back. I feel other hands binding me now as the rough edges of rope scratch my skin.

"You don't care about me at all do you?" I ask Jorvik, even though there are other men around us.

"All you had to do tonight was let Harald catch you, and none of this would have happened. You're stubborn, you're selfish, and all you care about is being out there." Jorvik waves to the tops of the mountains looming over us.

"Let me go then. Please, Jorvik, let me go, and you'll never see me again," I plead, hating every pathetic tear collecting in my eyes. *I hate feeling helpless.*

"Bring her here," Harald yells, and I look over to see Ivan on one side of me, smelling like vomit, and Jorvik on my other. They walk me to the Yule log, and I look around at my clan members who are frightened. Some have their weapons and are whispering to each other.

Harald raises a closed fist, and a horn blows to quiet the crowd. Joanna and Katrine are side by side, holding hands, mixed in with the other women. I have to trust that Shaw will come for me, or that he is right, and the gods will protect me. Maybe he is retrieving

Skadi's bow from the tomb under the ice, and this is one big nightmare that will be over when the sun rises?

"Rasha admitted to killing Axsel. It has been brought to my attention that she was involved in releasing Katrine and Ingrid from Bjorn's care. He was severely injured in the process."

"Witnesses!" someone from the crowd yells and is shushed by Harald.

"I will finish her sentencing so we can carry on with Yule," he replies, and tension reverberates through the throngs of nervous people. "This bow" –he raises the bow the women gave me– "is a symbol that she is something she is not. The rumors that Rasha will take Skadi's place and lead the women, who I have protected, to freedom in the mountains is horseshit!"

He waves the bow around the circle like he's showing off a badger he killed for stealing eggs in the chicken coop.

"Skadi was a whore, which is why her tomb is untouched, and we don't pray to her. You will not disappoint me by exalting this heathen who is here to carry my children!" he screams. My body convulses, and I fight to stand up straight. Both Ivan and Jorvik grunt against my shoulders as they keep me still.

"Bring her to the fire," Harald calls. Jorvik pauses, but Ivan, who apparently has never had free will in his life, starts to drag me, so Jorvik follows. Harald grabs me around the waist, ripping me away from my brother, and hits me so hard in the stomach my face falls forward, almost grazing the intense flames. Pulling me back up by my chin, he squeezes my jaw, bringing my face to his.

"Burn the bow." His wet voice is a humiliating demand in my ear.

"No," I reply. He pushes my face closer to the fire, and the edges of my red hair singe in the glowing, yellow flames. Letting me go, he holds the bow high for everyone to see and clears his throat.

"Burn the bow," he says to me and me alone. Around us, I feel tension coming from the clans. Everyone I traveled with has a hand on their axe or knife, which will only lead to them being slaughtered. We are outnumbered three to one in every way.

I will not be the cause of innocent people losing their lives or limbs tonight, but if I don't do something, then who will fight for these women and their daughters? With so many women watching, my defiance ignites.

"Untie me then, and I'll do what you ask with dignity," I say, and Harald brings me close to him. The heat of the fire is replaced with a hollow chill. He unties my hands, and I rub my sore arms before holding them out to accept the bow.

Harald keeps the knife pressed against my ribcage. "Go on."

The bow is heavy in my arms, like the weight of my whole life sits in this moment. I lit this Yule log over a week ago, and I asked the gods to help me. I have used every available moment to offer myself to Skadi in hopes that her bow and the power inside it will help me lead our clan away from Harald and the King. I have no choice but to believe Shaw when he said I will be protected. Dropping the bow into the flames, I hear a few women stifle a cry, and the men from our clan exchange displeased glances.

"Skadi is a whore!" Harald shouts, and I stumble backward, feeling lightheaded without the bow in my arms.

"Skadi is whore!" the men who follow Harald's every word shout the phrase, attempting to gain unity amongst the clans.

"Harald that's enough," Jorvik says, turning to give me a look of pity.

"You're right, Jorvik, we need to end this with a marriage," Harald replies, and I see a chance to run. Taking off through the ceremonial circle, I find women who are standing so incredibly still it forces me to stop.

"No, no, little Rasha, not unless you want them to die," Harald chides, walking over to where I pace around the edge of the circle. All of my friends have slender knives to their throats. *Outnumbered.*

"Sacrifice me. I won't marry you. Not in a thousand years. So sacrifice me to the gods and be rid of me." I press my lips together, still tasting Shaw on my flesh. He's the only one who knows about the bow, the real bow, underneath the ice, and he came into my life with a lynx from across the Vanheim. He didn't have to explain it. Where else did Aslaug come from? He might have run away to save his reindeer herd, but he promised I'd be protected. He's never failed me.

"Do you accept me as your sacrifice?" I scream, opening my arms wide to the circle.

"No, Rasha. Don't do this." Joanna elbows her captor in the balls, and he doubles over enough that she runs to me, intertwining her hand in mine. I know she'll offer herself right along with me. No one bothers to chase her. We are now trapped in the circle with Harald and Jorvik.

"I killed Axsel. I rescued my friends. Yes, Bjorn and I fought. So offer my life to the gods, and all of this will be forgiven. Jarl Harald can go to the King a cleansed man without the stain of a heathen woman." Whirling on Harald, I refuse to give up.

"All those in favor?" Harald asks the crowd, and more people than I want to admit cheer for my demise. My heart lurches in the dangerous game I started. What if I can't fake my own death? There are too many factors to think about, and I don't have time to change my mind.

Shouts and chants blur together, along with the popping flames eating the bow in the Yule log. Suddenly, an older woman breaks through the ranks of burly Viking men and scared women. She bangs her walking stick on the ground, emphasizing her presence. Due to her elderly nature, the crowd once again quiets.

"Siggy? What do you have to say?" Harald asks, having a neutral level of respect for the medicine woman. The memory of the first time I met Shaw crashes through my senses, seeing him laying on the cot and the way his face was horribly bruised. His helpfulness and lack of judgment made it easy to open up to a stranger.

Clearing her throat, she speaks to everyone. "In the years long past, there was always a couple sacrificed on the solstice. Their bodies were chained to a longboat and set ablaze on the fjord. Jarl Harald, you are being punished by the gods for not keeping to the true ritual."

"But, Siggy," he whines, and I squeeze Joanna's hand.

"Sacrificing Rasha will bring back the balance I saw in my runes when I channeled the Seidr," she explains.

"And you expect me to die with her?" Harald asks, starting to sweat his choices.

"I will die with her," Shaw speaks, walking through the crowd. Gutted at his request, I hoped he'd save me and not give up our lives so easily. Unless his faith in the fates is stronger than mine?

"The blacksmith?" Harald questions, looking between both of us, as if to say how disappointed he is. "No, just Rasha will die. Tie him up." Harald's words send the ceremonial circle into complete chaos.

18

SHAW

Due to my distrust in Harald, I don't join the ceremonial circle immediately. Instead I threw my things in my sled and found a longhouse roof to watch from. I had an arrow pointed at Harald's heart, and when he punched her in the stomach, I almost ended his life. Then she offered herself as a sacrifice, and I had a better idea.

The malice coursing through my veins drove me to make Harald watch her choose me instead of him. So I slid off the roof, and not coincidentally, into Siggy. Siggy was on her way to stop the shattering of the sacred rituals of Yule, and we quickly came up a plan, but I didn't expect Harald to not let me die with her.

Now we are fucked.

"Harald!" I yell across the crowd, but he's taking her away, through the snowy village roads to the gates. His men pummel me before I can reach her. Too many men throw punches and grab my limbs, making it impossible.

"Are you insane?" Jorvik asks, landing a decent punch to my jaw. Given the way this played out, maybe I deserve this from him.

"You could have stopped him from beating her at any time. You told him about the map when she asked you not to. You didn't care that she didn't want to marry Harald. Don't fucking come for me now," I gurgle at the little shit as he hits me again.

"Make him watch," Jorvik instructs, and they haul my sorry ass down the road too.

Her red hair is tangled in the crown still on her head. I have to believe there is dormant power in me that she can bring out. After years of seclusion, searching for forgiveness and a way home, I found her. That kiss we shared will not be our last. It is only the first of many once I figure out how to save both our asses from the mess we've made.

The snow outside the village wall is past my knees. I know from touching her in the maze she has nothing underneath that flimsy dress to keep her warm. If she dies before me or I can't complete the ritual, I will be stuck here for another thousand years, and her fight, her ferocity, will be in vain.

Taking heavy steps though the snow while being held at sword point, I look at the moon casting an iridescent glow over the icy fjord and pray.

"You're an idiot. You could have had anything you wanted from Harald if you brought her to him," the man closest to me says.

Spitting blood at his feet, I reply, "A woman comes to you when she's ready. Soon there will be a reckoning, and the gods will remember whose side you are on."

The mention of the gods instills fear into the fragile minds of the men around me. Swayed by the false narrative of Harald and the flashes of riches, most have forgotten how we once lived mutually with the gods. They have forgotten how to seek the divine.

Grinding my jaw at my ignorance, I remember spending a lifetime acting like my position didn't matter. Instead, I wallowed in my own self guilt and lack of purpose. Maybe I was just like them and that is why I was cast out. They slam my back against a tree at the edge of the fjord, and I look over to see Rasha trembling.

"It's going to be okay." My words fall flat.

"I know," she answers, but she doesn't look like she believes me. "Will the gods welcome me when I die?"

"Trust Siggy. She can stop the flames from hurting you. You're not going to die."

"We will run the rest of our lives if I don't die tonight," she murmurs, her body shivering in the thin dress.

"You are beautiful," I say, and her mouth forms a little smile. "You are, and not just because I remember how it felt to hold you in my hands, but because you are willing to stand up to them."

She strains her wrists against the ropes, letting her head drop. Tears hit the snow, and I realize she doesn't want me to see her scared.

"Rasha, look at me," I murmur, pulling my elbows taught against the binding to get closer to her. Her face is red and splotchy, but she looks over at me anyway. I want to tell her what I am, and that there is far more at play than petty Harald. But there will be time to explain everything. Men are coming for her now after they hauled an old, beat up longboat down the snowy embankment and onto the ice. Vikings slide and march along the path we created, carrying dry evergreen boughs from inside the stronghold.

Fuck, what if this doesn't work? Siggy is here, thank the fucking fates, and muttering all sorts of ancient prayers. Her arthritic hands slip over Rasha's limbs, coating her in oil so that the flames hopefully won't burn her. In the rush of everything that is happening, I hear soft cries from Rasha. The woman I am supposed to be saving can no longer hold back her fear. And where's her brother?

I crane my neck to see Jorvik holding Joanna, who is rightfully sobbing against his chest. *That is a problem for another day.* I focus on whittling away the rope in between my wrist and the tree bark.

"Let's get this over with," Harald hollers, standing by the haphazardly decorated funeral longboat. Siggy gives me a small shrug of encouragement before following Rasha down the fjord.

Harald renounces the gods in front of the clans while I desperately try to untie myself. He pledges his allegiance to the King who will come and bring order to the heathens. Everyone walks by me, gathering to hear him and see the Maiden give her life for Yule.

Rasha is stripped of her crown, and the ties of her dress are opened. Katrine is shaking through sobs when she steps in front of

Harald and paints Rasha like we would a corpse with black lines and dots. Rasha's whole body stiffens as she gives Katrine a kiss on the cheek.

Harald uses the chains I forged to tie her to the boat, sliding the heavy iron across her legs and around the bench. He forces her to lay down and threads the chain through her arms, latching the clasp against her heart where she won't be able to reach the lock.

"You are taking too much time." I recognize Enora's voice and still my hands as she cuts the ropes. "Do something," she urges, and I can't blame her.

"I am. I need your help. I packed a sled and need you to move it out of the gate while they are here. Can you do that for me?"

She says yes, running toward the village. Retreating to the shadows of the forest, Aslaug hot nose bumps the back of my knees, and I bend down to scratch her head.

"Take this to her without being seen," I ask, and the great cat looks at me like she's waited her whole existence for this task. "Wait till they think she is lost to this world, Aslaug. We cannot afford a mistake." I bring my face against her warm head.

Desire and jealousy can wait till after we have the bow, and Rasha is safe, miles away from this mess.

19

RASHA

I will never again wait for a man as long as I live, I swear as my teeth clatter together. I am about to die because I waited for my brother to make the right choice and for a fucking blacksmith to save me. This ends here in a funeral longboat.

By the looks of the archers readying their arrows with flames, I have maybe ten minutes to escape alive. I don't have time to let dread interfere with my resounding fate because Harald is growling obscenities at me.

"You could have had a throne right next to mine," Harald hisses when he clicks the lock closed over my chest. Since I'm tied down, he can finally touch my face and get a good look at my chest, which disgusts me.

"I'd rather die than be anywhere near you," I say, glaring through my tears. Looking down at where his hands touch my body, smudging the runes that Katrine shakily painted on me, I realize it doesn't matter if my body is marked. My soul will not be traveling across the Vanheim tonight, not if I can help it.

Harald moves to the stern and shoves the boat. "That is one wish I can grant you," he yells. Watching the stars zoom by above me, I feel the rickety boat skid across the rough ice until it slows. I rest my cheek on the wooden bench, trying to see if I am any closer to where the tomb lies below, but it is hard to tell where I've landed. I am too deep in the well of the boat to see the fjord or the men standing on the snowy crust of earth, waiting to set me ablaze.

Drums start beating what we play for a funeral, and I close my eyes, listening to my heart pound in my ears. Recounting all the precious prayers my mother taught me keeps me from shattering. A horn sounds as I try to feel the chain around my wrists. Shaw is the only blacksmith that makes this type of iron work, so this must be part of the plan, or he would have fought harder to free me. I need to succumb to the tomb to find the bow.

Suddenly, hot fire streaks across the sky, and I hide my face against my shoulder in vain as arrows rain down into the boat. Listening to wood crack and snap with each volley makes me dry heave uselessly against the bench. Flames erupt around me when the smoldering arrows catch the dry holly leaves and pine needles from the evergreen boughs.

My arms slide under the chains, making my skin buckle and bruise. Flames rise around me, licking my skin, but the oil Siggy doused me with is working, and though I feel so hot I want to scream, my skin stays intact.

Over the tall flames, I see two tufted ears and two amber eyes, but where the fuck is Shaw?

"Aslaug help me!" I wince as the flames start to eat away at the oil. She gets on her hind legs and opens her mouth above me. With a thud, a small amulet falls onto my stomach, and I try to shrug my shoulders to bring it closer, but it stays nestled in the chains tying me down.

"Aslaug!" I scream. She's gone or maybe she is going to summon Freya? Can she do that? My mind races through the possibilities. I look at the mountain range to one side of my vision and try to figure out if I am close to the spot Aslaug brought me too before.

Fire eats the old wooden longboat in seconds, and I close my eyes, waiting to burn. The wood cracks and splits underneath. My rib cage tightens as I hyperventilate. Any moment now, my flesh is going to peel away in the flames. Wiggling in the chains, I feel the weight of the iron suddenly slip away, and I roll off the burning bench without thinking. Moving my arms, expecting to feel ice and snow, I hit a solid smooth slab instead and pat my body for the amulet.

I fear I have died, and in my shock, I didn't feel it because the boat is no longer underneath me, and the chains are nowhere to be found. Flames as tall as the walls around Harald's village burn so deeply crimson they match my hair.

The amulet Aslaug dropped on my stomach lies at my feet. Picking it up, I graze my fingers over the metal lid and shiny clasp. It's exquisite. There is only one man I know who can craft this type of piece. Shaking out my wrist, I see the bracelet he gave me slide forward, and I compare the engravings. I wish I could be surprised, but something nags in the well of my soul. A tiny morsel of truth that this is how it is supposed to be—that he gave me these gifts because he felt that tug as well.

Assuming I am closer to the Vanheim or dead, I bravely wave my hand over the blood red flames and feel no pain. The next place to go is out of the circle of fire. I haven't been burned yet, so I take one step at a time, and with a shaky exhale, I move past the burning crimson wall.

The amulet gripped tightly in hand, I try to think of helpful thoughts instead of miserable ones. Like how Shaw could be dead because they think I am burning alive. Our runes predicted our deaths only a few nights ago. I should have seen this coming. Did Shaw? And that's why he let them drag me away? Maybe I am dead, left to wander what our parents called the inbetween. Glancing up, I see the flaming boat fracturing in the ceiling of ice above me.

Panicked laughter escapes my swollen lips as I think about how we traditionally pack seasonal outfits in funeral longboats to give the dead soul plenty of clothes to wear in the afterlife. I rub my arms and legs for warmth, knowing I am an unlucky soul who only has the snow and mud covered dress I'm wearing.

Keeping the amulet in my palm, I roll it over, watching the thick, scarlet liquid coat the inside. It is either my blood from the ice or Shaw's, based on how I am drawn to its contents..

Wherever I am, it looks like it was once beautiful and has since been left to ruin. Columns resembling tree trunks give off a liquid glow, and hesitantly, I touch the structures, following the rivers of gold in between groves of the rich brown wood. Taking long steps into the darkness, I feel the corners of the stone crack and crumble under my feet. With no leaves or colors of life, I feel like I am in the forest on the last day of fall, right before the first snow, when everything is dead and awaiting a triumphant return.

One foot in front of the other, I walk into what can be best described as a shrine, but has been forgotten by man and left barren. In the middle of the room at the top of the nine steps the columns change to resemble trees. The number nine is always used when speaking about the Immortal Realm. Nine runes were also represented in the Divination night.

In the center of the shrine lies an altar. Picking up my pace, I lean over the giant slab to find a strange set of wheels. Three interlocking wheels are carved into the stone, and around them is a groove no bigger than my pinky finger. Tracing the outline, I catch the bracelet on my wrist out of the corner of my eye and slip it off to examine Shaw's carved scroll work.

This must mean something? He isn't the type to give a woman a trinket. Rolling the bracelet around, I feel a tiny slit on the inside. I slide it forward, and an audible gasp escapes my shivering lips. Shaw's broken chain necklace falls out and slides down my dress, but I scoop it up before it can fall to the floor.

Holding it up in the strange light of the shrine, I watch each tiny link sparkle and want to scream. What does any of this mean? Skadi didn't wear a necklace to my knowledge. What does this have to do with wielding her bow? Looking back up at the icy ceiling, I can still see the boat burning, and I'm not sure what that means either.

Where the fuck are Aslaug and Shaw? The overwhelming feeling of frustration makes my eyes burn with tears. I hate crying, and so far all I've done during Yule is cry over my inability to accomplish anything.

I lay the chain on the top of the altar and walk around the space. The light continues to reflect off the silver and gold, but then again, so do the edges of the wheels, so maybe…

Pushing the chain into the grooves around the interlocking wheels, I pray that Shaw is really as good a blacksmith as he claims to be and give the chain a tug. The wheels move, releasing ancient dust into the stagnant air. Keeping the chain taut, I pull until the wheels have made one continuous rotation. *Thank the fucking fates,* the lid slides open.

Carefully, I take the chain out of the grooves and slip it back into the bracelet, making sure it is secure around my wrist. My excitement pushes my heart to keep beating as I reach into the oval opening and pull out an ancient deerskin quiver with the tip of a bow sticking out the top.

The slender trees shake and vibrate, giving me no time to examine the bow. Dropping the amulet into the quiver, I grab it and look for another way out. I run down the long shrine steps and see the cracks in the ice before I hear them. The burning boat overhead is melting the top crust of the fjord, and glacial water is starting to pour in from the narrow cracks.

Clutching the bow to my chest, I run to where the crimson flames shone through the ceiling, but there is nothing now. Water drenches the trees, dripping onto the pristine floor, and the sounds of snapping ice and wood reignite my panic.

The chains that Harald used to tie me to the long boat come crashing through the ice ceiling, and a deluge of frozen water closes the space between the shrine and the fjord. In one massive wave, I am swept away.

Bone crushing, frigid water slices through my nerves, worse than taking any knife or arrow through my flesh, and all at once I am drowning. Opening my eyes, I force myself to stay calm in order to swim.

My knees refuse to work, tightening with every frozen inch I try to gain to find the surface. The current created by the flooding shrine throws me through the water. My jaw clicks, and my ears pop as I fight with one arm to get upright.

Nerves fire in all the wrong ways, forcing me to want to breathe, even though I will suck in ice water and ruin my lungs. I can't understand which way is up or down, and the cold is making my eyelids heavy.

Ready to open my mouth, I pray to Freya that drowning isn't the most painful way to die and close my eyes. I pull the bow to my chest and see him above me. Somehow Shaw crashed through the ice after the heavy chains that Harald used to restrain me. Seeing him trying to reach me makes the will to live explodes through every part of my hypothermic body.

He dives down for me while kicking away the heavy iron. Still clutching the bow to my chest with one arm, I use my other arm and reserves of strength I didn't know I had to move up, up, up.

His arms are around me, pulling us both to the surface, and my vision blurs from the lack of air in my lungs. The sounds of cracking ice and wet limbs sloshing into the absolutely freezing night keep me from losing all sense of reality.

"Rasha." I don't know if he's whispering or yelling. His voice is muffled from the water logged in my ears. "You have to open your eyes." He keeps talking, telling me things I can't understand. His hands are everywhere, ripping off the front of my dress to roughly rub my chest, and I don't mind.

"I have it," I choke out, finally opening my eyes. He rubs my back so hard I spit water all over him, coughing and choking up the salty fjord water until my throat burns. At least I feel more alive than dead.

"Mhmm, you do. You almost fucking died," Shaw says in disbelief, but there's a hint of something there. I don't usually see it from men close to me. Fear hinges on the words, *you almost fucking died.*

"Cold." Is all I can formulate. The bow falls from my shaking arms, and Shaw pauses to pick it up. I panic, thinking it was all he wanted, and he's going to leave me here to freeze to death. But he presses it to my chest, wrapping my numb arms around the quiver, and picks me up under the knees.

"I am so sorry, Rasha," he murmurs, almost running over the

ice covered fjord to the darkest part of the woods. "I should have killed him when I had the chance."

I can't think of an answer. I am too fucking cold. My heart can't beat in a normal rhythm, stopping and starting, making it hard to breathe. "Cold," I murmur.

He's shaking as he runs toward what looks like a sled hidden in the trees. Wiping my eyes, I squint in the darkness to get a better look at the horses, but they are not horses at all.

"Is that?" I ask, and he walks to the front of the sled to set me in the driver's bench.

"Two reindeer, yes. I came with a horse, but the gods have heard your prayer, Rasha. These are for you." He pats the reindeer with a heavy hand. The reindeer look warm as they snort hot, impatient breaths that curl up through their wide antlers.

"We have to get into the Sacred Forest," he says, nervously gazing at my dripping dress. Climbing up to sit next to me, he rubs my arms, creating friction, but I need more.

"Take it off," I beg. Staring into my insistent eyes, he hesitates, and I start to yank the slick dress down.

"I'll make it up to you," he replies, grabbing the ruined fabric with both hands and ripping it from my shivering curves. He kneels to strip the rest of the dress down my body. His mouth is level with my womanhood, but I cannot fathom spreading my legs apart.

Throwing his dry, black coat over me, he shivers, and I thread my fingers under his tunic. He understands and struggles to remove the soaked leather vest and tunic from his muscular shoulders.

I climb, unashamed, into his lap, taking the coat and covering us both. A nudge from a warm nose prompts me to look over at Aslaug who's soaking wet and climbing in the bed of the sled. With a flick of the reins, Shaw has the reindeer breaking into a run. We move fast, skidding along the snow, and I wrap my arms around his broad shoulders for warmth. He pulls me closer, tucking me into his chest.

Frosty wind nips my cheeks, and my ears must be logged with frozen water because I swear I hear the little bells I passed around at the Divination feast. Nuzzling my face into his neck breaks his concentration.

"Don't close your eyes, my lady, the gods are welcoming you," he says over the crunching ice and the wisps of pine needles brushing the wooden sled.

Looking up at the sky, I am stunned to witness iridescent rivers of colors running through the darkness. Yellow and green dip and swirl with the vast indigo making every silver star more pronounced.

"We haven't seen the lights in years," I choke over my tears. We stop deep in the woods. Shaw's wet legs shake uncontrollably, and I rub his chest to keep his heart beating.

"We need to rest," he says and covers me completely in the coat when I move into the bed of the sled next to Aslaug.

"If they figure out my burned body isn't sunk under the ice, they will come for me," I add, peering through the wide pine trees.

"Between the oncoming snow storm and your supposed death, we will have time to get to my cabin without worry." He gently lays down. His gaze stays fixed on mine instead of my nudity as he reaches into a bag to throw a blanket around us. But I grab his waist and claw at his belt till he peels his pants from his solid legs.

"It's humbling to see each other this way," I laugh, my teeth clattering together, and he palms his cold balls.

"Are you amused?" He smiles, *thank the gods,* and settles in the blankets beside me.

"I want you, but I'm numb," I reply, reaching for him again. He does one better and moves on top of me.

"I'm here, Rasha. I'll warm you," he murmurs, his hands traveling down my body. If I could feel my core, I'd be immensely aroused at how our bodies fit together, but my bones are so frozen I'm left fantasizing.

He's moves his knees in-between mine. Rubbing my thighs to create friction my blood returns to the surface of my skin. He lays his chest over mine again, and I let his heat seep into my skin, glazing over my bruises and minor burns. My mind is too tired and frayed to over think, so I let my hands lead.

In the cocoon of blankets, our mingled breaths start to warm the air, and finally, I feel at peace. Shaw plants a delicate kiss on my forehead and lifts the blanket enough to find the bow. Securing my hand around the ancient wood means not all is lost.

Finding his palm, I press my tear streaked face into his hand. With the bow and Jorvik leaving me for dead, nothing will ever be the same. I will not wake up in the morning ready to accept apologies or excuses. Moments ago, I drowned. But now, I am holding Skadi's bow in one hand and this man I've come to adore in the other. I was so sure I could wield the bow for my people, but can I wield it for myself?

We lay, slowly falling asleep, watching the purple and pink lights flow like a dam broke open over the stars. The Northern Lights were the highlight of my parents' fireside stories, but I have never seen them until tonight.

Shaw doesn't say a word, and for that, I am thankful. He's right here, solid and secure, with his arms keeping me warm. Maybe that is more than enough for right now. Listening to his breathing and Aslaug snoring, I finally fall asleep.

20

SHAW

The sight of Rasha under the ice, sinking with the weight of her dress and the chains, rattles me awake. Reaching under the blankets, I find the curve of her hip and grip her warm skin.

She's safe.

A moan slips from her lips, driving all my blood into my cock. I'll never admit it out loud, but laying here with her in the security of my arms is my vice. For once the morning sky is bright and blue, drenched in sunlight and the clarity of a new day.

My thick length sits against her ass, and she sleepily grinds into me. Arching her back in the layers of blankets, she gives me space to slip my arm underneath her shoulders to bring her closer.

"You are naked," she murmurs, trying to move to see me, but I keep her spine flush to my chest.

"We were about to freeze to death," I reply.

"Thank you for coming for me. I was ready to die, Shaw."

Shushing her admission, I can't think about losing her today when we are finally ourselves and alone.

"Do you want to get dressed?" I painfully ask, knowing if she gets up, I'll be content with how far we've come.

"No, this is nice." She squirms against me. I can feel her smile in the crook of my arm.

"Rasha," I growl, and she uses more strength to push away and lie on her back. Her body takes my breath away. While I try to regain my patience, she traces each dip and groove of my torso, moving lower beneath the blankets. I want to tell her to stop, but I groan instead.

Taking her hand before she touches my cock, I kiss her bruised knuckles, and she catches me staring at her exposed breasts. She covers herself with her other arm and starts to pull the blanket up, but I stop her.

"You must have me mistaken for a man who isn't dying to etch the curves of your body into my eternal memory." It's my turn to touch her alabaster skin as her breath becomes erratic. I mold my hand to her breast, watching her fight the urge to close her eyes. "Where did all that bravery go?" I ask. She leans up, and I give in, just a little, letting her pull me into our first real, unbound kiss. "There you are. I thought you grew shy."

She kisses me harder, and I love it. Goading her into showing me what she wants, I feel her drag her nails down my back and can't help it when my hand finds her soaking wet cunt.

"Shaw." My name out of her mouth warrants a pause. She lays back again, skin to skin, and reaches over. I don't have it in me to stop her hand from encircling my throbbing cock.

"You'll stay a virgin this morning unless you tie me up and use me, which I'm not against," I say, and her face breaks into a blushing smile.

Stroking up and down my shaft, she asks, "Where is the fun in that for you?" Her inexperience makes me take a levelheaded breath. I want to show her how this is supposed to be. Sitting up, I take her arms and gently hold her wrists to either side of her head and trail my lips against her neck. The feeling of her body underneath me is enough to make me lose control.

"Seeing you come is what I want. And you might want to hold on to that virtue now that you have the bow." Holding myself above her, I memorize the swell of her breasts.

"I meant what I said before. That I'd give myself to you." She fights my grip, leaning up to nip my lower lip.

"Let me give you this, please. I love your stubbornness, but I need to touch you," I plead. She doesn't move when I release her wrists this time. Stroking up and down her soft legs, I guide her thighs apart till I can see all of her. Rasha stays quiet, intently watching as I run my knuckles through the outer edges of her cunt.

"Do you touch yourself?" I ask. She hums a yes, which piques my curiosity. "When did you last?" At that question, her piercing blue eyes widen, and I push two fingers inside her; I can guess when. Her cunt flutters around the new intrusion, and I push further, feeling how beautifully wet she becomes with every stroke.

"After the bath in the forge," she admits. Her mouth stays open, and I withdraw my fingers, dragging them over her chin.

"Did you think about my cock?" I ask. Feeling the absence of my hand, she reaches between her legs and touches herself. I put my fingers in her mouth, and her tongue swirls over the calloused pads of my fingertips. My cock pulses a drop of pre-come on her leg.

"Fuck, Rasha, tell me what you thought of." I work my fingers back inside her as she bows her legs wider, as if I need the encouragement

"Riding you," she says, and I slip a third finger in. Instantly, her body turns rigid, and she squeezes her eyes shut. "Too much."

I watch the tension in her face ease as I pull out, giving her a reprieve. Circling her drenched clit, I wait for her to want more. With one finger, I stretch and stroke until she bites her lower lip, and I feel her muscles relax enough for me to use a second finger again.

The moans slipping from her mouth make me want to drive my cock deep against her throat. I grip her ass, holding her in place, while my coated fingers stretch her in ways no one ever has. I want to lose myself in her until no part of her body is untouched.

"Look at me," I whisper, and she strains her head the other way, caught in what I hope is the cusp of an orgasm. "Rasha, please." I press my whole body against hers and keep two fingers buried inside with my thumb pressed into her perfect clit. "Look at me," I whisper, and she slowly turns, her mouth parted as heavy breaths cave in

her chest. "Look at how you make me come without touching me."
I can't keep it together, grinding my own sensitive tip into her leg.

She reaches down to squeeze my shaft with her trembling hand,
and I bite her shoulder.

"Promise it will be you." She suddenly twists to face me, rocking
herself into my palm, taking my fingers deeper.

"Come and I promise I'll mold your virgin cunt to my cock."
Inhaling the sweet smell of her come dripping down my wrist, I
watch an orgasm shake through her as my name falls in repetitive
moans at the end of each pant. I bring her on top of my body and
pull the blankets around us, gently stroking her ribs.

I want to tell her that it's been a very long time since I've
touched a woman—that I am equally as nervous to fall for her—but
is that what she wants to hear? Or should I tell her the truth about
the unfinished chain and let her hate me. Shattering her comfort
seems cruel, so I kiss the top of her head and let her trace her
fingers over the broken bits of my tattoo, wondering if she will get
the chance to see my body as it once was.

"Shaw?" She breaks the silence. Snow birds chase away an eagle
soaring overhead. All the creatures are relishing in the dawn of a
new day. "Your ancestors made the tomb for the bow?"

"Something like that. Do you want to tell me what happened
down there?"

Rasha moves away, wrapping herself in a blanket, and brings
the quiver into her lap.

"I was ready to die, but Aslaug brought me this." She pulls the
bow out and tips the quiver over so the amulet falls into her lap.
Laying the bow over her crossed legs, she holds up the amulet and
waits with patient eyes for me to explain.

"The amulet protected you and opened the path to the edge,
which is like a pocket between the Vanheim where things are sometimes stored." I take the small oval piece out of her hands and hold
it up to the sunlight, slowly turning it to move the coagulated blood
around.

"That's your blood or mine?" she asks.

"Ours," I answer truthfully.

"How did you get my blood, Shaw?"

I hand it back to her and start opening bags to find clothes. The sun is strong, but it is still well below freezing, and I can't think clearly if she's naked.

"I carved it from the ice. You left an offering, and it didn't need to go to waste."

"You didn't tell me," she said, plainly letting her aggravation infiltrate her words. "I didn't need to make a spectacle of myself. You could have said at any point that you had the key to getting the bow. That you knew about pockets between the Immortal and Mortal Realm."

"Rasha," I sigh and hand her my shirt.

Letting the blankets fall, she keeps talking. "I am not a child. I don't want to be consoled. I needed the truth. I left all those women behind."

"It wouldn't have worked if you knew the truth. We won't leave them behind. The clan thinks you're dead, which gives you time to learn how to wield the bow. I don't know if it will work the way I think it will," I tell her, and she huffs a glare my way for good reason as she puts my shirt over her perfect body.

"You asked me to trust you, and I almost died." She slips on pants that are far too big for her.

"I have tried to find the bow for many years to no avail. You" — I put my own tunic on and turn to face her— "you've been so deter-mined, and it hit me when we did our runes at the divination feast."

"What?" She looks down at the ancient bow. Her fingers are bruised from fighting with the men, but she glides over the carvings and marvels at the intricacy of the details all the same.

"That I have been carrying the empty amulet and the broken chain, not for myself to find the bow, but for you. And the gods wouldn't have accepted you if you had previous knowledge. It would have clouded your judgment."

"So where do we go from here?" Her anger is written all over her face. I broke her away from everyone and let her get hurt in the process, but I didn't want to chance that I'd be left here for eternity. I need the bow to make amends with my family just as much as she needs it to save her clan. If I tell her that, I run the risk of her leaving me.

"We go to my cabin in the Sacred Forest and make a plan to cut Harald's men off before Spring, when they will be able to reach the mountain pass. We will find the herd with my map and lead them to the other side, where they will be safe."

"Are you asking or telling me?"

My shoulders fall, and I fear the desperate lust we felt an hour ago is shrinking in the cold, like a dying fire in the forest. When I approach her, she doesn't move away, so I cautiously take my coat from the bed of the sled and wrap it around her shoulders, fastening it tight, which brings us closer.

"I am asking you," I say, and she swallows, loosening her tightly clenched jaw.

"We will need to stop at my village and warn them," she adds, wrapping her hands around my forearms.

"Alright. After we see how the bow works. Now, you can stay back here if you want to rest, or you can sit up front with me. I can't answer the thousands of questions swimming behind those beautiful eyes all at once. Is that fair?"

Watching her suck her pink bottom lip into her mouth, I almost say fuck it and tell her everything, but Aslaug jumps into the bed of the sled with a fuzzy, white rabbit between her strong jaws. Rasha moves away from me to scratch Aslaug's head and take the rabbit from her.

"Fair for now. We should cook this before we go so we aren't hungry and grumpy the rest of the day," she says, climbing down from the sled.

21

RASHA

The warm, little rabbit is dead when Aslaug drops it in my hands, but I break its neck anyway to be sure. Knowing how easy death could have found either of us last night makes my stomach turn, and maybe it softens my anger at Shaw, if only for a heartbeat.

He knew what was down there and never told me, which pisses me off. On my way through the snow, the massive reindeers paw the ground, and I stop to give them a closer look. Last night in the dark, through my frozen eyelashes, I couldn't see how beautiful they were. Reindeer this large haven't been seen in a hundred years. I move closer to the left one's velvety nose and reach for the bridge of her fuzzy face.

"Hello," I coo, and she lifts her head to see me. Her rectangle eyes are bright gold with a black center. I try to stay mad at Shaw, but how can I now? I am here, face to face, with an epic reindeer because he trusted me to open the tomb. Leaving the reindeer, I pat the pants he gave me to wear, looking for a knife. I realize I'll have to return to the sled to get one.

"Here," Shaw offers, walking casually toward me with the handle of the blade out.

"Thank you." I kneel to strip the fur from the rabbit's body. It comes off in one clean pull, and then I start to gut it.

Shaw brings over a small pile of wood and builds a fire. I feel him watching me, but I stay focused on gutting the rabbit. The warm, little organs slipping through my chapped hands remind me of my fear from last night. I don't know if I shiver from the cold or from the remnants of my ordeal. Shaw lights the fire and hands me a decent stick to skewer its body.

"You're very good at cleaning that rabbit," he says, taking a seat across from me. I ignore his feeble attempt at a compliment. He takes the bloody organs out of the snow where I tossed them and hand feeds them to Aslaug. She's purring like a giant barn cat and licking his hands in a lovely way. The *hands* that were all over me earlier. The foolish part of my heart wants him to touch me again.

Shaking my head as if I can shake away my problems, I sit by the fire to slowly turn the skewer. Aslaug trots into the woods, leaving Shaw to rub his jaw with tangible apprehension.

"My parents taught me how to hunt." I give in a fraction. Keeping his elbows on his knees, he lifts his face to look at me across the dancing flames.

"They are no longer in this world?" he asks, and I shake my head.

"They married without consent, and my father refused to pledge a clan, so they left civilization. From what they told us, my mother was happy to be free, and they lived alongside the creatures of the forest. Jorvik came first, and I came second. Sometimes I am afraid that what I remember of my childhood is all but a lovely dream, and it wasn't as wonderful in reality."

"I am sure there were hard days. No one can control their body the way you did in the fjord if they haven't experienced plunging into ice water before."

A laugh escapes my lips. "At the rise of Spring, my father used to make us dunk ourselves in a defrosting lake or river so we would know what to do if we ever had to escape freezing waters."

"Sounds like he was a good teacher."

"He was." I shut down and wrap my arms around my legs.

Talking about them is always hard. They thought what they were doing was right and that we would live abundantly in the mountains, but they didn't plan for the clans and their death. Shaw doesn't pry, instead he walks around the fire to turn the skewer when I all but give up.

We eat while the reindeer dig up enough underbrush to make themselves happy. After covering our tracks, Shaw takes a small knife and slits his palm. I pretend I'm busy securing our things to the sled as I watch him draw runes on the tree trunks and in the snow. Sliding over on the bench when he comes to sit next to me, I can't keep my eyes from darting from his to the reindeer in front of us.

"Are you going to ask me about the runes?" he questions, taking up the reins.

"Nope," I reply, and he snaps the leather, making the reindeer move forward and gain momentum.

The trees shimmer with melting snow as we leave our safe clearing and head deep into the unknown. Midday sun streaks through the ice, casting rainbows of color across the untouched forest. Aslaug leaps into the bed of the sled and curls up in our blankets to hitch a ride the rest of the way. After a while, my eyes grow heavy with the smooth movement of the sled, and I start to drift into Shaw's shoulder.

"You can be mad and rest at the same time," he whispers over the wind whipping around our faces. His leg hooks onto mine to keep me from being tossed as the reindeer bank a hard left to avoid a frozen brook.

"Can I trust you?" I twist into his body.

"I want to say yes, but there are things you don't know. They are my burdens to carry." He keeps his eyes forward.

"I can carry them with you? I am no stranger to burdens." I don't know why I'm offering when it seems he's already given me his burdens without explaining what they are.

"I don't deserve that kindness," he says.

I feel his sorrow like the slow ache of a frozen heart, coming from the amulet tucked away in the pocket of my shirt. If I didn't feel the heartache, I would ignore the tiny, slow pulses connecting our blood. It matters less that I didn't know about the magic when I remember he could have let me burn or drown once I had the bow, but he saved me instead. I would never have known how strong I am without that opportunity.

Whatever he's keeping to himself, maybe his guilt is too great to explain it. I know that feeling, so I press my hand over his heart. His body moves in response, bringing me closer. Resting my head on his shoulder for a few hours, I fight sleep, telling myself I don't want to miss the beauty of the quiet woods.

Safely sitting together on the sled we gain altitude, moving through thick pine trees and dense evergreens. I don't know how Shaw remembers the way because everything starts to blend together. Without a word, he slips his hand over mine, reaching up my wrist to find the bracelet wedged against my forearm.

"I need the chain, Rasha," he explains. I wiggle my wrist to slide the pretty silver metal down my hand. Removing the delicate chain, I give it to him and wait for some chasm in the forest to open.

It looks like he is counting the links or saying a prayer, and suddenly, my peripheral vision vibrates, shaking my line of sight. With another hard turn of the sled, I am thrown further into his lap, and I reach around his waist to hold on.

Snowflakes fall fast, tickling my nose and blurring the scene in front of us. Tucking his arm around me, he yanks the reins, and the whole sled moves forward a few inches before slamming back into the snow.

"No one can find you because you use magic to hide?" I ask in disbelief.

"I use remnants of what I have left to protect myself."

"Sounds like the same thing to me. Why do you have magic anyway?" I retort and jump off the bench. His cabin is bigger than I expected. Aslaug perks up behind us, shaking abruptly to remove the caked on snow that coats her thick fur. I take the quiver before anything else, making sure the amulet and bow are safely inside.

Aslaug brushes her happy body against mine and runs around the snow like a puppy. Her huge paws propel her toward the door.

"She's happy to be home," I can't help but point it out. He looks at his cat with that core-heating, satisfactory smile and unhooks the reindeer. They make their way behind the cabin like they've been here before.

"You are welcome to go in and get warm. There should be fire-wood by the hearth." He gestures to the door where Aslaug is plastering her body against the handle.

Taking two bags of blankets and clothes out of the sled to carry with the quiver, I walk through the knee deep snow to the door and expect it to be locked. But the same feeling I had when I held the amulet returns, and I wrap my hand around the handle till it slowly opens.

Aslaug doesn't even wait, pushing past the half opened door to run between my legs and inside her home.

"What magic has Shaw shared with me?" I whisper into the shadows of the cabin. We are connected clearly by something I didn't know existed. Dumping the things on the first table I see to follow Aslaug to the hearth. Everything in here is carved, from the door frames to the table legs, to the many palm sized statues along the mantle. Shaw's skills are on full display.

A pang of sadness hits me that no one has ever seen this in all the years he's lived alone. I take wood from the rack to set up a fire and use one of the many strikers from a nearby basket to light the hearth. Aslaug rolls around on the rug, showing me her pretty white belly.

"Can I pet you there or will you nibble on me?" I ask, stroking the sides of her freshly healed ribs. The door opens and closes with a gust of snowy wind swirling around the cabin. Getting back to my feet, I keep the table between us and watch Shaw set his things in their places.

"What else can I help with?" I ask, needing to do something to distract me from the one bedroom with one bed past the kitchen.

"First, this goes back inside the bracelet." He reaches across the table, holding the chain, but I hesitate. "Or I can keep it. But right-fully, the next steps are yours to take."

"What does that mean?"

157

"The chain needs to be finished. You are smarter than you give yourself credit for. I know you felt something when you opened the door, when we crossed into the Sacred Forest, and when you touched the amulet."

"We are bound by magic from the gods, aren't we?" I ask, holding out my hand for the chain.

"It was the only way to make sure you didn't die."

"Just own it, Shaw." My words are short and harsh. He walks across the room, and Aslaug runs into the bedroom to get out of his way. "Don't make excuses. Own the fact that you knew what you were doing, and you chose to bind us together because…" I stop, flinching at how he's looking at me.

"I knew what I was doing because my soul is bound into every link of the chain. Now you're the only one that can help me forge the last two links. You are the only one who can draw the bow using ancient power," he admits.

"And?" I ask, boldly stepping into his space. What happened this morning was not nothing, and he knows it.

"And because now that I've met you, I can't stay away," he whispers. Slipping his fingers through my hair, he finds the back of my neck, and I melt.

"Was that so hard?" I breathe, my lips so close to his, but I want to make him fight a bit more. My need to be close to him despite what he said about his soul is foolish, but I can't stop myself.

"We need to clean up and get the animals settled." He rubs his thumb under my earlobe, and my thighs tighten together, trying to hide how aroused I am.

"Sure." I wind the chain back into my bracelet. Securing the clasp, I push it over my knuckles and under the sleeve of the shirt to protect it. His *soul* is bound to the metal. The small admission is huge, and yet, I am suddenly conflicted. He was never as free as I thought.

Alone in the part of the cabin designated as a kitchen, I decide to familiarize myself with what is in the many baskets and boxes. Being completely and unabashedly nosey, I find more flasks of honeyed wine and take note of his collection of herbs. He can write, which makes me feel hopeful and inadequate at the same time.

Aslaug slinks out of the bedroom and makes herself comfortable by the fire while I figure out where he keeps grain or flour. Cooking takes my mind off of my problems usually, and even though my problems are bigger and harder than ever before, it won't hurt to do a familiar task. We need to eat and keep our hands off each other until I know what it means to be bound to him.

Shaw is outside long enough that I have a pot of stew with left-over rabbit meat from this morning bubbling away by the time he returns.

"I didn't know you enjoyed cooking," he says, pulling off thick gloves and laying them next to the hearth. No coat, no vest, just his cream tunic clinging to his chest and torso.

"I need to eat," I answer, adding dollops of ground grain mixed with an egg I found in his dirt cellar. I put the lid back on the iron pot to let the contents crust up. Aslaug saunters through the legs of his kitchen table, rubbing herself against him until she purrs into his knees.

In my need to be useful, I already set out two bowls and spooned herbs into the bottom of two tea cups. We ladle each other food, filling the tea cups with hot water from the second kettle I stuck behind the stew pot, all while awkwardly dancing around the cracks in our newly formed relationship. I want to ask so many questions, but in truth, I am scared to know the answers.

"You're very quiet," he says as I stand from the table with my empty bowl and spoon.

"It's been a long day." I sigh. "Actually it's been a very long few months." I turn my back and dump the cooking utensils into the awaiting wash basin. Being prepared to clean after cooking was a lesson my mother taught me for being efficient when there is little light in the winter months.

Shaw comes up behind me, sliding his arms around to put his own bowl in the basin, and takes my soapy hands.

"Do you want to talk about it?" he asks, and I shrug. Sliding from his grip, I dunk my hands in the lukewarm water to rinse them off. I set the bowls to dry on a rag and walk the length of the kitchen.

"I don't know. I feel as though I got what I wanted, but at what cost?" I ask, spinning on my heels to look at him. He drags the chair from the table so he can sit while I pace.

"Go on," he urges, filling up the tea cups with wine this time.

"I hastily offered myself up as a fucking sacrifice, and no one batted an eyelash. Harald is doing what right now? Planning on taking over the Beaivi Clan, most likely, and corralling all the reindeer for himself because Jorvik knows what the map looks like."

"We will get to the herd first." A hint of concern brushes through his face.

"How can you be so sure? And what about the bow? I don't even know what the bow does because you apparently have magic that you've had the whole time and haven't used. I should go back to the village, back to the women."

"Slow down, Rasha."

"I can't!" My voice breaks, and he leans back in the chair like I've wounded him. "I can't stop thinking of the events of Yule. Maybe I let my feelings for you get in the way." I say what has been on the tip of my tongue all day, and he holds my glare with that sorrowful look in his hazel eyes. Not even Odin could stop me from having some compassion, even when it is probably why I am failing.

"That may be true. Maybe we shouldn't have let it go as far as it did," he replies, and now I am the one wounded.

"I didn't mean it like that. I know what I did. And what I wanted to do, but it is at odds with helping the women and keeping the reindeer's resources hidden."

"Is it? Or are you scared now that you hold power?" He slides the cup across the table.

"Why can't you explain what that power is exactly? Magic chains and hidden goddess relics in a place that I had to sacrifice myself to get to? Are we still in the Mortal Realm or can you travel between realms?" I start to unravel, shrieking through the last question, but he stays annoyingly calm.

"Have a sip or three," he softly says. The wine tastes better than it did in the forge, and it reminds me of how kind he was that night. "The chain is ours now, and a time will come when you'll need to decide if you want to make the last two links or part from me. The choice will be yours, I swear. And the bow holds the last of Skadi's power. The ability of the huntress will determine if she can wield it. That is why you cannot go running back to your brother."

"Maybe I can change his mind?" I harp on the topic of Jorvik instead of Shaw telling me I can decide my own fate. He picks up my deflection, and his quiet demeanor fractures.

"That's ridiculous, and you know it. You're more capable than he could ever be. Why can't you see that you don't need him?"

"Because, Shaw, when you have a family, you don't abandon them," I seethe and walk away. I know it's his room with only one bed, but I need space. He doesn't follow me as I close the door and lay down. Staring at the ceiling, I listen to Shaw and Aslaug move around the cabin as guilt gnaws away at me, and my eyes swim with fresh tears. It hurts to think about my brother—how he condemned me to death without so much as saying goodbye, and how our parents would be ashamed of what has become of their children. Both are unable to complete a Yule and make good decisions to support each other.

22

RASHA

My longboat is surrounded by a flaming fjord. Waves rock back and forth, licking the sides of the wood. Burning hair and flesh sting my nose and eyes. Blinking my surroundings into focus, I can see my torso is secured to the bench with rope. I try to turn around on the bench, but fire scalds the sea as far as I can see. The boat rocks up and down in swells larger than I remember, and I try to pat my dress down for the amulet.

"Aslaug!" I am screaming, but I can't hear myself. I try to scream her name over and over again. Maybe I am screaming for him too.

Fire-kissed water dumps into the boat as the waves crest higher around me. Yanking my hands back and forth, I am stuck, tied to the burning boat with nothing and no one. My skin sweats with each lick of the blaze.

Rasha

I hear my name, but it's so far away, and I cannot row. The oars are gone; they must have slipped away or burned. Wood splits, and flames erupt over my legs, and I thrash against the sinking boat.

Rasha

More insistent now, my name is being called, and I try to call back, but my chest hurts. My muscles throb like I am burning from the inside out. I want to fight the flames with my arms, but nothing moves.

"Rasha!" Bolting up at his voice, I gasp for air. Shaw's arms are securing me to his chest, but I push away. He releases me, and I move to the edge of the bed, throwing the blankets off.

"The amulet? Where's the amulet?" I croak out, patting around the bed in a frenzy.

"It's here."

"Where?"

"In the quiver. You were having a nightmare," he explains. I know he's right, but I squeeze my eyes shut anyway. "You're safe." Another comforting word comes from the man I yelled at earlier.

His hand touches the tense muscles in my back. My tears have no more barriers and fall in earnest down my face, into my lap. I dry heave as I move to leave the bed, afraid I might vomit. Shaw swings his legs over and is suddenly kneeling at my feet.

"Breathe, it was just a dream." He rubs my legs up my knees and down the backside of my calves. "I heard you screaming for me." His voice shakes, and I grip his shoulders, trying to hold onto something real.

"I was on fire in the sea." I gasp between sobs. My nose is wet with tears, dripping down my chin in salty rivers.

"You're safe. You will always be safe within these walls," he whispers, and I give up. Sliding off the bed and into his lap, I feel him pull me to his chest, holding me close as I let my sadness take over. I didn't cry on the way to Yule, no matter how much I wanted to over the many days of arguing and fighting with Jorvik. I had to be strong for the clan and the women. They couldn't see me falter. But here in the dark, when I have nothing else to be strong for, the tears cleanse me.

Aslaug scoots close, resting her body against us on the floor, as if she knows the grief in my heart. Shaw strokes my hair and down my back in slow circles while my body settles. The memories of fire are still there, but not as threatening.

"I didn't mean to yell." I sniffle up at him, and he takes the corner of the blanket, wiping under my eyes and across my nose.

"Don't worry about it. You have every right to be frustrated. I didn't come in because I thought it would be best."

"It's your room," I reply, resting my head against his shoulder.

"Do you want me to stay here?" he asks, loosening his arms to allow me to lean back and look at him.

"If you can handle the occasional frustrated Maiden, then yes."

He chuckles, which makes me feel like I said something right, and picks me up. Aslaug jumps onto the end of the bed like she's finally getting her comfy spot back, and Shaw tucks me into the pillows.

"I'll be right back." He leaves, and I sit up to pet Aslaug. She's warm and fuzzy, which is comforting. Shaw comes back with fresh wood and lights a fire in the hearth in the corner of the bedroom. The crackle of a new flame makes me clench the cat's fur tighter.

Aslaug shows me her big, white fangs, and I let go. Almost launching halfway out of the bed when the bright-orange sparks shoot out over the dry wood. Shaw moves besides me, taking my face in his hands, but I can't focus on him. My gaze darts between the fire rustling in the corner and his rich hazel eyes.

"You're a hunter, Rasha. You can be afraid and keep moving at the same time," he instructs, and we lay down, wrapped in each other's arms.

"This nightmare is so different from any other. I have no control," I murmur into the darkness. Shaw's scent envelopes me in the comfort I've grown surprisingly used to.

"If you want to regain control, we can start at the beginning with the bow in the morning. Let's try to sleep." He moves to take my leg and drape it over his waist, sealing our bodies together.

SHAW IS sound asleep when I wake from a deep, unbothered rest. We are both mostly clothed, but with the heat of his body next to mine, I mindlessly took off my pants in the night. Picking up the blanket gingerly, I see his arm slung low around my waist and his cock peeking out of the top of his pants. I could easily sit on top of him and lose myself in his touch once more, but my outburst last night guides me to slide out of the bed instead.

Aslaug is waiting at the door to hunt, I assume, as I pad out into the main living area, wearing Shaw's long tunic.

"What time is it, Aslaug?" I coo, pushing the heavy wooden door open. She prances around in snow that covers her paws, and I wrap my arms around my thinly protected chest to block the cold. The sun is hidden in a thick layer of clouds, disorienting me to the time of day. I know we slept longer than I would normally, but it is hard to tell if it's almost midday or still early morning.

When Aslaug disappears into the forest, I go back inside and put a fresh kettle of water on the fire. Adding more logs to the hearth makes my heart thunder past my common sense as the dream comes roaring back. It is foreign to feel afraid of fire when I make one a few times a day. I light candles and hold torches so now is not the time to succumb to my fears.

Tip toeing back into the bedroom, I grab the pants from yesterday and slip out, closing the door gently behind me. He is entitled to sleeping in every so often. Putting on boots, I trudge outside to explore the self-sufficient home Shaw created for himself. The forge is far more extensive than Harald's, with a home for every tool and designated places for each step of weapon smithing.

Around the side, our reindeer are sleeping in a cozy bed of hay under half a roof. There are goats tucked next to them, which he must keep for milk, and a small chicken coop.

"He's got you all safe and warm in here, doesn't he?" I ask the nine sleeping hens. Reaching my hand underneath the middle one, I watch her open her yellow eyes at my intrusion, but she allows me to take two eggs all the same. By the time I am done checking the chickens, I have over a dozen eggs in a basket I found hanging on the wall.

"I thought you made a run for it," Shaw says from the bedroom door as I set the basket on the kitchen table.

"Aslaug wanted to be let out," I reply, swallowing hard at the sight of him. "There are a lot of eggs." I focus on the blue and brown, smooth shapes in the basket and not his messy hair falling over the tattoos on his skull.

"We should get out and use the bow before the snow comes. Let me find you something warmer." He walks back into his room. I nervously comb through the ends of my hair until I hear him call, "Rasha?"

"I know how to use a bow," I reply, going into the bedroom. It looks less frightening in the daylight as Shaw lays out options on the bed, and the fire crackles at a quiet pace in the corner.

"This isn't a normal bow." He looks at me from his bottom drawer and hands me thick pants. "I don't mind if you cut these tonight. There's plenty of sewing supplies, and I'm sure we will have a few days of heavy snow."

"I can pay you back when we get to my clan," I say out of habit.

"You can think that if it helps you come to terms with whatever you're feeling. Take anything you want and meet me outside." He brushes past me, walking out.

Quickly piling on all the warm things, I roll the top of the heavier pants over, securing them to my round hips with one of his belts, and head back outside. I follow his footsteps and hurry along the back of the cabin, past the animals and into the trees. He left a single track of steps leading to a clearing. When I walk through the sparse trees, I am blown away by the view.

Shaw is standing with the quiver in his hand, against the backdrop of a cliff, waiting for me. I didn't realize how high up we drove the sled. The mountains and trees make a semicircle of frosty, snow-capped terrain, followed by a mind numbing drop down into the sea. He turns upon hearing my boots crunch through the snow and fully takes in the mismatched outfit of fur and wool.

"We are tucked away into the mountain, aren't we?" I ask.

"Yes, the Sacred Forest is in the largest of the Elkthynir Mountains. So I have an idea," he says when I lean over the edge to gaze down at the sheer drop. "Can I see the chain again?"

Walking away from the cliff, I wiggle the bracelet off and give it to him. He pulls the bow out and hands it to me, then takes the amulet from the bottom of the quiver. He opens the amulet, careful to hold it flat so our blood stays inside, and fits each end of the chain into the delicate filigree cover.

"If this works, tonight I'll attach a clasp to the ends with silver." He holds the amulet up, and I instantly see that he's made a necklace for me to wear.

Putting it over my red hair, I ask, "So why do I need all this to wield the bow?" The amulet rests between my breasts, and I cover it with the coat as Shaw backs away with the hint of a smile across his lips.

"Because you need to create the arrow."

"You're a blacksmith. Why can't you make the arrows?" I counter, walking around him as he strides to one side of the clearing, away from the cliff's edge.

"There was a time I could." He glances around, looking for what would be the best target.

"I'll stand here." I already scouted the widest tree trunk on my walk here, but he doesn't need to know I planned ahead. The bow is unexplainably light and almost as tall as I am. Turning it around in my hands, I line up my palm with the grip and pinch the silver string between my fingers. The amulet pulses against my chest, spreading the strangest sense of warmth over my body. Heat radiates along my arms, and I picture an arrow.

"What do I do now, Shaw?"

From a good distance behind me, I hear him say, "Lean into whatever feeling the amulet is giving you."

"Is it supposed to be hot?"

The amulet is making my skin sweat and arms tremble. Squeezing my eyes shut, I picture every fucking arrow I've ever shot flying through the sky, but nothing happens. I've used a bow since I was old enough to pull the thin string my father crafted for me, and his face winks into my memory. Disappointment, coupled with the heat emanating from the amulet, whips my focus into a storm of emotions.

"Open your eyes," Shaw murmurs, and a chilly tickle of wind seeps down my clothes. "You have to see the target," he adds. I don't just open my eyes, I glare at him.

"I know, but I don't feel the arrow."

"Relax and try again. Would it help to send off a few normal arrows with a normal bow?" He nudges his foot into a bag, slumped into the snow with an array of weapons sticking out.

"I didn't think you'd want a rematch of our first time." I give him a snarky answer and lower Skadi's bow. Glancing at it again, I have no words to describe the feeling of holding something so ancient.

"Nothing will happen to it if you put it down," he reminds me, so I put the bow in the quiver and lean it against a tree. The forest is suddenly eerily quiet as an eagle finds a perch high in a tree, causing all the bunnies and song birds to stay hidden.

"It's humbling," I add, meeting Shaw back in the middle of the clearing.

"What is?"

"Holding what was once Skadi's. When my parents died, I thought maybe the gods weren't real. That our suffering was a condition of mankind, but hunting taught me otherwise. Being in the shrine confirmed it."

"The forest holds many lessons. Are you ready for the one I am about to give you?" He passes me an arrow and a yew bow.

I laugh at his cheekiness. "What lesson is that?"

"What having a real opponent is like." He draws back the huge bow. Matching his tall form in height, the yew belly bends to his will with ease as he sends an arrow flying into the farthest tree trunk.

I line up my own arrow and pull the string back, expecting the weight to be heavy, but it's perfect. How would he know how to string a bow for me? The thought rattles my focus, and I let the arrow loose, watching it hit a few inches below Shaw's.

"Stop thinking about everything." He passes me a second arrow.

"How'd you know how to string my bow?" I ignore his request, lining my arrow up first so he keeps his pointed down.

"Lucky guess."

I shoot, exhaling all the tension from my muscles and bones. The arrow hits a tree behind the one he shot, putting my arrow further away.

"You're a terrible liar." I walk behind him with a smile on my face.

"I'm not a liar. If I had told you I restrung a bow for you, it would have scared you off." He lifts his bow to take his turn. A breeze swirls around us, picking up sparkling snow and rustling the evergreen trees. His arrow flies so fast my eyes miss the shot, but I hear wood split. Excitement gets the better of me, and I hurry through the trees, away from the cliff, to see Shaw's arrow lodged against mine, deep in the soft wood.

"Giving me an equal advantage is the least frightening part of you," I counter. Try as I might, I can't stop my gaze from finding his. "Should I try again with Skadi's bow?"

Shaw touches the two arrows, nearly on top of one another, and yanks them free.

"You should not waste precious time, my lady." A strange voice makes us both whirl around. The eagle from the tree is gone, and at the base of it stands a man dressed in a rich black tunic and matching pants. *Where did he come from?* The cliff is unclimbable.

Shaw's hand is instantly at his belt where his knife is sheathed, but his face changes from aggression to shock so fast he never removes it.

"Vidarr," he says, and I nock the already used arrow back into the string, keeping my bow ready and pointed at the ground in case this isn't a friendly visitor.

"It's been a long time, brother," Vidarr says. I look from one man to the other, seeing the similarities.

"Rasha, go back to the cabin with what is yours."

Knowing full well what he means, I walk past the two men and pick up the quiver with Skadi's bow tucked inside. Aslaug trots through the trees, happily roaming around both men before waiting for me on the path back to the cabin.

23

SHAW

We don't move till I hear the door to the cabin close, too far away for mortal ears to hear. She locks it like a good girl, and I take a heavy breath.

"How are you here?"

Vidarr loosens his shoulders and walks through the trees till our bodies collide, and snow puffs out from our cold clothes. My heart twists as he throws his arms around me in an embrace.

"Nice trick with the amulet and your blood. She opened the channel in between realms, so for a brief moment, I could find a way in." His short words cover his emotions. I squeeze his bicep, making sure he's real and not an illusion.

"Can you take us home?" I ask, and his vibrant eyes darken.

"She has the bow. Not you. So sadly, no," he replies, and I sigh. This was what I was afraid of. "One more thing. You have less than two months to finish the chain," he spits out nonchalantly. Walking through the trees, I grind my jaw to avoid looking at Vidarr. Now that he's here, it feels like no time at all has passed, but I am different then how he saw me last.

"And if she won't?" I ask, thinking about Rasha's crimson hair falling over her smooth shoulders.

170

"She will. I've been watching her since she left the shrine," Vidarr says. I shoot him a glare. Rasha and I were fooling around together in the sled with no cover. He chuckles, patting me on the back with the same boyish smile he's always had, no matter how many lifetimes we've lived.

"I didn't stick around to listen to her call your pretty name. But it was nice to know all your talents haven't left since your exile," Vidarr teases. I have half a mind to wrestle him over the fucking cliff.

"How's Vali?" I ask about his twin and my youngest brother.

"He needs you. We all do. He just won't admit it," he explains, and I am crestfallen. We meander away from the path, winding through the snow covered trees. Everywhere Vidarr steps, animals stop to watch him. It's not everyday that someone from beyond the Vanheim walks in the Sacred Forest.

"I am sorry, Vidarr." My voice is rough with regret.

"That is nice to hear."

"You can give me all the shit you want. I didn't handle anything the way I should have. But Rasha is young. She has no idea what is in store for her. Is there a way for me to sever the bond and let her live out her life once I return home?"

Vidarr clasps his hands behind his back, his long, black seal coat billowing behind him and says, "She belongs with you. I was here the first time you traveled to this realm with a partner, and I didn't feel the same way I do now when I watch her."

"If you keep talking about watching her, we are going to do more than stroll through the forest."

"I'd love to stay and rile you up for old times sake, but I cannot keep this form for too long."

"If she uses the bow, will you be able to track her?" My concern for Rasha's safety is reaching a new height, but it won't hurt to have Vidarr keeping an eye out for Harald.

"I'll do what I can if it gets out of hand. But Shaw…" He stops and blocks my path back to the cabin. Staring my little brother down makes me feel gutted. I should be giving him advice, I should be keeping an eye out, and I shouldn't need his help. Vidarr waits till I am ready to listen and says, "You cannot tell her the truth about the ritual, or the ritual won't work. You know that, don't you?"

"That doesn't seem fair." I walk around him, wondering if he'd want to meet her.

"You forfeited fair when you lost your seat. This is the test you agreed to. And if it doesn't work, the vultures are already circling."

His coded words boil my blood. In the grand scheme of things, I have never been counted out completely.

"So because I have come out of hiding and it wasn't me who procured the bow, our line is in jeopardy?"

"You were supposed to retrieve the bow. Skadi died on your watch. Now, your eternal life being bound to that chain, that's another story."

"You don't have to remind me."

"I do because you failed once. For fuck's sake, Shaw, don't fail us now," he bites with a harsh tone, sending a flurry of snow over us from the skies.

"Vidarr," I call his name as I would have in our realm, and he straightens, pushing back his shoulders and leveling a respectful stare.

"What else can I tell you?" he asks.

"Tell me everything you can in the time you have left. Tell me about our sister and our mother." I lean my back against a large tree, folding my arms over my chest, and wait.

His cheeks rise as he smiles like the stately man he is and regales me with details of our home. Half of the time, it's hard to listen because my soul aches at the nostalgia, pulling me closer to my brother. When he's done, he takes to the skies as a magnificent eagle, soaring high into the storm clouds and back into the Vanheim.

Welcoming the shift in the air, I feel the breeze as it turns harsh and unrelenting. Snow quickly falls in wet flakes, coating my tunic and face, but I don't move faster. The afternoon is swallowed by bleak clouds and dropping temperatures. Vidarr's parting gift to halt Harald's progress and give Rasha more time to learn to use the bow.

Aslaug darts through the trees, almost invisible with her sleek silver and tan coat against the snow. To the naked eye, no one would see her coming. As I trudge back through the forest, the snow gives even my eyes a challenge. I hear Aslaug again, but I don't see her.

My ankles are swept out from under me, and I turn as I fall, hitting the ground with a cleaving thud. Ready to swing a punch, I figure it's Vidarr who can't resist a moment to knock me on my ass, but red hair flashes over my face. Rasha slams the solid handle of an axe into my chest and throws her legs over my hips.

"You have a brother, and he wants what exactly?" she demands over the howling wind. My hands instantly grip her thighs.

"He wants me to come home." I try to keep my blood frozen in my veins, but my cock awakens.

"Tell me the fucking truth, or I'll leave with the chain and bow," she threatens, and I don't blame her.

"I haven't seen Vidarr in many, many years. When you retrieved the bow, it sent a signal to him."

"A signal from where? You promised no one could find me here." She pushes the handle higher into my neck till I feel the razor-sharp edge of the axe. My hand roves up her back to the braid she must have secured while she nervously waited. Her clothes are splotched with wet snow, and I can see the shimmering chain hanging around her neck.

"From the Immortal Realm," I tell her, and she lets up. Wiping her nose on her sleeve, she looks at me with those bright blue eyes that look like pieces of sea ice. She parts her red lips to huff a breath and slams the long axe handle into my collarbones.

"What the fuck am I supposed to believe? That you are not mortal?" she growls. She's too alluring, and I buck my hips to disorient her, tossing her to the side. Before she's able to use her blunt weapon, I grab her arms and pin them above her head. She pulls her legs up and tries to kick me, but my hips over her waist are far too heavy for her to wiggle free from.

"Does it matter if I am?" Seeing Vidarr left me raw. Now my emotions are spilling out. "I am going to teach you to use the bow. We are going to protect the reindeer from Harald."

She wiggles underneath me, slower, more deliberately, and her hands relax open, letting the axe roll away into the snow.

"And the chain?" Rasha's eyes flick up to mine as her legs widen to encompass my body. The snow is melting around us, and the fresh falling snow is kept out of our circle. She's radiating heat beneath me, and although I'd like to take credit for her arousal, I can't deny the amulet sitting between her breasts, thrumming happily at our bond.

"The chain is yours to finish," I softly reply and push my knees into the cold mud to stand. Holding a hand out, I pull her up and into my chest.

"You promised we'd start at the beginning, so maybe it's time to tell me why you're here, away from your family?" Her face is one hot breath away from my lips.

"Because Skadi's death is on me. This exile is my punishment." The snow falling around us sizzles into tiny curls of smoke when it touches our clothes. I can't stop myself. I slip my hand into the opening of her tunic to cover the amulet and her chest with my hand.

For a moment, I feel the world stop moving and the snow cease to fall. Her heartbeat quickens like a racing rabbit through a summer field. She's undeniably worthy of this task. I just need to show her.

Rasha stares at me and then around us, taking in the prism we are creating from the heat rolling off our skin and the snow stuck in a lethargy of time. She covers my hand with her own, which opens the tiny bit of magic inside the amulet even more. The axe in the snow vibrates off the ground, and I open my other hand to catch it before it knocks into us.

"I don't know what to say," she murmurs, leaning into the crook of my neck. My devious mind wants to slip my hand over a few inches to cup her breast, but I don't dare break the concentration of magic while she's getting used to it.

"Help me get the cabin ready for the storm. We will have days to talk," I answer. She pulls away and gasps as the snow gusts down from the sky after being held back for the five minutes we stood with one another.

Walking back to the cabin is a mess; the wind pushes ice-crusted branches from the trees, and the snow comes down so hard I am not sure Rasha can see a few feet in front of her. Aslaug is there at her side, keeping her on the path, for which I am grateful. Before long, we are laying dry hay for the goats and checking on the reindeer, who don't seem to care one way or another about the weather.

Aslaug had left two fish nearly frozen at the door earlier, so first and foremost, I start a fire when we are inside for the night.

"Where do you fish?" Rasha sings to the cat, who's rubbing her stretched out side on the carpet. Stocking the logs to keep the fire burning all night, I watch the two of them trying to communicate and chuckle under my breath.

"She probably scavenged them from an eagle," I answer, and Aslaug sits up to purr at my assumption. "Don't wait to get out of your wet clothes."

Rasha looks me up and down, pressing her lips into a thin line, and walks away, closing the bedroom door. It's for the best anyway. After wrestling in the snow and touching her beautifully soft skin, I know we definitely need space.

When she comes back, wearing a heavy wool sweater I made, I take my turn to change. Sliding my wet trousers down, I know my cock is impossibly hard. Even wrapping my cold hand against it does nothing to soften the ache. Pressing it to the side, I pull fresh pants on and try to forget how much I want her.

Hunting is best when the animals come to you. The lesson we are taught as children in the Vanheim reminds me of Vidarr and Vali enough to replace images of Rasha's body in the sled. When I come out, Rasha is sitting by the fire, examining the amulet resting in her palm as the silver chain dangles down her forearm.

"Do you still want to know why the chain is my penance, and how the bow being left here was my fault?" I take a seat close to her.

"What did you do?" she asks, and I rub my hands up the stubble shading my jaw.

"I took my position for granted, and she died."

"I have a hard time believing that you would do such a thing."

"Being young sometimes means being foolish and arrogant." I stare into the fire to avoid her concerned glances.

"So the bow was left here for you to reclaim, but you couldn't open the tomb? Because?" she continues, and I watch her slip each link through her delicate fingers and open the amulet to slide the ends out.

"Because some wounds are too great to heal. Maybe? Or maybe there is another lesson I have yet to learn from the fates?"

"Do you think the women will forgive me when they learn I am alive?" Connecting the fragments of our journeys.

"I think they will, and more so, they will look to you as their guide. Leaving a horde of angry men is going to be difficult for years to come," I reply, remembering how determined Enora was to help me when Rasha was being sacrificed. I do wonder if the women know Rasha made it out of the funeral longboat, and what has happened to Harald, but selfishly, I am enjoying Rasha all to myself.

"You bonded us, and you can break the bond?" she asks.

I think I'm going to be sick. "Rasha." Fear hitches in my lungs as she passes the still-warm amulet to me.

"I don't mean tonight. But if you decide you don't want me forever bound to you, can you break the bond?"

Taking a deep breath, I reach over and trace up her arm to where she's wrapped the chain —my life in links, around her wrist.

"If you want to go your own way when this is over, I won't stop you. You'll have everything you need to put an end to Harald's reign," I say slowly, which is at odds with how I feel. I want her to want me. I want to make her mine thought that isn't how it works.

"Can you teach me how to forge the links, or do I have to figure that out all by myself?" She rolls those pretty blue eyes at me.

"I will teach you. We can also go into the caves under the mountain range. Maybe finding ore from inside the mountain will inspire you to make that arrow appear."

Taking the amulet back from my outstretched palm, she asks, "When I do make it appear, will it give me the power I need?"

"That depends on how much power you think you carry inside you," I explain, and she furrows her brow. Contemplating our conversation, she stares into the flames as they lap over the kettle. "I am glad you're up for the challenge," I tease and leave the coziness to prepare dinner.

24

RASHA

It snows worse than any storm I've seen this year, piling in drifts up the side of the cabin. Opening the door to check on the animals is a feat all by itself.

I work on sewing myself some decent pants and practice holding the amulet to grow more comfortable in allowing the magic to flow through me without using the bow. We sleep soundly beside each other for a few nights without any more than a lingering kiss. At the end of the first week, I wake up with blood staining my thighs and slip out of bed.

"Where are you going? I can hear the wind in my dreams," Shaw sleepily groans.

"I have to get some washing done," I tell him and stand, which is naturally the wrong move. Blood runs down my leg, and embarrassment flares as I try to find a coat long enough to cover myself.

"What are you doing?" He gathers the pillow under his chin to look at me.

Aware my messy hair is clinging to my sweaty face, I dart out, "I have to go." Taking the nearest rag I can find, I clean my leg and hold it to stop the flow from making more of a mess.

"Rasha?" Shaw isn't wearing a shirt when he comes out of the bedroom to find me tearing apart a second rag. He closes his mouth when he sees the trickle of blood that won't quit decorating my white skin and walks past me to where he keeps his herbs.

"It's okay to bleed. It makes you a woman," he says. Absurdly, I want to cry.

"This means a month has passed since Jorvik and I prepared to leave for Yule."

"Sounds about right. That gives us less than two months of winter to find the reindeer before the pass thaws." He counts the days of a moon cycle under his breath while muddling herbs in a stone mortar. "Go back to the warm bed." He picks up one of the rags I furiously shredded. I ignore him and watch instead as he spoons the herbs onto the cloth.

"You can't be serious. Why would you let me back in your bed?" I ask, and he leaves the kitchen table to walk me to the room. I try to fold over the blanket where I've bleed through the sheets, but he stops me and kisses my knuckles.

"What do you do when you bleed? Hide?" he asks. I sit, folding the clean rag nicely for myself.

"I don't tell anyone when I bleed. I usually stay in the women's longhouse, or if I am out on a hunt, I hide it." I feel about an inch tall now that the words have left my lips. Jorvik's whole plan was to use my womb to gain status. He was prepared to flaunt my dependable cycle, but here I am cowering.

Shaw tucks my hair behind my ears and gently pushes my shoulders so I lay back in the warm pillows.

"Can I?"

I nod, curiously watching as he lifts my tunic and spreads the herb-coated cloth over my abdomen. "I never would have taken you for a man who dotes on someone." I attempt to break the awkward silence.

"I'm sure you can return the favor in time." His hands work over my stomach, making me want to return the favor sooner rather than later. Deliberately, he massages my hips until my lower spine releases the taut stress of the past week. I melt into the bed as Shaw kisses my forehead and leaves for a moment, only to come back with hot water in a bowl, fresh rags, and cups of breakfast tea.

"I have a sister and a mother," he starts to say, and I sit up on my elbows. Wrapping my stomach in the hot, steamy cloth makes the swollen ache disappear.

"They live with your brother?" I gobble up the tiny morsel of information.

"My brothers, yes. Vidarr is a twin. I have two younger brothers and my sister. I wonder what my sister looks like sometimes. If she has grown into a woman like you, or if she's taken up a craft."

"I'm sure she'll be happy to see you. I can hear the trepidation in your voice, Shaw. Time heals," I assure him, even though I don't know if I am being truthful.

"Would it heal your relationship with Jorvik? Because I'm still ready to kill him," he says, and I laugh. Killing something would be terribly wonderful right now.

"If Jorvik could see reason and want to make amends or understand what I want in life, then sure, I'd forgive him. But Shaw," I take his shoulders so he looks at me from the bedside, "you can be forgiven by your family too."

He crawls into the bed next to me, passing me a cup of steaming tea, and we listen to the wind gusts rattling in between the long planks of wood.

"If the snow lets up this afternoon, I'll fire up the forge." He is quick to change the subject past our family troubles. I haven't thought much about Jorvik the past few days or the women. The panic that bursts through my body thinking about them is too great. Coming to terms with relearning Skadi's history is challenging enough. *I have her bow and am learning to use it.* I take a sip of the pungent tea.

We lay in bed throughout the morning, talking about all sorts of things, including our childhoods. From the first hunt we ever went all the way to the the worst injury we ever had. His intrigue prompts me to lift my tunic and show him the crescent scar over my ribs, left by a grumpy bear.

His eyes become a decadent swirl of gold and hazel as I pause with half my body exposed. His finger traces the thin white line under my breast.

"Did you kill it in the end?" Shaw asks.

Forcing cold air through my nose, I answer, "Yes, I wasn't alone though. We hunted in a group. Mostly women and a few men."

He takes the tunic and lowers it over my body, but the effects of being so close and comfortable have already taken hold. My nipples are hard peaks, and the amulet resting on the chain is pulsing heat over my skin. Shaw's hand drifts down my stomach to peel the now dry rags away.

"Shaw." I say his name for no reason. I have no idea if I am telling him I want more or less. Kissing my stomach so gently, he laughs against my skin and throws his arm around my waist to hold me tight.

"You're very flighty today. Tell me if I've done something to make you feel ashamed?" He rests his chin in between my breasts. His solid, heavy body over mine is too nice, too sweet, and it makes me overthink what he truly wants.

"Let's get up before we lose a whole day of practice." I run my hands down his muscular back.

"There's plenty a virgin could practice in a bed." He actually growls this time, and it ignites my core to the point of throbbing.

"Don't tempt me," I murmur as he moves to accommodate his pants around his erection. Not saying a word, he grabs clothes and walks out, giving me a moment to prepare myself for the day. Lately, I've been fighting the urge to fall for him – to fall for wanting more than my life in the clan. I know Shaw is not of this realm. What if I cannot follow him to his home? What if making the last two links to connect the chain takes him away from me?

While we eat, Shaw lets the kiln heat. When the wind takes a respite from howling through the forest, we walk outside to his forge. He pulls folding wooden walls around the back half of the space to protect us from the snow, thrilling the goats with the new warmth billowing up and around the forge.

"This is all the ore I have left. We will have to go into the mountains to get more when we can travel." He hands me the same pouch he had in Harald's village, and I drop the tiny pieces of silver and gold into my palm. "To make a link, you have to willingly give something of yourself," he instructs.

I take a small knife out of its sheath. "Like my blood?" Asking makes him set his long tools down and walk over to where I am at the workbench.

"What do you want to give? What is uniquely yours that I would recognize anywhere?" he asks as I watch his eyes wander over my braided, red hair. Loosening the tie on the end, I unwind the layers of the red plait and take a chunk from the bottom. The knife is razor sharp, cutting through a section no bigger than the length of my thumb without any effort, and I hand him the red lock.

"Good choice." He adds it to the crucible along with the ore. The amulet is singing against my chest, like it knows the ritual is beginning without being told. Taking the necklace off, I open the top and hold it out for Shaw.

"That is our blood, Rasha. Are you sure?" He holds the open crucible over the smoldering fire so the contents begin breaking down.

"I know it belongs in the link. I can feel it."

"Yes, but do you want to accept that feeling? Every time we use the bond, it strengthens it."

"I do." I take a small iron spoon to ladle half of our blood into the crucible. The colors of my red hair, the silver and gold ore, and the mixed blood from the amulet combine, melting into a swirling current.

My blood simmers, urging my body onward through the ritual. I take a pair of gloves to protect my hands, but the unwavering sound of the flames spurs me to set them down. Holding my hand over the blurry edges of the fire, I wait for pain to come, but it doesn't.

"It's already taking effect." Shaw glances at me, tempting fate over the fire. "Put on the gloves in case you lose focus for a moment. I'd rather you not singe off your skin."

I put the gloves on, following his instructions on how to turn the crucible so it melts evenly. We work together to keep the forge burning hot and prepare the clay mold for the cast.

Shaw tells me all the ways to make a normal sword or a knife, which I find endearing. Instead of telling me to clean up after him or stay out of his way like men I've worked with before, Shaw is eager to teach me.

"What makes the weapons I sell to Harald better than those made in the village is that I use animal bones to give the smelt every possible advantage when extracting metal from the ore. Honoring the animal in the ritual binds its strength to the metal."

"Does Harald know?" I ask, happy that Shaw is growing more comfortable talking.

"No one knows. That is one reason why I live alone, but still make a profit. I don't spill my secrets." He nudges me with his elbow. We set the tools deep inside the molten hot kiln and step back.

"But you've told me several." I slip the gloves off.

"I promised trust. And you've done nothing but given me yours, so it's time I put my faith in you," Shaw says. The gravity of what he's saying clings to the magic surrounding the ritual.

While we wait, he takes several long pieces of unfinished metal and shows me how to draw them out after a quench and bend them with a hammer to fit around a shield. I am in awe at how he knows what each weapon needs to be strong and sharp.

"Can you teach me how to do this?" I ask, after we've poured the bright yellow liquid from the ritual crucible into the link mold during, what he calls, the cast.

"Yes. Blacksmithing and decorating, or goldsmithing, are two different things. Or are you asking about learning to write?" He points out rune labels he's etched into the table to show the status of different weapons he's crafting.

"Jorvik made sure I had no ability to speak for myself or sign anything. That's why he kept ink out of my reach and parchment locked away." I touch the pretty details on a sword made for a man who must have paid Shaw handsomely.

"Here" – Shaw hands me a tiny tool with a sharp smoldering blade on one side – "you can't mess up. Draw what comes to mind and practice holding the knife like this." He takes my thumb and wraps it around the slender tool. Holding it tightly between it and my pointer finger, he guides my hand over a blazing hot loop that will be a hand guard.

My lines are wobbly at first as I try to create the key shapes for the majority of our rune language. It's easier than I imagined to sink the little blade into the metal, and my confidence grows. Shaw stands beside me with unending patience, showing me how to use the fat blade versus the pointy tip to draw the bends in the letters and make a border to accentuate my single word.

"Not bad for one day of practice. I can teach you to read if you'd like," he says, putting tools away and blowing warm air into his cold hands. We've been out here for hours.

"What about the link?" I wrap my hands around the hot clay to defrost my fingertips. The snow picks back up as the afternoon wanes, and deep-purple snow clouds block out any visible stars.

"We can bring it inside for now," he recommends, and I scoop up the mold, carrying it inside where the cabin is warm and cozy. Closing up barrels and feeding the goats on his way, Shaw follows me inside and takes off his heavy fur coat.

"Thank you for today." I brace myself on my tiptoes to give him a kiss. We smell like embers and smoke as he wraps his arms up my back, under my tunic. My lips part, and our kiss deepens. His rough fingers graze over my skin, buckling my knees in the best way.

"Rasha," his voice trembles against my mouth, and I fist his shirt to keep him close. "The magic of our blood mixing with the elements you provided is making you feel more."

"I've felt like this for days," I murmur. Slipping my hands under his shirt, I need to feel his skin against mine, and I pull the sleeves off his shoulders. My lips trail over the broken, blue lines of his tattoo.

"We need to go to the caves when you stop bleeding." He moves me away so he can kiss down my neck.

"If we stay in the same bed tonight, I don't know if I can keep my hands to myself," I whimper as he looks at me with pure depravity in his eyes.

"The alternative is that we sleep apart, and I can't have that."

He pulls me close again. "You must be starving for more than the taste of my skin?"

"I am hungry." I giggle as he picks me up, sets me down on the kitchen table, and begins pulling things out to prepare dinner. The clay mold sits on the floor by the hearth, each piece of our bond solidifying little by little as the link cools.

25

SHAW

Everyday we grow closer, and every day my restraint wanes. I've pumped my cock dry while she sleeps. Looking at the swell of her hips and the dip between her legs is enough to make me come. Some nights, she stirs, like her body knows and reaches for me, but I dare not wake her.

When she offered to use our blood in the link for the chain, I was both elated and conflicted. Should I have stopped her or kept my blood out of it? I never thought I'd have a partner when reclaiming my seat in the Vanheim, so I am at a loss. Are my feelings for her because I am a man starved or is she to sit beside me as an equal in the Immortal Realm?

She is so certain she understands what she feels. I haven't stopped her since I feel it too. Vidarr was right when he said this time was different. Rasha is different from Skadi, though she doesn't know it. She has no idea how powerful she is as she slowly learns to wield her new strengths.

We've practiced less with the bow, considering it frustrates her, but this morning she wears the quiver with the bow tucked inside as we follow Aslaug down to the icy river below the cabin to fish. Her flushed face as she descends the difficult terrain makes me think of all the ways I can make her sweat. Hiking down a mountain is ridiculous with a hard on. I swear at myself and take a swig of the honeyed wine she insisted we bring.

"What are you doing way up there?" she asks, gazing up at me with those big blue eyes.

"Watching you," I call, sliding on my ass a good ten feet down to where she is. Snow and ice cave-in under my legs when I stop. A massive piece of ice breaks from underneath, hitting the sides of the mountain on the way down. We are almost at the river bank where I plan on making a fire while I watch her fish with Aslaug.

"Out here, we are at the border of my protection, so don't be too complacent," I explain and watch her survey our surroundings.

"The snow stopped yesterday, and I doubt Harald will be on the move so quickly. I don't remember traveling through any river valleys, so Jorvik won't come this way if he is returning home." Her gaze travels up and down the river. The foamy current breaks the ice in places, sending fat sections careening down. Pushed by sliding snow drifting off the mountain and the sheer force of our ever changing nature, the river never completely freezes over.

"There are other predators besides man," I remind her and start climbing down the rest of the way.

"I still think I should go home before we try to find the herd. There might be people in the Beaivi Clan who would be on our side, people who would help us. Before my grandparents generation, they lived with the reindeer, never taking more than they needed. That's how they survived the winters before the other Vikings came from the South." She brings up a conversation from a few nights ago.

"You trust those who didn't try to stop Jorvik from giving you to Harald?" I choose the same line of defense I did in the first argument.

"Maybe if they see I defied Jorvik and have Skadi's bow, they will change their minds?" Rasha makes a decent point as she climbs down the rest of the way, walking gingerly over the river bank to a sizable spot where we can all fit.

"I have lived through many cycles of politics, and they all have one thing in common."

"Which is?" she asks over her shoulder.

"Most people will support whoever can protect and provide for them. You might have her bow, and there was a time you provided for them, but they will question your ability to protect them."

"I am trying to protect them. I can stand up to Harald. I have been spared by the Immortal Realm by evading my own death," she says, taking things out of her bag.

We sit in the snow while she ties large hooks to a line. Her mind is working, thinking about her options, and I hesitate at what to say. On one hand, she could stay here and lead her people; on the other, I am running out of time to complete my own penance.

She doesn't look my way, but I hear her ask, "Would you stay with me?"

"In the Beaivi Clan?" My face tenses as she slowly nods, casting her line with Aslaug darting around the fallen trees and blocks of ice. "I am not one for groups."

"Shaw, if you taught the women how to smith weapons, they would have skills beyond bearing children. They could be paid freely and defend themselves. They will need something besides living nomadically with the reindeer." Rasha makes a compelling argument, standing on the riverbank with her long fishing line in the flowing water.

"We need to get them away from Harald and sadly, your brother first," I add, and she whips around to look at me.

"Then you'd teach them?" Her excitement is hard to ignore, so I press my lips together, refusing to let a smile breach my cheeks. "It will make a difference, even if you aren't sold on the idea." The lightness in her voice makes me happy, which is something I don't think I've let myself feel in exile. To make someone else happy lifts the strangest weight off my chest.

"Walk up stream to catch the fish as they swim." I motion for her to move higher, and she rolls her eyes at my change of topic.

Aslaug crouches over the end of a tree trunk, her tufted ears moving back and forth, and she locates a school of fish upstream.

Working as a team, Rasha takes direction from the massive lynx and moves her line until they catch a trout the length of my arm. Every time they catch a fish, Rasha moves further up the river.

The sun's warmth is melting snow and ice, creating tiny drops of water that drip from every tree branch and rocky ledge. Bright rays of sunshine burst through the water, creating a kaleidoscope of colors across Rasha's red hair and in the fog wafting up over the water. For a while, I sit and watch her move around like an ethereal faerie.

Then her body stills, and I feel the ground rumble from a mile away. Aslaug leaps from the nearest ledge, where she's been devouring a fish, and raises her hackles. Suddenly, she hisses at the dense forest, those deadly fangs out in defense.

"Rasha," I call, and she walks backward, keeping her eyes on whatever is coming through the mountain. Glancing over my head, I don't see an eagle or Vidarr in human form, which causes me to worry. With the axe from my belt, I get low to cross the iced over parts of the river without being spotted by our predator.

She reaches for Skadi's bow in the quiver tied to her back and slides her body against a tree. The mountains shake, sending snow and ice crusted branches falling all around us. Tiny, white stoats and foxes run from their burrows towards the cabin without hesitation.

"What is coming?" Rasha asks when I reach her side.

"Something that is not from this world," I whisper, noticing she already has Skadi's bow out of the quiver.

"Are you doing this? Is this a test? You don't have to scare me," she mutters low as the rumblings become more methodical, like a group of deer running through the forest.

"It is not a test from me," I retort and look to the skies again. "Others want to prevent me from returning." I know I have opened a line of questioning for later, but she doesn't respond. Trees break at the roots, falling over the evergreens, sending sharp pine needles and shards of bark flying over our heads.

Rasha runs for Aslaug, and I sprint the other way to discover what is barreling at us. Black fur engulfs the fallen trees as the huge creature speeds toward me. His long, narrow snout and deep red eyes are unmistakably that of the Fenrir. Legs the size of trees and paws that could flatten a mortal in one crushing step draw closer. The wolf beast must have been conjured to end me now that my way home is nearly in reach.

"Run, Rasha," I yell, but she isn't, instead she's climbing a tree. "Rasha!" She turns to see Fenrir, and her mouth falls open in horror. Skidding into the riverbank, his coarse fur is covered in snow and ice. Bits of trees and rocks fall off as he shakes like a dog and bares his many rows of pointed canines.

"What is that?" she shrieks, locking her legs around a branch to situate herself in the tree.

"He's after me. Go!" I shout. Fenrir turns his huge head to stare at me. "Do you remember when we used to be friends?" I ask the beast. He growls so loudly that ice shatters in the river, and the rest of the water rushes down from the mountain, taking logs and rocks with it.

Running back the way the creature came, I use its path of destruction to make it easier for me to be chased. Hopefully, Rasha locks herself in the cabin until I can find my fucking brother and we send Fenrir back through the Vanheim.

Jaws snap too close to my back, and I whirl around with my axe at the ready. Aslaug tackles Fenrir's face, her agile body wrapped around his long mouth. She claws and bites while he tries to shake her off. Taking the opportunity she provides, I move left into the thick collection of trees.

I hear her yelp and look over my shoulder to see Rasha standing underneath Fenrir's paws as he's trying to throw Aslaug off of his face. She slashes her own axe, trying to reach the deeper ligaments and bones, but the wolf is too strong for her. Rasha sees me and darts into the woods to avoid being trampled.

"I told you to go. You won't survive a bite from him," I snarl out of fear and grab her arm to move her behind me.

"Aslaug is keeping him busy. Do you have a plan?" She ignores my anger.

"Rasha."

"I have the bow, remember." She places her hand in mine for a moment and squeezes. "Usually we hunt from both sides and box the animal in. With the cold running water, we should have the advantage."

Exhaling a ragged breath, I nod and leave her to maneuver to the other side of the aggravated Fenrir. When Aslaug sees me making a run for it, she jumps off his back, leaving blood trails and bite marks covering his face.

"Good girl," I tell the cat as we prepare to tackle the huge hairy wolf. "Try avoiding its mouth," I add, as if she doesn't already know. We run up a set of boulders, jumping with every last hidden bit of power left in my bones. Willing strength beyond my mortal body, I collide with his oily fur. The power of the two of us sends him down to the forest floor with a seismic quake, making the icy ground split on all sides.

"Fen, who sent you?" I groan as he rolls over, snapping his jaws when he tries to rip me off his body. Snarling and growling ensues, and I wiggle free to run further down to the water where I hope to the fucking fates Rasha is able to conjure an arrow.

Leaping, he almost closes his jaws around Aslaug as I hurl an axe into his chest. The hit distracts him enough that she is able to scurry up a tree, but Fenrir's fur is too dense for the blade to do any sizable damage.

Running back to the sound of the rushing river, he rams his ugly snout into my back, tossing me in the air. I hear my ribs crack as I hit the ground and roll away before he can sink his teeth into me. Fenrir growls, drool flying everywhere, but I grit my jaw and aim another axe at his eye.

Blinking back blood when the axe hits its mark, I hiss, "Go home before you regret this." Fenrir closes his wounded eye. Forgetting about Rasha, he hauls his angry ass through the thick trees to try to chomp on me.

"Here, boy," Rasha whistles. I use the slight turn of his head to run underneath and drive my seax knife into his belly. His ear-piercing howl deafens me, and I don't see his head whip around. Razor sharp canines sink into my shoulder and deep into my back.

Rasha's screaming pumps adrenaline straight into my heart.

Aslaug appears from nowhere and latches her strong jaw onto Fenrir's back leg. His teeth release me to change opponents, and I get to my feet, shutting out the agonizing pain to run to my cat.

"Fenrir, is this what you came for?" Rasha's voice is louder than it should be, silencing every sound in the forest. She's climbed up a wet rock in the middle of the river. The crazed wolf turns to see a formidable huntress wielding Skadi's silver bow aimed at his chest. Fenrir bolts for her. His open jaw drips blood and drool while his oily, black fur catches on the thick pine trees.

My heart feels like it is going to burst into flames, so I clutch my chest, dropping to my knees as the bond is overwrought with her determination. His massive paws hit the ground, too fast for me to intervene, and he leaps over the water to eat her.

The fibers of my mortal body are pulled to my limit. Holding my bleeding shoulder, I pray to my mother for the first time in a hundred years for her to protect Rasha. My joints and ligaments stretch beyond their capability in a blast of light, and I lift my head to see a long, silver arrow flying through the blue sky. Swirling snow circles behind as it sinks deep into Fenrir's chest.

With a yelp, the wolf crashes into the river and is swept away by the gushing water and ice blocks flowing downstream. When I try to stand, my vision darkens, and I grasp my knee for support. My shoulder is bleeding uncontrollably from Fenrir's immortal fangs when I lift my hand away.

"Shaw? Shaw, where the fuck are you?" She's yelling for me, but I can't seem to form words. Aslaug bounds over, her big amber eyes full of concern as she pushes her body under my arm. Rasha's footsteps are not far behind.

"Shit, Shaw, you've been bitten." She crashes to her knees at my side and pulls my shirt off my torn up back.

"You conjured an arrow," I weakly say into her hair. Threading the shirt under my arm, Rasha does her best to cover the deep bite wounds, pulling the sleeves of the tunic to make a knot.

"I did," she breathes. Gripping her hips in preparation, I succumb to blinding pain as she yanks the makeshift bandage tight. I focus on her thundering heartbeat and how my fingers are touching her, leaning into her sweat-licked skin. "Shaw, stay with me. We need to get to the cabin. Tell me what to do?" Her panic brings life back into my eyes.

"I can walk." I grind my jaw and stand but stumble into her. Aslaug helps to stabilize us. We make it to the easiest part of the steep mountain path back to the cabin.

"Where will his body go?" she asks, and I look over our shoulders to the rolling river. Fenrir's body is gone.

"He cannot die. You, my lady, opened the channel when you used the bow, so Fenrir will return." Vidarr's voice makes Rasha turn. Her quick movements knock me off balance, and I hit the rough bark of a tree.

"You took one for the realm, I see." Vidarr strolls over to me, lifting the bandages as I wince.

"Where were you?" I glare at my younger brother as he presses his hand into my chest. Grunting at the collision of my bond against Rasha and Vidarr's power, I start to feel my blood cease to trickle from the bite wounds, and my ribs crack back into place.

"What are you doing!" Rasha's here, pushing against Vidarr. I do love her fearlessness. My glare changes to smirk at my brother who gives me a final pulse of power and releases me.

"I'm healing him," he says, leaving an edge to his voice that doesn't phase Rasha one bit.

"How do I know you didn't send that beast?" She assaults his character. I laugh, bringing fresh air into my smashed lungs to reinvigorate my body.

"Why would I do that?" he asks. She steps between us, covering me with her arms. Aslaug runs to Vidarr, pushing her nose into his hands and sniffing around his long, soft coat for evidence of the rest of our family. Vidarr feels her all over for scratches and wounds, gazing up at Rasha. "I want my brother to come home. Though right now I am in the minority, which is why I couldn't intervene when Fenrir appeared. If they knew I was walking between the Vanheim, we would all be worse off."

"What do you mean? In my experience, brothers will do anything to get ahead," she says. Vidarr slides his stare beyond her to me. I shrug and find my footing, looping an arm around Rasha's waist to bring her ear to my mouth.

"I have more fear of Vidarr falling for your beauty than I do of him trying to kill me," I murmur, and she shivers against my chest.

"He's right. You are ravishing, especially now that you've finally got the hang of the bow." Vidarr comes to our side as we start the trek back to the cabin.

"Should I say thank you?" She raises an eyebrow at Vidarr.

"Hopefully, when Shaw comes home, it will be me thanking you." He offers his hand to help her up the mountain, and I watch her assess him. Slipping her hand into his, she allows him to pull her up a steep section. I wish I could hear her thoughts. The rich fabric of Vidarr's coat and trousers, the fancy leather boots, and his extraverted smile make for a much more impressive picture than me with a bloodied coat over my sore shoulder.

26

RASHA

"Where exactly is home?" I ask Shaw's handsome brother as he reaches past me to help Shaw up the rocky mountainside.

"Through the Vanheim. I am not going to spoil all the surprises, so you'll have to use your imagination. But I can assure you the accommodations are nicer than my brother's little shack," he scoffs. Shaw attempts to push him over, but his shoulder is still raw, the skin blistered in places.

"You healed him with magic?" I ask another question in hopes of some clarity on what happened.

"Yes," they both say together.

"When you were more like your brother, could you use magic?" I ask Shaw.

"I could do magic far better than Vidarr," he retorts, fixing his coat over his blood-stained chest.

"You're only saying that because you're trying to impress her," Vidarr counters.

"I am saying it because it's true. Though I was never good at shapeshifting, so maybe you could give us a demonstration by turning into an eagle and flying away," Shaw retorts, and I chuckle at Vidarr's feigned gasp.

"You have been following us?" I suddenly remember all the times I've seen a sleek, black eagle flying overhead.

"When you took the bow from the shrine, you left a small part of the channel open. Today, when you conjured an arrow, you widened the space between realms. Most likely, each time you've connected with the items Shaw's given you, the channel has grown."

"And what will close it? We cannot have angry spirit creatures running through the mountains." I look between both the men.

"It will close when I return," Shaw says.

Turning to Vidarr, I can't help but ask, "You're an eagle. Can you fly over the clans to be sure nothing like Fenrir attacked them?"

"I can if that is what you wish." Vidarr's quick appeasement makes me feel like I am missing a piece of the puzzle.

"Thank you." My thoughts revolve around everything that has happened. The channel will close when Shaw returns, but what will he be returning too if there are those who still wish him dead?

I lead the men back to the cabin with Aslaug at my side giving the brothers the chance to talk about the Fenrir and the Bow. Once we are inside the warm cabin it is easy to excuse myself and go to the bedroom. Gently closing the door, I set the quiver on the bed and peel off my sweaty clothes in exchange for my favorite sweater.

When I open the bedroom door to return to the kitchen, I hear them teasing each other about the state of Shaw's cabin. Listening to them squabble about things makes me think of Jorvik. He wouldn't have healed me or trusted me to take down a beast from another realm.

"Are you alright?" Shaw asks, coming to where I stand in the doorway to rub his hands up my arms until I look at his hazel eyes.

"Yes, why?"

"Because you're lurking."

"Take that off so we can get you cleaned up." I nudge his good shoulder as I walk around him to find a kettle for clean water.

Shaw undresses from the top down and sits by the fire that Vidarr blasted into the hearth with a wave of his hand. The magic is starting to shock me less and less. Vidarr pulls all sorts of things down from Shaw's kitchen while I come up beside him to take a clean cloth.

Stifling a giggle, I share, "I did the same thing the first night I stayed here."

"He's been alone for far too long, Rasha. I don't think you know yet what it would mean to him for you to help him get home." Vidarr's voice cracks over the last words. His eyes are beautiful now that I am calm enough to see him. In my hesitation to answer, his face softens to a visible ache.

"He isn't alone now. He has me."

At that, Vidarr's smile returns. He helps me carry a tray over to Shaw, who is petting Aslaug by the fire.

"I am so sorry, love. I have nothing to offer you," Vidarr tells the big cat. If she is displeased, she doesn't show it, instead she peppers him with affectionate kneading and purring.

"Tonight is a new moon. In the Beaivi Clan, we always offer something, but I think I dropped all the fish." I chat to keep myself from looking at Vidarr who is grinning at Shaw. Wringing the cloth out over a bowl of fresh, steaming water, I clean the dried blood off Shaw's back and notice a shadow of his tattoo beyond the usual border I've grown accustomed to.

He leans back to quietly whisper, "We can open the mold and see how the link turned out. That is more than enough for an offering."

"With your brother?" I ask, holding Shaw's anxious stare.

"He is more sentimental than most of my family." He watches as I stroke over the front of his chest and flinches when I trail over the deep fang wounds. Even though Vidarr sped up the healing process, Shaws muscles are still tender and swollen.

"How much longer can you stay?" Shaw asks Vidarr.

"Less than an hour," he replies. "Are you sure you want me here when she adds a link?"

Shaw stands, and I take the bowl full of red-tinged water away to dump out the back door. The amulet around my neck passed the threshold of soft pulsing as soon as I conjured an arrow. Since that moment, I have felt a steady flow of power running through my blood. A shirtless Shaw calls my name, and I turn to see him placing the clay mold on the kitchen table.

"Rasha, would you like to do the honors?" he asks. Suddenly a pang of nervousness hits me with the two of them watching. Vidarr takes a wooden container of salt and carefully pours the tiny grains out to make a triangle in the middle of the table. Grabbing dried mistletoe and the snow flowers that Shaw picked for me yesterday, he decorates the table as we would for a new moon offering.

"Are you sure I should? I could break it," I ask, but Shaw puts the pry tool in my hands, urging me on. Tempering the power simmering through me, I carefully crack the mold open down the middle. The dry clay breaks apart with ease, and I sweep away chunks from around the center. Through the dust, the shiny silver metal is unmistakable. Taking a deep breath, I feel the amulet's power thrum against my skin, calling to what is familiar.

"Brother, it seems your fate has changed." Vidarr moves to the other side of the table to give us room.

"For the better?" I take the amulet off my neck. Shaw separates the ends of the chain and lays it flat on the table.

"If you are my fate, Rasha. It is for the better. The link is yours to take and yours to add," he tells me. I pull the slender oval link out of the clay, dust it off with my fingers, and roll it over, finding it odd there is no space to slide it into the last link available.

"It's not as smooth as the others." I look at Shaw for an explanation or a hint of disappointment.

"I can teach you how to make it smooth with time, but nothing is smooth or perfect on the first try. The beauty of the imperfections is that you've poured your heart and soul into it." His words mean more to me than he knows, and my response catches in my throat.

Vidarr presses his hands together and opens them slowly, which creates a current of magic flowing between them over the table. The salt triangle vibrates quietly, and the various plants return to their vibrant green hue.

"My lady, do you want to connect the first link of your bond?"

Vidarr asks me. The swirling shadows of colors between his hands grow to cover the entire tabletop.

"You can wait, Rasha," Shaw murmurs against my neck. The warmth from his shirtless chest encompasses my back. Our pull is unshakeable, growing stronger every day we spend together, and we haven't even touched one another beyond the surface.

"There is no need to wait. How do I attach it without an opening in the metal?" I ask the men. Vidarr smiles and closes his hands only to open them again, using more magic to light the salt triangle ablaze.

"All you, Shaw. I am simply the witness," Vidarr says, his lovely, high cheekbones taut with focus.

Shaw takes my hands, bringing us over the purple and red flames that are stoked by Vidarr's magic. I have the link while he takes the end of the chain, holding it flat in his palm. The flames lick my skin, but I feel no pain.

"In the Vanheim, we pray to the deer goddess who has been driven into darkness. Will you bring her into the light?" Shaw asks, his hazel eyes glowing nearly golden like his brothers. "To accept the bond is to promise your blood to the god before you, Rasha," he pauses and slides his hand over my cheek.

"I promise, and I promise to finish the chain so you can go home."

Taking the link and the end of the chain from Shaw, I hold the pieces over the fire in the center of the triangle and feel the familiar channel opening inside my soul. Shaw's hand falls from my face, and he doubles over, keeping his palms firmly planted on the table. My fingers feel as though they will be crushed by the weight of the magic, but I know my link belongs here. I know with all my heart that I belong with Shaw.

Closing my eyes, I feel the magic channeled by Vidarr shake, and the flames spread over the table, searching for a more powerful conduit. I conjured the arrow, I almost died in that longboat to find the bow, and now, I can surely bend metal to strengthen this chain.

I hear Shaw grunt through the immense feeling of our souls

being stretched and tightened until something pops. He crashes to the ground as my eyes fly open.

Holding up the chain, I look down to my own hands that hum with glorious, golden vibrations zinging up and down my fingers and arms. It's like a million honey bees are buzzing underneath my skin. Shaw throws an elbow on the table to hoist himself up, and Vidarr loops an arm under his injured shoulder to bring him to his feet.

"She did it." Vidarr's excited whisper is encouraging.

"Try to extinguish the fire," Shaw says. Glancing at the two men who urge me on with hopeful smiles, I wrap the chain around my palm and gently bring my hands together – the way I watched Vidarr do moments ago. The heat from the fire dies down in my exhale. As I let the bond settle in the marrow of my bones, the fire smolders down to the white salt granules until it is completely gone.

"I would love to celebrate, but my time was up a while ago," Vidarr says. He squeezes Shaw's good shoulder and sweeps his coat around his formidable frame.

"Thank you, brother." Shaw's hoarse voice hides a sadness I feel inside my own heart. Bowing deeply to me, Vidarr kneels before Aslaug and kisses her fur before leaving the cabin. I heave the heavy bolt over the door, even though with the bow and the chain, I know we will be safe tonight.

Shaw lets out a ragged breath, filling the quiet space building around us.

"I don't know what to say," he finally whispers. I move around the table, threading my arms around his sore ribs and warm skin. Resting my head against his chest, I let my feelings flow unencumbered through the fragile bond we are nurturing.

"You don't need to say anything," glancing up at his rich but sorrowful eyes, "it was just one link," I murmur. He gives in, wrapping me in his arms.

He laughs softly. "That part is why you are incomparable. It wasn't just one link. I will honor you for your commitment, but sadly, it will have to be a night when we aren't exhausted."

He kisses my cheek. I move up to reach his lips, languidly kissing him as if time no longer exists. There is no point in cleaning, and I have no desire to eat. So we lay in bed, entangled in one another, needing nothing more than to let the flames of our bond continue to grow.

———

We wake in a fog of magic and desire. Needing space, Shaw slips from bed at the first break of the sun through the window. I lay curled in the blanket, looking at each link in the chain. A small part of me is crestfallen that he left the bed and didn't touch me beyond our clumsy, sleepy kisses last night. I won't admit it, but I dreamt of connecting more than the chain.

"We should get ready to go to the Elkthynir Mountains," Shaw says, standing in the doorway of the bedroom. Pushing the blankets off, I don't shy away from stretching my naked legs and shaking my messy red hair from my shoulders. I want him to see me after everything that we've done together the past month. I don't want to beg, but I am not above being a temptress. He stays gazing at me but doesn't move. I want to ask why he's waiting.

"Do you think we will see Vidarr again?" I ask instead, giving up my game and beginning to dress.

"I do. I think you'll meet my whole family soon. Can you handle that?" There is a hint of happiness in the question, which makes me grin.

"Sometimes I am not sure I can handle you."

He breaks and pulls me into him from behind, even though I am wrapping a tunic over my chest. Dipping his nose into the crook of my shoulder, he holds me tight when I push against him.

"I am sure you can handle me just like you handled all that magic last night." At his deep guttural groan, I melt.

"How are we traveling?" I breathe, trying to keep up the charade between us.

"We will take the two reindeer with us so we can bring them to the herd after we see your clan."

I spin in his arms. "You want to ask them?" My cheeks hurt from the smile beaming across my face.

"I owe you the opportunity to try to gain their trust and help. So yes, we will ask them," he says. "Can you ride a reindeer without a saddle? I should have asked you if you've ever ridden a horse?"

"Yes, I'll be fine on the reindeer." I laugh.

"Don't make a joke, or I'll lose all my honorable traits, Rasha." He looks at me in warning. I glance at the long strain in his pants and giggle to myself. I begin packing extra clothes for our journey into the mountains, making sure I have enough to stop at my clan after.

Working together, we close up the cabin and head deeper into the Sacred Forest. The Elkthynir Mountains on this side are untouched by man, the trees dot the snowy mountainside like the tattoos on Shaw's arm, and the animals aren't afraid of how we encroach through the boulders.

The sled would never have made it through the uneven snow and rocks. Riding atop the giant reindeer, I feel like one of the goddesses drawn in our many scrolls, but I don't have the same confidence. The enormity of our task, coupled with what lies beyond this trip, stirs up fresh apprehension.

When it seems the reindeer won't fit through the sharp, narrow mountain terrain, we dismount. Shaw opens his palm with a knife and uses his blood to paint runes over the cold rocks.

"Are we going to leave them alone?" I ask as Shaw tucks the reindeer in a small collection of short trees.

"Aslaug will come for us if there is a problem. Don't look so worried. She'll be fine." He kneels to pet her arched spine. She saunters over and bumps her head into my palm as if to encourage me to trust her master.

"Off you go." I rub my face against her prickly whiskers, then she runs into the trees to scout.

"Hopefully, you're not afraid of tight spaces," he teases and leads me through the entrance to the mountain. The huge boulders are covered in ice and snow, and I have no idea how Shaw knows where he's going.

"After we find ore, there is a special place where the water from inside runs hot into pools." He walks ahead of me as the space between the rocks narrows. I have to step one foot in front of the other and turn sideways to shimmy through.

Inside the cave, Shaw lights a torch from a mounted iron holder and keeps moving down a long pathway. Every so often, there are other unlit torches and runes. Sometimes tiny rivers of iridescent water flow over the little cracks and crevices.

"Do you come here often?" I ask when we stop to climb a carved set of stairs.

"Over the course of my time here, I guess you could call it often?"

Raising my eyebrows at him, I climb half the staircase. "Enough times that you carved stairs?"

"It is easier than using a rope to climb through the hole that was once here," he mocks, following me up. The walls along the staircase are detailed in looped and curved lines that I have come to recognize as Shaw's favorite design. Grazing my fingers in the deep grooves, I stop at the ledge and look out into the unknown.

27

RASHA

"What do you think?" he whispers at my back. Shivering at his voice, I scoot to the side so he can lead me through the path, winding around massive pieces of the rocks that jut up from the cave floor. Some almost touch the equally sharp rocks that form dagger-like structures coming down from the cave ceilings, and everywhere in between, the iridescent river flows.

"It's unlike anything I've ever seen," I murmur, careful to step only where he steps.

"The water down here hasn't been this active and full in years." Shaw cups his hands under a ledge where the shining water is running like a stream in summer.

"We haven't seen the Northern Lights in years, so maybe they are connected." I hesitate to touch the water, wondering if there is magic held within the particles. "Just thinking out loud."

"They are one in the same." He beckons me closer.

"What do you mean?"

"The lights are a reflection of the Ivalo River flowing through the mountains. In the coldest months, the magic left by the gods casts the light into the sky, revealing the path to the Vanheim."

Slowly shifting my gaze to him, I remember opening the shrine and how it felt to move between realms in limbo. The lights I saw the night he rescued me were the first in my lifetime.

"So here we could cross over?" I ask, and his lips part in an effortless breath like he could kiss me.

"You could, maybe. But I have the map to the reindeer because I need them to accept my penance when I cross over," he reminds me. I shove down my strange need to touch the amulet.

We walk through the cave, letting the magnificence of the underground river guide us. After a while, I understand the colors. Those near the inside of the mountain run pink, and the ones dripping down from the ceiling are yellow. Under our feet, the slow, oozing water is blue, picking up the fragmented colors of the cave. When the stream flows outside to the plants under the snow, the sheen is green.

Shaw is deep in thought, I can tell by how often he rubs his jaw and avoids looking at me. His reservations are making me question if I should be here. I could have stayed with Aslaug and let him get the ore. Have I spent too many nights sleeping soundly next to him that I have forgotten what my purpose is? The thought that maybe taking my virginity doesn't interest him has crossed my mind more than once.

"Rasha?"

I start to answer, but my throat closes in trepidation.

"Do you want to swing the pickaxe? It's very satisfying?" he asks, holding it out. A sweet smirk crosses my lips as I take the heavy tool. Dropping the bag from my shoulders, I motion for Shaw to step back, and he does.

"Where should I aim?"

"For the deepest vein, but don't overthink it." He gives the instruction, and I slam the pointy tip of the axe into the mountain. Everything shakes like I hit the center of a ceremonial drum.

"Again," he calls from behind me, and I oblige. The ceiling shakes as tiny drops of water sprinkle over us. The rock bed vibrates. I don't need him to ask me again as I wait for a pulse in the amulet. I focus on that beautiful strength woven in our blood and aim for the crack in the cave wall. "You did it," he exclaims.

My chest is heaving as I lower the axe and gaze at the cave floor. Plain shards of stone are everywhere, but the light coming from Shaw's torch flickers over several shiny, misshaped pieces. We bend down to gather the precious ore, but his hand finds my cheek instead of the silver.

"I don't know how to say this," his voice cracks over the words while I sit on the cave floor.

"You never thought a girl could swing an axe like that?" I coo, propping my tired arms on my bent knees.

"That's not what I was going to say." He presses his lips together, and I give up. Leaning into his lap, I crash my lips into his. "Rasha," he murmurs as I break away to find his hazel eyes searching mine.

"Save whatever you want to tell me for these fancy hot springs you keep promising." I scoop up the remaining pieces of silver and gold. There's a clear stone that fell from the opened vein in the mountain. He studies it with the torch and then slips it into the pocket against my breast.

Finding the ore seems to have brought us back into our usual rhythm, like I passed an invisible test. My unexpected, brave kiss might have helped us along as well. I am still smiling to myself behind his back when he crosses a narrow stone bridge. Skipping down a few uneven slabs of granite, I follow Shaw around bubbling purple and blue pools of water.

"These are the hot springs?" I balance my bag over my shoulder, waiting for him to say we are stopping, but he continues around the corner. Keeping up with him, I am suddenly hit with fresh, cold air, but we aren't at the same place where we came in.

There are too many places to look at first as I stand by Shaw on a wide ledge providing a view of the outside world. We are nestled in the vast mountains, not at the very top, but nowhere near the bottom. Below lie the valleys and frozen rivers that create the map of our land, the Beaivi Clan included.

"The pools were once used by the gods to replenish themselves." Shaw stays in the shadows of the rocky, arched entrance while I peer over the side.

Turning back to him, I ask, "Do they still hold that power?"

"Do I look old?" His quick answer makes me laugh, and I walk back to drop my things by the collection of pools. Shaw follows me with determination.

"I'm going to take your clothes off," he whispers, threading his arms around my stomach.

"I am more than capable," I answer, knowing it's fruitless.

"You are very capable of making pants that show off your ass, but I like stripping you."

"Why?" My question dies in my throat as he pulls the laces open and slides his hands over my curves to loosen my pants.

"Because it makes you wet." His fingers graze my clit. Yes, he is right. Of course, I am wet. "Then in your infinite creativity you made this perfect tie so I can unwrap your top."

"I had you in mind." I whimper when he opens the double-wrapped tunic to let my chest free. My head falls on his shoulder as he explores my body while his cock presses through his pants into my back. He lifts the chain off my neck and detaches the amulet, stowing it inside our pile of clothes.

"Get in the water for me?" He takes a step away. I sit on the edge and ease myself into the hot water. Swimming over to the other side, I drape my arms along the rocky wall and sink deep enough that the water is to my collarbones. Shaw takes off his clothes, springing his large cock free, and stares at me.

"Shaw?" I ask when he doesn't move.

"You are beautiful. I know you know, but you don't see what I am seeing."

"What do you see?" I ask. He splashes steamy water over the sides as he joins me in the pool and swims over to my spot.

"I see all of you. Your stubbornness and perseverance. Your intelligence and beauty. We've both been holding back, but I have run out of reasons not to worship you. I can no longer pretend this is anything less than extraordinary."

He pulls me into a kiss. Wild and unrelenting. My arms are around him, stabilizing us. His hands find my legs, wrapping them around his body. Even in the hot water, my arousal is tangible.

Guiding us back into the edge of the pool, he props me up on smooth rocks that form a shallow seat.

"I don't want to hold back." I am out of breath from kisses and desperately need more. The water around us flows against the muted colors of the caves, heightening every feeling I've ever had until I'm dying to be released.

"Sit up here for a moment." He lifts me higher so my body is exposed to the cool air. Tiny, opalescent water drops catch the light, making my skin shimmer. "Can I use this to help you?" He shows me the chain dripping with water.

"How?" I ask.

He holds the last link I added two days ago and says, "Put your hands on your knees."

My eyes flare up to his, knowing how this will look with my bigger breasts, but I'm so turned on I do it anyway. My nipples swing forward, and my cunt floods with sweet heat as he takes in my vulnerable position.

"When I'm done, you can tell me you want to stay like this or not. Either way, I'm making you come in this pool." He meticulously fixes the links over me. Looping the chain around one breast in a triangle position, he threads the end behind my neck and does the same for the other side.

As I watch him wrap the chain around my ribs and twist it up my front, the notion isn't lost that he made the links multiply right in front of me. He pulls the chain tight, and the sensation of being held securely engulfs me, dowsing all my fiery nerves in a wave of stability. With his free hand, he takes the ribbon from the end of my braid and ties the two ends of the chain together.

"Fucking beautiful," he groans and flicks one of my pebbled nipples. "How do you feel?"

"Safe," I murmur. He helps me slide halfway into the water where the heat makes me want to beg.

"What do you want, Rasha?"

"Can I taste you?" I feel bold, wearing his eternal life strapped against my chest.

"Mhmm." He sits out of the water and pumps his cock for me.

208

Moving to my knees, I feel the water lapping at my back, urging me on.

"Tell me if I'm horrible." I wrap my hand around his base.

He runs his fingers over my nipples while he says, "My cock between those lips will never feel horrible."

Sliding him past my lips, he feels huge in my mouth and my hands grip his hard thighs for leverage. My tongue explores every groove and twitch, relishing in how he tastes.

"Look at me," he murmurs. I open my eyes to glance up, and he gently thrusts his cock in and out of my mouth. Roaming my hands up his thighs and over the light hair trailing each ridge of his abs, I marvel at how much I want to please him.

Shaw scoops up my wet hair and thrusts faster between my teeth, hitting the top of my mouth until I gag. He removes himself, and I catch my breath. Scooting closer, I take his balls in my hands and roll them through the hot water.

"I want to," I offer. Wanting him back inside me in any way possible, I grip his shaft and pump his slick cock. He takes my other hand in his, and using the water from the pool, he guides my fingers to trace runes over his body. I move my mouth back over him as he uses me in the most delicious way. Relaxing my jaw to take him deeper, my enthusiasm elicits a moan I haven't heard before falls from his lips.

"You can stop," he groans. I know with every pulse down his shaft that he's about to come. Sucking hard, I run my teeth over the tip of his cock and dig my nails into his knees. The friction between my lips is what I imagine fucking must feel like, and it makes me want to finish him.

"Rasha." His voice unravels. He fists my hair hard enough that I can't move, but not hard enough to hurt. Exploding deep into my throat, he loses all semblance of control, and I fucking love it.

After I swallow, he slips out of my raw lips and pulls me up to his chest, sealing the moment with a hard, wet kiss. The water running off the chain is hotter than the cave pool. Curling torrents of smoke waft from my skin, making the air hazy to match my light-headedness.

"Did you like that?" I lower my gaze as he guides us back into the pool. The water soothes my shoulders and spine, so I take it upon myself to dunk my head under and fully wet my hair.

"One day, I am going to loose my fucking mind and ravish the deepest parts of your body." The promise of being pursued relentlessly is melodic to my core, and I throw my leg over his lap, grinding into him.

My heart pounds, and my nipples are painfully sensitive from my breasts being bound. Taking a better look at how intricately he's twisted the chain down my ribcage, I watch his fingers graze over my body.

"You were not gentle with those lips." He finds my ass and squeezes.

Leaning in for a kiss, I whisper, "You don't have to be gentle either."

It's the permission he needs, and I am more than willing to give it to him. The chain tightens around my body, and I let the pressure of each link hold my fears and nervousness, making room for the new sensations of being with him.

He moves me effortlessly in the water so I am laying across his lap. His hands hover over my nipples in an excruciating pause, and I wiggle my bum against him.

"Patience," he rasps. The chain holding my flesh is making me feel exposed in ways I didn't think possible. I assume he's going to suck my nipples when he leans over me. I am ready for it, but he blows instead, the cool air releasing a needy sigh from my throat.

"Are you going to come as I play with your perfect breasts?" he asks, and I open my legs. Chuckling, he presses the palm of his hand into my aching slit, holding me while he delicately pulls on my nipples. "I will never make you beg," he says, taking my peaked, pink flesh in his mouth and keeping a cold breeze over the other with magic.

"Shaw," I whine, squirming underneath him. My nerve endings are on fire and freezing at the same time. His hand reaches behind my neck, and I feel him notch the chain with his finger, tightening it so my breasts are fully propped up for him to play with.

"Can you take a bit more, or does this drenched cunt need attention?" he asks. I moan through a *please* and *I need you.*

Flicking my nipples, he matches every minor twinge of pain with immense pleasure from his lips kissing and sucking my flesh. I feel my orgasm starting to pound against my core without him ever touching my cunt.

Traveling down my stomach, he finally spreads me open, rubbing over my clit fast and hard. My breath stills. Gripping his bicep with one hand, I cover my mouth with the other to stop from crying out.

"You can be as loud as you want." He drags my hand away from my face while he keeps swirling his fingers over my cunt. With a lung full of steamy air, I can't stop the noises I make from filling the cave in a cacophony of moans and splashing water.

He plunges two fingers inside me, and I half sit up to hold on to him as he slides them in and out of my throbbing walls. My hips rock against him until I am about to come, and he stops. Hauling me out of the water, he lays me down on the edge of the pool and pulls my legs over his shoulders.

"Shaw, we can. You must be hard again." I want to tell him how badly I want him inside me, but his mouth is on me. His teeth nick my sensitive clit, and my back aches against the rough cave floor. Holding my legs open as I try to close my thighs around his head, he licks down my center all the way to the bottom.

Releasing me for a moment, his deep voice echoes, "I'm the hardest I've ever been, all for you. Is that what you want to hear? That I want to fucking worship you into eternity."

Raising my ass higher, I invite him to devour me with his tongue. Swirling through my slit, he dips deep inside and out again, gently slipping in two fingers. He stays pressed against the most tender spot inside me and rolls my clit through his teeth. I reach for him, needing something to hold as my orgasm ruptures through my core. My muscles wring out ecstasy like water spilling from a cloth, and I stare at the cave ceiling. Starlight from the evening sky has drenched the rocks in a rainbow of celestial colors.

Shaw comes out of the pool and lays next to me. He's hard and out of breath. Rolling to my side, he reaches for my ribs, pulling the end of the ribbon so the chain loosens, spilling over my shoulders and into my lap in a hot pile of delicate metal.

I search for the words to tell him what he means to me and only find one. But what happens once I say it? Deciding its best to not say anything, I lean over, my wet hair cascading over us in a dripping red waterfall.

"Are you satisfied?" he asks, and I grin.

Getting to my knees, I can't help but look at how big he is. My throat runs dry.

"Take me here."

"Rasha." He sits up, taking the chain from my lap, and reaches for our clothes.

"You told me how special these caves are. How connected the water is to the Vanheim. And the chain." I hear the pleading in my own voice. Crawling over to him, I brace his shoulders with my waterlogged hands, and he holds my hips. "I am sick of waiting for my fate to happen to me. I want to make my own choice."

He holds my stare. "I thought I gave you a choice tonight. Back in the sled?"

"You have always given me a choice. And being with you is what I want."

"The ore in your pocket will make the last link. Connecting the chain will bring you to a place where I cannot cloud your judgement, Rasha." He winds the chain around my wrist. I succumb to how fucking elated I feel around him as he takes my face in his hands, and we dissolve into needy kisses.

"I am not going anywhere if that's what you're afraid of. Hundreds of years have passed since I have truly been with a woman. Forgive my patience," he murmurs against my lips, which quells my rising panic for tonight.

We lay together for a long time, letting our bodies air dry while the stars change over the ceiling of the cave. Shaw takes the ore out and holds it to the tiny streams of moonlight, showing off the beautiful yellow and milky silver.

In between glances and soft touches, we make a bed with the

rolled up blankets and piles of clothes. Settling next to him, I clutch onto the feeling he's evoked in me. We will finish the chain and rescue the reindeer from Harald's grasp so my clan can live in freedom in the mountains. But behind the optimism I see in my relationship with Shaw, there are moments with Harald that wear on me. Harald has pledged to the King, and King's don't forget who owes them.

Conjuring an arrow with Skadi's bow when I faced Fenrir was one thing, but doing it to stop Harald will be more important than our relationship in the coming month. Spring will begin, and the thaw will make the pass easier for everyone to travel.

"You've grown quiet?" Shaw stretches out next to me on the cave floor.

"I was thinking about Harald and the King. Will the King come for my people regardless of my ability to wield the bow?"

Shaw tucks me into his chest, kissing the top of my head as if he alone can protect me from the world we have run from. "A part of me wishes to meet the King, but it has been my experience that men who rule through control don't take kindly to other men telling them what to do. I fear any meeting will result in bloodshed.".

Dipping my chin into his chest to look at him, I say, "If it comes to that, I want to be there. I could hold a seat on his stupid Harald's or my brother's council to stand up for the women."

"I'll clear your path," he murmurs. We keep talking about the reindeer and the stars until he falls asleep. Sleep doesn't come for me though. The shimmering lights weaving around the corners of the cave walls hold my curiosity.

28

SHAW

A hot nose presses into my face, urging me to rise.

"You're going to wake Rasha," I murmur to Aslaug who is determined to wake me. Throwing my arm around the sturdy cat, I try to wrestle her into my chest, but her claws poke into my skin. I open my eyes. Black wings rustle over us through the cave as Aslaug nips me with her teeth.

"Get up, brother. She's gone." Vidarr's voice bolts me awake. "Put on your fucking pants." He tosses me my clothes as black eagle feathers float down into the hot pools next to me. Reaching through the blanket, I can't feel Rasha's tender body.

"Where did she go?" My stomach clenches like I am going to be sick. Getting to my feet, I force my legs into pants and call my magic to the surface of my skin. It's easier now that the ritual has begun.

"I don't know. I wasn't watching, but I felt the Vanheim open," Vidarr spits out. His anger wafts through his coat.

"What!" My scream shakes the cave and makes the water slosh over the edges of the pools. Aslaug is pawing through Rasha's things. Bending down, I shake out the clothes she left, and the amulet falls to the rough stone floor.

"Where is the chain?" Vidarr asks, helping me sort through our things and stuffing them into her bag.

"She has it. I wound it around her wrist as we fell asleep," I explain, my voice dropping to a whisper as the gravity of what I've done sets in. "She opened the mountain and found ore so her naive magic will have left a trail."

"Let's try before it dims or the channel closes and she's trapped," Vidarr's voice is full of panic as he opens his hands slowly like he did in the cabin. Together we illuminate the runes in the cave.

"I didn't feel her wake." I trace the trail she left through the mountain with Vidarr behind me, keeping his flow of magic pouring through me for support. "Who wants to see me fail?"

"Vali temporarily assumed your position when you were exiled. Deals were made so our bloodline could stay in power."

Whirling around, I take out my fucking frustrations on my brother by cutting him off. "What kind of deals?"

Pushing gently against me with his shoulder so he doesn't break the magic, he says, "The mortals need a King. Without the god of the forest, our worlds are collapsing into chaos. So Vali reached out to an impressionable, rich mortal."

"For fuck's sake!" I slam my hands on the cave wall by Vidarr's ears, making rocks rain down from the ceiling. "You should have told me."

"I am not even supposed to be here helping you! I am not supposed to interfere in your penance, brother," Vidarr growls, pushing away from me to follow Rasha's trail of illuminated runes. Gathering my composure, I follow him, digging deep within my bones to find the tiny fragments of our bond. I give our bond what is left of my magic to keep her mortal body alive wherever she is.

Vidarr is quiet, leading the way and allowing me to stew in my feelings. So many things should have gone differently. Last night, we should have made for the Beaivi Clan instead of staying here in the hot pools. Am I a fool for denying her every night and not making the links sooner? Skadi was so unhappy in the Vanheim that I brought her to the mountains in the Mortal Realm, thinking she would be free, but her freedom came at a price. I cannot let Rasha fall to the same fate.

"Stop thinking so loudly. Rasha is superior to you in most ways, so give her some credit why don't you?" Vidarr jabs at me to lift my spirits, and I offer a wincing smile.

"There are parts of the Vanheim I wish for her to never be subjected to."

"Vali is only trying to finish his deal. He knows he cannot keep her in between worlds."

"She found the first reindeer," my voice slips into a whisper when we arrive where Rasha left the realm. Deep within the stone is a carving of the first reindeer my father sacrificed, marking the center of the Mortal Realm. From the carved antlers, all rivers flow. The largest vein of gold water connects the Immortal and the Mortal Realm, which we call the Ivalo River. With her new strength, she must have wandered through the caves like a moth to the flame. She is searching for our home without realizing, which is my fault to be honest.

Vidarr squats to put his hands into the glossy water flowing from the large carving down the rocks and under our feet. Immediately, his fingers sink into the slow flowing current.

"I cannot follow you," I remind him. We head back to the entrance I used yesterday with Rasha, minding the multicolored streams of water winding and weaving through the mountain.

"The rivers haven't been this full while you've been exiled here. It's a sign, brother. A good one. I will stay as long as I can." His offer comforts me, though I don't deserve to feel comforted. The amulet in my vest pocket grows cold now that we are far away from the carving. Vidarr wipes his forehead on his coat sleeve and marches past me with Aslaug on his heels. "How do you finish the ritual?"

"I need the herd to accept my penance. They were Skadi's creatures," I explain. Bright sun from what was supposed to be a glorious morning blinds me when we cross the last expanse of rock at the entrance of the mountain. We walk to where Rasha's reindeer is curled up under an evergreen tree, sleeping. Clicking my tongue, I see my reindeer gracefully bow his antlered head, coming to greet me. The amulet lurches in my pocket, and I grip my chest. Our last conversation gives me an idea.

"So do you still have that star map to find the herd?" Vidarr hauls his limber body up to her reindeer.

"We need to get to her clan first." I find my own plan unfolds as I speak.

"You're going to trust the mortals?"

"She trusted them. Maybe for her, they will do what I am failing to accomplish," I tell him. We mount the reindeer to ride to the Beaivi Clan.

It doesn't take us long to descend the mountain and pick up speed in the snow covered valley. Being immortal has its advantages, which Vidarr uses to the fullest by keeping the reindeer running so they barely sink into the snow and bending the forest to reveal the easiest path. We stop once so I can show him the antler map that Rasha risked her life to retrieve for me. Using his power over the sky, Vidarr changes a small section of the day to night so we can read the stars and make sure we are traveling in the right direction.

"When you were an eagle, were you able to see if Harald left the Aske Stronghold?" I only ask to be sure, but he scoffs like I am questioning his abilities.

"He is on the move. What is set in motion will be hard to stop, even with willing Vikings from the Beaivi Clan," he retorts, slamming the magic shut and returning the small swath of sky back to its properly bright blue. Pulling the reins of his reindeer, he spurs the magnificent animal along, and I shove down my arrogance to follow him.

I am reminded of taking Vidarr and Vali to the Mortal Realm when they were young as we ride through the frosty forest. When our father's soul left his body, he became one with the stars, and it was up to me to take his place.

I was responsible for guiding my brothers and teaching them how to keep our worlds revolving and thriving. Most of the time, they were getting into trouble or testing each other like young boys do. But seeing Vidarr ride beside me now, I realize how much I have longed to go back to those days. Bringing my reindeer flush with

Vidarr's, I send a flurry of snow over his head, and he flares his nostrils at me.

"I am sorry for failing you."

He shakes the snow from his dark hair. "I forgave you a long time ago."

"Though I appreciate it, I still left you to fend for yourself. I shouldn't have been so clouded in my decisions." Admitting to Vidarr what I have felt for hundreds of mortal years eases the twisted tension in my chest.

"There were many times I wanted to come here and pound your face into the ground for Skadi's death. But I've grown up, Shaw. I am not so little or so foolish to think it was all your fault. Skadi could have stayed in the Vanheim." Vidarr's words release the guilt, if only by a fraction, that I have held onto and moulded into every link, save one, on that fucking chain.

"See, the Beaivi's haven't been bombarded yet." He points through the cliff to a valley below where hot smoke drifts up in ribbons from a collection of thatched roof huts.

"Now comes the difficult part."

"Keeping them from killing us?" Vidarr chuckles, and I shake my head, guiding my reindeer down to the well-traveled, muddy road.

"Convincing them Rasha is alive," I tell him. We keep our weapons at the ready as we travel closer to the old wall surrounding the village. I tell Aslaug to keep to the forest for now. Jorvik wasn't lying when he said the clan needed Harald's coin; some posts are tilted to hold up parts of the wall that are about to collapse. There are longboats half finished, and only a few pelts drying on racks, which means the people have sorely missed the huntresses who attended Yule in Harald's clan.

"Look who is alive." Bjorn slides his body out from the other side of the gate, swinging his axe through an already beat up post. Wood chips fly in every direction, and Vidarr's magic rises around us.

"I can say the same about you. What are you doing here, Bjorn?" I ask, dismounting and leading the reindeer behind me.

"I traveled to the Beaivi Clan with Jorvik, the new head of council. Harald is with his own party, locating the reindeer herd. Then this miserable clan will be dissolved. Who's your friend, and where did he get his clothes?" Bjorn misses nothing, eyeing the golden threads in Vidarr's long coat.

"This is Vidarr." I have no plans on giving Bjorn any more ways to torture me. He swings his axe a few more times, trying to make sense of what we want before letting us in, so I ask, "Is Jorvik here?"

"Came to offer your condolences?" He's quick to reply with the information I need. They think Rasha is dead, which will make it hard for Jorvik to see reason.

"We need to have a word with your new head of council." Vidarr's commanding voice is nice to hear. He steps between us, nearly knocking into Bjorn, and I walk the reindeer through the gate into the village.

"Shaw!" Joanna barrels toward me in a mud covered dress, and I drop the reins. When she throws her arms around me, I whisper in her ear, *"Rasha is alive."* Her arms stiffen against my neck, and she pulls away, her muted brown eyes searching mine.

"I need help to find the herd for her," I whisper. Joanna hears me and looks to my left to see Vidarr. His charm works its way back as he dips his chin in a smile that would melt an icicle.

"Vidarr." He outstretches his hand, and she blushes like they all do.

"This is Joanna." Introducing her, I let a moment of normalcy cross my tired soul.

"She's spoken for," Bjorn drawls, walking by us.

"Don't mind him. He limps since Yule and has been sent here by Harald," Joanna explains softly so only I can hear. Holding out my elbow, I beckon for her to slide her arm through, and we fall in line behind Bjorn to walk to the center of the clan. "Did she find the bow?"

I nod to my back to answer her. Tucked under the leather wrap in the quiver rests Skadi's bow. She raises her eyebrows, squeezing my forearm with her overworked hand.

"I'll tell you more when we are alone," I say, hoping to bring her some comfort. I know they were very close. To lose Rasha for more than a month and to think she's dead is a pain I had no intention of bringing up.

"We have company!" Bjorn shouts as we walk up the steps into the longhouse. Women are cleaning and stocking the fire basins, all in similar dresses to Joanna, with heavily worn fabric and lacking the security of a weapon on their belts.

Jorvik comes through a door in a wall that cuts the longhouse in half and stops dead in his tracks when he sees me. Letting Joanna's arm fall, I shrug off the hidden quiver so she can take it. Vidarr steps aside, taking Joanna with him. Jorvik gains speed as he crosses the empty hall, women take heed to find other places to be, and I shake out my arms, knowing he's going to be full of bravado.

"What the fuck do you want?" Jorvik hisses, the gold chains around his fur coat clinking in his anger.

"Rasha needs your help." I say her name, and he swings. His knuckles connect with my jaw, and I feel all of Vidarr's wrath exploding around him. Joanna screams, but I take the hit. I couldn't protect his sister, which is why I am here. Needing to gain any form of complacency if this is to work, I still my torso, not engaging, but I block his next punch with my forearm and take a step back.

"Rasha is dead because of you," Jorvik seethes.

"She's alive. We need to find the reindeer herd before the next full moon in two weeks."

Jorvik lunges, ready to swing at me again, so I take the hit to my shoulder and punch him in the gut. He doesn't go down. Instead, he launches himself at my waist, and we collide with the wooden floor. Holding a hand out to keep Vidarr from intervening, I open myself up to Jorvik who punches me in the ribs. In return, I swing my legs around his scrawny ass and bash his head into the floor.

"You fucked with her head. Kissing her and sneaking around with her. Our clan is in shambles because you got her killed," he shrieks, grappling his hands at my neck, trying to strangle me.

"She's alive, Jorvik. She didn't die. The only pain she's endured is by you using her." I hold his shirt to pick him up while he's trying to claw my fucking eyes out and slam the both of us back on the floor. His teeth grind together, and he lets me go.

"Don't lie to me. Is my sister alive?" He spits blood on the floor. I let him go and back away, dusting off my clothes.

"She's alive. I have the bow of Skadi that she pulled from the burial site." I give a bare bones version of events, causing Jorvik to survey the room, taking in Bjorn who is sitting on a table and Joanna tucking herself behind Vidarr with the quiver pressed against her chest.

"Prove it," Jorvik says, beckoning Bjorn to him. "And who the fuck are you?" He looks at Vidarr.

"I am the proof you need. I saw Rasha use the bow against a Fenrir from the Immortal Realm," Vidarr explains. Jorvik coughs out a laugh.

"Are you two related? In blood or simple delusion. Fenrir are creatures from bedtime stories. This is crazy. Lock them up." Jorvik motions to Bjorn who slides his axe into a better position.

Vidarr claps his hands together, and magic erupts throughout the hall. He opens his hands to reveal the deep purple, shimmering channel between this world and the next.

"What are you?" Bjorn points the axe at Vidarr, to which my brother smirks and waves his hand pulsing with ancient magic. The axe hurls out of Bjorn's grasp and into Vidarr's in one smooth motion.

"I walk the Vanheim. I have seen the Maiden wield Skadi's bow and use the power that she gained for her sacrifice." Vidarr's eloquent speech makes Jorvik's dumb face fall in utter shock.

"Enough," I softly tell my brother as he slides the axe to Joanna before closing his hand and sealing his power into the channel.

"Why does she need the reindeer?"

"Are you really that stupid, Jorvik? We all saw the Northern Lights the night Harald sacrificed her. We knew something changed and we've been ignoring it," Joanna interrupts. Letting the leather flap fall from the quiver, she takes out the long silver bow as tears gather in her eyes. "We all saw the runes on Divination night. We are to find the herd, and this is why. This is our fate. The people will help you, Shaw." Joanna looks at the bow like it might catch on fire at any minute.

"There aren't any arrows?" Jorvik asks, walking around the table, wanting to come closer to Joanna, but clearly afraid to do so with Vidarr by her side.

"Only the archer can conjure an arrow," I chime in.

"So what? We are going to convince the people to trek to the pass in the snow and find the herd? Which is where my sister is?" Jorvik is full of questions that aren't easy to answer without shaking his confidence in the plan. Not even knowing if the plan will work, I ignore him for the moment.

"Why don't we show our guests some hospitality and get them cleaned up. The Hall will be full of hungry Vikings in an hour, and many will be happy to see the blacksmith alive and well," Joanna intercedes, handing me back the quiver as she dissipates the tension in the room.

"Fine," Jorvik calls. Taking Joanna's upper arm, he walks her to the doorway where we cannot hear and whispers who knows what into her ear. I know that look on her face. She is being threatened, but I have to trust she can handle herself. Jorvik will pay for what he's done when Rasha is back by my side.

29

RASHA

Shaw fell asleep quickly, but my thoughts couldn't find peace, so I wandered through the cave, admiring the glowing runes. Curiosity got the better of me as I followed them deeper into the mountain until I found a huge carving of a reindeer depicted on a cave wall. From its bowed antlers, several streams of water flowed down and into the crevices in the stone.

The water called to the very marrow of my bones, so I dipped my hand in like I saw Shaw do yesterday. Without even a moment to retreat, I was swept into sparkling darkness.

Wobbling on my achy legs, I feel as if my joints are too loose, like there is nothing holding my body together besides my own withering veins. Around my wrist is Shaw's chain, but I don't have the amulet or the bow, and I don't know where I am.

I assume I am near the Vanheim, or in it. The walls are covered in iridescent waves, forming ribbons of scrollwork in the stone. Shaw said the mountain is a place of connection where the earth meets fire, wind, and water. This room has none of those elements. It is hollow and airless like the shrine. My feet timidly shuffle over the smooth floor. I expect it to be icy cold, but it's warm in the lack of natural light.

Vidarr can travel back and forth through the open channel in the Vanheim. Should I be able to as well? With the chain looped around my fingers, I press my hands together and remember what it felt like the night I attached my link to the chain, focusing on the expansion of my blood and bones to hold the magic it took to bond our souls. I open my hands and pour all of my focus into finding any magic inside me. Tugging and pulling at tiny fragments floating around, I can tell my blood is trying to make each tidbit come together.

"Please work," I whisper. Shaking, I feel heat and bone crushing pressure, but nothing happens. I crash to my knees and pull my legs underneath me, taking deep breaths.

"Okay, so where do I go from here?" My voice sounds far away like in my dream. All around me the runes flicker and glow brighter, leading into more shadows. *Do I walk through the shadows? Or do I wait for help?* I stand back up with determination.

The last time I waited for help I almost died. With newfound courage, I step into the shadows, and the blue scroll waves understand my need. Letting out a breath, my fingers graze the walls while the errant magic I've been harboring moves to my hands the way I wish it did a few minutes ago.

"Shaw," I whisper to myself. The corridor is growing colder the further I walk, but the designs are becoming familiar. They are the same as the broken tattoo on Shaw's shoulder, which is encouraging.

The ground trembles, and I reach for the walls to stabilize myself, but wind comes from nowhere and everywhere, engulfing me in blustery, cold gale. Currents of blue illuminate the room, and I exhale, watching my breath curl in the freezing air. Rubbing my hands over my arms to get warm, I grip the chain tighter, willing all my strength into the links.

"I need you. Where are you?" I whisper as my lips start to tremble against the cold. In an instant, wide beams of light come from above, showing a woman walking my way with long white hair and a strong body. I recognize the bow that she's carrying and the markings drawn across her cheeks.

"Skadi?" I call out, but she doesn't hear me. I am starting to think she isn't real. Maybe I am not either, and my body is still sleeping next to Shaw's in the cave. Running to her, I push my hands through the beams of light and through where her body should be. The edges of her elegant form falter, vibrating through the channel we must be stuck in.

"Show me," falls from my lips. I have been in her shrine and have listened to the stories of the forgotten goddess since I was a child. No one has ever been through the Vanheim and lived to tell about it. But I have fought to stay alive and have drawn out magic from a man who is not of my world. The tugging at my heart is not solely from Shaw's chain. The delicate fabric of my soul remembers and is reaching out, looking for our story.

"Please, show me what I need to see so I can go home." I pat my coat down, landing on a small hunting knife, his hunting knife, and take it out of the sheath. Dragging the razor-sharp edge down my ring finger, I rub the skin until blood forms. It's easy to find her runes because they are the same as in her shrine under the ice.

Preparing myself for what will come next, I trace the runes with the blood beading on the pad of my finger, and the temperature plummets to freezing. The walls sparkle, blinding me in blue and white lights coming from every single rune until I am forced to close my eyes. My eyelids turn orange from the hot light filling the room, and panic grips me that the icy floor will melt.

The nose buzzing scents of Spring awaken my senses, and I open my eyes. The walls and ceiling are gone, the runes are gone, and I am standing in a blooming field on the edge of the fjord where I found the bow. Behind me, I see the mountains are glorious peaks of flowers and green grass. Swaying back and forth in the warm breeze, the trees house birds of all sizes, and I hear waves lapping at the black sand beach.

My head swivels as I feel a thousand hoofbeats thundering this way. Reindeer are running as fast as their slender legs will carry them between the mountains, through the same spot Harald's stronghold now sits. I hide, but then I remember this is not my reality, it's hers.

Thousands of long, curved antlers group together in a mass of hazel and gray fur, coming through the flower-drenched field. They make a circle around me like they are following a path that cannot be seen by human eyes. In the fray of hooves and wet velvet noses, I see two reindeer together, nudging one another at a much slower pace. One is pure white and the other a rich hazel.

They are breaking from the massive herd and trotting through the trees. Following the line of peeling spring birch trees, I run on instinct. I am a hunter. If I was to hunt deer, I'd kill the ones who have broken from the herd.

The chain wrapped around my wrist grows hot like it did the day I connected my link. Pushing through the first few lines of reindeer, I manage to get past the loops of focused creatures and see Viking men coming through the trees on the other side of the fjord.

It happens before I have the chance to take a breath. With bows at the ready, they let arrows fly across the narrow inlet where the beautiful white reindeer is drinking. She falls. My body clenches, and I rub my chest, trying to rub away the heart shattering death.

Looking at the massive, hazel reindeer who is momentarily frozen, I try to scream, but my voice is lost. He runs, his reindeer form changing into a man's as he pushes his way through the forest and out of sight. I move too but not after him. Before I can register what I am doing, I am kneeling at the white reindeer's dying body. The first arrow hit her neck, the second, close to her heart.

With minutes to live, she transforms into a goddess. Legs and hooves become womanly limbs while stark-white fur becomes long, braided hair, stained with oozing crimson blood.

"This moment is yours alone, Rasha. A promise kept will bring our worlds back into balance," Skadi declares, gazing up at me with crystal clear blue eyes. I stroke her white hair even though my hands are coated in her blood. The punctured vein in her neck gushes in a horrendous and unstoppable way.

"What promise?" I ask, trying to staunch the bleeding anyway I can. "What do I do to make this right? He never wanted your death," I assure the dying huntress. Her long fingers wrap around my wrist where Shaw's chain is tightly resting against my skin.

"You must take my place or our gods will be lost. I couldn't fulfill my promise, but you took up my bow." Her mouth fills with blood, preventing her from continuing. I don't understand. Rubbing her chest to try to keep her alive, I pull her into my arms and hug her so that she doesn't feel alone.

"How?"

She grips my wrist tighter, pressing the chain between our skin, and tears gather in my heavy eyelashes. I hold her as her heartbeat slows, and her lungs stop expanding in her broken chest. Rubbing her back in slow circles, I cry, my emotions spilling out in messy tears and running down her soft skin. Gradually, Skadi's soul leaves her body.

Another hand presses into my shoulder. I expect it to be Shaw, but it isn't. Strikingly similar to Vidarr, this man must be the brother I haven't met. By the look in his dark eyes, I am not sure I want to.

"It is time for you to leave the edge."

"Where are Shaw and Vidarr? You're the twin?" I answer, collecting myself and stringing the chain around my neck in long loops. I am covered in her blood, but it doesn't matter.

"My name is Vali. Yes, I am the older twin. Vidarr shouldn't have helped you. Shaw lost his seat as King, and that is how it will stay. Skadi's soul showed you a false hope."

"You sent the Fenrir after me so that I couldn't finish his chain. Her death was by man, not by Shaw." My teeth clatter together as I accuse him. Forcing myself to be stronger than I am, taller even than I am, I search that place deep inside my soul for my own brand of magic.

"He should have never brought her there. Marrying her and bonding their souls was his purpose to keep our realm alive. But they couldn't have cared less about us."

"I don't believe that Shaw didn't care for you. They were young and foolish. She wanted the freedom to choose," I cry out, flailing my arms over Skadi's lifeless body.

"Freedom comes at a price, which he is paying. So I will keep the both of you where you belong. The Vanheim is mine, and your wasteful world will soon have a new set of rules."

"I can feel your magic. You have no one bonded to you, which puts you equally at risk."

"Don't worry about me. This is a lesson for you, Rasha. Take heed."

"I am done with lessons from men. We will be returning together." I don't know where the words came from, but I find them all the same. He watches me like a hawk, waiting for me to fail most likely. But if I want to keep my promise to Skadi so her soul isn't trapped in this pocket the same as the bow was trapped, I cannot fail. Pressing my hands together, I look past the imposing Vali and focus on the many reindeer feeding in the tall grass.

Hunters keep the balance. The forest is a loop of life ensuring the survival of all.

My mother's voice, soft and graceful, sings in my thoughts. Our worlds, the mortal and immortal, revolve around the balance found between gods, humans, and a land that is teeming with creatures. I made a promise to Skadi, but more than that, I made a promise to myself. At that thought, my heart lurches, sending my own brand of magic through my soul.

Vali's mouth falls open, and I stare back at him. Between my hands, I have opened my own channel of swirling, shimmering red and pink. I almost smile, but I don't want to break my concentration, and I sure as fuck don't want to look like a fool in front of a man who is trying to push me away. The chain pulses with delicate heat as my body radiates magic.

"Tell him our mother misses him," he whispers. In a seismic flash of god-like power, he disappears. I close my hands in absence of the threat and gather flowers to bury Skadi.

Clouds tilt the field in shadows, and the reindeer who have eaten their fill find safe places to sleep among the thick trees. Every so often, I gaze into the forest to see if Shaw will come back. I felt his grief the first time we mixed our blood in the amulet. I know he cared for her, but did he love her?

Finding a sturdy reindeer who hasn't fallen asleep yet, I bring Skadi's body to its back and walk my one woman funeral procession out into the fjord. Her white hair falls from her braids. I try to smooth it out over her shoulders, but the white strands are sticky with blood. The color almost matches my own hair.

The fjords warm water seeps up my pants and over my hips as I walk into it, followed by the reindeer. It backs away, and Skadi's body floats into my arms. As the water washes her wounds, I gaze down at her, wondering why I don't feel any jealousy?

Surely he cared for her if she was to be his bonded partner? But I don't feel inadequate in comparison or remotely inferior. Thinking back to the nights of Yule and how I hated all the women who looked at Shaw, I know I can be jealous. Something about Skadi's blue eyes and soft words make me feel more like I am looking in a pool of reflection.

I swim her body to where I remember her tomb lying. Diving to the sea bed, I haul up rocks to weigh down her corpse. Her precious form sinks into the deep silt, and I cover the rocks with flowers picked from the fields. No doubt, the current will wash them away or the bottom feeding fish will eat the pretty petals, but it doesn't seem right to let her body disintegrate without some lovely reminder of the place she always longed for.

Back on the soft black sand, I lay down and stare at the clouds overhead. My thoughts drift to Shaw and how he should be the King of the Vanheim. I am in love with a man, no, an immortal god who is returning home to become a King. The idea isn't as frightening as it should be. Before long, the blue sky is gone, and night is beginning to permeate the strange edge of the Vanheim.

"Fire will light your darkest nights." I remember the words my mother used to tell Jorvik when he complained about cutting firewood for the long winter nights in our small outpost cabin. Finding logs big enough to make a fire is easy. In no time at all, I have a nice bundle sitting on the black sand.

Pressing my hands together, I feel the magic come easier now as my hands burst into flames. Similar to how Vidarr did in our cabin, I set my palms over the wood to keep my new magic flowing like a river running down stream. Suddenly, the logs crack into tall, fiery flames.

Rewrapping the chain around my wrist, I watch the flames grow to an enormous height, sending sparks and burning chips of wood flying into the fjord.

My link on the chain is tucked into my palm, and I open my heart, reaching for the tiny moments that our bodies became stronger over the past few months – the places we've touched one another and the feelings that have grown into something beyond explanation. I hold on to the feel of him around me. His voice reminds me I can be afraid and keep moving at the same time. Despite the anxiety at war with my desire to find him again, I press my wrist into my chest, keeping the chain close to my heart, and step into the flames.

30

SHAW

Last night, Vidarr left for the Vanheim and returned with a new idea. A Dísablót ritual calls a goddess to the Mortal Realm. If Rasha is alive, then the women will be able to call her home.

Convincing Jorvik to allow Joanna and Katrine to perform a Dísablót ritual isn't the easiest task. And Vidarr is risking his magic every day that goes by, staying with me in the Mortal Realm while we argue with Jorvik. He wants to wait for Harald's word to find the reindeer herd and would rather forget his sister ever existed. Now that we've told him our plan to call her from the open channel he laughed like a fucking maniac, prompting Joanna to close the meeting room for several hours.

I don't want to ask what Joanna promises him, or if it is our constant bluffing and willing her to be alive that finally wins him over, but he does have a soft spot for Joanna. I remind him the clans will never let him keep his seat on the council if his sister is alive and well. So to prove us wrong, at dusk, he marches his slithery ass through the snow and into the forest.

"These are her closest friends?" Vidarr asks. His power is waning, and he refuses to tell me what happened when he crossed back over. "I don't know about the old woman."

"She wouldn't take no for an answer." Between Katrine and Joanna stands a sturdy elder who cussed me out and told me her name was Edith. She gave us no choice. Insisting she'd come to honor the offering given to the female goddess, she grumbled about how the feminine power of three, Maiden, Mother, and Crone, would make the ritual stronger.

"I won't be able to stay." Vidarr winces as he keeps himself upright.

"Can you feel her?" I ask, gripping his shoulders. Being without Rasha for four days is a torture worse than exile.

"I feel Vali, and he's furious."

"We have never done this before. Shaw! Are you coming?" Katrine's voice carries on the wet wind blowing through the trees. With winter shedding the bitter cold to usher in Spring, the storms have been dumping tumultuous amounts of heavy, wet snow instead of crystal clear flakes.

"Harald will kill us if he finds out we are worshipping the goddesses," Jorvik whines from his post under a tree with his scrawny arms crossed like he has a hundred other places to be.

"Well, don't tell him." Vidarr snorts.

"Alright, make a triangle in the snow. The vertex point needs to face where the Ivalo River flows into the sea to open the sacred space to femininity," I explain. The women, including Edith, map out a large triangle in the forest clearing.

"When I was a girl, we had a Dísablót every year to call forth the goddesses, especially when we were worried about a woman ready to give birth or before a battle to give our Shield-maidens strength in the fight." Edith takes over explaining the ritual while Vidarr and I gather snowdrop flowers and any holly berries that haven't been eaten by passing creatures. Aslaug's amber eyes flash through the dark trees, and I beckon her closer.

"We are being hunted," Jorvik whispers, but no one so much as flinches. Aslaug pounces out of the tree line and into the clearing, causing Jorvik to reach for his axe.

"Relax, she's a friend," Joanna calls. Aslaug sits with her paws holding down the wings of a raven so the frantic bird can't fly away.

"Do you remember me?" Joanna's voice is small as Aslaug peers up at her, blinking in recognition. "Can I take your offering?" she asks. Aslaug retracts her long claws for Joanna to pick up the dying raven.

"Why a raven?" Katrine grimaces at the way Joanna quickly snaps its hollow-boned neck.

"Once upon a time, ravens were used to call the Valkyries. It is our best chance at using the three of you to call forth a goddess," I explain.

Katrine's concern shifts into a smile. "So we are Valkyries?"

"Perform the ritual and find out." Try as I might to keep a straight face, I match her smile with a smirk. The women are intelligent. They know there is more happening here than a simple prayer. While they are busy, I take out the amulet and drip tiny amounts of our bonded blood on the wood. Striking the iron, I watch as sparks skitter over three torches, and the bundles erupt into flames.

"Edith is the oldest," Vidarr starts. The elder woman huffs a glare his way. "I don't mean to insult, but your connection to this world is strong, so you should lead." He walks back his instructions in a smoothing tone, and Edith picks up a torch on her way to the bottom of the triangle.

Joanna slices the black bird's chest open and dips her finger into its warm blood. Painting a solid line down Katrine's and Edith's lips, she stops to look at Jorvik, and her body tenses like she wants to ask but already knows the answer.

Walking through Vidarr and I, Jorvik finally comes to her side and takes one finger to coat Joanna's lips with a thin red line down to her chin.

"Thank you," Joanna whispers and places the dead raven in the middle of the triangle. Joanna takes her place across from Katrine. Jorvik falls back by the trees while Aslaug stays on heightened alert by his side.

Edith clears her throat to say, "Once, we worshiped the goddesses. Once, we prayed for their might. Tonight, we reclaim that power in the name of Rasha."

The women close their eyes. Vidarr uses the moment to open his hands and call his remaining power to light the triangle in beautiful flames. Joanna jumps when the raven's body bursts into orange and yellow fire, but she holds her place and the torch high.

"I will see you at home." Vidarr flashes a clever smile and steps into the flaming triangle. The world shifts. His magic and the combined power that the women have unknowingly brought forth connects, yanking my heart through my ribcage. I clutch the amulet in my palm and desperately search my soul for the fragments of Rasha's connection to my realm.

It is easy to find. I don't know why I doubted us. Every ounce of what I have to give is met with her unending love. There is sadness and hurt forming around the bonds, being quenched in the deepest well of our connection, but it never falters.

A thud hits the fiery, triangular channel, and all the flames are doused instantly. I feel her before I see her, but I can't bring myself to enter the sacred feminine space. Smoke wafts over all of us, and Joanna's elated voice breaks through the chaos.

"You're alive!"

"I am. It's good to see you," Rasha chokes out. Aslaug runs to her, pummeling Rasha with big, furry paws. All three females are in a heap of dirt, snow, and ash with smiles on their faces.

"How did you know how to reach me?" She looks to Katrine who turns Rasha's shoulders so she can see me. It's a strange feeling of embarrassment to want to love someone beyond comparison when she is fully capable of caring for herself. I am humbled.

Rasha moves to her feet with that gorgeous glossy look in her eye and my chain wrapped around her arm.

"Where were you?" Jorvik doesn't miss much, I'll give him that.

"I had to die because of you," Rasha snarls. Her ferocity makes me hard before I know what my body is doing.

"Do not blame me for your fucking foolishness. Where were you?" he asks her, then turns on me without waiting for her to answer. "And where did your brother go?"

My body heat rises in tune with hers.

"Vidarr was needed elsewhere," I say, my eyes colliding with Rasha's for the first time. Her beautiful lips fall open, but Joanna interjects, stomping over the threshold to cajole Jorvik.

"Obviously she didn't die in the longboat because she is standing here, good as new. Let's have a feast to welcome our huntress back home." Joanna's flat tone leaves no room for argument.

"Where is Harald?" Rasha asks her brother, stepping over the threshold to square herself to him with Katrine right behind her.

"Not here. Not yet anyway. Bjorn is staying with us to protect Harald's interests."

Hanging back, I walk around the triangle, picking up torches. Aslaug rubs her square head up and down Edith's little body as the sturdy woman wipes tears from her eyes.

"You are not what you seem," she says to me. I take off my coat, giving her an extra layer against the cold night.

"That may be true. I have to ask. Who is Rasha to you?"

"One of the many orphans I have cared for over the years. When her parents were killed, Jorvik dragged her here. She was an unruly child, so when he pledged their lives to the council, Rasha was thrown into the kitchens to work for her meals," she explains. I am listening, but I can't take my eyes off *my* maiden huntress, glowing from her time in the Vanheim. My chain is pulling us together, but I stay away while she is speaking with her brother. The glare she is giving Jorvik holds decades of pain that I want to wipe from her memory, but it is what gives her a multifaceted heart. A heart I certainly don't deserve.

"Thank you for putting your neck on the line with Jorvik," I tell Edith. We start to walk back to the village, and I watch Rasha fully embrace her friends.

"I have participated in many rituals, but I have never felt a man leave the Mortal Realm until tonight. We are in the presence of the gods are we not?" Edith quietly asks, her wrinkled face roaming over mine. "The better question is who is Rasha to you?"

Patting Edith's hand, I let my guard down. "She is a goddess in my eyes."

Edith pokes me with a boney finger, and I look to see the old woman grinning from ear to ear. Shuffling away from me to join the women, I watch as they loop their arms around her. Rasha looks over her shoulder to see that I am still behind them.

Jorvik is leading the way, hopefully to catch Bjorn before he has a chance to find a horse and get word back to Harald's traveling party. When we come to the edges of the huts and longhouses, Rasha hugs her friends and turns to me.

"Are you alright?" I ask. Against everything raging inside me, I stay planted across from her.

"I saw Skadi die. I met your brother Vali, and I learned how to open my own channel." She speaks in an unrelenting tone, and I fight back the urge to kiss her. She went to the Vanheim and came back unscathed, which reaffirms everything I know in my soul.

"Vali is hurting," I reply.

"I am hurt too. I am hurt that you didn't tell me what happened the moment I came back from the shrine with her bow."

Needing to touch her, I move closer. The air fractures with sparks from the chain, our bodies desperate to touch.

"I couldn't. I am in exile because I tried to give Skadi everything she wanted. But what she wanted was mortality, and gods cannot change their fate!" I yell, giving my emotion an outlet. Rasha crosses the snowy ground with a swirling torrent of utter arousal and anger.

"From where I am standing, you don't want to fulfill your fate either! You've been here pretending you are a blacksmith instead of being a leader." Her fists are clenched, squeezing the chain, and my lungs collapse in my chest.

"You say that like you know what it is to deny yourself for hundreds of years,' I shoot back, and her eyes widen. Why didn't I remember that arguing with a woman is like trying to breathe while drowning?

"Vali showed me the moment Skadi was struck down. I held her as she died while you ran away. Is that all you're capable of? You took me away from my clan. We hid in your cabin for weeks, to what end? To keep me from leading my people because you cannot lead your own." Rasha's voice drops so low the ground shakes at her mercy.

"I wanted to protect you." My response is weak.

"You don't even want to sleep with me because you're afraid."

"Stop." I bring myself to touch her, taking her face in my hands.

"I am afraid that you won't stay because I won't be enough for you." To say my heart is breaking is an understatement. Rasha's crystal blue eyes have pierced through me since the first day I met her and have forced me out of hiding. Tonight she deserves the truth. "Denying the bond is how Skadi and I found trouble in the first place. I have lived with her death on my hands for so long I don't know how to let you in." My admission crushes Rasha's blazing temper.

"We need to make the last link in the chain before the next full moon, or Vali is going to take your place forever," she says. Infusing hidden gems of love and acceptance over every torn and fractured particle floating without direction in our frayed bond, I cradle the back of her head, threading my fingers through her crimson hair.

"Making the last link will bond us for all of eternity. Do you want that?" I whisper. My resolve falters, and I brush a delicate kiss over her cold lips to invite her in.

"I made a promise." She is slowly unraveling.

"Eternity is forever. Will you be happy arguing with me forever?" Our bodies are sealed together against the cold, and I drag her leg up my thigh to hold her as close.

"As long as you promise to hear me out, but, Shaw?" she says my name, and I am ready to fall to my knees here in the dark, unnamed forest.

"Ask me anything you want." I don't care about the rules. She is right, I am the King of the Vanheim, and it is time to go home.

"I need you." She grips my tunic. Running my nose down her face, I nip her lip, and she finally lets out the moan I have waited to hear.

"You don't need me. Ask me a better question." I know the same feeling building inside me is also driving her to madness. She leans up, and I pull her hair gently aside to expose her neck to my lips. Kissing down her throat, I want to lay on snow covered ground and please her until Spring blooms.

"Who am I?" she whispers a new question with a hot and needy breath in my ear.

I give her the truth.

"You're mine. You will be a Queen."

We cannot stop the chain from constantly bringing our souls together, even though the last link isn't made. Rasha stands before me a maiden, which I am about to change. She is the other half of me for all eternity. We can die together or fight through our short-comings, but we will always find one another. Life exists in balance, and it starts with the gods.

31

RASHA

Arguing with Shaw is unbearable. Half the time, I want to forget why I am mad in order to keep his lips on mine.

"Do you have the bow and the amulet?" I ask, dropping my leg back to the ground.

"Of course. Do you want to go to the Hall?" He peels himself away from me, which is the right thing to do. Joanna must have announced my return by now, but I can't stop the pounding in my core.

"We should make an appearance."

He nods, reaching into his pocket, and pulls out the bracelet. I haven't seen it since the cabin because I've been wearing the chain as a necklace.

"For safekeeping. I know you trust your people, but Jorvik and Bjorn would sooner kill us both then allow you to bring your clan to the mountain pass." He hands me the bracelet as we walk through the last of the sparse trees, and I tuck the chain inside.

Sliding it up my arm, I hide it under my sleeve. "What happens when we connect the chain? Do we both leave?"

Taking my hand and tucking it around his arm, he says, "I need to leave to fix the mess between Vali and me. I would like you to come with me."

"I sense a *but*," I reply, my eyes fixed on his tall frame and clean-shaven jaw.

"But I am not going to take you. It's your choice," he answers. I don't know what to say, so I press my lips together and look out at the village I have called home for half my life. Every torch and fire basin is lit, leading our way to the Hall. People are lining the dirt path to see if I am truly alive. The last time they saw me, I was leaving for the Aske Stronghold.

Aslaug nudges me with her soft nose and drops the quiver at my feet. Before I can bend down, Shaw picks it up and slips my arm through the leather strap to put it on my back. Reaching behind my head, I feel the silver tip of the bow peaking out the top and pull my hair over my shoulders, shaking out the bits of ash and leaves.

"You are beautiful," Shaw whispers, leaving a ghost kiss along my neck. His words hit me, making my stomach tumble with nerves. After everything I witnessed on the edge of the Vanheim, I am having trouble believing that this man, who is the most powerful being in all of eternity, thinks I am worthy of being at his side.

"Walk with me." My voice runs dry. With Aslaug and Shaw by my side, we make our way into the village. People cover their mouths with their hands when they see it is really me. Some, I recognize as those who traveled to Harald's stronghold. They saw my longboat burn and believed me to be dead.

"The Maiden lives!" Girls and women shout from the railing of the longhouse I've shared with them for years. Waving, I allow a smile to grace my cheeks at how many of them look well, maybe thin because it is winter, but still full of vivacity. Men pound their torches into the ground and bang drums for my ascent into the Hall.

"The huntress has returned!" They cheer, and I struggle to breathe. I have done nothing to earn this welcome. I left them. Katrine, Edith, and Joanna are standing at the double doors to the Hall, beaming with pride. I let them think I died. I left them to deal with Jorvik, Bjorn, and Harald. My lungs are on fire as I dig my nails into Shaw's arm.

"Breathe," he murmurs.

"I don't deserve this." I force the words out. Sucking in cold air through my nose, I keep looking straight ahead, trying to wrap my head around the things I've done. I needed to eat, women needed to eat, so I hunted. I didn't want anything more than freedom.

"Breathe, Rasha." Shaw's voice is low but soothing. "Be yourself," he suggests. I let out a controlled breath. Behind me, the rest of the village is coming up the road to follow us into the Hall.

Jorvik is sitting at the council table on an elevated platform with Bjorn, Oslo, who is Katrine's father, and two other men who have been councilmen as long as I have lived here. Shaw lets me go to blend in with the women. All around me, people are sliding into benches and passing around hot wine. More fires are lit, the crackling sounds of wood awakening the last memories I have of being surrounded by Vikings.

"We are intrigued to know how you survived," Bjorn calls, his loud voice booming over the crowd, making the buzz of conversation die down. I look to my brother, the person who is supposed to support me and care for me in the ways I have always cared for him. I fed him, fought for him, and bent who I am for him, but Jorvik only nods in agreement with Bjorn.

"It was not my time to die, according to the gods. Do you believe in the gods, Bjorn?" I boost my voice the best I can and walk to the table. Pulling the bow out of the quiver and over my shoulder, I catch the silver shine in the firelight. People let out a mix of gasps and prayers. "This is the bow that the goddess Skadi used to hunt. It is by her will that I am here. Our gods need us. They need us to remember them." I turn my back on the men at the head table to speak to the crowd.

"Prove it." Jorvik's voice counters mine. I whirl around, our blue eyes clashing like combatting waves fighting for the right to push the current to calm waters. "Only a maiden who is worthy can conjure an arrow."

Another barrage of murmurs and shocked faces overwhelm Jorvik's demand, but he calls for me to prove myself again and again. Glancing over at Shaw who is standing off to the side with the women, I see him raise his eyebrows as if to tell me to unleash my newfound skills.

"Why don't you hold a shield for a target, Bjorn? Since you and Harald don't believe in the stories of the goddess anyway."

He looks at me with those awful, dark eyes, flashing me a quick smile before picking up a shield from the corner of the Hall, and walks down the side aisle.

"When nothing happens and you prove to all these people that the goddess isn't coming to save them, I want you to kneel before Harald when he gets here with the herd," Bjorn snarls. My heart thumps against my chest as I gaze over the many people I have given fresh meat to and whose goats I've found wandering through the woods. The people who have pushed me around and taken me for granted.

After everything that I have given, is there no one besides Joanna and Katrine who are willing to stand up to them and support me? All this time, I thought I didn't deserve a place in their clan, but maybe I have it wrong.

Jorvik stands. The noise from his chair scraping over the floor makes the room forget about Bjorn for a moment.

"Do you know why she was given to Harald?" Jorvik asks the crowd. Turning to Shaw directly, he says, "Do you know what she's done? Did she tell you while the two of you were locked together in the Wild Hunt?"

My blood runs cold as the bow slides through the sweat forming on my palm.

"I am a maiden, and that is what Harald asked for," I murmur, panic clouding my thoughts.

"You killed our parents. You owed this clan your fucking life, and you couldn't make good on that promise!" Jorvik shouts, walking around the raised platform to meet me on the same level as I am standing with the rows of tables and benches. People know what he is about to say, but Shaw doesn't.

"I hunted when I was a child to keep you fed, and the Beaivi Council deemed me a trespasser in lands that are free for all people." My voice recedes, and I wish to be anywhere but here.

"What else, little sister. What else did you do?" he continues. I can't stop the blood rising in my veins, tingling my flushed cheeks.

"I didn't mean for it to happen, Jorvik. You know this. You were there," I plead.

"Enough!" Shaw's voice shakes the rafters, and the fires blow over, causing people to scream before the flames return to a normal height.

Jorvik says unrelentingly, "Tell them what the perfect maiden did."

The room is deathly quiet. Still, there is no one besides Shaw to tell Jorvik this is unnecessary. No one, who has a full belly because I stalked a moose through the woods until my feet were frostbit, comes to my aid. Shaw's anger is flowing through me, coupling with my anxiety and surging into my heart. My biggest fear is that when I tell him, he'll take his chain back and his love.

"Tell them, little Rasha," Bjorn calls from the back of the Hall, near the double doors where he waits for me to shoot the bow.

"There are those in this Hall who know me," I start, finding my voice through the layers of resistance in my throat. "There are those who know I hunt and return with more than enough for our people. I was brought here as a child because I killed a boar on the clan's land. I didn't pay a due, so they took me to lure my parents out of the mountain and punish them. Instead of pledging myself to the Beaivi's, I ran the first chance I could. My parents were killed in retaliation."

"I have brought her back and have devoted our lives to this clan and council. Rasha never showed the same allegiance," Jorvik adds to my speech. I genuinely would have rather died in the longboat than be forced to recount a history I've always tried to bury.

"She owes you nothing," Shaw says, his tense body falling in line behind me. "I came here to ask for your help because she said I could count on her people. No clan has ownership of the forest. That is written in our oldest scrolls, is it not?" he asks the crowd. Gaining confidence, he walks around the room, choosing families to shake hands with as he speaks.

"Shaw is a blacksmith with no clan. Do not listen to him." Jorvik

243

picks up momentum, coming to my other side to face me. "This ends right now. Put that bow down and take a seat until Harald gets here," he spits in my face. I straighten my spine a little more.

"No." I have said it before but this time it is different. "You asked me to prove this is Skadi's bow, and I will."

"She is the huntress. Let her prove it." A voice from the head table brings order to the chaos. Katrine's father is standing with the last two men who have raised their arms to silence the crowd. "We have been on this council longer than you, Jorvik. We took your word when you and Bjorn came back from Yule, but Rasha is here, which already proves you a liar." Katrine's father is unforgiving, and the crowd erupts into clapping.

I grip the bow tighter. "I didn't kill our parents, and you know it. I was a child," I hiss at Jorvik as he walks away. Shaw stays in between the table, where the men have returned to their places, including Jorvik who takes the head seat. The Hall settles quietly, and Bjorn stands opposite me, holding a shield like he would in combat.

Raising the bow, I pull the silver string back effortlessly, grazing my ear, and widen my stance to hold my form. Everyone fades into the edges of my vision, the noise of the flames dies out in the background, and I bring the power I found sitting on the black sand of the magical fjord to my fingertips.

The bracelet peeks from my sleeve on the wrist that is holding the bow by the slender grip, like it was crafted for my hand. Shaw's energy is here, surrounding me, shrouding me so that nothing matters beyond the tip of the arrow. It's there, hollow and shimmering, with short silver bristles tickling my cheek.

I release, sending the immortal arrow flying through the air. I hear it hit the shield before the blurred cocoon of protection dissipates. The Hall explodes into an uproar of cheering and clapping. People are calling my name, calling me the Maiden, and raising their cups to the goddesses. Tucking the bow under my arm, I rub my tingling hands together. This isn't over.

Bjorn is on the floor across the room. The force of my arrow knocked him on his ass. He drags the shield into his lap to see the silver bow sticking through the wood. Taking his axe off his belt, he swings it through the shaft, and I slam my palms together on instinct. The arrow disappears in a cloud of red and pink dust.

"This isn't possible," he curses and swings his axe in front of him, warming up his arm. Everyone is pouring each other more to drink, satisfied with my display, but Bjorn and Jorvik will not retreat after tonight.

Drawing the bow, I yell, "Leave, Bjorn. Take my fucking brother with you."

Bjorn sneers and swings his axe again, moving closer to me. He throws his arm around a young girl, knowing it is my weakness, and nicks her neck with his axe.

"You want to lead these people to where? The King will come with armies so large you'll all be slaughtered in an hour." He presses the blade into her neck and blood beads along her white skin.

"Let her go," various people say. Men stand from the benches, axes and knives raised. Bjorn backs up, dragging the girl with him as she struggles against his blade. The bracelet against my wrist is burning so hot the thought that the silver will melt off, revealing the chain, crosses my mind.

Lowering the bow, I stride quickly down the center aisle to catch up to him and hear the snapping of wood and pummeling of bodies behind me. A quick glance over my shoulder shows Shaw is wrestling a knife out of Jorvik's hand.

"I told Harald that the blacksmith arrived here four days ago, and you were nowhere in sight. Word came to me that Harald is already marching with men to locate the reindeer herd for the King. You are too late to save the reindeer or your people." Bjorn hauntingly laughs, backing into the darkness beyond the double doors where Aslaug is waiting. She lunges the same time I do and sinks her teeth into Bjorn's shoulder. He lets the girl go, the axe slicing through her hand, and I reach for her.

"Fucking animal," Bjorn shrieks, swinging his axe like a maniac. Aslaug jumps over him with her strong hind legs, putting her huge, furry body over the injured girl. Squeezing her torn hand into her chest, the girl shrinks back into the Hall, and men bombard the door.

"Let him go," I say, standing at the foot of the stairs. "If what he says is true, it won't matter if we kill him or not."

Seeing the sheer number of people coming out of the Hall, Bjorn takes off running off balance, due to his leg, and his arm hangs limp at his side. I don't wait to see him reach the horses, though a group of men take off down the road to make sure he doesn't cause any more trouble. I fit the bow back inside the quiver and walk through the surveying crowd.

Katrine and her father are coming to meet me.

"The girl needs attention and probably stitches." The first order of business is to get this night under control.

"I want to apologize, Rasha," Oslo says, his eyes reaching mine in a solemn gaze. "We shouldn't have agreed with Jorvik."

"What's done is done. We need to prepare the people to move, but not tonight. Let them find happiness in each other's company," I tell him. The plans come easier as I find my confidence. Joanna is pressing a cloth into Jorvik's bleeding eyebrow, but I don't care to see if he's okay.

A large hand finds the small of my back, and the bright bond I've continued to strengthen burns through me. Sinking into his embrace, I look at Shaw with too many emotions to count passing between us.

"Can we disappear?" I ask.

"Yes."

I give Katrine a hug, whispering my appreciation into her blonde waves. Her father proceeds to find the musicians to lighten the atmosphere. Shaw threads his fingers through mine on our way between the throngs of people. We smile at those who raise their cups as we walk around full tables of relaxed Vikings, avoiding glares from Jorvik, who swats Joanna away and downs a cup of wine without so much as a thank you.

32

RASHA

There's only been a handful of times I've been in the rooms behind the Hall. They were originally constructed for the families of the councilmen and the highest ranking group of men. Katrine's family has their own large home with fields for livestock, so they do not take up residence here, and the other men might stay in a room or two. As we walk through the hallway, I have the sense that Jorvik took over the Hall, using all the rooms to house Joanna and Bjorn.

"I've been in here with Vidarr," Shaw says when we reach one of the last doors.

"Did Jorvik offer you a room?" I raise an eyebrow. Shaw opens the door and lets me in first, locking the door behind us. The room is small, holding a fireplace, a few pieces of furniture, and a decent sized bed.

"Joanna did. Your brother thought Vidarr and I were delusional, so he was more apt to converse before you appeared."

"I was gone for four days?" He nods. "Jorvik only helped you because he figures I'll still be complacent," I admit.

"He pulled a knife on you." Shaw's voice brakes. I try to shrug it off like this is normal. My brother is an ass as always, but I bite down on my lower lip, struggling to build up my facade. "I hit him to protect you," he murmurs, taking off his own axe and knife to put them on the bedside table. He slides the pointed knuckle rings down his swollen fingers. The guilt that Shaw is exuding has no place here.

"I'm sorry. I should have told you about my parents. That was not how I wanted you to find out." Taking the quiver off my back, I set it on the chair. Shaw sits on the bed, spreading his legs so I can stand close to his strong body.

"There is nothing to be sorry for. I only wish I had been there to…"

"Don't say it." I press on his shoulders until he succumbs. Falling back into the bed, he drags me with him, pulling my legs around his torso so I am riding his hips.

"Okay, I won't say I wish I could have protected you. Instead, I will say that the pain you have harbored over what happened has given you empathy and understanding. I will say, if you'll allow me, that I love you. I have loved you in all of my lifetimes, though we only just found each other."

My heart swells. Leaning over him, I gently devour him with my lips. The words I want to say are lost to guttural moans and wet kisses, caressing the dips of our mouths. His hands pull up my shirt, calloused fingertips grazing my skin, and I help him ease the material over my head.

My hands slip under his shirt, feeling the ridges of his abs as I peel the tunic off his body, and kiss down his chest till my teeth find the ties of his pants.

"Rasha," he sighs from his tense jaw. I peer up at him.

"I love you. I might not know what it means to love a god or what I am getting myself into, and I know I am inexperienced, but I don't want to wait to finish the chain. We can do that after or tomorrow."

"Rasha, slow down." He brushes my hair off my naked shoulders with a smile on his handsome face.

"I'm nervous," I say honestly, sitting up to feel his hard cock pressing into the seam of my pants.

"Don't be. Say the first part of what you said again?" Shaw asks, his fingers traveling up and down my arms.

Looking to him for clarification, I repeat the first thing I said. "I love you. But, Shaw."

He leans up fast, throwing his arms around me and pulling my lips to his. The kisses are hard and fast, replacing my words with the bond we share in our souls.

"That is all that matters." He kisses down my chest until he puts my nipple in his mouth. My head falls back in bliss as he sucks hard, swirling his tongue around my ridged skin. Shaw finds the top of my pants and unties them. Pushing me off of his lap, he eases my pants down my legs, and I lay back on the bed.

"I missed you," I softly say. The glow in his hazel eyes still holds a flicker of hesitation, even though I am naked before him. "Shaw?" I almost beg, but I see him take out the ore and a tiny iron cup.

"Fire?" he asks. I move to the end of the bed, rubbing my hands together and remembering the feeling of my veins filling with power. Flames light the fireplace, and Shaw drops the ore into his iron cup. Taking the amulet, he waits for me to agree and pours our blood inside the cup as well.

"Here." I kneel naked on the floor beside him and cut a piece of my hair the same way I did for the first link. "My hair is red because of the blood spilt on the bond, isn't it?" I ask, adding my offering to the smelt cup we are using as a smaller version of a crucible.

"I didn't think about it that way, but I see it now. You were made to become a goddess, Rasha. It would be wrong of me not to honor you." He secures the lid on the cup and wedges it deep into the flames. Taking a thin, smoldering piece of broken wood out of the bottom of the fireplace, he hands it to me to hold while he pours clean water from the pitcher into a cup.

"I promise to honor you always," he says.

I repeat, "I promise to honor you always." Dipping the blackened wood into the water cup, he lifts my chin and draws a line over my cheeks. After setting the wood back into the fireplace, he stands and pulls me up with him. I watch him take off his pants as I ease into the bed. His solid cock bobbing in freedom makes my mouth fall open in anticipation.

"Do you want all of me?" he asks.

My throat is tight, so I nod. Leaning back into the pillow, I spread my legs, dipping my fingers inside my aching cunt.

"I need you to say it. Tell me you want me to fuck you, please." He asks, stroking my thigh and circling my knee. I bow my legs wider to show how wet I am.

"I told you the truth every time I said I wanted to give my virginity to you. Tonight is no different. Bond or no bond, I am yours, body, heart, and soul." As I tell him my truth, my limbs move more confidently than I thought possible. Moving to my knees, I run my hands up his naked chest till I reach his strong jaw.

Our kisses sear promises into each other's skin as the fire burns brighter around the smelting cup. Shaw touches me all over with his mouth and hands, leaving nothing to his imagination. My body softens under him, and I wrap my legs around his waist to keep him close.

"I have dreamt of you on top of me," he whispers. Rolling to the side, he situates himself on the bed in the most intimidating way. He strokes the ridges of his long cock up and down with drops of his own need dripping down the sides. "Come here and set the pace."

"You are the King of the Vanheim. You can have me any way you want," I coo, getting closer.

"This is what I want. I want to watch you use me." He runs his hand up my ribs as I rest my knees around his body. My chest rises and falls quickly out of the slightest tendrils of fear that in this moment, I won't be enough.

Shaw fits the tip of his cock inside me and glides his hands up, around the curve of my hips. His cock is wider than his fingers, and sliding down only a fraction causes my whole body to tremble. My walls spasm as he watches my eyes squeeze shut with pressure building against the single barrier between us.

"Eyes on me," he says. My gaze snaps to him. His fingers trace my lower lip, keeping my mouth open, and I grip the sheets underneath us for support. The tension in my jaw slowly releases, allowing me to encompass more of him until we reach my limit.

"I can't," I whimper. His cock is nestled inside me, along with the acute sting of being stretched far too wide.

"You're doing so well. I promised to bury myself in your tight cunt. Do you still want that?"

I hum a *yes*, and he pulls me down to his chest. Nuzzling my face in his neck to absorb the scent of embers and snow, I dig my nails into his skin. With one ripping thrust, combined with his hands pushing my hips down, *we become one*.

My cunt opens, leaking hot blood between us, but he keeps thrusting until the pain is replaced with devastating rapture. Leaning up on his shoulders, I look at where we are connected in all our uninhibited glory.

"Fuck, I want you on top of me every day," he grinds out, rocking my hips forward. Taking the initiative, I roll myself forward and back, succumbing to the deep pleasure of being seated on his cock. My chest is exposed when I return my hands to his thighs, and his mouth claims one of my nipples. Ripples of pain web out over my breasts in the best way. I am so close to coming I want to cry.

He wraps his arm around my hips. "I'm going to lay you down."

Kissing my forehead, he pulls out and scoops me up, switching positions, but my hollow cunt flutters around the emptiness. He drenches his knuckles in my soft, swollen slit and guides his strong thumb up and down my clit.

"Please." I am fully begging, and his smile turns wicked above me.

"Do not beg. You are too beautiful like this." He takes the chain out of the bracelet. Wrapping it around my wrist and looping the ends through my fingers, Shaw clasps his hand in mine. "Touch yourself." His raw voice sends a fresh flood of arousal through me.

With my free hand, I circle my clit, basking in the exhilaration of him watching me. He slips his cock back inside, and my walls stretch at the new angle. Shaw pushes his hand into mine, and the links on the chain begin to glow. I raise my ass higher to get more of him as he pulls out halfway to torture me.

"I want to lose myself in you." He gazes down with reverence.

"Stop being gentle." I blink back the gravity of my own admission. "Fuck me like a god."

He sinks into me, capturing my groan with his mouth on mine. Kissing his lips, his neck, his collarbones, I call his name while he thrusts long and hard over and over again. He grabs my ass, keeping me still so he can withdraw and plunge inside like I am the well from which all pleasure begins and ends. My first orgasm catches me off guard, erupting over my body. Shaw slows his thrusts, staying deep inside me while I squirm and leak down his balls.

"Don't stop," I whimper. He steps off the bed to drag my legs up to his shoulders.

"Never. You're mine." He shudders and pushes himself inside me with a new purpose. Holding my legs tight to his shoulders, he releases every pent up moment of desire with unrelenting thrusts. My body soaks in his power willingly. I focus on returning the exquisite love, drawing the fragments of our bond together until there is only one beautiful flowing river of gold between us.

"I'm coming." I can't stop myself from writhing beneath him on the bed. My thighs shake, and I feel his cock twitch, hitting my walls with such force the bed moves.

"Stay with me." He collapses on top to keep our bodies flush together. When the chain on my hand touches his skin, he comes so deep, my stomach flips over, and I sink my teeth into his shoulder. Hooking his arm under my leg, he keeps us together and pushes us into the middle of the bed.

We lay tangled in each other, catching our breath and reveling in the quiet of our union. Tenderly, I stroke his back up and down, circling his shoulders. With every second that passes, his tattoos sprawl out down his arm.

"Shaw, your tattoo," I murmur. He rolls off me to twist his arm so he can see the blue scrollwork darkening his muscled shoulder.

"Hopefully you like it. I will continue to change until we return to the Vanheim."

"And me?" I ask, suddenly worried I am going down a road I cannot return from.

"You won't look different until you cross over. But with the last link still not connected and both of us living in limbo, we are at our most vulnerable." He stands from the bed to find the water pitcher. "Are you satisfied?"

"I am," I answer, but my fierce smile fades when I see my blood smeared on both of our legs.

"Come to the edge of the bed." He pulls the sweater I wore everyday in the caves out of our bag. It smells like us, and I suddenly have the urge to have sex all over again. Shaw takes a damp cloth and cleans us. The friction from the cloth renews my desire.

"We should sleep, but if you keep looking at me like that, I don't know if I can show restraint," he teases. "Let's pour the last link before I give up and taste you." I shiver in his boldness and wrap the sweater around myself. He puts on pants and places the little mold on the stone hearth. Taking the smelt cup, he passes me smaller tongs so I can help remove the lid.

"Did it look like that back in the cabin?" I watch the molten metal swirl in a circle like it is set in motion by an unseen force.

"No it didn't. The metal has changed because we, well I…" He nervously pauses to meet my stare, struggling to find words that won't diminish what we did.

"Your blood. Giving yourself to me. It was the final piece of the ritual. Now our bond is infused in the link, which will seal our fate as one."

Watching him pour the shimmering liquid into the mold, I reply, "That's why you held out for all these weeks. So I was ready to accept the bond." I wrap my arm around my stomach and sit back on the bed, feeling a trickle of our come between my thighs.

"Mhmm. If you are worried about me finishing inside you, I can't make a child with anyone but my bonded partner, and it has to be under certain celestial conditions." He explains what I had been far too lost in the throws of my orgasm to think about until now.

"I would like to imagine we would be good parents." I beam at the thought of teaching a little girl how to be a Viking.

"One day." He puts another log on the fire, keeping the clay mold safely cooling to the side, and crawls back into bed with me.

"First, we need to find the reindeer with the star map. It will tell us the location for our ascendance into the Vanheim. I know Bjorn thought it showed the path to the herd, but the herd is ever changing."

"They will be coming after us. Bjorn is riding as we speak to tell Harald that I am alive." Talking it out makes it real, which scares me. Harald will try to kill us again, simply out of spite. Shaw covers us with the blankets, letting me cuddle against his ribs. Resting my head on his shoulder, I can hear our hearts beating in unison and feel the profound flow of power connecting us.

"Rasha." Shaw's quiet voice is soothing. "I don't want people to suffer any more than you do. We can take as many as we can into the mountain pass, but I don't want to make a promise I can't keep."

"I know. I don't know if we can keep them safe either," I murmur as sleep washes over me.

"Hope lies in rebalancing the realms," Shaw whispers, holding me close while our bodies fall into a peaceful rhythm of rest.

33

SHAW

Rasha releases a hunger so insatiable from within me that I part her legs in the lilac-colored dawn, unable to wait till we are fully awake. Her drowsy, pouted lips open in a soft moan when I drag my cock through her wet entrance. Taking her gently from behind, I feel her grind her ass into my hips as I drink in her perfection.

After, we are sitting up in bed with the mold in her lap and the chain laying across my thighs. She asks about the links, and if I made them all alone. I tell her about the first few I crafted when I lived every day in dark despair then about the links I created when I started helping the clans make weapons.

"Why did you keep smithing all these years if you didn't believe you'd find your way back home?" She trails her fingers from the last section to the end where her link is attached.

"I gave up for years. Long stretches of time passed, and I put the mold away, thinking eventually I'd die like a mortal, but death never came for me. Something would push me to keep going after a while like Aslaug or the beauty of Spring. The thought that Vidarr, Vali, and my sister are waiting kept me searching for a way home. And then the stars led me to you."

"Would you believe me if I told you I never wanted a husband." She slides me a gaze that could melt an iceberg.

"Am I your husband, my lady?" I tease, tucking a section of her crimson locks behind her ear so I can shamelessly kiss her soft shoulder.

"Do you like hearing me exalt you?" She chuckles.

"Of course, husband, King, god whatever you call out when you're coming is what I want to hear."

Throwing her leg over my waist, she mounts me like she is destined to be on top of me for the rest of time. The mold between us unmistakably pulses, emitting from the link inside.

"Ready?" I ask, trying to not stare at the swell of her breasts near my eye level.

Rasha nods, and I cover her hands with mine so we crack the top of the mold together. I don't need it anymore. The thought that this is my fate, to have her at my side, makes the bond smolder in contentment between us.

Rasha breaks off the rest of the mold, and the last link comes into view.

I honestly don't care what it looks like. I only care about the person who gave up everything to be with me. Caressing my hands across her cheeks, my lips crash into hers, offering her kiss after kiss, having no words to describe my thanks.

"Look, Shaw. Just for a moment." Coming up for air, she brings the small link between us and sits back in my lap. Her center glides over my hard cock with nothing but a blanket between our skin.

The link is different from any link I have ever made. It's different from the one Rasha made before we had sex and before she traveled to the edge of the Vanheim.

"It's already engraved with your runes and whatever these ones say?" Her voice catches in hesitation, thinking that something is wrong. A habit of self doubt I fully intend on breaking once we are safely home.

"These are your runes." I run my finger over the unpolished metal. She looks at the tiny markings and elegant loops in the link with disbelief in her big blue eyes.

"I have runes?"

"You have prayed to Skadi, Freya, and the rest. Now, if we can put everything back into balance, the people will be able to pray to you." Easing her off my lap, I reach for clothes to put space between our aroused bodies.

"This feels like a dream," she replies as she starts to braid her hair.

"Let's get dressed and see what your brother is getting himself worked up over today. If we connect the link, the bond will run so hot neither of us will be able to think straight."

Dressing with a raging hard-on is easy enough because I've been hiding my cock from her for weeks, but before last night, she didn't look at me the way she is now. Like a woman who knows what she wants. Fuck me, I want to give it to her. But the banging coming down the hallway is putting an end to any and all thoughts of today being less stressful than yesterday.

"Rasha, are you awake?" Joanna's panicked voice comes through the loose door frame. Rasha glances at me for the okay before opening it. Joanna bursts in with a flushed face, her hair falling in wisps around her head, and Aslaug follows her. The huge cat pushes through the woman's legs to see me and rubs her arched back into my knees with a heavy blast of purring.

"I'm sorry. I'm sorry. I tried to tell him to stay. You have to stop him."

"Who?" Rasha asks, adding a fur and leather vest over her green sweater.

Joanna avoids my stare. "Jorvik."

"Where is he running off to?" I interject. Rasha adjusts the quiver over her back and holds Joanna's shoulders to calm the poor woman.

"Where is he going?" she asks.

Joanna's lip trembles. "He's gone to meet Harald. He drank himself silly after you two left and mumbled something about Harald being closer to the entrance of the pass than we thought."

"We need to leave," I tell them.

"I am sorry, Rasha. I thought I could change him." Joanna's tears lace her cheeks, and she sniffles into Rasha's embrace.

"Whatever happens, I won't abandon you," she says, giving her friend's shoulders a squeeze. "I need you to take the lead here and keep our people fed. Hunt in our usual places. Don't go far, and let everyone stay in the Hall for warmth."

Her instructions make pride ring through my chest at how quickly she is adapting to setting plans and inspiring others to follow through. Slipping the link in my pocket, I take stock of the bracelet around Rasha's wrist. We leave the room with Joanna and Aslaug in tow.

"We will have to allow Harald to be here. There is no way we can fight him," Joanna explains, to which we agree.

"Just until I can come back with help," Rasha replies. "I won't leave you to his wrath."

Joanna stops before the door to the Hall, looking at me and back to her friend. They console each other for a fleeting moment, and I push through the door to give them privacy.

It feels wrong to be taking Rasha away from her friends when she's only been here one night. But I am running out of time. The last link is struck, and I need to close the ritual. Telling myself this is for the best and Rasha chose me, I keep moving through the Hall as people clean the grimy floors.

"There are men who wish to help Rasha," Oslo says, quietly meeting me in front of the double doors. Katrine's father's change of heart comes as a shock since he sent his own daughter to Harald's winter solstice, not caring if she would be safe. The sway of men's conversations was never something I excelled at before being exiled, so it is a task I will need to practice.

"That is kind of them. It would be best if they fortify the people who need the most help. Winter will end soon, I can promise you that. And with the thaw, you'll be able to seek refuge."

"To what end?" Oslo asks. Katrine sees us speaking, and I gesture to the back of the Hall where Rasha and Joanna are.

"Harald must have reported to the King, but speaking from experience, a King won't march his men until he is sure of the outcome." I give him hope, which will serve him better in the coming weeks.

"For our sake, I want to believe you, Shaw. I am sorry the girls dragged you into this mess." Oslo turns a tired glance back at the three women coming up the centre aisle of the Hall.

"I am not sorry at all. Rasha was taken for granted, which will never happen again. Don't let anything happen to Joanna or her siblings. She had pure intentions with Jorvik, and there will be consequences if I find out she's been treated unfairly."

Oslo takes my forearm, shaking on what I've told him, and I let go to allow the three women into the conversation.

"I was telling your –" Oslo pauses to find his words, and Katrine stabs the silence.

"Her husband." She nudges Rasha with her shoulder, and the smile on Rasha's face makes me weak.

"Husband," Oslo repeats the word like he's speaking a foreign tongue. "Right, well I was telling Shaw that there are a few we can spare to accompany you. They can act as scouts and report back in a day or two."

We wait for Rasha to realize it is her decision.

"That is fine. And if I find Jorvik before he meets Harald?" she asks the group.

"Tell him he has no place among our people," Oslo firmly states. Katrine throws her arm over Joanna in an attempt to stifle her heartbreak, but Joanna wipes her eyes and walks out of the Hall alone.

"She'll be okay. Jorvik was bound to fuck up," Katrine adds. Oslo stays in the Hall to set up a table for accounting and hiding the precious, ancient scrolls Rasha's clan keeps buried in a dirt cellar.

Outside the Hall, more people have gathered, men strapping weapons to their bodies and women preparing the land for an attack. They all quiet as we reach the middle of the road, as if they are waiting for Rasha to speak. Katrine beats me to the encouragement.

"Say something," she whispers as Rasha's blue eyes grow wide.

"I have no authority over them."

259

"They don't need authority. They need your resilience. My father is great and all, but he doesn't know what it is like to live out there in the mountains. Harald doesn't even know what it is to be hungry or to wait knee deep in the snow for one deer to walk by in three days. But you do."

I find a place with Aslaug outside of the stables and prop our bags on the wall to give Rasha her own moment. It's a strange thing to witness a woman have a tumultuous relationship with people who have both fed her and kept her decently safe, but who have also used her and left her for dead.

"Jorvik sold us out!" a few families holler, forming a group around Rasha as they wait for her to speak. The bond is pulled taut by her sudden upswing of nerves. Sending soft waves of reassurance to smooth over her fear is the best thing I can do while she gains her own confidence.

"I know. I am sorry. He sold me out too," Rasha starts, her voice shaking.

"Will we kneel to a King?" another man takes the lead to ask.

"Not if I get to the herd and drive Harald away from our lands. Then you can all move into the pass for the Spring and Summer." The crowd mutters between themselves, probably wondering if the risk is worth it. "If I leave now, I might be able to find Jorvik before he reaches Bjorn and Harald. We are taking three of our fastest riders."

The two men and one woman that Oslo mentioned come around me, saddled and ready to go, leading our two reindeer.

"Thank you." I keep my voice low and mount the reindeer beside the horses.

"When we hunt during the dead of winter, we stick together. We take turns sleeping and watching each other's backs. I need all of you to stick together. I'll be back, I promise," Rasha calls while mounting her own reindeer. The group on horseback leads the way out of the Beaivi Clan with our reindeer trotting at an easy pace. Some reach up to hand Rasha or me wrapped loaves of bread and flasks for our journey.

Out of ear shot, I bring my reindeer close to hers, letting our legs bang together.

"I don't know if you can come back once you've crossed over." I can no longer lie to her. Keeping her gaze forward on the rounded curves of the antlers in front of us, she tightens her jaw without answering. "Rasha, I don't want to lie to you. The group coming with us will have to go back in a day or two. They will need to relay what they've seen."

"I know. But I will find a way to do both. Help you and help my people. I cannot let them kill Jorvik, even if he is wrong all the time. Vidarr traveled through the Vanheim, so why can't I?"

"I am coming with you!" Joanna's voice sends Rasha's reindeer into a run, and she yanks the reins to bring the creature around.

"What are you doing?" Rasha yells, her face flush with the effort of controlling the reindeer.

"I can't let you kill him. I love him." Joanna's solemn tears have dried up and been replaced with determination.

"I wasn't going to kill him. Joanna, this is crazy." Rasha moves her reindeer against Joanna's horse.

"Katrine is better than me in every way at managing the clan. She doesn't need me to stay. You, Shaw, are trouble." Joanna steers her horse around my reindeer.

"I have done nothing but keep Rasha alive," I reply. She's upset and heartbroken, which I understand.

"You would sooner see Jorvik dead and Rasha lost to wherever she was when you arrived at our doorstep," Joanna spits the furious words at me. Rasha's bond ignites through my veins.

"Joanna! That is not fair!" Rasha yells, but Joanna is already moving her horse to the front of the group. The party greets her, but the solitary woman glances back to make a shocked face at Rasha. Shrugging it off, I keep us riding at a steep incline over swaths of melting snow and the sounds of rivers being brought back to life.

When the group stops to let the animals take a drink, I walk my reindeer over to where Rasha is scooping fresh ice water into her hands. The two women haven't spoken since Joanna blasted past us. I bring my reindeer close to hers and slide off.

"Talk to her?" I ask, unaware of how female arguments work.

"She has her mind made up." Rasha turns behind the reindeer's large antlers to see Joanna fixing the straps on her horse's saddle.

"Do you think Jorvik cares for her?" I try another route of conversation.

Rasha's chest rises and falls in a sad breath. "I have known my brother to rotate women in his bed quicker than the changing seasons. Though, Joanna asked me if I was okay with her pursuing him to keep her siblings cared for and to give herself a better position with the clan."

"You gave her your blessing?"

"I did. That was before all of this." She raises her arm to jiggle the bracelet between us. I take her hand, bringing her closer, and let my fingers explore the skin down her wrist. I shouldn't be thinking about taking her pants off while she's deliberating over her friend's love life, but our bond is overpowering my common sense.

"Do you regret promising me your life?" I ask like a nervous boy who trembles when given his first axe. Rasha steps closer, bringing her body into my embrace, and leans her beautiful face to mine.

"No, not for a second. Shaw, I am not ashamed to admit I like who I am becoming. I want to sit by your side and do more good than I could have done by staying here." She leans in, sealing her words with a kiss.

34

RASHA

Walking away from Shaw, I remind myself that I've known Joanna since the very first day I came to the clan. We have been through awful nights and sweet berry-filled summers together. My brother should not be the reason we fight.

Joanna sees me coming. Her brown eyes have changed in the past few months. Instead of darting all over, looking for threats, she is staring at me like I am her adversary.

"We should keep moving," she says sternly.

"Five minutes for the horses and we will be." I come around to the boulder she is sitting on. Saying a prayer, I plant myself next to her. "I never thanked you for showing me the way home."

Letting the fight out of her lungs, Joanna says, "I didn't believe there were other realms and no longer had any faith in the gods. But Shaw was so certain, and of course, his brother is very persuasive."

"Vidarr is a charmer." I think back to his sweet face, and the strangest pang of missing him strikes me.

"Did you know they were different?"

"No, I didn't meet Vidarr till I escaped my own sacrificial funeral. Realizing I was capable of loving Shaw, didn't happen until recently."

"Katrine is correct in saying you two are wed?"

"We weren't wed in the normal ways of the clan. But yes, I am his wife." It's the first time I've said the word *wife* out loud, and the bond buried inside my bones shakes to life with the acknowledgment. "I understand that you love my brother, I do. But, Joanna, how can you support him when he condemned me to death?"

Joanna runs the edge of her heavy coat through her red, blistered fingers. Constantly being worked by my brother or other men, Joanna is always willing. She believes pleasing them will prevent her from being left behind. This whole situation should be showing her otherwise.

"You died. Or so we thought. I watched the boat burn, and I didn't think you were ever coming back. You told me it was okay to fall for Jorvik days before the Wild Hunt. For a month, I thought I was making the best of the worst situation. I lost my closest friend." Joanna presses her lips into a hard line. The guilt in my chest creeps up in a nauseating wave, and I stand to shake out my hands. Our party is mounting the horses, and Shaw is bringing my reindeer over.

"I am so sorry. I left you, and I am going to do it again." I tell her the truth, now knowing what following Shaw means for my life. Joanna looks over at me, her eyes searching for that girl who always does what she is told. I am not that girl anymore.

"I won't listen to my brother to make nice, or Harald. I am sure as fuck not going to kneel to a King who is prepared to eradicate our gods. But I won't stop you from trying to change Jorvik's mind."

"That's all I ask," Joanna replies. I find Aslaug nudging the back of my knees.

"You and Katrine know how to communicate with Rasha." Shaw carefully chooses a moment to come between us.

"You said in the Dísablót that we were Valkyries calling for the goddess? That will work again?" Joanna asks both of us.

"It is always worth a try until I set my own family problems right," Shaw admits what he can and extends a hand to Joanna to help her on her horse. "When we were in Harald's stronghold, I should have helped the women get out from under his rule before

Rasha was sacrificed. You have my sorrow for my lack of judgement."

Joanna stares at Shaw with her mouth open. I know this is the first time a man has apologized to her. Settling into the saddle, I break the silence between them, calling to our three scouts.

"We need to ride fast to find Harald by sundown."

Taking off, Shaw and I lead, using our connection to the underground routes of the mountain river to guide us. Shaw cannot use his star map until it is dark, and we won't risk using any of my magic around the scouts. They might be happy to help me, but in the face of Harald, it would be too convenient for them to switch sides.

Aslaug blends into the mountainside. Sometimes I see flashes of her fur high on the ridge above us. After another hour of riding, she's fallen behind, wrestling with a vole in the snow. I stop at one point when I see tracks made by a single horse near one of the freezing rivers. Jorvik must have stopped to give his horse a drink, which means we are going in the right direction. Underneath the crust of crunchy ice, the middle is melting, causing the land to shift beneath us and on the side of a mountain. One wrong move will start an avalanche.

"We are catching up." I motion to Shaw to see the path that tracks up a narrow break in the mountain path. "We will have to go one at a time." His reindeer takes a chunk of bark off a tree as he surveys the options.

"If Jorvik understood how to read the map and Harald has a planned route, they will end up where the herd might be."

"Why do you say it with doubt?" I ask, keeping our conversation away from the rest of the riders.

"Because the reindeer will circle for me, for you even, and that can be wherever we call the ritual to a close."

Taking the antler map out of his pocket, he slides off his reindeer, and I follow as we kneel in the snow near the small rolling river. Shaw dips the smooth antler into the water, his skin so warm with the constant pull from my side of the bond that steam evaporates as he takes the antler out of the water and lays it in the snow.

We watch as the water drops connect over the embedded, silver stars to make a web covering the curved edges.

"That's the way, isn't it?" I ask, brushing my body against his – I can't stand not touching him.

"It is, but the gorge could be a dangerous path for the scouts and Joanna. It's narrow, and we'll need to go one rider at a time. If Harald has his own men watching us, we won't have much in the way of defense."

"Joanna won't leave now no matter how dangerous it is." I look over to my friend. We've never fought like this. I appreciated our conversation, but I don't know if it made me feel any better about what she wants to do. Shaw's hazel eyes are steady on mine as I wish I could make the choice without so much concern for my former home.

"We have a few days before the full moon, so we go after Jorvik like we promised. But if they are already herding the reindeer, I won't have a choice. We need to connect the last link and circle the reindeer to ascend," he responds.

"I know." I give him the assurance that I am with him. We head down the narrow path, through the gorge in the mountains. Jorvik or someone's horse bolted through here recently; the tracks hit the ground hard and deep. Unfortunately, I am struggling to keep my reindeer moving fast when she's concerned about her antlers knocking into the loose rocks.

Shaw is in the lead when we see the edge of the blue and gray, rocky trail. Overhead, rocks skid down, falling on our shoulders with pieces of ice. I scan the top of the crevice we are guiding our animals through, searching for the shadow of a man or the raised curve of a bow. I am bringing up the rear of our party, which is too far away for me to say anything to Shaw.

The snow shimmers in wet, melting piles on every ledge and surface. As if the sun knows the King of the Vanheim has found his bonded partner and is on his way home. The earth itself is warming to our arrival. Melting snow is not good for traveling, but I force myself to calm down with each pained breath as I make it to the end of the tight trail.

"The tracks stop?" Joanna questions.

"How is that possible?" a scout asks. But I gaze up at the cliff, looking for the reason why the snow and rocks were falling on our heads.

Shaw is almost at the end of the trail, and I hear too much movement for it to be animals, especially this late in the day. Joanna moves her horse horizontal to block the last few paces of the trail. Patting my vest down to find the link, I have the sudden urge to expel the power in my hands. The cold trickle of snow across the back of my neck makes my heart plummet. The link is in Shaw's pocket; I didn't even question it when he packed our things.

"Wait!" I shout, but it is too late. Arrows fly down into the gorge, and I barely get off my reindeer to slide against the rocky wall. Shaw is moving out of the gorge to turn his reindeer around, but the sunlight reveals the edge of an axe, and I feel his body break open.

My knees give out as arrows hit the three scouts around me. The horses try to run or back up as their riders dismount, looking for shelter amid the chaos. One pushes past me and runs out the way we came with an arrow in his arm.

"JORVIK!" Joanna screams, pulling a banged up shield off her horse to protect herself as she crawls to me.

"Did you bring her?" I hear my brother's voice as I throw up in the snow. I don't have the link, and Shaw's blood is spilling out of his chest. My ribs crack from the pressure of pouring the fragile power I've built up over the last months into keeping our bond alive.

"She's here," Joanna yells back. I need to move before she gets to me. I push my reindeer back, pleading with the creature to run away, but I can barely speak through the pain of Shaw's injuries.

Barreling toward Joanna, I drive my shoulder into her shield to knock her off balance and run past.

"Stop shooting!" Bjorn's voice is next. One of the scouts is bleeding out, slumped over in a pile of crimson snow and rocks. Keeping my feet moving, I see Shaw on his knees at the entrance with his chest torn open in a terrible way.

Behind me, Joanna screams, throwing her shield into my back, and I topple over. She jumps on me, wrestling me into the icy mud.

"What the fuck are you doing?" I grind out, rolling my body over hers. Her small fists collide with my collarbones and cheek. My power is recalled into my palms, and I shake, trying to hold her down without opening the channel or setting her on fire.

"I'm saving our people!" she yells, using everything in her wheelhouse to throw her leg around my waist to knock me off. "Jorvik and I will be in charge of the clan. I am taking your place. Harald is going to reward us," she shrieks. I get a better grip and pick her shoulders up enough to bash her head on the ground.

"Little Rasha, he's dying," Bjorn mocks, walking down the side of the ridge. Jumping off the last ledge, he's standing next to Shaw, who is clutching his chest, staunching the blood flow with his hands. I swallow back my vomit.

"Get her off me," Joanna yells for her partners, but they don't come to her aid. Jorvik obviously used her feelings to twist her against me, but I don't have time to reason with anyone. Shaw's bond is pulsing down my spine.

Pushing off of Joanna, I take the axe from my belt and hit her clean across the face with the blunt wooden handle. Something breaks between us at that moment. She hits the ground, unconscious, not able to watch what I plan to do next. I pray to Vidarr to help me and to Vali for forgiveness on Shaw's behalf. I sense in my blood that they are here on the edge of the Vanheim, waiting for us.

Jorvik slides down the path, wet, heavy snow slipping beside him, and rocks begin to fall from the disturbed mountainside. At the end of the gorge, there is a cliff overlooking the pass where the reindeer should be. Keeping my axe at the ready, I need to make it to Shaw and the link before he truly dies.

"Come here, Harald will have you still." Jorvik reaches for me, and I drop the axe. I have more powerful weapons to help me get closer to Shaw. "That's it. This is over. He's dying."

I calm my breathing, settling the air in my lungs so I don't explode, and wait for Jorvik. He kicks my axe over the cliff, and I watch it tumble down the mountain. In the valley below are hundreds of oval shapes. Some are moving, and others are still, but there is no mistaking the amount of reindeer right below us.

His hand slaps my cheek, breaking my concentration. The second hit to my face today draws blood. My teeth rip through my lip, and I land in the cold snow at my husband's knees. Reaching for Shaw, I push my hands over his wounds with tears blurring my vision and look for the link in his coat.

Bjorn twists my hair, yanking me away as I scream, but Shaw moves to his feet.

"Thank you for finding the bow and the map. You won't be punished too harshly." Bjorn's words sink like a stone in my stomach. "He can watch us punish you as he dies."

Shaw moves with the reserve strength I didn't know he had. His fist collides with Bjorn's face, and I use the opportunity to search the snow where Shaw was kneeling. Blood coats my hands along with melting snow. Following that humming power, I finally feel the fucking link between my fingers. Shaw is wrestling with Bjorn, throwing punch after punch while Jorvik doesn't seem to know what to do.

Connect the link, Rasha.

Vidarr's voice is in my mind, and I look up to see a huge black eagle circling overhead.

"How?" I shout at the sky. Aslaug comes from the top of the ridge, and my worst nightmare unfolds. Claws out and jaw wide, she leaps at Bjorn, but he's learned from previous encounters.

"No, Aslaug!" I yell while Jorvik wraps his body around mine, suffocating me.

"It's for the best," he grunts in my ear as I push and hit him.

Shaw screams when Bjorn twists his axe and slices through Aslaug's pretty white belly. Swinging the axe again, Bjorn hits the cat clean across the neck, splattering blood on himself and Shaw. Shaw is spent, lying in the snow, trying to breath with broken ribs and exposed muscles.

"Fuck you." I slam my knee up into Jorvik's groin, and because he's a complete pussy, he releases me. The bond is threatening to break between Shaw and I, my bones shaking as I try to hold it together. I remember what it felt like to bond the first link between us. What Vidarr's magic felt like flowing through my hands.

That's it. Bring the mountain down, my lady.

Vidarr's words of encouragement are enough to spur me to run. Jorvik reaches for the quiver on my back, but he doesn't reach me because I leap off the cliff.

I don't look down. I don't let my fear take hold. I have no business scaling the side of the mountain, but I'll die if I don't try. One foot over another, I am running far too fast to keep balanced as my feet trip over icy rocks. Hitting wet, prickly evergreen branches, I grab hold of anything to stop my descent and try to catch my breath.

Bjorn and Jorvik send another slew of arrows through the brush in my direction, but it doesn't matter anymore.

"There is nowhere to run." Jorvik's words reverberate off the rocks. Pulling the bracelet off my wrist, I open the hidden compartment and find the unfinished end.

He promised this was enough to bind us forever.

Tears slide down my cheeks as I hold our new link against the two open sides. I need to make a triangle. After a minute, I don't see any arrows coming down the mountain, so I run again. As soon as I make it past a line of trees, Jorvik's accuracy lessons from our mother kick in, and his arrow buries itself in my thigh.

The pain is beyond anything I've ever felt. My screams are swallowed by the absolute shock that my brother shot me with an arrow.

"Come on, Rasha. I don't want to kill my own sister," he sneers. Looking up at him, I can see he's half way through the path my body carved out as I tumbled down the steep tree-dotted incline. Over the gorge we all came from, there are massive sections of melting snow. Snow that could break at any moment and blanket this side of the mountain in another layer of frost.

I struggle to stand, blood streaming over my knee and into my boot. My muscles rip against the iron arrow embedded in my thigh as I bite down on my lip to not scream. Taking out Skadi's bow, I plant my feet in the ground and aim high.

If I can cover the gorge with snow, no one will get through for months until Spring, and by then, the reindeer will have moved on. Katrine will make sure of it.

"Vidarr, if your fucking listening, I need Katrine to know what happened," I call to the skies. I don't see his feathers or his yellow beak anymore, but I am out of time. Jorvik has his shot lined up already, and Bjorn is not far behind, carrying a dazed Joanna.

Shaw's heartbeat is a dull thump in my own chest. Pulling the silver string back, I close my eyes. I can't watch myself kill my own kin.

"I never wanted it to come to this," I whisper, knowing Jorvik will never listen. The arrow comes easily, dusting my cheek with the familiar silver bristles. I open the channel with my hand pressed into the forefront of the slender bow and leave all that I am here on this mountain. I was always destined to wield this bow. Releasing the solid arrow, I watch as it flies fast and true into the weakest part of the snow-capped mountain top.

"You missed!" Jorvik hollers. Dropping to the ground to avoid him, I put the bow between my legs, letting the sheer pain explode through my body. After laying out the chain, I hold the last link over the two edges and press my palms together.

I promised to be yours. To bring you home. You promised you'd find me in all our lifetimes. Find me now.

Pink and purple dust swirls as I open my palms over the chain. Above me, the snow rumbles, making the most feared noise in the mountains.

"What have you done!" Jorvik yells as he realizes that he cannot outrun an avalanche. I repeat my prayer, knowing I don't need fire to ignite the triangle. My connection to the Vanheim gives me all the power I need. Flames shoot out around me, protecting me from the arrows that Bjorn is volleying my way.

Holding the chain and the link together in my own power, I persevere the bond we worked so hard to make. As I close my eyes, I feel the plume of wet air coming down the mountain as rocks and trees begin to roll toward me.

I am not of this realm, I don't belong here, and I am going home with my King.

271

Connecting the link pulls in all the available air around me for a moment before sending it sprawling out in every direction. Trees are felled, and birds are sent flying high over the avalanche racing down the mountainside. Aslaug and Shaw's bodies are covered in a tomb of ice and snow.

Massive waves of white snow hit me, and there is nothing I can do besides hold on to the finished chain. The first heavy bout of snow sends me rolling down the mountain, and my pain is suddenly nonexistent. I feel the arrow snap out of my thigh and blood pour from my wounds.

When the snow picks up speed, my body is released, only to be pounded down again by another heavy wave. Rocks are tumbling in the unrelenting waves of cold, airless snow, and my body is tossed around, compressing and fracturing in all the wrong ways.

Fighting to keep myself alive, I feel the chain slip from my broken hands, and the world I know is, all at once, gone.

EPILOGUE
SHAW

Cocooned in a tomb of snow and ice, I scoop Aslaug closer, running my hands over her transforming body. Dazed and immensely proud that Rasha connected the last link, I take my first breaths of renewed immortality. She has shattered the barriers that held my god attributes at bay.

Pure power emanates from every vein, healing my bones and muscles. Eradicating my exile, the expansion of our bond seers up my spine, through my skull, where sharp antlers are poking through my head.

"We must find her," I say, holding the giant cat closer. I push my hand up through the layers of icy crust. Snow blasts everywhere in my first uncontrolled use of blind power. Fuck, I missed this.

Connecting with another rough hand, I know it's Vidarr who pulls us up.

"She's going to die if we don't hurry." He doesn't wait for me to catch up. I sling the slow breathing Aslaug over my back so her head is resting on my shoulders, and we run.

"Are the others dead?" I glance behind us where Jorvik, Joanna, and Bjorn are buried in the onslaught of snow.

"Her brother and the girl are the only ones who have survived.

Their life force is dim, but I feel it. I might have aided a tree in landing on the shit-head who hurt Aslaug," Vidarr explains, his chin gesturing to the lynx slowly coming into consciousness. The quick moment of pride at Rasha's courage to wipe everyone out with an avalanche is replaced with fear that if I can't bring her body to the ascendance, she'll die before her transformation is complete.

Following our connection, I sift through massive snow drifts and felled trees at the bottom of the cliff. Reindeer begin rising out of the snow with Vidarr's help. Their noses instantly brush through the ground, their hooves digging through the heavy piles until I feel Aslaug stir near my ear. Kneeling, I let the lynx slide off and nimbly trot to a spot in the center of what will be a field come Spring.

I aim both hands at the snow, tempering my explosive power, trying to smooth the snow away from the place Aslaug is digging. Reindeer come in full force with Vidarr in the fray to encircle us. He glides on his coattails to where I am, helping to steady my magic so I don't crack the earth.

"Stop, I see her." He releases my shoulder, and we break into a run. Aslaug peers at us, the unsure look in her amber eyes making my stomach clench. What if Rasha is dead? Is my fate perpetually doomed to find a partner and watch them die on my behalf? I can't stop the emotions bubbling up through my skin, sizzling the snow off my torn clothes.

"Give me the map," Vidarr says. Tossing the silver-star antler map to him, I barely register him criss-crossing the open space, making the runes. I don't know how to hold her as I sink to my knees. Tears I haven't shed in hundreds of years drop onto my cheeks. Her body is broken, limbs twist the wrong way, and blood seeps out of her nose and mouth. Yet, she tucked Skadi's bow into her vest all the same.

"Rasha?" Her name is all I can manage as I remember I am a god. Soon she will be too. Aslaug whines, her big teeth pressing into my bicep, as if to tell me I am wasting time. Running my palms over Rasha's broken arms, I pop her shoulder socket back in place, keeping the bond smoldering between us, and she stirs. "You're going to be okay," I murmur, making her hair wet with my salty tears. My fingers find the gaping hole from the arrow in her thigh, and I open my chaotic flowing magic, threading her muscles back together.

"Are you ready?" Vidarr shouts. He's standing with his arms wide, beckoning magic to expand through his hands. The reindeer sense the three of us and nudge each other into a perfect circle.

Lifting Rasha into my arms, I watch her body tremble, and she reaches for me. "I'm right here." I grip her hand, feeling the finished chain crumpled inside her blood-stained palm. I whisper over and over again that I love her, hoping that I can keep her heart beating until we ascend.

A thousand reindeer circle around me as I hold Rasha, and Vidarr stands with Aslaug at his side. Their hooves and curved antlers blur so we can no longer see the forest or the mountains, kicking up sparking snow into the air over our heads. I press my palm into Rasha's and kiss her knuckles.

I am returning with my Queen to reclaim my throne. No one, immortal or mortal, will stand in our way to rebalance our worlds.

ACKNOWLEDGMENTS

First, I have to thank the online book community! Without bookstagram I never would have picked up a romantasy. I might not have renewed my love of literature and writing. I certainly would not have had the balls to self publish.

You all inspire me with your daily perseverance, your endless nsfw posts, the courageous and equally hilarious reels that brighten my day and you make me giggle through the hard times. I genuinely feel lucky to have found such an amazing group of writers and readers!

Azala Press, thank you for giving the original short story "A Huntress's Heart", a spot in the valentines anthology in 2024. You gave me a chance and it opened so many doors.

Kate, having you edit this story taught me so much! You're a gem of a human and your attention to detail while keeping the integrity of the story is next level. Thank you!

Lacey! There is too much to say here but I'll try. From writing sprints to being critiquing partners I am so lucky to have you as a friend. You supported me from page one till the very end, reading every draft, chatting over all the epiphanies, character arcs and squealing in the spicy scenes. I don't think I would have finished without you and I thank you from the bottom of my heart.

Holly, the ultimate alpha reader! A thank you isn't enough. Where would I be without you? Your thoughtfulness while reading is irreplaceable and ever so appreciated. To all our sprints and editing sessions! The reading and chatting helped me learn more than any storytelling book.

Ruth, when I was putting a list of people I would like feedback from you were at the top! Thank you so much for reading and being supportive no matter how many times I change my ig handle. I can't wait to see our books on the shelf together!

Lindsey, I might tear up writing this but they are sweet salty tears because you have shown so much bravery in your own journey that it spurred me to be brave as well. When I doubted my ability to write fantasy and be unhinged you were there to give a loving nudge into the chaos! I truly appreciate the epic voice notes about plots, characters and smut. I cannot wait to see where this road takes us!

Tj Lundin, Kat, Nicole, Bri, and Qilanna! I have grown all because of our group, our prompts, the sprinting and daily encouragement! Thank you all beyond words for reading and helping me edit! For having a place where we can all be ourselves and thus let our creativity run free.

Last but not least, I have to thank my family and most of all my husband. He is nothing short of amazing and a long time ago he showed me what perseverance looked like against all odds. It started this chain reaction of believing that I could also do incredible things. Over the years of our marriage, I've heard it all - we got married young and some might have believed my dreams over but in actuality they were just beginning. So, for all your love and unwavering support, for bringing all the mmc vibes to my world THANK YOU.

ABOUT THE AUTHOR

L.C. Petra believes that stories have the power to shape the world, to breathe life into our vivid imaginations and capture our innate humanity. Her love of literature began when she was a child like so many of us, and led her to attend the University of Rhode Island where she studied English Literature and Art History. A self proclaimed witchy wife, she lives with her family and cats in coastal Virginia.

Made in the USA
Middletown, DE
18 January 2026

27243497R00175